ALL
THE
LITTLE
CHILDREN

PRAISE FOR JO FURNISS

"What a truly fantastic book. One of my favorites of the year! It's a feminist version of *The Road*. Jo Furniss has created a powerful female heroine: a successful career woman, wife, and mother who will do whatever it takes to protect her children. I devoured this novel in one day and [found] myself still thinking about it and Marlene long after I was finished. Jo Furniss's characters are gripping, and the [plot] is fast-paced and relentless, each chapter leaving you breathless. I'm still reeling from the powerful story and the heart-stopping conclusion of this incredible debut novel."

—Hollie Overton, author of the international bestseller *Baby Doll*

"When the world changes overnight, all that is left is instinct—survival and maternal. This tense, emotional, and wholly absorbing book makes you wonder: What would I do?"

—JJ Marsh, author of The Beatrice Stubbs Series

ALL
THE
LITTLE
CHILDREN

JO FURNISS

LAKE UNION
PUBLISHING

Text copyright © 2017 by Joanne Furniss

All rights reserved.

No part of this book may be reproduced, or stored in a retrieval system, or transmitted in any form or by any means, electronic, mechanical, photocopying, recording, or otherwise, without express written permission of the publisher.

Published by Lake Union Publishing, Seattle

www.apub.com

Amazon, the Amazon logo, and Lake Union Publishing are trademarks of Amazon.com, Inc., or its affiliates.

ISBN-13: 9781542045681
ISBN-10: 1542045681

Cover design by David Drummond

Printed in the United States of America

For
Lydia and Frank

Into my heart an air that kills
From yon far country blows:
What are those blue remembered hills,
What spires, what farms are those?

That is the land of lost content,
I see it shining plain,
The happy highways where I went
And cannot come again.

—"A Shropshire Lad," A. E. Housman

Chapter One

Crouched in the lea of an ancient oak tree, the safest place I could find on the sparse margins of the forest, I hid from my own children. Hunkered down like prey, I ferreted out my mobile phone; I just needed five minutes to take a work call, that's all. Then the little terrors could have me. But Billy came crashing through the undergrowth, forcing me to flick the ringer to silent. Late-summer foliage shrouded me.

"Mum-may?"

His voice was close. I imagined his kissy lips pursed in confusion. Maybe he could smell me, like baby birds do? His footsteps faltered and he called, "Marlene?" The realization that he thought I would answer to my adult name more readily than "Mummy" sent me into a swoon of guilt. I knew I should jump out and gather him up. Play the role of fun mummy—surprise! But the phone vibrated in my hand. Billy's footsteps moved away; he trotted toward our campsite, still calling. His aunt's voice sang out in reply, as I knew it would if I waited long enough, and Billy whooped as he was swept into one of her hugs. Their entwined laughter tumbled through the trees to taunt me.

If only I could stack up my life like one of Billy's wooden towers, into an edifice of compartmentalized blocks. If only I could turn my back for five minutes without those pretty boxes tumbling down. *Oopsy-daisy*, as Billy might say. I tapped the screen to answer the call. The line connected to a hollow wind tunnel and cut off. Return call. Line engaged. I tried again, but a voice said the number was not available. And finally, the connection cut altogether.

"Sod China." I hoped the sentiment would reach my unreachable Chinese employee who was screwing up my day. "And Shropshire," I said to this remote hole in the forest where I'd dragged us for a long weekend in order to bond with my kids. "Sod them all," I said to a rare patch of blue sky visible through the canopy. It was hard enough raising three children without my staff regressing the moment I went off-line.

One of those sudden forest breezes caused the oak to shudder around me. A lilt of Billy's laughter wafted by. Amid the green of the forest, it sounded magical, like fairy music. I pushed myself to my feet, too big and too cumbersome for this realm. Too adult.

It was Saturday. Still morning. Cloudy with a high risk of tantrums. The kids had spent the whole summer bugging us—my sister-in-law, Joni, and me, that is—to go camping. The trip was a consolation prize for Joni, something to look forward to after she'd had to cancel plans to visit her mother back home in Pennsylvania. But as the school holidays ticked by, I had so much work, so much travel, that we left it to the last weekend.

I booked a rare day off work so we could get away early on the Friday, but a crisis broke out at my factory in China. My business partner assured me she would handle it; I should go. And when I wavered, my husband got his knickers in a knot. I'd promised Julian that I would keep our progeny out of his preened hair for the weekend while he packed up and moved out, in order to, in his words, "give you some head space."

As I sneaked out of my hiding place and followed the path out of the forest, the trees swelled and roiled in the breeze, their leaves like thousands of tiny hands applauding in sarcasm.

My car door opened with an echoing creak. It really was dead quiet in the forest. I stepped up onto the running board of the Beast, breathing in the new-leather smell of the SUV's boat-like cabin. Don't know why we'd even bothered packing tents; we'd be more comfortable sleeping inside this cocoon. My father always said you had to run in a new vehicle, but the long drive into the countryside had done the Beast good. Its gleaming flanks had been blooded with a go-faster stripe of authentic off-road muck. It was in its element. Shame it had to be demoted back to the school run on Monday morning.

I plugged my phone into the car's charger, skimming past e-mails and texts that Julian had sent before I'd even been gone a day: he probably couldn't find something in the house. But then again, he couldn't find his arse with his own two hands, and I'd had enough of mollycoddling him. He wanted time on his own; let him find out what that entails. The man was an oversized Alice in Wonderland, just as rigid and self-righteous, whose world had shrunk when it should have grown. It held no job, no childcare duties, not even one of his pie-in-the-sky business schemes or, since his knees had given out, a vague plan to train for a triathlon. His life had grown so small that the tiniest detail now loomed large. Minor changes to the household routine—the cleaner putting the breakfast cereal in the wrong cupboard, for example—would rile him. Heaven forbid he should have to locate one of his innumerable gadgets. I deleted his pleas for a return call; let him go it alone—see if he could survive one weekend without me.

After Julian's messages, I'd received nothing else—no e-mails or calls—which was the point of coming away, but still. When I tried to call Aurora, my business partner, an electronic voice told me the network was busy.

"So I can get a connection when I'm in China, but not in bloody Shropshire?" I muttered.

Something standing right behind me gave a gruff of assent.

Adrenaline flashed up my spine. The phone slipped out of my hand and bounced once on the seat. *I should jump into the car and lock the door,* I thought. *I should scream for help. Go on, scream—scream! Warn the children.* I tried to arrange my throat, but when nothing came out,

I twisted round and saw a dog, some kind of giant mastiff. A starburst of relief prickled my limbs.

"Hello," I said, only for the dog to advance a pace and press the side of its head against my abdomen. I laid a palm across its skull, which was a good couple of inches broader than my hand. "You're a big fellow," I told him. "I've ridden ponies smaller than you." His tail swatted the ground once.

I looked up the path for his owner, but the track twisted away and ran across a field to the road. I scratched the dog's ears and, when he gave a gruff of pleasure, built up into a massage over the folds of his face down to his meaty chops. And then I was a teenager again: the yeasty smell of his damp hair, the muscles knotting under my fingertips, the earthquake rumble in his throat; this could have been my dog, my Horatio, from all those years ago in Africa. If I closed my eyes, I was there again, leaning against his back under the shade tree in the yard while Dad loaded up the overland truck, my skin glowing like baked earth.

But my eyes opened on a dank English forest with a dog's hot breath on my legs. He gazed at me like I was an angel. I took a moment to shake off the feeling that he was one too.

"So who are you, anyway?" I ventured into his pleated neck to retrieve his name tag. Chap.

"Chap?"

He looked down at the ground.

"Doesn't do you justice, my ginormous friend."

As I moved toward the camp, I saw that the dog's back legs were streaked with blood. When I tried to touch them, he stepped away, so I let him be. The blood was fresh, from small cuts under his hindquarters, as though he'd scrambled over something sharp.

"Did you get hurt and run away? Come on, I know some people who'd like to meet you." And when I headed up the short slope to the tents, he followed.

The kids tripped over each other to get to him. "Everybody," I announced with a theatrical wave, which the dog recognized as his cue to step forward and draw up his chops, "this is Horatio von Drool, guardian of the camp."

"Horatio!" said Billy.

"Horatio von Drool," I corrected him, "likes to be addressed by his full name."

The dog swatted his tail on the ground and walked to a spot in front of Joni's cooking pot, where he lay down to rest.

"But there aren't any houses round here," said Charlie, my eldest and—at the grand age of nine—the wisest. He stared at the dog while twisting his trousers into tight buds.

"So where did he come from?" asked Peter, a classmate who was tagging along for the weekend.

Before I could answer, Charlie's attention skipped away like a needle over scratched vinyl and Peter followed. They were fretting over the campfire. Charlie's *Survival Skills for Girls and Boys* book said we needed to stockpile fuel. I knelt down in the dirt between Charlie and Peter.

"This is great, isn't it?" I grabbed Charlie round the shoulders and crushed him into my side. "Being outdoors."

He glanced up at me. "Are you okay, Mummy?"

The lack of phone service was forcing me to go cold turkey. But I was okay. A little giddy at being cut off from my usual responsibilities, but then a swell of contentment hit me like the head rush from a first slug of wine.

"Let's build a big, cozy fire," I said. "To keep away the bears."

"There aren't any bears. And we mustn't start a forest fire." Charlie read aloud the safety instructions from the book in ponderous detail. I knew he wouldn't settle until he'd created a pile of tinder that exactly resembled the one in the book, so I said we should take a walk into the forest to gather some firewood. Hopefully, we'd also find someone who might know where Horatio—Chap—came from.

Joni was pulling Tupperware containers out of my cooler, getting ready to cook dinner as soon as the fire was going. As I came over to explain my catering system, she was already pointing at the sticker on one of the lids, grinning up at me from where she squatted in the dirt.

"Color-coded tubs," she said.

"The ingredients for each meal are packed in labeled containers so they don't get mixed up."

"Does it come with an Excel spreadsheet?"

I made a face like that was ridiculous, but *of course* there had been an Excel spreadsheet.

As soon as everyone was ready, we set off. Joni tramped away in one direction with my seven-year-old, Maggie, whose foghorn voice sent birds skittering into the sky as she harangued her aunt to hurry so they could get back first.

"It's not a race," Joni said, fading into the tree line.

"I want to get the biggest log," Maggie bellowed.

Joni's own kid, Lola, refused to leave the camp. With the infinite disdain of a teenager, she said there was no need to fatigue ourselves. *Fatigue ourselves.* Lola went gliding in her slow-motion gait to pluck dead twigs from the trees, like a nymph picking enchanted fruit for a heartsick knight. She high-stepped off into the undergrowth and, for all I knew, changed into a deer, such was the inscrutable nature of my niece, the Lady Lola.

By contrast, the all too scrutable Billy was screaming to go with the big boys, who I knew would abandon him up a tree given half a chance. "Carry me," he said no more than five feet from the camp. So he scrambled onto my shoulders, his arms clamped in a fierce little grip around my forehead.

Charlie ran to catch up with Tagalong Peter. I could hear the boy farther up the path, whacking a stick against trees and singing some awful ditty about piranhas eating his nether regions: "Dumb Ways to Die" it was called. Surprisingly, the list of dumb ways to die didn't include pushing your best friend's mother to the end of her perilously short tether.

The path turned uphill, so I swung Billy down onto my hip as I wheezed along after the boys. I was wondering how it was possible that I could run for ten miles and yet a few steep steps left me sweating and speechless, when we rounded the corner and emerged on the summit.

If fairies existed anywhere, they would set up home here.

The woodland gave way to a stage set with oaks, their trunks bright with moss and their lower limbs strung with ferns. The uppermost branches, though dead and bald, protruded from the canopy as proud as antlers. Charlie was capering about at the foot of one tree that was as wide as my car. My eyes followed his gaze up and up, and I performed my own little dance of consternation as I realized that Peter was already far above us in the branches, making his way, with a methodical coolness, ever higher.

"Peter, come down! That's high enough," I shouted, and he stopped. Somehow, looking up at him looking down at me gave me vertigo.

He cupped his hand round his mouth and shouted, "I'm going to the top so I can see out."

"No, absolutely not. You need to come down right now."

"It's fine, the branches are really thick," he said and climbed up another one, like it was nothing more than the rung of a ladder.

"They're slippy," I warned his retreating backside.

"Peter's really good at climbing," said Charlie. "His mum lets him climb trees all the time."

"Well, bully for her."

So there we stood, watching a nine-year-old perched several stories high, with nothing to break his fall but a few leaves—and me. I'd read once that it's nigh on impossible to catch a falling child, but I could hardly stand back and let the kid plummet to his death. It would make the next PTA meeting most awkward. So I moved around the trunk, shadowing him from below, unclear of the correct heroic procedure should he actually slip.

"Peter!" I tried again. "Come down right now. Do you hear? Peter?"

But the boy had stopped and was staring into the distance at something visible only from his vantage point. He put his hand above his eyes, lookout-style. He glanced down as though he was going to say something, and then scanned from side to side again.

"What can you see? What is it?" yelled Charlie, tugging at my arm and adding, "Can I go up, too?"

I gave him a hard stare and carried on prowling the base, while Peter kept searching the horizon.

"Peter?" I shouted, curiosity killing me. "What can you see?"

He shouted something.

"What did he say?" Charlie and I asked each other. Then we kept calling, "Peter? What is it? *Peter!*"

The boy wended his way back down until he reached one of the lower branches, where he hung by his arms, milking it.

"Fires." He dropped twice his own body length into the leaves below. "Fires and smoke all over the place."

Chapter Two

We found Joni and Maggie in a clearing, where the skeletal remains of foxgloves stood in groups like crucified corn-husk dolls. A haze clouded the dell. It was only dampness—I flipped a log with my toe and it flaked apart, its core furred with mold—but the white mist made me sniff the air, thinking of the smoke Peter had seen.

After we told Joni about the fires, she had asked all the same questions as Charlie and I. Peter's answers were no less obscure the second time around: it looked like lots of volcanoes going off. As I had done ten minutes previously, Joni patiently explained that there were no volcanoes in this country. "Not actual volcanoes," Peter insisted. "*Like* volcanoes. In the distance. Plumes." He wobbled his hand upward to indicate smoke rising. Joni and I shrugged at each other. Whatever the truth of it, it sounded far away.

Nevertheless, Peter's story had given us all the willies. We agreed the clearing was creepy and followed a barely discernible path out of the trees.

The long grass was sopping wet despite the warm air; we couldn't hope for many more days as mild as this. Even the crickets sang about the end of summer. Maggie had light-fingered a Tupperware container that she called her "happy box" and was busy filling it with things she found lovely, such as scabs of lichen and knuckle-shaped twigs. When she snatched a pine cone from Billy, he stood his ground and screamed at her, "You little bucker!"

"Shush, you two," said Joni with a hand on Maggie's shoulder. "Listen to these locusts mating." She started fishing about in the undergrowth, hunkering down to press her ear to the grass.

"I want to see a locust." Maggie jostled closer.

Joni beckoned her into the undergrowth. "Come and listen to the grass."

Maggie got on her knees. "What's it saying?"

Joni nudged her down farther. "Can you hear it drinking?"

"Yes!"

When Joni sat up, she held a cricket in her cupped hands.

Maggie peeped between her aunt's fingers and let out a cry of triumph. "I got a grasshopper." She scrabbled it into her own fist, shouldering Billy out of the way to show the others.

Once we'd negotiated the release of the grasshopper, we followed the path to some pastureland. I'd expected to arrive back at the camp, but instead we reached a post-and-rail fence, so new it was green and sappy.

"Are we lost?" said Maggie.

"It is not possible to establish our precise coordinates at the current location," I said.

"We're lost," said Maggie. She pulled herself up to her full four-feet-nothing, made a great show of inspecting the sky for directions, and strode out into the field. Joni looked up from rooting in her bag and chuckled. Charlie and Peter chomped on apples. Peter asked what Maggie was doing.

"Showing me what's what."

Charlie kept his eyes on his sister long after the rest of us lost interest. Joni finally found what she was looking for amid the chaos of her bag: a compass and an Ordnance Survey map. She and Peter crouched over it, pointing out the contours of hills and landmarks, and even

Charlie was divided in his loyalty. "Aren't you going after her, Mum?" he asked as he got down on his knees beside the map. Maggie strode, up-tiddly-up-up, to the crest of the field and disappeared, down-tiddly-down-down, without looking back once.

I heaved myself off the fence and set out into the long grass, which sopped through my canvas shoes in an instant. I ploughed along until I heard Maggie calling. She was pointing across the valley at an eyesore of a farm, where a Georgian house that could once have been prettified to have a degree of curb appeal was now dwarfed by an industrial behemoth of a shed. The function of the hulking unit was clear even to a seven-year-old: "Cows," said Maggie.

Their noise floated like a cloud of methane, a fat lowing punctuated by screams that sounded more like trumpeting elephants. Even from this distance, we could see the movement of the herd, with most of the black-and-white shapes in a mosh pit around the gate to the dairy shed, while a few stragglers made mad dashes—most un-bovine—around the edges.

"Are the cows hurt?" Maggie's hand slipped into mine, and I held her cool fingers between my warm palms. A pulse ran through her thumb, rapid from the walk across the field or maybe the unsettling sight of the cows. Neither of us took another step toward the farm.

"I guess they haven't been milked today," I said.

"But I thought the farmer milked his cows?"

"I thought so, too."

"Should we ask the farmer about Horatio?"

This is what we'd set out to find: a place where someone might know the dog. But there was no one to be seen. And the cows were screaming.

Maggie's hand clenched. "I don't want to go down there," she said.

My shoulders convulsed in a shiver, and I heard my mother's voice: *Someone just walked on your grave.* I came to as though I'd been hypnotized. What was I thinking? We couldn't go down to the farm; the kids couldn't see animals suffering like that. The cows' pain was as palpable as their smell. I pulled Maggie away from the sight, but I couldn't block out the noise. The wind had shifted and the screaming swelled, washing across the land like surge waves, swiping at our ankles as we waded through the grass back to where the others were waiting, listening.

———

By the time we reached the camp, dusk was leaching out of the trees, and we raced to get bedded down. We'd spent the first night squeezed into my family tent, after Joni's yurt proved too difficult to erect without its missing instructions. Now that she'd unearthed them from her copious luggage, she wanted to put the thing up. Easier said than done.

"Your tent is a total B-A-S-T-A-R-D," I said.

"It's fine," Joni answered as methodically as she worked.

"What does B-A-S-buh-buh-buh spell?" Maggie called out from inside our pop-up tent. I sat on a log by the entrance, struggling to snap Joni's poles together.

"Mind your own beeswax, hawk ears," I replied.

Billy wandered over and asked to play with my phone. When I refused, he asked Lola for hers instead. She gave the canvas a shake to unfold the fabric and said she'd left her phone at home.

"You didn't bring your phone?" I said.

"Mom said we have to unplug. I brought a book."

"But—" I stared at her narrow back, the canvas enveloping her legs like a crinoline. "What kind of teenager are you?"

"I'm reading Sylvia Plath."

"Jesus, Lola, you've got your whole life to be miserable. You should be on Snapchat."

Her delicate fingers unraveled the guy ropes, but her smile remained beatific, like a nun remembering something pleasant.

Our camp was contained in a corral of trees that gave the reassuring illusion of walls. We had three tents—mine, Joni's yurt, and a mini marquee-style shelter that I'd thrown in the car at the last minute so we'd have somewhere to prepare food when it rained. We reached our little settlement from the car park up a short but steep path that was flanked by granite slabs. When we'd first arrived, I'd told the boys that the camp was remote, but its elevation meant we could better defend it in the event of attack, which pleased them to no end. Billy asked me what *remote* meant. It meant he mustn't fall out of a bloody tree.

"You're sure these poles go on the outside of the tent?" I asked Joni.

"I'm sure. And it's a yurt."

"Goodness, I do hope we don't run out of fermented mare's milk." I turned to see Billy unsnapping the pole I'd already built. "So a yurt. Why?"

"It's circular," said Joni. "You know, sacred, creates good energy."

"The Native American thing?"

She stopped to tie her thick hair into a knot that held itself together by magic. The sheen from damp air and hard work threw her rounded cheekbones into high relief. "It's like day and night, life and death, the sun and the earth—all circular," she said.

"Shouldn't you have a wigwam?" I asked. Joni snapped her poles together.

My antipathy toward Auntie Joni and her easy bond with my children could never be aired. Too much depended on it. She kept our family ship afloat with all the babysitting and school runs and sleepovers. But I could never let her go unpunished, either. If she had only ever passed one judgmental comment, let slip one sneer about "having it all"—if she'd just given me a little ammunition, I could shoot her down like I did the holier-than-thou mums at school drop-off. They never skipped a chance to harp on about how I'd missed Sports Day, and then exchanged smirks when I said I'd been at my factory in China, as though I was making it up and was actually getting botoxed or whatever it is they imagine I do while they're posting pictures of cupcakes on Pinterest. Unlike the SAHMs and MILFs, though, Joni never criticized. It was as though she genuinely relished the thankless task of co-raising three extra children alongside her own turbulent teen. I was indebted up to the eyeballs to my sister-in-law, and I had no currency with which to pay her back. Sometimes, it made me so sharp I got this sensation in my fingers like I was pressing a scalpel into flesh: the resistance of skin and a sickening release as it burst open. I massaged my fingertips together to push out the feeling.

Once the poles were in place, we hoisted the canvas and stood back. Naturally, all the kids wanted to sleep in the novelty yurt with Joni, so I left them to soak in the sacred energy and started blowing up my air mattress now that I had enough space for it in our profane but practical tent. After a while, Joni joined me.

"Hello, neighbor." She opened up a side flap to let in what was left of the daylight. "You got yourself a giant window here."

"All the better to see the wolves with. And I just found a built-in wardrobe at the back."

"You are kidding me. A tent with a closet!"

"One of Julian's many purchases." I switched on the million-candle integrated ceiling lamp. It burnt yellow squares into my retinas. "He researched it on the Internet for a solid week. He was all giddy. And when I got the bill, so was I. Of course, he never took the kids camping. First time the bloody thing's been unpacked."

Joni looked over her shoulder to check the kids were occupied in the yurt. "So is he really going to move out?"

I nodded without looking at her. If she wanted me to go through the motions of talking about my problems, I'd prefer to do it later, when there was darkness and gin.

"So where's he going?" she asked.

I shrugged.

"What's he going to do?" She pressed together the studs that fixed the flap, making out like we were just chatting.

"He could start by getting a job," I said.

"Doing what?"

"Sucking cocks for loose change."

"Marlene!"

"What do you want me to do, throw myself on a funeral pyre? He's the one who's leaving his wife and three children."

Joni rolled her shoulders as though she could shrug off that unpalatable truth.

"Anyway, he won't suffer," I said. "If he divorces me, he'll get half of everything."

"You've spoken to a lawyer?"

"First person I called."

"The way he's let you down, that's got to hurt. But I guess he's entitled—"

"*Entitled* is exactly how I'd describe him."

"—because he's your husband, even if he doesn't act like one most of the time. But, then, you could say the same for me. I haven't brought home a paycheck in years."

"It's not the same at all. I'm talking about partnership. David can put in the long hours because you keep the household running—you and he are two cogs in the same machine. But Julian? You know what he's like. A spanner in the works."

Joni nodded her acknowledgment at the ground.

"I can forgive the fact that he doesn't work—never has, never will—what I can't forgive is that he doesn't contribute anything. Never cooks. He won't attend school meetings or help with homework. He refuses to collect our dry cleaning even though he walks past the place every day. You do little things like that for David, right? But Julian . . . he acts like it's beneath him." I rolled out the flaccid air mattress. "Believe me, having a husband is not the same as having a wife."

Just looking at the foot pump lying next to the mattress filled me with exhaustion. Joni placed one hand on my shoulder blade like a warm compress. "And it costs me," I said. "That detour on the way home, the time it takes to pick up my shirts or buy a pint of milk or whatever—something he could easily do during the day—that costs me the chance to read the kids a bedtime story." My voice started to thicken, so I bent down to screw the nozzle into the pump, but the thread spun and wouldn't catch. "Fuck's sake!"

"Go easy on yourself, Marlene." Joni took hold of the nozzle and twisted it into place. She started pumping, slow and deliberate. "For the record, David and I won't be taking sides, even though they're brothers."

I was about to point out that Julian avoided his brother whenever possible, but one of the kids fell over in the yurt, and Joni ducked off to see to it. "Sorry, later—" she said. I wasn't sure if her wave indicated me or the mattress.

———

The forest was poised in anticipation of the night, like a playground in the moments before the school bell rings for break. The kids had accepted the crushing news that it was bedtime. Even Lola disappeared into the yurt with her book, and Horatio was snoring beside the fire. I had my hand in the cooler, hoping to chance upon a ready-mixed can of gin and tonic, when Joni whistled from down by the cars. I grabbed two cans and picked my way down the slope, the granite slabs black as sleeping dogs in the darkness. "Look at the stars," Joni said as she accepted the drink. I tipped my head back, gazing up through the canopy, waiting for my eyes to adjust. Joni grunted as she lay down on her back. I did the same.

Layer upon layer of stars revealed themselves, shyly at first and then—as though veils were being drawn aside—in droves: some twinkling, some shooting, some strobing through colors, some that weren't stars at all but satellites, some so tiny and numerous they formed shadowy dust-cloud galaxies.

"That must be north," said Joni, "because there're the two bears, Ursa Minor and Major, dancing around the polestar." She pointed out planets and a galaxy where baby stars are formed.

"How do you know this stuff?" I asked.

"There wasn't a lot to do, growing up in rural Pennsylvania."

"There wasn't a lot to do in rural Kenya, either," I said, "and even less in bloody Burma." Although, come to think of it, I had spent some time stargazing as a kid. My father bought a telescope once on a camping trip to the Ngorongoro, and we had seen stars like this then. I remembered how he'd told me that we could see so many stars—a picture book of stars like the ones we could see now—because there was no light pollution for miles around.

"Is there still no phone signal?" Joni asked.

"I've had a couple of messages, but nothing since this morning. A call came through from China earlier, but the connection was so bad we couldn't speak. We're a long way out here and the signal seems to come and go—"

"You know what I saw on the map earlier? Up on that ridge?" The dark shape of Joni's arm pointed toward the skulking hills that surrounded our campsite. "A phone tower. The signal should be fine." The abyss of space daunted me into silence. Chattering bats skirted our orbit. Sighing wind. Shallow breath in my chest. Joni sat up to loom over me in the dark. "We're only fifteen miles from Church Stretton—that's a big enough town—and thirty miles from Shrewsbury, and that's a city. We should be able to see lights, even if it's just a glow behind the hills."

We got up and went to the Beast to get my phone and check the signal. Joni was right: there was coverage, but when I tried to call a couple of numbers—her phone, my home—the line was permanently busy. I left the handset on charge, just in case.

The glow from the car's interior light made the darkness all the more intense, as though it had taken a step closer. I flicked on the headlights and they shot out into the night, a pure white lance whose tip faded before it could pierce the heavens. Joni and I stood in the streams of light while long shadows of ourselves strained to get away. Common moths glinted through the beam, shining briefly before blanching to nothing.

We stood there for a long time, drinking our gin, each finding her own silent reasons for why there was no electricity as far as the eye could see.

Chapter Three

I grasped for Billy in the purple part of the night, certain he was frozen through. I dug into the covers for his hand, which was warm, and laid my palm flat across his shoulder blades to check for the rise and fall of breathing. I fell back onto my mattress, listening to a silence so deep it had its own complexity—the pitch and roll of waves—and when I woke again it was to an ashy dawn, as gray as the remains of the campfire where Horatio still slept. Wherever he'd come from, he was in no hurry to get back. I shrugged on a fleece and unzipped the tent flaps, which were laden with dew.

Maggie was already outside, fussing about something.

"What's up, Princess Margaret?"

She held up both hands. "Which one is my favorite finger?"

"The pinkie?"

She dropped her hands into her lap, looking away. I had done wrong; now I was dead to her.

"The sore thumb?" I tried.

She ignored me. One strike and you're out. Game over. For a second, I shone so brightly through my daughter she became translucent, and I saw myself sitting there, raw as a ripped hangnail. No wonder I found it hard to like her sometimes. I reached over and kissed her unwilling head. Charlie was subdued, too. Even Peter managed to sit still for a while. Our listless mood was in contrast to the bustling forest, which chattered with life. I wouldn't have been surprised if Mrs. Tiggy-Winkle or some other woodland creature straight out of Beatrix Potter scurried past wearing a bonnet and carrying a pattypan. Maybe that would have pleased Maggie.

I went back to the tent to get dressed, and Charlie sidled up, slipping his hand into mine and making me startle.

"What happened to the cows, Mummy?"

You can protect kids from everything but their own curiosity. I told him I didn't know exactly, but for some reason they hadn't been milked.

"Why didn't the farmer get help?" he asked.

That was a very good question.

"What will happen to the cows?" he said.

"I don't know. They might get mastitis."

"Will we get *mashed eyes*—"

"You can't catch mastitis. Try not to worry about the cows."

He looked away into the trees as though he could still hear their screaming. I stroked his hair back from his forehead.

"I'm scared," he said.

"How big is your worry, Charlie?"

"The cows were horrid. But it's good that Horatio's here. About a seven or six?" He went quiet, fingers seeking inside my grasp, velvety as a mole.

"A six isn't so bad." I squeezed his hand three times, our secret code for *I love you*.

"Peter reckons their udders will swell up with milk and burst." He scanned my face for signs of confirmation. Of course, I lied. He squeezed my hand four times—*I love you, too*—and ran off to tell Peter.

Joni stumped up the slope and dumped shrubbery into one of the big cooking pots. By way of a morning greeting, she told us how she "wiped out down by the crick," ripped her shirt, but found this pile of edible greenery from which we could rustle up all manner of herbal treats. "It's a fricking supermarket out there," she said, jabbing a finger at the wilderness, her eyes lit up like a kid peering into a golden treasure chest. I poked at the forage with a wooden spoon. Joni gave the kids a bucket and sent them to fetch washing water from the stream. They raced off and she turned on me.

"There's a whole bunch of big birds way off. Buzzards. Circling." She mashed the pond weed into the pot, lips pursed with effort.

"That's what birds do, isn't it?" We'd wound ourselves up tight the night before, lying outside under the stars like teenagers with a Ouija board, but in the pragmatic light of morning, the knots slipped and the anxiety eased. In my experience, there was a rational explanation for everything. "Peter's on about fires. Charlie's fretting over the cows. Now birds? Please don't tell me you think this is some kind of omen."

"It's not a fricking omen." Joni separated watercress leaves from the stalks like she was wringing a neck. "The buzzards are circling over that farm. Think about it: the cows are dying."

I opened the cooler and stared at the contents—*we're out of milk*—while I thought about it.

"So let's drive to the village." I let the lid drop. "We'll find out what's going on. And if we can find a shop that's open on a Sunday, we'll get some fresh milk."

We gathered the kids, squeezed Horatio and the big boys into the boot so we'd all fit in one car, and for the first time since we'd arrived on Friday morning, left the camp.

I slid my foot off the accelerator and let the automatic engine haul us along the dirt track out of the forest and across the field. We had the windows down, patrolling the landscape on all sides. A kids' CD was playing quietly on the stereo: a scene from *The Wind in the Willows*. A plummy voice intoned, "There seemed to be no end to this wood, and no beginning, and no difference in it, and, worst of all, no way out." I clicked it off.

We watched the buzzards soaring with the brutal grace of skateboarding teenagers, up to nothing that was ostensibly no-good, but menacing all the same. Their cat-screech cries cut through the uproar of rooks until, in response to some secret signal, the birds swept away and silence revealed itself like a genie. At the top of the dirt track, the Beast splashed through a ford in a shallow stream, and we accelerated onto the main road.

It was just over five miles to the outskirts of Wodebury. The town was little more than a village, but it must've at least had the basics—a shop, a post office, a pub. Somewhere we could find an explanation for why we were the only car on the road. We passed St. Sebastian's church, with its standard-issue Norman tower and gnarled yew tree. The grass, diligently mown into cricket-pitch stripes, only emphasized the decrepitude of the graves, whose stone faces were streaked with tear tracks of mascara-black algae.

"They used to plant yew trees in graveyards"—Lola's voice so close it made me jump—"because people believed they drank the poison left by the bodies."

An empty church on Sunday morning? Maybe the service had already finished. I had no idea what time people went to church. In any case, it was deathly quiet. Silent as the grave.

"Hey, kids, this must be the dead center of town!" I said. No one laughed. My brain churned out wisecracks, passed down like family heirlooms from my father, on some kind of inappropriate autopilot.

We rolled past a handsome rectory, and then a school, windows dark, as were those in the row of sandstone almshouses opposite. We followed the road to a junction, where I accelerated away. Billy whooped as he bumped back against his seat. Charlie urged me to go faster, and I complied—anything to distract them from the traffic signal, which no one else seemed to notice had no light, no power.

At the next junction, I turned toward the town center. We cruised round a bend, and I had to swerve around the rump of a car that was sticking halfway out of a driveway. I could feel Joni staring at my left cheek, wanting eye contact. But I couldn't face the discussion, the speculation; giving voice to my worries might make them real.

I squinted at the road ahead and pulled over before a single-lane stone bridge that arched across a shallow river. Beyond was a village green with a pristine cricket pavilion to the left and a pub off to the right. There was no one crossing the bridge, or fishing in the river, or playing on the green. I turned off the engine, which tutted in the awkward silence. The kids started to move and unstrap their belts.

"You all stay here with Joni," I said and got out. "No exceptions. Do not get out of the car." I looked at each one in turn, including Joni, to make sure they got my point. "Do not follow me." And, just as I pushed the door closed on Billy's wide-eyed face, I added, "Mummy always comes back. Okay?"

The door slammed as they broke out into protests. It muffled their noise, and the hush enveloped me. It was as quiet as fresh snow, and I was loath to be the first to sully it.

My wellies clopped as I walked onto the bridge. Greenish lichen prickled my fingertips as they trailed over the stones. Tree limbs creaked. The bridge narrowed at the highest point, where I stopped and looked across to the pub. There were a few cars lined up in the car park—a Range Rover rubbing shoulders with an old banger—and one van stood with its doors open, blocking the driveway. A refuse sack lay ripped and eviscerated, its contents scavenged. A barman's tray sat on a lone picnic table—the smokers' table—a pint glass still upright with murky liquid and fag ends floating inside, the rest in a shattered pile on the ground below.

I crossed the bridge and walked into the car park, past the abandoned van—keys still in the ignition—and the picnic table, which was thick with wasps. Then around the corner into Wodebury high street, toward the front door of the pub, whose artfully distressed signboard promised real ale, gastro fare, and good cheer. I stopped beneath the painted crest of the Whiten Arms, which swung and moaned on its gallows.

There were three bodies on the pavement outside the pub. All men, all face down and sprawled in a semicircle, as though they'd been flung from the door and dropped where they fell. The body nearest me—an age-withered man, swamped by his clothes—held in his outstretched arm a lead with a threadbare collar still attached, as though he were being dragged along the ground by an invisible dog. Another of the men had his glasses trapped uncomfortably between his pudgy forehead and the paving stones. The third wore shorts and sandals with socks. There was no blood, no rictus grins of pain, no hands grasped around swollen, air-blocked throats. No sign of what might have killed three blokes outside a pub.

I staggered back half a dozen steps and clattered into the signboard, which folded up and crashed down with a backfire crack that echoed up the street. Would the kids have heard that? Would they come running? As the echo faded, the muted atmosphere returned; there was no sound of car doors opening on the far side of the bridge. I moved out into the middle of the road and walked along the white line until I was level with the pub door, which was propped open by an overturned bar stool. The interior was blank, silent—no music or voices or fruit machines spitting out jackpot coins. But the sunlight picked out a female hand—wearing too many rings—still grasping the leg of the bar stool, though the rest of her body was hidden by darkness. I backed away to the other side of the street and slumped against a parked car. Farther down the road, a hatchback was wrapped around a lamppost, a hanging basket embedded in its windshield. In the other direction was the desolate cricket field. There were no signs of human life.

I drew in a slow breath, let my ribs expand, and blew out through my nose as I counted to five, then pushed away from the parked car. *This is actually happening*, I told myself. *This is happening right now. You need to think. Get your ducks in a line.*

In a smooth motion, I turned my back on the bodies and steadied myself by planting my hands on top of the car. And screamed.

Staring up through the driver's-side window was a silently screeching woman, teeth bared, lips stretched where she had slumped and slid down the glass in a macabre parody of the blowfish that Charlie liked to perform on the patio doors. I staggered out into the road and ran a few steps down the white line until I realized I was surrounded: pub to my right, blowfish woman behind me, the crashed hatchback up ahead. And my family waiting in the car.

Oh, God, did I just scream out loud? Did they hear that*?*

I sucked air through my nose and panted it out, each breath more ragged than the last. I needed to think. But my thoughts overlapped, speeding up to a blur like the colors on a pinwheel, so I couldn't focus on any one thing. I turned round and round in the middle of the road—a broken toy—my wellies clop-clopping over the white line, and the creaking hinges of the pub sign goading me. My mind strobed with thoughts of a man's face pressed into the pavement, a woman's teeth grating against glass, virus or poison or plague, an empty dog lead, bodies like carrion, infection everywhere, Joni demanding answers, *Mummy always comes back.*

Do something.

I pulled my phone from my back pocket and dialed 999.

"Sorry. The service requested is not available. You have not been charged for this call."

I hit redial. The robotic voice returned. "Sorry. Please hang up. Sorry. Please hang up."

Sorry.

For days we had thought there was no signal, but maybe the network was overwhelmed. Maybe the police themselves were overwhelmed. All at once—the thought seemed to whip around me, looking for a way in—I knew these bodies were only a glimpse of something bigger.

Blackness writhed in my guts, and I pressed it down, kneading my belly with both fists until the bad energy frothed into my legs. Then I could hardly hold them still. I kicked off the wellington boots and marched down the middle of the road, away from the pub and the blowfish woman, breaking into a run as I neared the second car, which became the starting line of a sprint. I raced the full length of the high street, pressing down through pistoning thighs, pumping elbows and fists in wide arcs, gulping oxygen until the metallic tang of blood iron filled my mouth, and I was forced to slow down.

I stopped at a mini-roundabout. The town fizzled out into a country lane, the white lines sweeping off along the tree-tunneled road. I let my hands rest on my knees, my stomach heaving with air but voided of the fury. It took a few seconds for the sparkles to clear from my eyes.

Mummy always comes back.

What if they come looking for me? Little feet stampeding, desperate to be the first over the stone bridge, racing around the corner of the pub. Billy, always bringing up the rear, overtaking the others when they stopped in their tracks—thrilled to be winning for once, running right past them, right into the bodies. Falling over them. Onto them. Touching them.

I had to get back to my children. Pounding along the white line again, snatching up my discarded wellies, glancing at another body lying half-hidden down an alleyway, too fleeting to register beyond the simple jolting shock of it. *Keep running.* As far as the pub, where I pounded to a drumroll stop in the street again.

The bodies were still there, in my peripheral vision. I hadn't touched them or gotten close enough to breathe the same air; surely I hadn't been exposed to whatever killed them. I pulled myself back together, literally: hauling my disheveled hair into its band, tucking my shirt into my jeans, pulling on the wellies. Otherwise, I could hear the conversation:

"Mummy's got no shoes on!"

"Why have you got no shoes on, Mummy?"

"Why, Mummy, why?"

At some point, I was going to have to explain, but not now.

Directly across from the pub was a village shop. It was painted British racing green and had a display of quaint bags and biscuits in the window, every last thing decorated with a retro Union Jack. I pushed at the door, which opened with an old-school tinkle. The store smelled of dusty newsprint and stale chocolate, but nothing worse: I could see no bodies in either of the two aisles. A drinks fridge, dark and silent, was within reach to my left. I grabbed two liters of semi-skimmed milk that were still quite cold. Then I jogged back across the high street and over the bridge to the car, the shop door jangling a warning behind me.

Chapter Four

"Let's go for a nice walk," I said to the kids on the way back to the camp. We agreed to climb to the top of Bury Ditches, the hill fort, which was the highest point for miles around. With no phone, no Internet, no TV access—nothing but static on the radio—I needed to get a wider view. Joni was drumming her fingers again, staring out of the passenger-side window; the kids were hyperactive with tension. Maggie and Billy fought over elbow room and traded bizarre insults, while Charlie and Peter, hidden by the bulk of Horatio, sang "Dumb Ways to Die" in falsetto, until Lola screamed at them to stop. Everyone—even Maggie and Billy—shut up until we got to the fort.

As usual, the older ones ran ahead up the path, and, as usual, I had to carry Billy. Joni plagued me with questions, but there was both too much and nothing to say. Yes, there were three D-E-A-D people and more inside the pub and cars. No, I couldn't tell how they'd . . . passed away. No, there was no B-L-O-O-D, nothing to suggest V-I-O-L-E-N-C-E. Lola started sniveling, and Joni walked with her, holding her round the shoulders in an awkward moving bear hug.

I was glad to stop talking as I lugged Billy along the earthworks to the summit. The ground tumbled away down the ramparts, which had been built with unimaginable industry eons ago, and left us in a bleak but lofty position that seemed both exposed and protected. Shropshire rolled out ahead of us; Wales lay out behind. The kids clambered over a cairn, while Joni and I tried to decipher the view with her map and compass. I looked east, toward home, but saw only hills, fields, more hills, and more fields. Some kind of castle. A road: a black river in the sunlight. Charlie dragged me over to the cairn, informed me there was an orientation plaque that told us what we could see. Now the hills had names, the fields were populated with barrows and flint factories and standing stones, and the settlements became real once I could pinpoint them on the map. Charlie prattled on about ancient forests and Stone Age tribes, and I snapped that I could read the tourist information board myself if I wanted to. He trotted off to inspect the defenses, leaping about in a jubilant display of not having hurt feelings. I picked at a scabby skin tag behind my ear, dabbing the blood onto my tongue, savoring the metallic taste of myself.

"We need to go home," said Joni.

We could talk now that the kids were upwind, but it was so quiet; it seemed the world had been put on mute. The absence of sound felt anything but peaceful: it declared the presence of nothing.

"If the Druids or Romans marched up here today, it'd look the same as they left it."

"I said, we need to go home. I want to get to a computer or a landline, try and call David. He's supposed to fly back from New York today. It is Sunday, right?"

Was it still Sunday? I hadn't had a moment to think about Julian—the frenetic tedium of feeding and refereeing the kids had forced my brain into standby—and I'd been grateful for the emotional oblivion. As happened during my business trips, I'd settled into a new persona so distinct from myself that even strangers reacted differently: hotel staff more deferential, men lingering over eye contact, women more wary. Sneaking glances at photos of the kids on my phone would ground me again, stop me from floating away. But I still had stabbing moments of clarity when I understood how people could up and leave their home, their family, their friends without a qualm. In fact, I reasoned, they probably didn't leave—it was something more passive—they simply woke up one morning, distracted, and their old life had receded like a tide. Then later: "Oh, my husband and children? Why, yes, I simply forgot all about them. How remiss of me."

But the top of the Bury Ditches, with the wind snapping its fingers in my face, was as sobering as seeing my own front door from the taxi. The tide rushed in, bringing with it Julian and his brother, David; I turned as though I might see their heads bob up over the ramparts. I half expected to hear Julian's forced laughter, gabbling about some bullshit venture so that David couldn't ruin his fun with practical questions.

"I can't remember the last time I saw a plane," Joni was saying. "Like Saturday morning maybe? Or Friday?"

And that was it. The eerie silence had a prosaic explanation: there were no planes. Joni and I watched the sky, but there were none of the vapor trails that usually carve up our congested airspace and, so obvious now, no persistent background drone from high-altitude aircraft.

"You don't notice until it's gone," I said.

"How's David going to get home?"

We went over our timeline, trying to piece together when we last heard cars, when we last saw someone, when the dog arrived, when we spotted the cows. All the clues we had missed. I remembered that I'd deleted a couple of messages from Julian. I found his e-mails in the trash folder on my phone. Both sent late on Friday:

> Call me—urgent!
> Can't get through. Pls call.

"You're right," I said. "We need to go home."

But Joni was leaking into a tissue, and I looked around for Lola to come and give her a hug.

"What if it's not just here?" Joni sniveled.

I stared at her, incredulous. If it were "just here," the village would be crawling with emergency services. The police would answer a 999 call. There would be planes in the sky. "Of course it's not just here, you—"

Before I could finish my point, an almighty boom surged across the landscape, ricocheting off hillsides and gathering momentum as the initial blast was joined by a further barrage of cracks and bangs. I spun round to look dead north, where flames and a column of smoke rose from some far-off industrial buildings. We gathered together on the edge of the earthworks and watched a factory explode and burn, long after the heat went out of the day, and long after the kids stopped asking questions about it.

———

Once upon a time, I made a rule never to start drinking before I'd finished cooking. But, "We're on holiday, right?" I said to Joni while she rooted through the cooler, and I chugged back a warm can of gin and tonic. She looked at me sideways and said a pointed nothing, but accepted a can nonetheless. Then she put it to one side, unopened.

We decided to sleep at the camp again rather than drive back to the city at night, not knowing what we might stumble upon in the dark. Bodies seemed likely, maybe lots of bodies. Or chaos, looting, unrest. I'd been in London for a night during the riots; it didn't take much to set people off, especially under cover of darkness. So I wanted to see what we were facing.

Peter was worried about his mum and asked if we could phone her. He wanted to climb to the top of a tree to get a signal, because all the phone towers were up high, so obviously the signal was up high, if only he could climb up: Could he, could he, could he? He could not.

Joni gathered him into a stifling embrace and told him a long story about a coyote who lost his mom in a canyon, and she got all the way to the end of the saga, some fifteen minutes of it, before Maggie piped up with, "But what's a coyote, and what's a canyon?" and I snorted into my third can. It was late before we got them settled and then only by putting them down top to tail in the yurt. I crammed my mattress in, too, but Horatio would have to brave the night alone in the other tent.

Not long after we bedded down, Billy sought me out and rolled over to lie with his back pressed into my stomach, head tucked under my chin. We lay there, in a human Zz. I found myself shushing under my breath like I did when he was a baby, and his hand found mine in the dark and gripped one finger. I don't know how long I slept, but I woke with twitchy legs and brain.

I extricated myself from Billy, rolled over, and pulled my phone from my bag. Facing away from the others to shield them from the light, I opened up a new page in Notes, a to-do list: self-soothing for insomniacs. *Pack up camp, find police station, contact Peter's mother, find Horatio's owner.* I hit done, but knew I wasn't. My legs still fizzled. *Contact Julian.* That should be top of my list, even if I wasn't top of his. In the darkness, Joni smacked her lips. I reopened Notes, added *Contact David* and *Check on intl flights.* Then a second wave came, and I let practicalities distract me: *shelter, food, fuel.* On and on, I emptied my brain until the red battery told me the phone was going to die. I wasn't about to creep into the night to put the phone on charge in the car, so just after 3:00 a.m. it shut down. I lay back. Still couldn't close my eyes. Deep inside my bag I found a notepad and a stub of pencil. I scribbled until I punched a hole through the thin paper. I screwed up the sheet and stabbed it again and again onto the floor with the pencil, punching a hole right through the ground sheet and pounding the scrap into the soft earth, covering it over with a blanket, and dropping back onto the pillow.

My head was leaden, aching like my thighs after an especially masochistic run. I rested my eyes, and sleep wafted in and out on the breeze. I woke once to footsteps outside the yurt. A cold rush of air told me the flap was open. I laid a heavy hand on Billy's leg in the sleeping bag next to me. He was fine. My body was mattress thick with fatigue. Another stumble in the leaves outside and the sound of liquid splashing. A whimper, distinctly in fear and recognizable as Peter. *He shouldn't be out there alone in the night,* I thought, as my eyes closed again.

Gray light and bird calls, and Billy's face against mine woke me again. "Awake, Mum-may," he told me and rapped his knuckles on my forehead. I tried to pull him back down for a cuddle, but he was having none of it, and when I realized that Joni was already up and brewing tea, I let him go. I tried to sit up, but dizziness forced me back down. A cough dredged up something from my lungs that had to be swallowed. I held out a hand and saw it tremble. Then I was fully awake, scrabbling around in the bedding for socks, jeans. I was a bloody idiot to get as close as I had to those bodies—whatever killed them had to be contagious. And I'd spent the whole night pressed against Billy, breathing it over him. Over everyone in the yurt. I should get away from them.

I bolted out of the tent straight into Joni, who was coming my way with a cup of livid-green tea.

"So you *are* living and breathing," she said.

"Why, what's wrong with me?"

"You look like shit." She thrust the cup into my hand, stumped off. "Not surprising, after finishing all the gin and pissing around in the dark all night."

I didn't feel so dizzy now that I was up. The weird tea seemed to settle my stomach. And I was ravenous. It could just be a hangover.

"I was making a list," I said.

I heard her mutter "fricking brainstorming" as she carried the cooler down the slope to the car. I went back into the yurt to pack, but ended up sitting down again, watching the trees play shadow puppets through the canvas. Maggie scurried across to lie beside me.

"Are you scared, Mummy?"

"No, love."

She put her arm around my shoulders, pulling me awkwardly down to her level. "It's okay, Mummy. You can be scared."

I lay there with my head on my seven-year-old's chest. *No,* I thought. *I can't be scared.*

———

Joni was bandaging Peter's latest injury. I was wrestling the inflatable mattress into its bag. Charlie was supposed to be holding it open for me, but kept wilting. I snarled at him to concentrate. Maggie eyed the cooler in the back of the Beast.

"There's nothing in it, Maggie," I called out to her. "I'll get you a drink in a minute." She pulled out a bag of dirty clothes, emptied them all into the mud, and abandoned everything when she found no drinks.

"Maggie! Leave things alone. Hold up the bag, Charlie, for God's sake."

The mattress was mostly in. I heard a scraping thump and a scream. Maggie was prostrate, pinned down by the cooler she'd pulled on top of herself. I pressed my fingertips into my eye sockets until I saw stars, dragging in a long breath that whistled through my hands. They were pressed together in a prayer gesture. "Give me strength," I whispered. Next to me, Joni tossed the grill into the remains of the fire.

"Let's just leave the fricking camp." She held her arms out like a cormorant, cooling herself.

Lola stopped untying the yurt cover and watched us both for confirmation. My niece gave a little cough and said, "It might be wise to have a place of refuge."

I shrugged in agreement and watched her retie the canvas with prim double bows. I picked up the biggest torch—hefty enough to function as a makeshift weapon if necessary—as I walked to the car and bundled everyone in.

"Bye-bye, camp," we singsonged as we powered up the dirt path across the field. "Bye-bye, wabbits," I encouraged them to silliness. Bye-bye, (massive, flesh-eating) birdies. Bye-bye, (mastitis-doomed) moo cows.

"Bye-bye, Bury Ditches," said Maggie as we passed the hill fort.

"Buh-bye, buried witches," echoed Billy.

Joni and Lola managed to keep up in their car all the way to Wodebury, where I cruised past the now-familiar church, houses, and school, confirming that nothing was changed by the arrival of Monday morning, the day we should get back to normal: there were no children raging around the playground, no mothers one-upping each other at the gate. I didn't need to see the pub to know that the bodies were still in the street, and there were no police making notes and scratching their heads and taking statements. In fact, judging by the long expanse of empty road that streamed over the hill before us, we might have been the only remaining statements.

After a few miles, we approached the motorway roundabout. Although the road was still clear, we stopped. Perched on the vantage point of a grassy mound was an armored vehicle, the kind you see on the news, its desert camouflage conspicuous against a sky washed out by rain clouds. Unease circled the inside of our car like a chill breeze that made us draw closer together.

"Mummy?" Charlie said. The windows of the armored vehicle were too dark to see if there was any movement inside, any response to our approach.

"Must be a monument," I said. "Maybe there's an army base nearby." But as we set off along the motorway, my lie was exposed by a second military vehicle embedded in the central reservation. Tanks on the streets? I wondered if I should have left the kids in the safety of the camp and gone back to the city alone.

Back on cruise control, the car barreled down the middle lane into the city, doing a little over eighty miles per hour at rush hour on a

Monday morning. I glanced in the rearview mirror and realized that the children were not asleep, but staring out the window with cement eyes. Even Charlie, who was in the front to make space for the dog in the back, only blinked occasionally, his eyelashes wilting down over his cheeks. I checked that Joni's car was still in sight and returned my attention to the road ahead, just as we passed yet another crashed car on the opposite carriageway. This latest wreck was a silver sedan, the first nonmilitary vehicle we'd seen on the ninety-minute drive between the camp and the city. It made me wonder: *Dead or alive, where is everyone?* Charlie raised himself a fraction to see the upturned car before letting his head loll onto the seat belt. I went back to counting lampposts, my thumb tapping a rhythm on the steering wheel with each one we passed: lamppost, tap, lamppost, tap, two lampposts together, tap tap.

But as we swooped under a bridge, my thumbs fell silent. In the mirror, I saw a line of cars clogged nose to tail along the elevated road. A few doors had been flung open, but there was no movement. Buzzards perched on the parapet.

"Hospital," said Charlie.

"What?"

"The road sign says 'University Hospital.' That's where they were going."

For a long stretch after that, I saw nothing unusual. Not even buzzards. It started to feel normal, like any long drive where the car would fall quiet after the kids and even Julian went to sleep. Eventually, a blue sign warned that our exit was coming up, and I indicated out of habit. I took the bend too fast and had to brake in jerks, shuddering over the rumble strip. I rolled to a stop on the summit of the overpass and surveyed a service station below. A plume of smoke rose from scorched restaurant buildings; frames of cars could be seen beneath the collapsed roof of the petrol forecourt; a coach lay on its side with wheels burnt to the rims. But no emergency vehicles in sight. I glanced around the car:

the kids had nodded off. Even Charlie. That was a blessing. I slipped the Beast into drive and headed into the city.

We breezed through the outer suburbs of Birmingham, where the windows of the bookies, Cash Converters, and kebab shops were murky. With no delays from old ladies at crossings or delivery vans performing illegal maneuvers, we soon turned onto a high street riddled with charity shops and estate agents. At the touch of a button, my window slid down to let in the incongruous city air: as silent as our camp, and with an unexpected pall reminiscent of the campfire. The car bumped over something in the road, and I saw in the mirror a fireman's hose, abandoned on the street. We drifted past the burnt-out remains of the police station, the entrails of its gracious Victorian building still smoldering, sunlight streaming through its collapsed roof. My wheels crunched over glass, and I steered around a brickwork drift from the front wall of a house that had partially collapsed. It looked like a picture from the Blitz. Scorched interior revealed, original fireplaces, remains of a sofa facing onto the street. You just don't expect it, do you? Not when you've invested in heritage paint.

At the curry house on the corner, I turned onto Joni's terraced street and drifted along the tight middle lane between parked cars. After the carnage of the high street, the sense of normalcy was unsettling, as though I'd walked onto a stage. Maybe if I turned around, they'd all be watching me from the cheap seats, all the missing people. Again, I wondered, *where is everyone?* I stopped outside Joni's green door, engine running. She parked behind me, and in a second, she was out and trotting up to my window, tapping even as it was winding down. Lola joined her, fingers interlocked across her stomach.

"What do you think?" Joni said, sucking on a lump of her hair.

"There are fewer walking, talking human beings than I'd hoped to see," I said.

She stared at her front door, sucking away. After a few seconds, she spat out the strand of hair, and her eyes returned to mine. "Thing is, we should stick together. I'm going to check my e-mail and try the home phone, okay? See if there's a message from David."

I asked if she wanted me to come in with her, and Lola could stay with the sleeping kids, but she said she'd be okay. She squeezed herself between two parked cars and up the tiled steps to the front door, leaving it ajar when she disappeared inside. Lola waited beside my open window, staring down the road as though she could see more than a row of tatty cars and feral rosebushes and litter.

I got out, too. The wind picked up my hair and slapped it across my face—a mischievous squall racing between cars, whistling like a child trying to hide its loneliness. I stepped up to the porch outside Joni's front door. There was a sheet of paper inside a plastic sleeve that Joni had tacked to the wood. *Take What You Need,* the paper offered in a cheery font, and underneath were tear-off strips printed with inspiring words. No doubt Lola and David would each have selected a word that they knew would please Joni—something like *serenity* for Lola and *fortitude* for David—and not even have rolled their eyes. Most of the strips had already been taken, leaving me with a choice between *faith* and *patience*. I had no belief in the former and no time for the latter. One strip was caught up behind the sheet, though—I untucked it with my little finger: *healing.* In the circumstances, it seemed churlish not to take it. I tore off the strip and tucked it into my pocket, then turned back to the car to say something reassuring to Lola about her dad, but Joni was already coming out behind me.

"Can't turn on the computer, there's no power, and the phone's dead, so I guess I'm done here."

She held a small pile of books. The top one was *A Complete Guide to Foraging for Food.* I was tempted to say that I'd be sure to pick up my copy of *Roadkill for Dummies*, but Joni was talking to me again.

"On the calendar it says David was due to land last night, direct flight from JFK. So I guess he's still there." She reached out to Lola, who took her mother's hand in both of hers.

"Don't worry, Mom, Papa will call when things get fixed up." They nodded rapidly at each other.

"Shall we track down the other husband?" I said, and Joni jumped like she'd been electrified. She prattled about how poor Julian must be desperate for news.

"We don't even know if *poor Julian* is at home," I said, and waved her toward the car so we could set off again. We looped back to the main road and turned uphill for a mile until we entered the next district, but the deli and bakery and florist were empty of the usual Bugaboo crew. At the park, I turned onto my road, where long blank windows of double-fronted houses surveyed the green with doleful spaniel eyes. There were two permit-protected spaces right outside my front door, and we both pulled in and switched off the engines, climbing out onto the pavement.

The chunky thud of my car door echoed across the park. A rope on the kids' climbing wall slapped in the wind. On the far side of the common, a pair of foxes stopped to watch us before trotting on their way. Joni said she would watch the sleeping kids; we agreed she would take them over to the playground if they woke up. I stepped up the box-bordered path and scratched the key into the lock.

The heavy door opened with a dry suck of air and swung back to reveal the hallway and its curving mahogany staircase. The scene perfectly resembled my house: everything in the right place, but too quiet, too shiny. A facsimile of home. An elaborate trick. My keys clattered onto their hook, the sound magnified by silence, and I trailed my fingers over the back of my silver Burmese Nat, a figurine of a spirit that writhed across the console with sword in hand to protect the household. I stroked his smooth back, tarnished from years of devotion, and the habit brought me home again.

"Julian?"

My voice didn't carry far, the heavy curtains and rugs doing their job. All I could make out was a buzzing, like the inside of my head when

I wore earplugs to get to sleep. I called again, but it was obvious Julian wasn't home. I opened the cupboard under the stairs, and there were his boots and shoes, lined up on his red shelf above my yellow one, and the kids' stuff arranged on their painted shelves: blue for Charlie, pink for Maggie, and green for Billy. Julian's coats were still there, too, although the suitcases were gone. *Curiouser and curiouser.*

I moved down the hall toward the kitchen, noticing there was no post in the tray. The buzzing seemed to be getting louder, like a metallic humming. The door to the kids' playroom was open, revealing the devastation of a toy bomb. Either the cleaner had not come on Friday, or I would find in the kitchen one of her terse Eastern European notes: *House too dirty to clean.* I pushed on into the kitchen. The buzz was loudest here, and I wondered for a moment if it was the fridge, but it couldn't be—the light switch and the stench of rotten food told me there was no power. I hardly needed lights anyway as the room was greenhouse warm from the sun glaring through the glass roof, illuminating the island workspace and the family area in front of the foldaway doors that led to the garden.

My eyes settled on the sofa. It seemed to be covered with a shiny-black blanket that I couldn't place. On the rug, a jumble of fallen cushions and Julian's Converse shoes. On the arm of the sofa, a mobile phone with a leather cover; it was his, Julian's. I took a step toward it, but the strange onyx blanket that stretched along the seat caught my attention again. It shimmered and seemed to heave slightly, like an oil spill. The buzz was intense now; I could feel it as well as hear it. I took another step forward, and just as I realized that the blanket was not a single entity but a writhing mass of living creatures, the flies broke away from the body beneath and rose up, meaty bluebottles engulfing me in a roiling bombardment of filth that enveloped my head even as I ran from the room and fell face down onto the hallway rug with my hands clamped over my mouth and nose to keep them out. The furious cloud lifted away, and the buzz faded back into the kitchen, leaving a couple of languid stragglers to fly a torpid circuit of the stairwell before heading back to the feast.

I drew myself into the recovery position and then onto my hands and knees. The buzz. My guts kicked once, and I vomited onto the rug. I waited to see if there was any more: had an irrelevant thought about staining the sisal. I spat out bits and sat back on my heels. I could still hear the buzz. I forced myself to my feet and dashed across the tiles to pull closed the kitchen door. It had to be Julian in there. His shoes on the floor. His phone on the sofa. His body covered in flies. The source of that sickeningly sweet smell.

He'd never left. Or maybe he'd died before he had the chance. Either way, that was my husband. Hidden under that . . . filth. That buzz.

A dry heave caught me unawares, bending me double like a fist in the belly. I stayed down for a long moment. I had to make sure Joni kept the kids away, from the horror and—I looked at the brass doorknob I had just turned—the contamination. I turned back to the console table, opening and closing drawers to find my stash of disinfectant wipes. I scrubbed my hands, working a cloth under the nails, and threw the dirty wipe away. Then I grabbed another and wiped it over my face, across the back of my neck, in my ears, inside my mouth. That buzz was everywhere, on my skin, inside my skin. I wiped and wiped until the packet was empty and my mouth was stinging with chemicals.

In the cupboard under the stairs, I rooted out some giant plastic boxes, looking for heavy boots. In the last one, I found them: snow boots that Julian had made me buy for one of our extravagant "date weekends" in the Alps, which he had organized in the belief that hedonism could be a substitute for actual pleasure. I don't think I ever wore the boots. It had been too late in the season for snow.

I kicked away my tennis shoes and hauled the boots on. Then I picked my keys off the hook and strode out the front door, slamming it so hard the knocker cackled behind me.

Chapter Five

The green refuse bin lay flat on its back in our front garden, offering its "No Hot Ashes" warning to the sky. I crossed the road to the park. The kids had dispersed around the playground. Even Lola was swinging, lying back to let her long hair ripple behind her.

Joni turned to me with pursed lips. "Has he gone?"

I waggled my head from side to side. "Yes and no."

"What does that mean?"

"He's there in body, but not in spirit."

Joni blinked at me.

"He's dead, Joni."

We looked at each other for a while. I wanted to put my finger under her chin and close her mouth. She expected me to talk, but there was nothing, nothing in me needing to come out. She launched into a litany of "oh my Gods" and "poor Julians" and "poor everyone elses," and you'd never know that only twenty-four hours ago she had felt quite strongly that her brother-in-law was an arse. It was like she'd opened a drawer marked "Grief," and the contents were spilling down her face. Her words of comfort, however much they were intended to help, struck me as so inadequate—belittling almost, in light of what I'd just seen—that I had to turn away. I had that sharp feeling in my fingers again, the one the marriage counselor had told me was a physical manifestation of the way I channeled hurt into anger. "Have you ever noticed that every time you need to cry, you get angry?" She had told me it was a coping mechanism. Well, now more than ever, I needed to cope.

"Stop, Joni, just stop it!"

Surprised, she did.

"We can't do this now. The kids will start asking questions, and I can't deal with that on top of everything else. We need to get them away from here," I started saying. "We can't risk them seeing—"

"You can't gloss over finding your husband dead in your home. What happened in there?"

"He was on the sofa. The denim one by the garden doors." What more did she want me to say? My drawer was firmly shut and was unlikely to open without jimmying. "I didn't touch him—there were flies. Loads of flies."

Joni nodded.

"I mean really shitloads of flies. And a buzzing. That's what the kids can't see—the fucking buzzing." I ground my fingertips into my forehead.

"We'll go back to my place," she said, "and work out what to do next."

I thought of all those front doors, cheek by jowl down that sordid little street, a buzz behind each one. "No, we need to get out of the city. There must be bodies everywhere. Every single one of these places"—I jabbed at the gracious, smug, contaminated homes circling the park— "is full of buzz."

"Where we going to go?"

A desert island, I thought, *or a lush valley with a salmon-filled river in perpetual spring, or a Mediterranean village with oranges falling from the trees and a fishing boat sitting atop its own reflection in smooth waters. We could get in the car and drive somewhere like that, through the Channel Tunnel and across to the Continent, just keep going until we got someplace where the living is easy.*

"Marlene?"

That was a fantasy. "Back to the camp," I said. "It's the only place we know is safe."

———

"Mum-may, I'm hungry," Billy whined. As usual, we didn't get anywhere fast. I was still revolving on the roundabout in the park, trying to think straight. The other kids climbed on board and surrounded me, their pleading-chick mouths gaping. Joni produced some tiny boxes of raisins, but soon enough they were at it again. I swatted the midges away, hissing that I couldn't just pluck food out of the air and why can't they let me concentrate for five minutes? Then Joni remembered that we still had baked beans in the car and stumped off to fetch her tiny gas stove, which she set up in the sandpit. The kids sat cross-legged in the dirt, while Joni settled into a primitive squat to poke at the food cooking over a naked flame.

I walked along the pavement, away from the houses overlooking the park and the dark windows that seemed to be eyeballing us. People could be watching through those windows. Survivors. If we were alive, there could be others. Maybe I'd watched too many TV shows, but I wanted to be away from strangers, at least until we knew more about what had caused this to happen. So I eyed the parked cars. Before we could leave the city, Joni needed a Beast of her own. Something reliable. Her knackered hatchback was kept on the road by the constant attention of a local mechanic, whose magic touch we lacked. The last thing we needed was to break down and get stranded where there might be buzz—or strangers.

I ignored the endless SUVs and coupes and minivans. I knew exactly what I was looking for: the souped-up Land Rover driven by that surgeon who lived on the next street. It would suit us just fine. It would keep us mobile. Just in case.

The vehicle was hulking in its space right outside the surgeon's house, and I gave it a proprietorial pat on the bonnet as I passed. I rang the doorbell. It chimed. I waited. Rang again. Then I took a step back and shoved the front door with my shoulder. It didn't budge. I stepped back and kicked at it with the full heft of my new boots, but though it bent in, the lock held. I turned and looked up and down the street for inspiration. The sight of the new Beast drove me on.

Above the door was a portico, decorated with fancy ironwork. I pulled my sleeves down over my hands and jumped up to hang on it. I swung both legs back and, using the momentum, pounded them into the door, which burst open and wedged against a body that was lying at the bottom of the stairs. A frenzy of flies heaved itself from the corpse and swarmed out the door. My fingers failed, and I dropped down into the cloud, my left knee and shoulder taking the brunt of the awkward landing. I scrambled away, squashing bluebottles under my hands as I struggled for purchase on the concrete steps. I fell onto my backside among the purple slate that covered the garden. There wasn't even any grass to wipe my hands on. I scraped away the guts as best I could on the concrete and got up. I gave the Land Rover one last look, but I wasn't going anywhere near that body to find the keys. Farther down the street was a cluster of half-decent urban tractors, no doubt tanked with fuel and primed with snacks, ready to tackle the rugged terrain of the school run.

Outside the gray door next to the first vehicle of interest, I pressed my ear to the letter box. No buzz. I lifted it and peered inside. No body. I took a step back and slammed my foot right against the Yale lock. Pilates be praised for flexibility and strength; the door gave and swung open. Gray walls, wood tones. A chalkboard hanging off the banister requested that I wipe my feet. A quick scan showed no obvious place to find car keys. In a closet bathroom under the stairs, I washed my hands in a tiny sink before I went out to the next house and listened at the letter box. A kick and a slam revealed mid-century modern lines, ruined by a toppling pile of clutter on the sideboard. Too messy to know where to start. The third door was deadlocked, and I succeeded only in hurting my hip.

But the fourth door slammed back against a wall of family photos, which started in the hallway and spread back through the generations up the stairs. Funny-face-pulling kids, a mum in her salad days, a glammy granny on a cruise ship—all looked down at me. The buzz was audible behind the closed bedroom doors above, but it seemed to be contained and didn't bother me as I approached a console table where brown carnations festered in white water, giving off a sleazy smell like bodily fluids, not unlike the one in my kitchen. I picked up a set of car keys and bounced them in my palm. If the residents of number 42 disapproved of my theft, their holiday grins didn't show it. I gave them a nod, hoping they understood that while I was sorry they didn't need this car anymore, we did, so I was taking it.

I pressed the button on the key fob. An SUV parked outside flashed a complicit reply. I pulled the front door shut and drove back to the park to present Joni with her new car.

———

It's quiet because all the people are inside their houses. They are inside their houses because everyone got sick. No, we can't go inside to check on them because they might be contagious. Con-tay-jus means that we might get sick, too, so we have to leave now. No, we can't get the rabbit; we have to leave the rabbit. Yes, we have to leave right now. I'm sorry about the rabbit; I'll let him out of his cage so he can live in the garden. Look, throwing yourself on the ground won't change anything.

As soon as we started explaining, I realized we should have split the kids up and told them separately in their own respective languages. Lola knew already, of course. As did Peter, it seemed, who accepted the news with dark eyes and a sangfroid request that I check on his mother and pick up his Star Wars Lego. If Maggie heard what we said, and I'm sure her eyes were darting about beneath the fringe, it didn't stop her frenzied digging up of sand. Charlie asked about his father—a question I sidestepped for the time being—and then released such a deluge of questions covering arcane practical measures that Joni gave him a pencil and told him to write it all down. I let my fingers toy with Charlie's floppy hair. His bent head and square scribble reminded me of Julian at university.

Loss closed in on me. Really, I'd lost Julian weeks ago, when he first told me he wanted to move out. I was, if nothing else good could be said of me, a fighter: I'd fought to keep my family together. But this was different. Death, even I couldn't fight.

Sadness gripped me in the fierce hug of an angry parent. What a waste! For years, I'd lamented how Julian wasted himself. His potential, his privilege, his intellect. And I'd clung to the hope that the man I first met at university would return. We used to sit up all night back then, brainstorming. The possibilities crackled around us like static electricity off the nylon carpet. When Julian received his family trust fund, he bought what we then called a "home computer," which David trained us how to use just before he took his payout to some place called Silicon Valley and promptly lost it—though he did find an American wife to bring home. Julian and I stayed in most nights with that first iMac, programming, writing business plans, playing Lemmings; we must have led millions of the creatures away from certain death. We were geeks long before that was cool. And after three years of techy bliss, we shot out of university, right into the jet stream of the dot-com era. I picked my best plan—online retail; no one else thought it would catch on—and rode the bubble higher and higher while Julian . . . didn't even try. He didn't need to; he had the trust fund. And by the time that was spent, he had a successful wife. So.

It wasn't that I ever stopped loving him, but it also wasn't the first time I'd wondered: Did I marry the man—or his potential?

Billy sneaked up and huddled into my side.

"You're crying, Mum-may."

"I'll stop soon," I said.

"Good girl."

I kissed the fluff behind his ear.

Joni called out that the new car had fold-down seats in the boot, so all the kids could fit inside, buckled up. They would stop quickly at Joni's to pick up her stuff and then start a slow drive back toward the camp, while I got a carload of supplies and caught up with them. I could stop by Peter's house on the way; better to do that alone, so the boy couldn't rush inside and find, well, who knows what he'd find. His mother was a nurse, at the hospital, which must have been ground zero. Horatio von Drool stepped up beside me as their car turned at the end of the park, the yellow indicator bright against the black railings. He thumped his tail on the pavement and then spun round, startled, to see who had made the noise.

I waited outside my front door, key in hand. I had to go back in, get clean clothes for the kids, enough for a few days at least. It would be easy to avoid the buzz. The front door swung back, and this time I left it wide open. I stepped inside and went straight up the stairs. The handrail was smooth and cool, softened by a hundred years of fingers. It was calming, the sense of running my palm against theirs, as I caressed the full length of the wood, the perfectly hewn joint that turned onto the landing. Up the smaller staircase to the master bedroom in the attic. Two suitcases lay open on the bed, seemingly exhausted from their efforts to expel their contents all over the room. Every drawer of the tallboy was open, with clothes retched up over the sides.

So, Julian had been planning to leave after all. He'd started packing.

I moved across to open the windows. The curtains blew into the room like flags on a pole. At half-mast they slapped around my head.

In the en suite bathroom, I found disinfectant spray and disposable latex gloves inside an old first-aid kit. I scrubbed under my nails with a toothbrush, scoured a flannel up my arms and over my face, and finished by splashing antiseptic over my cheeks and mouth like it was Old Spice. Then I watered down some in the bottle top and gargled with it. *My God*, I thought while my throat burnt, *maybe all the helicopter mums were right about hand sanitizer. What might Julian have touched before he died?*

I pulled on the latex gloves and went over to my office, built into the eaves off the bedroom. My planning board caught my eye. A mood board of photos and color swatches and pencil sketches from a year's worth of business trips to Denmark and China with—in pride of place in the center of this thought cloud—a snapshot of me next to the design world's Next Big Thing, my smile so wide with relief I looked like I was about to eat him. Beside that, a single photocopied page with a red circle around his signature on a contract naming me the exclusive supplier of his overhyped, overpriced furniture to the overexcited consumers of Britain. A year of courting and kowtowing signed into cold, hard cash just last week. The press release from my PR agency still lay in the printer tray, livid with the red-penned changes that made up my final approval.

Still, with no electricity and no computers, I had no online store to worry about. None of it mattered. None of it even existed. Like the proverbial unseen tree in the forest, my life's work had fallen without making a sound. I pulled from the pinboard a tweed swatch in the bright green fabric of the season, which we'd described as emerald but I now realized was the exact color of the thick moss on the roots of the trees around our camp. Beech trees, Joni had said. The fabric should be called beech moss. I placed the tweed alongside my collection of trinkets and talismans in the desk's top drawer. I cast an eye over the bookshelf for anything that might be useful to take along, but there was nothing that could help us now.

The bedroom was an even worse mess from this angle. I shoved the suitcases off the bed and let them slump to the floor. I pulled out a leather weekend bag and stood it open. But the contents of my wardrobe just hung there, the work suits redundant, the party dresses with nowhere to go, the versatile coat stubbornly impractical in the current climate.

From the tallboy I grabbed a clean bra, threw it into the bag. Gathering up a handful of knickers, I found a hard stone, a big pebble from the garden that was painted with two black dots and a smiley mouth. Billy's work left somewhere he knew I would find it: the drawer where I was always packing and unpacking, coming and going, apologizing and comforting while one of the babysitters tried to lure him away with chocolate and Octonauts. And then Maggie would start emoting in the only way she knew how, by making trouble, and I would end up bawling her out right before I stepped into a cab and disappeared for a week. Five whole sleeps. And where was Charlie in this mundane scenario? Was he even in the house or was he off with Peter and his mum, who always seemed to be just getting back from her hospital shift? Or maybe with Joni, if she'd staged one of her to-the-rescue dashes to pick him up from after-school club on the occasions that Julian forgot—actually forgot—to collect his own son (and the school always called me, every single time, to ask where I was and sounded miffed when I said, "Denmark"). And now all that was gone, too, and it was just me and a big pair of boots and a hippie and four kids—no, five, including bloody Peter—against the world.

I lay down on the floor and surrendered myself into child's pose. My heart thumped like it used to during childhood night terrors, echoing through the caverns of the mattress. I concentrated on long breaths and talked myself down as I'd been taught: *You can't change the past, in this present moment you are okay. The plane will not crash if you sleep, you are not in control of the plane.* At least there would be no more flights now.

The floor was uncomfortable. As I pushed myself up, I caught a glimpse of a faint green LED at the bottom of a hillock of Julian's clothing. Covered by one of his ironically uncool-band T-shirts was a flashing light—an electronic light. Belonging to his laptop. I grasped the machine. With my fingertip covering the LED, I saw it flickering under my skin like a heartbeat. Sitting with my back to the bed, laptop propped on bent legs, I opened it up. A box popped up to warn me, 5 percent battery remaining. I okayed it away.

I clicked to open an Internet page: "You cannot access the requested website. Please ensure you are connected to the Internet." I hissed. No Wi-Fi, of course.

All right, then—browser history.

Last opened on Friday, the day we had left to go camping: a long list of dead links to Facebook pages, Google maps aimed at Shropshire, and finally the BBC. I clicked on the most recent headline—or, at least, the last one that Julian had been able to access—posted on Friday evening, some twelve hours after we got to the forest: "Deadly Virus—Curfew Imposed."

I clicked on the previous story, posted a few hours before: "Fatal Virus Triggers Epidemic."

Farther down, the first headline in the list, posted just an hour after we had driven out of the city: "Terrorist Bombs Leave Many Dead."

I snapped the laptop shut on the graphic images that had flashed before my eyes: a domed building flaming like a torch. Bodies in the road. A woman in one shoe running past the camera, a boy in a football kit running behind. Was the child with that woman? I opened the laptop again, punched in the password, and the image appeared. He was looking at her. She wasn't looking back. I steepled my hands over my mouth and nose. *Did she get to safety? Did he? No, of course not. Terrorist bombs. Fatal virus. Epidemic. She died. He died.* I closed the tab, and her eyes vanished. It's surely the mother of all mummy guilt, when your dying thought is: *I ran away.* I ran away from my child to save myself.

All this had happened while we were building tents and gathering firewood. We'd missed it by hours. My hands prickled with adrenaline sweat inside the latex gloves. *I could have been that woman. That could be me. Would I have run away too?* I was a very fast runner.

I scrolled the page down to the very first report Julian had seen on that Friday morning, "Breaking News: Terrorist Incident," and read each subsequent update, reliving a timeline that started with multiple bombs across the country and speculation that the suicide bombers were homegrown, then took a twist to synthetic viruses, overwhelmed hospitals, and martial law—the curfew and soldiers—that was why there were so few people on the streets.

The news reports ended with an abrupt statement from the prime minister, photographed on the steps of a helicopter, confirming that "a despicable group of unidentified terrorists has attacked the people of Britain with a manufactured virus that is both fatal and virulent." A man-made plague spread to all corners of the nation by dirty little bombs. Apparently, "the perpetrators would be held accountable for their actions." *By whom? Were they planning some kind of response from inside a bunker? If so, there was no sign of it.*

I searched the browser history for more, but that was all Julian had accessed. How long the BBC hacks had limped on, informing a dying audience of the latest, I could not tell. Maybe they were still there, holed up in a studio, like during the war. I jumped up and pulled out a storage box from under the bed. There, under the spare blankets, was my collection of treasures. The material wealth of my childhood contained in a Quality Street tin. Among faded snaps and bits of coral was my ancient Roberts radio, the one that had kept me connected to the outside world during the long school holidays visiting my parents, wherever in the world they happened to be posted at the time. The set was my source of music, gossip, and sanity during long nights in the bush. When all the teenagers back home were watching TV and going to discos, I passed the time with other trailing offspring who were orphaned from their real lives.

I clicked the radio on and the hiss filled me with a familiar yearning for voices, ordinary voices. My fingers knew their way around the dial. Shortwave was an art and a science, and the middle of the day wasn't the best time to get good reception, but I tuned through the busiest frequencies. There was only static.

I scrabbled in the tin for the antenna, but it was missing. I kept trying anyway. I roamed the waves, through banshee cries and mourning howls, and eventually slammed the radio into the tin with the other worn-out old tat, which I threw back into the box under the bed.

There were no familiar voices out there. Only static.

Chapter Six

The laptop's little green light fluttered bravely on even though its end was nigh. I cruised around the browser history, trying to squeeze out every last drop of information before I lost contact with the digital world. Julian had shown a frustrating lack of imagination for news sources, sticking only to the BBC and the *Daily Mail*. And, of course, the information ended as abruptly as he had. I still had questions. The main one being: "What happens now?"

I closed down the Internet browser. The laptop warned that it would shut off shortly. I scanned the room for its power cord, but of course, there was no power. Expecting things to be normal had become like a tic; I couldn't stop myself. In any case, without Wi-Fi, the machine was obsolete, the entire World Wide Web rendered as impotent as a history book.

I had taken long enough. I should be catching up with Joni and the kids. But I ran the arrow across the icons, wondering if I could pluck out any last data from this virtual scrap: the calendar of events that were presumably "cancelled due to apocalypse"; an address book of acquaintances who would not be needing a Christmas card this year; and Julian's inbox, which, unless it could connect to the other side, was equally useless. I launched the e-mail program anyway.

There was plenty of activity on Friday, but nothing since then. I scanned down a long list of social media notifications from people he barely knew emoting banal statements, everyone hoping that everyone else was "all right." No wonder Julian never had time to get a job. There was no word from David, but was that a good sign or bad? It could mean the networks were overloaded in the States, just as they were here. Or possibly, safe and sound at his conference venue in New York, he hadn't realized how serious the situation in the UK was until it was too late, and we'd already gone off-line. There was, though, a message from Julian and David's little sister, who was in quarantine at Heathrow Airport after a terrorist incident: the usual stream of consciousness from a woman who lived so much "in the moment" she had no use for full stops. One of the news articles said bombs had gone off in each of Heathrow's five terminals, which suggested that her moment had probably passed. My thoughts wandered to the scene—bodies propped against luggage as though waiting for a delayed flight, security officers slumped at their posts, the departures board going through the motions, urging all these Sleeping Beauties to wake up and get to their gates. My mind explored the scene until I realized I had edited out the panic, the fear, the buzz. I retreated from my own fantasy.

That was it for Julian's e-mails: not much to show after dedicating nearly forty years to socializing. One sibling and a bunch of profile pictures. Where were all the mates from his ironic "darts league"? Just as the machine begged me again to plug it in, I clicked on his sent messages.

Two e-mails addressed to me—the ones I'd ignored on my phone. I wondered what I would have done if I'd phoned home as he had insisted. Presumably, driven back to the city, into the cool arms of my husband and the cold clutches of the virus. Nestled between those two e-mails, a rose between two thorns, was one addressed to Aurora.

Why had Julian written to my business partner?

He knew very well, or at least he'd been told—therein lay the difference—that I was camping with Joni, not Aurora. Like Aurora would go camping. She wouldn't even go glamping. The mail had been sent late on Friday. The subject line was "Desperate to reach you." I took off one latex glove to pick at the scab behind my ear as I read it.

> Hi Rory,
> Ive been trying to call, but cant get through, the network is overloaded. I don't know WTF to do. I just tried to RUN to yours, but some military cordon in the high street turned me back. The guy had a gun.
>
> Obviously Im not going to make it tonight. But we need to talk. About all of it. I cant get through to M. I dont even know where the kids are.
>
> Fuck we need to talk. Maybe when its dark I can get to yours by the back streets or through gardens or something.
>
> I'll get to you somehow. Love Jules

The blood from my scab tasted tangy and fresh. I dug at the spot behind my ear, but it was clotting and withholding, already busy forming a new scab over the wound. I pulled my latex glove back on, stretching and snapping each finger into place. Then ripped it off again.

It was beyond belief that Aurora would lower herself to a thing with Julian.

I read the e-mail again, absorbing the details. A plan to meet. A need to talk. Since when did they meet? Or talk? My eyes came to rest on "all of it." When I tried to read on, the sentences broke apart and re-formed into "all of it." No meaning in the letters, just shapes of a secret code.

All of it.

The black hole of not knowing what "all of it" amounted to sucked me in. The light drained from the room into a dark place in my gut, where I could feel it gathering, fomenting. I dropped my head in submission, braced against my own ferocity, straining to keep it down. None of my thoughts had form beyond the pure energy that fueled rage. My mismatched hands, one a latex death pall and the other heaving with veins, gripped each other in my lap. I closed my eyes as white-hot fury shuddered up and over me in a rabid contraction, and I found that a metallic grating noise was my teeth grinding together.

The chaos passed. I was still there, sitting on the floor, holding myself. Everything was intact. I released my jaw, my breath, and my hands. In my lap, the palm of the latex glove flapped open like torn skin, shredded by my nails.

The laptop peeped a meek warning that it was shutting down now. Icons started to disappear, and I put my fingertip over the green LED as it flickered a couple more times in an irregular pulse. An hourglass turned. And then darkness. The light glowed for a while under my fingertip, but I knew it was gone. I had a last image of an action-man version of Julian, scaling fences to rescue his woman. *I'll get to you somehow!* Although he obviously hadn't fulfilled that promise, so "Rory" got a glimpse of what life would have been like as Julian's partner and—the thought actually made me smile—at least they would start their new life in eternity with an almighty row.

———

The leather bag crashed into the wall as I threw it over the banisters to the hall below, taking a framed holiday photo and a mirror with it. I shrugged as the glass shattered into the carpet. I pulled my best running top out of the dirty linen basket and threw it down after the bag. It spread its long-armed wings and floated like a wraith down the stairs. Wading across the clothes-strewn carpet, I returned to the bed and grabbed my best pillow, which I lobbed in an overhead throw out the door and over the banister. "Whee," I called out. I heard a thump and a tinkle of glass as it landed below. Finally, I went to my bedside drawer. Inside was the jewelry that I only ever wore on flights so it didn't get lost in the luggage: my modest engagement ring, bought when we were just starting out, which got replaced by a garish eternity ring after I made both Charlie and a fortune; my mother's huge brooch, whose provenance was assured by every single photo I had of her—always smiling without showing her teeth, beneath a broad sunhat draped with a scarf held in place by the jade. I wrapped everything into a soft fabric bag and tugged the drawstring tight, slipping it inside my pocket.

I went from kid's room to kid's room, pulling out clean clothes, shoes, weather-related kit. All of it went airborne to the ground floor. I grabbed from the airing cupboard towels and flannels and extra blankets and a bucket. I peered over the banister to see the pile below, which seemed to be crawling up the stairs to get back where it belonged. In the family bathroom, I stuffed a wash-bag with Band-Aids and bandages and toothpaste and disinfectant and DEET-formula bug spray and as many random medicines as I could find. Over the banister. From the sideboard in the hallway, I pulled out fleeces that we'd need if the weather turned, looking more stained and bobbled than when I'd packed them away, as though they'd started decomposing. In a drawer were hats and socks and gloves, but I couldn't gather them all into one handful, so I dumped them back into the wooden drawer, pulled that out, and sent the whole thing sailing over the railing where it smashed onto the Minton tiles. I followed down the stairs, climbing across the mound of stuff to get to the kitchen door. I stood outside, pressed my forehead against the freshly painted wood, breathing hard. I listened to the buzz.

Trust him to die in the kitchen.

All the important stuff was in there. Pans and knives. Food. "We need to fucking eat, Julian," I yelled, pounding at the door. The buzz swelled in reply, and the metallic sound needled my anger.

"Judas," I hissed through the keyhole. "After fifteen years of bleeding me dry. Like a tick. All the shit-brained schemes. Pissing away your trust fund. You've not done a single thing in all that time. Not for us. Not for me. Not even for yourself. Not one thing." I pounded the door three more times with my forehead. *Not. One. Thing.* The dull pain calmed me. "For fifteen years, Julian. How could you be such a—" I could hear the buzz receding. I pictured the flies, bloated and dopey. "Parasite."

I slumped to the floor. Except, of course, for the first time, he *had* done something. He'd had an affair and decided to leave me. Finally, a decision—two whole decisions. "Well, you know what, Judas?"—I was back on my knees, spittling the keyhole—"I'm okay on my own. I'm fucking brilliant on my own. What doesn't kill you makes you stronger, right?" My hands fell from the doorknob as a swell of laughter doubled me over. "Oh, God, sorry, that came out wrong." I punched my thighs. "That sounded really bad." My ribs hurt. Pass that woman a corset; her sides are going to split. I held myself together with my arms until it passed. Wiped the tears from my eyes. Got to my feet. I gave the door one last petulant bang and turned back to face the hall.

Do we need all this stuff? Or none of it?

The tears had washed me out, like an enema for the heart. I was hollow. Light.

I didn't want all this baggage. Into my leather weekender, I pushed medicine and clothes. All the food was trapped behind the kitchen door, contaminated, so I'd have to find some elsewhere. From the console I picked up the car keys and my silver Burmese Nat. I walked out the front door and didn't bother locking it behind me.

———

We made quick progress along the high street, Horatio and I. I leap-frogged the speed bumps, weaved around traffic cones that failed to calm me, jumped the lights. As the road widened, I watched my speed dial reach "100 mph" and pushed the Beast into the red. I swept through a spill of rubbish, scattering bags and wrappers into the air; they flapped to the ground behind me, like old ladies waving their hands in disapproval.

When I turned my eyes back to the road, I hit the brakes hard, and the car fishtailed to a halt, but not before we ploughed through a gang of a dozen or so dogs sunning themselves on the warm asphalt. I caught flashes of movement in the side mirrors as they dashed out of the path of my steaming wheels. They yapped in protest, while I sat with my knuckles bulging round the steering wheel.

Horatio hauled himself up in the back seat and gave a magisterial gruff. I told him to stay there as I got out. Most of the dogs backed away, though a couple of the more craven breeds approached on their bellies. I patted one on the head and immediately regretted it, as the musky scent of the pack reached me. Two of the bigger dogs started snapping at each other's legs in a fussy dispute. The ones on the pavement hadn't even bothered to move, just lifted their heads to check if they were required. Beyond them, I saw the reason they were gathered here: a pet shop, dark behind two glass doors. But I wasn't sure if it was the smell of food they were after or the fat golden Labrador that lay flat on the linoleum, trapped inside her gilded cage. I made to turn back to the car, but the Labrador locked eyes with me. "Oh, for God's sake," I breathed and stepped up to the pavement.

I rattled the doors, but they were locked. One of the fighting dogs edged closer behind me. When I made eye contact his lip twitched, showing his teeth, like a cowboy raising his shirt to reveal a gun. The Labrador whimpered a plea, but I didn't know how to help her. A growl made me whip round, but the fighting dog was snarling at Horatio in the car. That gave me an idea. "Go back"—I flapped my hands at the Labrador inside the store—"go on, move back!" She just scuffled her legs against the lino and remained prostrate. I went round the bonnet to get in the car, and reversed up onto the pavement, inching back against the glass doors: in the side mirror I saw the Labrador struggling away. I edged back, giving the accelerator more pressure when the car made contact. There was a second of resistance, and then the glass burst in a glittering shower that spattered down over my rear bumper. Right, that was it. I'd done my bit; she could get out and fend for herself. I'd grab some food for Horatio while I was here and get moving. I crunched into the shop.

The Labrador tottered forward on arthritic legs. I used my key to slice open a few sacks, spilling dog food across the floor. That would keep the pack going until the scavenging instinct kicked in. I pocketed some dog treats and heaved a bag of food over one shoulder before picking my way across the broken glass to the car. The old Lab followed me into the sunlight. "Sorry," I told her, as she came up to the car, "you're on your own now." As though she understood, she doddered away along the pavement, while I stowed the food and treats on the back seat. But the fighting dog stayed, eyeing me or the food, I wasn't sure. He was standing between me and the driver's door, head low, lips drawn.

I lifted a piece of paper from the back seat, one of the kid's drawings, slowly scrunched it into a ball, and threw it into the road. His eyes followed, but he didn't. His focus swiveled back, and he pulled the trigger, lunging forward to grasp one ankle and whip my legs from under me. I sprawled hard onto the ground, realizing the dog's massive strength as he gripped the leg of my jeans and dragged me along a foot or so, until I swung my loose leg and slammed my boot down onto his muzzle. He released me and started shaking his head frantically, distracted by a scrap of denim stuck between his teeth. I scrambled up and got into the car. Through the shock, my ankle started to sting where he'd broken the skin.

The car gave a shimmy as the engine fired. The fighting dog had selected a new victim and gone after the Labrador, who cowered, one front leg lifted in submission. I thunked the gear stick into drive. From the back seat, I grabbed the treats. I let the car roll closer and ripped a packet open, holding the meat sticks out the window, calling out— "Hey!"—to the big dog, who ignored the food even when it landed between his front legs. Maybe he wasn't even hungry; maybe this was just pack mentality, the alpha male asserting himself. He loomed over the old Lab, up on his claws, tail high, teeth bared. The old girl gave a yelp, a cry of incomprehension or perhaps defiance. In a thrash of movement, he went for her neck.

An ammonia smell of dog and my own fear sweat filled the car as I over-revved the engine. *No more heroics,* I told myself: *Get out of the city; stop for nothing; don't look back.* But I did look back, and as I pulled away I watched the Labrador haul herself onto her front legs and make it about six inches back toward the pet shop, before slumping onto the pavement, either dying or resigned to it.

———

Less than a mile along the motorway, just outside the city, Joni's new car was parked at a careless angle on the hard shoulder. It rocked slightly, and I could see the kids climbing about in there. As I pulled up in front of it, Lola was picking her way delicately down the steep embankment from the direction of a bridge above the carriageway. I assumed she had gone for a pee, but then I saw Joni coming from the other side of the central reservation, shouting as she jogged, pointing up to the bridge.

"We must've scared him off," Joni was yelling as my window rolled down. Lola made it over to me first.

"There's a child," she said, "on the bridge."

Joni straddled the metal barrier and arrived in a few steps. Her cheeks were flushed, hands businesslike on hips as she scanned the surrounding fields. I restarted my engine.

"I can take Billy and the boys the rest of the way," I said, putting my seat belt back on. "Are you okay to have a girls' car again?"

Joni's eyes swiveled round to my face and stopped there. "We saw a boy, Marlene. He ran off, but he's here somewhere." She and Lola watched me, as though waiting for a cue.

"I hate to say it," I grimaced, "but I rather think everyone's dead."

Lola looked down at her feet, tossed her hair back up, and moved toward the other car. Joni pursed her lips. "We saw a child. A boy," she said, "in pajamas. He was up there, and when we stopped he ran that way." Her arm swept from the bridge to a copse on the far side of the carriageway. "And now we need to find him," she finished in her best don't-fuck-with-me voice. "Come on, Lola," she called. "Now that Marlene's here to watch her own kids, we can climb down to those trees."

"Why?" I asked. They both stopped and turned back to me again. "Pardon me?" said Joni.

"We can't take him with us. He might be infected."

I adjusted my rearview mirror so I could see my kids in the car behind. Billy in front, arms stretched across the steering wheel as though he were driving a bus. Maggie pulling her hair over her face, inspecting the strands. Charlie propped up over the back seat, looking my way and batting an upside-down Peter's feet away from his head. I waved and he waved back.

"Infected how?" asked Joni.

They both stood in the middle of the motorway, arms folded, squinting at me like I was the sun and I was guilty of burning them. I told them about the terrorists, the bombs, the man-made virus. "We only survived because we were in the forest. We can't risk making contact with anyone who's been exposed."

Lola looked back in the direction we had come. "You saw a body. Maybe you've been exposed too. Maybe we were all infected while we were in the city."

The slight wind dropped, and the bordering trees stopped bristling. All living things held as still as the asphalt beneath our feet. I undid my seat belt. Opened the door and slid down onto the carriageway.

"Actually, I've seen several bodies. Three men. A woman in a car. My husband." I paused to think if that was all. "A neighbor. A dog." Lola winced at the last one, as though it were the final nail in the coffin. "But I didn't touch them and if I'd been infected by those bodies yesterday, I'd be dead by now. We all would. I don't know how this works, but I do know we survived because we were shut away in the forest. So I just want to get the kids back there, because we don't know who's infected and who's not."

Joni grabbed a gobbet of hair and started sucking on it. "You know how people always say they live day to day? Take it one day at a time? That's what we're going to do." She spat out the hair and looked over to the copse again. "If we're not dead because we were isolated, then maybe that kid was, too."

"So why's he on his own? Where are the parents?" I asked. Not giving them a moment to jump in, I carried on. "Dead, that's where they are. Which means he's been exposed and he's not coming with us."

"Shh," said Lola, "he'll hear you." We turned to see a little Asian boy, holding a gray blanket, peering down at us between the bars of the barrier on the bridge. We all stared at him, until Lola gave a finger wave. The boy raised his gray blanket and waved it back.

"So," said Joni, hands on hips, up on her toes to look down at me, "are you going to drive away and leave him there?"

"I'm thinking of all of us."

In fact, I was thinking *for* all of us. I turned away from the child, back toward my own kids in the car. Billy had stopped "driving" and was staring up at the boy on the bridge. Charlie's face was also pressed up against the glass, alongside Peter's, both looking as stunned as the blowfish woman back in the village. I really wished the kids hadn't seen the lost boy—I could cope with Joni and Lola thinking I was broken, but not my kids.

"I say he could have been exposed, and I'm not risking my kids' lives," I said.

But Lola was already marching toward the bridge. "And I say he's just a little kid, and we're taking him."

Joni gave a shrug and jogged after her.

I let them go.

When I opened the door to get Billy and the others out of the car, the din drowned out any voices from the bridge. I explained that the child was lost and would come with us for now. By the time I installed the four of them in the Beast, Joni was coming back across the carriageway with the boy following a few paces behind. I got up into the driver's seat and closed the door. Now that he was close, I could see that he was six or seven, about Maggie's age, wearing supermarket pajamas and plastic shoes. A big leaf that had stuck to one sole scraped against the road with every other step, giving the effect of a pitiful limp. His lips were grayish and cracked. I opened the window just enough to throw a water bottle to Joni, who caught it and crouched down to help the boy drink. He choked and coughed, spittle flying everywhere, but got some down. Joni offered the bottle back to me.

"Don't want it back."

She rolled her eyes. "He's just dehydrated."

"Maybe. You can take him in your car," I said, "the kids are coming with me. What's his name?"

"He doesn't want to speak yet," said Joni.

"Must be traumatized," I added in a whisper, "from watching his parents die."

Joni shushed me, but the boy was totally zoned out. "If he survived, then he's immune."

"Could be a carrier." I started my engine. "Anyway, you'll soon find out after being cooped up together in the car. I assume Lola's riding with me?"

Behind us, Lola hauled open the back door of the other car and started shifting the detritus left behind by my kids, making room for herself and the boy. "I'll sit in the back with him," she called out.

"Really?" I said to Joni. "Like a canary down a mine shaft?" She gawped at me as I put the car into drive and rolled forward onto the carriageway.

"When did you get so hard, Marlene?" she said.

Hard. I slipped the car into reverse and backed up. How to explain to Joni the gradual process of my hardening. How it builds up without you noticing, like lime scale. How you steel yourself to sit rigid on the plane that might crash and leave your children motherless. How the long-distance phone calls make them cry, so you stop calling. Or should I tell her instead how I paid the mortgage each month for ten years? How I provided—provided everything—even a team of babysitters once Julian reneged entirely on his side of the parenting deal. How I did it because I never had a choice. All these much-celebrated choices that we have, apparently, us modern women. There are no choices, only higher expectations.

Except that now, sitting in the Beast with my kids, on the side of an empty motorway, I did have a choice. If I had to be hard, I would be hard for all of us. I would choose for all of us to survive.

"People aren't hard, Joni," I said. "But decisions are. It's up to you, it's your call."

"Wait," Joni said as she started off along the hard shoulder toward Lola. After several minutes of rapid hand gestures, Lola high-stepped over to my passenger door and managed to slide in without ever unfolding her arms.

Chapter Seven

In hindsight, I probably should have consulted my lists. I sat on the empty cooler, poking at the fire with a long stick. But there was nothing to cook. And nothing to drink except water. The kids sat on logs on the far side of the clearing, eating salt 'n' vinegar crisps in a steadfast rhythm, licking their fingers down to the knuckles to get the last few crumbs. They were hushed and dopey, humbled by hunger.

At my insistence, the kids kept their distance from the Lost Boy, but Maggie still subjected him to a stream of information about the camp and our life here. Joni had him out of his filthy pajamas and into some of Charlie's clean clothes and, even with the trouser legs rolled up twice, the family uniform of head-to-toe Boden meant he looked the part. He remained mute, wide eyes taking everything in, while he dabbed every last speck of salt off the foil of his crisp packet and sucked crumbs from his chapped lips. The boy was hungry. How many days had he been alone? I cut up our last apple into a bowl for him. Maggie never stopped talking while he ate.

I watched them while I pondered a fact that had been pushed to the wayside while we were busy disagreeing over what to do with the Lost Boy: his presence meant there were definitely other survivors.

"Did you bring medication?" Joni was stamping to and fro between the cars and the camp, dragging back to the tents all the stuff we'd hauled the other way only that morning.

"A few bits."

"Disinfectant?"

"No."

"What about food?" Lola chimed in.

"Nope."

"You were supposed to be getting supplies."

"There was a dead bloke in the kitchen."

Only now I thought about the tools in the garage. The fully stocked pantry in the utility room, which opened into the garage. The massive gas barbecue on wheels, also in the garage. In hindsight, I probably should have gone into the garage. In hindsight, I should have gotten my ducks in a line. And, thanks to Julian and his lovelorn e-mail to Aurora, I'd even forgotten to let the bloody rabbit out.

"Lucky I stopped and got this," said Joni, coming up the slope holding the yellow feet of a headless chicken. "And this." An axe landed in the dirt. I didn't ask for details, but she answered anyway. "We passed a farm, and I grabbed this old girl from a little coop in the yard. She'll do us for tonight. I should've brought them all, they could roam free."

"The foxes would have them," I said.

"Take this," said Joni. She held out the chicken by the stump where the head used to be. "Come on, I'm going to skin it—quicker than plucking." I reached out and took the bloody stub, which slipped straight through my hand. I caught the chicken before it hit the ground. "You're going to have to stand up, Marlene. I can't do it down there." I straightened up, juggled the chicken so that I was holding it with one hand around the throat and the other under its backside. Joni went to work on its neck, pulling back the skin, using a penknife to cut away the white tissue that held skin to flesh. "Higher," she said. I raised my arms to hold the chicken right in front of my face. Joni's fingers ripped down under its collar, and one of its taloned feet kicked up and clawed at my chin.

I jumped back and dropped the chicken, feeling my chin for blood. "It got me."

Joni chuckled, bent to pick up the hen.

"Just a reflex." She handed me the chicken as I inspected my fingertips. "There's no blood." I took hold of the chicken again. Joni smiled as she worked. Again, she tugged sharply at a gristly bit and, again, I dropped the carcass into the dirt.

"Jesus, Marlene—shall I get one of the kids to do it?"

She started nipping away at the white tissue again, and when she was ready to tug said, "Hold on," so I managed not to drop it. We stood face-to-face over the chicken, feet planted wide for stability as we worked. "Hold on." I gripped the stump. "Hold on." I held on. The feathered layer peeled down until the headless animal looked like it was wearing a tutu, its ugly feet dancing beneath my hands. Lola came up and prodded the swollen food sack that hung from its neck.

"That's her crop," said Joni. "Some people eat that. It's a delicacy."

"Gross," said Lola. "But it's about all we're going to have left for breakfast tomorrow." She huffed off to find the kebab skewers for dinner.

"I'll make a broth, we'll be fine," Joni called after her daughter. She stared at me until I raised my eyes to hers. "There's food all around. We'll be fine."

"Banana," said Billy, an hour later when dinner was served. I explained again that we didn't have a banana or a mango or a minty Viscount biscuit. He would have to eat his food if he was hungry because there wouldn't be any more. He didn't believe me, of course, because that's what I said in our kitchen at home, leaning over his booster chair with my back turned to the cupboards stuffed with food. But now, with my back turned only to the darkening void between the trees, I realized he would have to work this one out for himself. He would go hungry. And learn to eat. I took away his plate.

Charlie and Peter descended to finish off Billy's chicken kebab and watercress salad, which they still couldn't believe was made with actual watercress that Joni found in actual water in the actual forest. There was also a bucket of blackberries for dessert. They lolled around afterward on their logs, as stuffed as Romans. Joni hunched over her stove, boiling up leftovers into a soup for the morning. But unlike those of us who were confident our survival was assured by the presence of watercress, I couldn't stop thinking about the garage at home. It was too far to drive back now, but a garage was a garage. They all contained roughly the same things, didn't they? Things we needed.

"Can you get the kids into bed?" I said to Joni. "It's my turn to go out foraging."

"Now?"

It wasn't dark yet, but night was just over the hill and coming our way. I kissed the kids and went down to the car. "I'm taking the axe."

———

According to the map, there was another village south of the camp, in the opposite direction to Wodebury. With luck, I would see a farm or a house on the way and check it out for useful kit. I started up the hill to the lane and by habit switched on the radio, but there was only static. I let it scroll through the stations, the regular bursts of white noise forming a bleak soundtrack like a marching song. The frequencies scurried past and started all over again. I began to hum during the pauses between bursts of static.

The lane turned onto a bigger trunk road, where I switched on my headlights, although they didn't venture far into the gloom. The road pitched and rolled between the high walls of hedges. I accelerated past a black-and-white pub with a couple of hatchbacks in the car park—I didn't want to repeat my pub experience. Less than a mile on, I braked hard and just made the turn into a mechanic's yard. I stopped in the driveway, with the security barrier lifted high above me, its open padlock dangling up in the sky. As I got out, metal chimed against metal to sound a feeble alarm.

The sliding doors of the workshop were open on one side to reveal a long slit of blackness. I picked up the axe and held it by the heavy end in one hand, the Maglite in the other. My boots scuffed across puddles of gravel, then fell silent over mossy patches that had reclaimed the forecourt. At the shed, I laid my hand on the wooden door, feeling the blue paint crumble and patter down over my toes. There was no buzz, so I used all my weight to press the door farther back. Inside, the darkness gathered in corners. The only sound was my own breath going in, in, in and out; in, in, in and out. I fumbled the torch on.

An ice cream van took up most of the space, straddling the mechanic's pit with its serving window open. My light revealed pictures of cones and sundaes and something called a "screwball," which evoked a distant memory of childhood desire. The gaudy images emerged from the dark like the hieroglyphs of the future.

It was hard to linger, though, with the dark tweaking my ponytail. I swung the torch down into the pit and around the sides of the workshop. Along the back wall hung the tools. I glanced the light down into the dark pit again, just checking, before I stepped over and grabbed a crowbar, a hammer, a saw. A pair of pliers. Working as quickly as I could. In and out. I spotted a car battery. I scraped it across the floor to the entrance, dumped the lot, and went back for a sledgehammer and some metal cutters.

On the way out the door to fetch the car, I struck gold: fuel canisters. I washed the flank of the Beast with most of the first one, but got the knack and topped the car up to overflowing. The heady smell of the jerry cans took me back to Africa: my father loading the roof rack of the safari truck before dawn, while I huddled in the warmth of the headlights. The Beast's headlights glinted off the sopping canisters, and I wondered if I was just imagining the shimmer of rising vapors. Those fumes would be overwhelming in the car. I found a short ladder and some bungee ties inside the workshop. The ladder swung into place on top of the bike rack. Securing it was simple, but hauling a full jerry can onto the roof was not; it weighed as much as Billy. A dead weight. I apologized to the Beast as I gouged scars into its side by pushing the canisters up onto the bonnet and then scraping them over the windscreen, swearing all the way. Finally, the fuel was fixed onto the modified roof rack, and I jumped back down into the gravel.

"It's okay." I patted the Beast where I'd scratched it. "You look the part now."

I slid the workshop doors closed to hide the ice cream van, a strange little secret for someone else to discover.

The first gray houses of the village straggled down the hill, but I flashed past them, braking hard when I spotted the green sign of a grocery store up a side street. I reversed and turned up a steep concrete ramp into the small car park. Empty. A good sign. I bumped up onto the pavement and across a short pedestrian area to stop right outside the double doors, leaving the lights on full beam. The windows were covered by vibrant pictures of tempting delicacies: red wine gushing from a bottle, tomatoes as big as my head. But the doors were shuttered. I picked up the axe, crowbar, and sledgehammer from the passenger seat.

I found the lock at the bottom of the shutter and heaved at it with the crowbar. The metal slats roiled and clattered, the loudest noise I'd heard for hours. I glanced up and down the street, reassuring myself there was no one to disturb. The windows of the surrounding bungalows were as blank as their inhabitants. As if to brazen it out, I grabbed the sledgehammer and slammed the lock, felt my spine rattle like the metal slats. I tried lifting the shutter an inch or so with the crowbar and hacking at the lock with the axe. Nothing budged. I stood up and arched to stretch my back. The moon was just rising over the slouching rooftops. I was grateful for the light.

I picked up my tools and switched on the Maglite to look for a back door. In fact, there was a side door, which did little to resist the crowbar. I shone my light down a corridor, strode past a staff toilet and a windowless office, pushing through swing doors into a loading area, and then into the shop itself. I listened for buzz, but there was just the sticky sound of decay. And a smell like the bottom of the fridge after my longer business trips. With the crowbar, I forced the main entrance doors from the inside, and found a simple padlock that held the shutters closed. An axe blow to the chain and the shutters rattled up to knee-height. I pushed them up, letting moonlight luster the checkout and magazine racks.

Outside, I dropped the tools on the passenger seat and walked over to pull free a trolley. It bucked out of my hands, and I realized that it was chained, needing a coin. "You are kidding me," I muttered. My handbag was back at the camp. I had no money. I checked the car for coins—the center console, the door pockets, under the seats.

"Fuck's sake!" I shouted into the night. *Ache, ache, ache,* the echo came back down the street.

"Fine." The axe was back in my hand and I swung it high, bringing it down onto the tinny little chain that held the trolley. "Don't worry," I shouted to the other trolleys as I dragged one out, "the rest of you can go free." I swung the axe and smashed chain after chain, pulling a few trolleys out and pushing them off into the car park, where one collapsed onto its side, but two others gathered speed down the slope toward the road. "That's it!" I called. "Go! Go on, run free!" I hacked more trolleys from the pack and sent them off in singles and pairs, shouting after them as they jiggered away like shackled ponies. When I had freed a line of trolleys, I let the axe drop onto the paving stones and caught my breath. I rubbed my hand over my face. "Ducks back in a line," I said, and pushed my trolley into the supermarket.

———

I finished stacking the first trolley-load in the boot of the car. The shop was small, but densely stocked, so I went back for more. Against the back wall, I compared types of charcoal. Decision made, I shone the torch across and saw disposable plates and cutlery. As I pushed the trolley along the aisle, I heard the twin rattle of a trolley outside.

I stopped dead.

Silence. I opened my mouth to breathe more quietly.

Another burst of trolley rattle from the car park. I clicked off the Maglite and crouched down to the floor, instinctively looking for something to crawl under, but there was no cover.

Silence again. Long silence.

Maybe a trolley had rolled down the hill by itself?

I waited a few minutes longer and stood back up. I clicked on the Maglite, moved to the end of the aisle, keeping the torchlight low to the ground. I could see the moonlit entrance, the railings outside, the headlamps streaming in from where the car stood out of sight to the left. I should turn those off, I thought, in case the battery dies.

As I took another step toward the entrance, a moonlit shadow darted across the path. Tall, fast, human. I hit the floor again, scrabbling the torch off. As I did, the shutter came rattling down in a shower of noise, and I was huddled in darkness.

"Quick!" A voice outside signaled a burst of trolley rattle. Running footsteps, fast and light. I crawled back toward the loading bay and crouched along the corridor to the side door. Creeping round the outside of the building to the pedestrian area, I saw dark shapes engulf my car.

They were everywhere. I held a hand up against the glare of the headlamps and saw that they were inside as well as out, small silhouettes pulling out stuff and dumping it into trolleys: raiding the car. Their scuffling footsteps consolidated, and I gathered there were about eight of them, a couple inside the cabin, the others clustered around the boot. A box came flying out of a side door, and round shapes the size of hand grenades rolled away: avocados. "Gross!" said a shrill voice, and another one giggled. One trolley left the scene, pushed down the slope by someone who jumped on and rode it as it picked up speed and jangled off.

They were children, boys. Behaving like a pack of wild things. Like the dogs back in the city. They were taller than mine, older than Charlie, not little ones; old enough to know better. Injustice burnt in me, and I fought an urge to run forward and grab my stuff, fight for our supplies. Our lifeline. I stood upright and stepped out into the light.

"That's my food."

The scuffling stopped, as if a bunch of mice had been caught in the glare of a cat. There was a beat, and then one of them shouted, "Leg it!" The shapes streamed away from the car and scattered, some pushing a second trolley away, while others vaulted the railings and dropped the few feet to the pavement below, where they had bikes. I chased the closest figures, but they separated, so I headed down the slope after the trolley, but it was already turning into the dark alley of another side road. I stopped after a few steps, too slow to stand a chance.

"Little shits," I yelled after them. "I'm coming after you." I turned back up the slope toward the car. Ahead of me: a quick footstep and the scrape of the axe as it was lifted from the paving stones. A taller boy, the one who had closed the shutters, swung the axe into the air.

He darted through the headlights, the beam bleaching out his electric mop of hair so it blazed for a second like a filament. His face fell again into darkness and he swung at the wheel. "No!" I screamed as the axe landed with a muted thud in the tire. The breath left my body with the same dull rush as air through rubber. The Beast sagged like a wounded bull. The axe clattered to the ground, its clang echoing down the now-empty street, as the boy leapt onto the pavement below. I ran after him and teetered over the railing, pivoting on my hips and flailing at the air through which he'd fallen. I leaned out and screeched a long cry of pure fury into the night—the sound of outfoxed prey. Below me, the boy made a running jump onto a bike.

"Witch!" he shouted back, his voice cracking. "Get a broomstick!"

Chapter Eight

"Fucking feral scouts," I ranted. "Shitting little Wild Things got the car battery and the Special K. It was the last bloody box."

"At least you got this." Joni topped up my red wine, which was medicinal because I'd managed to slice open my shin while changing the tire on the car. Now, I lay flat on my back next to the campfire, while Joni shone the Maglite into the wound to pick out any bits before disinfecting it. I'd gotten disinfectant, too; the thieving little buggers had gone, predictably enough, for the least practical items.

"Ow!"

"Man up, Marlene, keep still."

"Man up?"

She just laughed.

"Speak for yourself." I craned my neck to slug some wine, dribbled most of it down my chin.

The night was still. High strips of cloud were lit up by the moon like a giant X-ray of a sick lung.

"Julian was having an affair with Aurora," I said. "I found an e-mail on his laptop earlier."

Joni picked up the disinfectant and poured a lid full over my cut. I sucked in a breath and blew out the pain through pursed lips. Joni dabbed away the runoff and started opening a bandage. She didn't say a word.

I came up onto my elbows to confront her. "Did you know?"

"Course not, I would have said something. But I guess I'm not surprised. She was kind of a bitch."

"She funded my start-up, back in the day," I said.

"She was a total princess. And Julian was—" She floundered a beat too long.

"Emasculated by his wife?" I saved her from saying it.

"Jeez, go easy on yourself. I was going to say weak. Or lazy. Weak and lazy. Hold this; the cut's not deep, but I don't want it getting infected. No clue where we'd find antibiotics." She placed a line of gauze pads along the length of the cut and started cutting off strips of tape. "But, yeah. I guess your success humiliated him. He never found his *thing*."

"That's what she said—"

Joni snorted. "True, maybe it was nothing more than sex. Hold still."

I scrunched forward to keep the gauze in place. "We went to marriage counseling." My voice came out cramped from the position.

"I remember."

"He told the shrink my anger was traumatizing the kids. She made me sit in a chair, while my anger sat in another chair, and I had to tell it—myself—how I was hurting my kids."

Joni nodded.

"He said he had to leave so I could take responsibility for my own negativity."

She nodded.

"But he couldn't care less about me or the kids. He was just upgrading. To a first-class bitch."

Joni nodded again.

"Stop fucking nodding!"

"He was a prick."

"Prick!" I slammed my hand into the dirt, pulling the bandage out of Joni's grasp. She pushed me firmly back down, adjusted the Maglite, and carried on wrapping.

"You didn't deserve to be treated that way, Marlene. You work harder than anyone I know. And even if it hasn't always been easy at home—"

"For him or me?"

Joni snapped the sharp teeth of an elastic clip into the bandage. "For all of us. But you work hard for those kids. You made a life for them, a home, security. You did that. That's what he should have told the counselor."

While she packed the first-aid box, I rolled over to sit with my back against a log. Turned my face away from the light of the fire and blotted the tears with my sleeve.

"You okay?" Joni looked at me intently.

"It hurts," I said.

"Sure it hurts. However much he wronged you, you're still going to mourn for him—"

"I meant my leg hurts."

Joni snorted. "Right, of course. And we're done discussing it."

She topped up our wine again. I slugged mine more successfully this time. Joni unraveled the remaining bandage into a pile at her feet, and then set about wrapping it into a neater roll around two fingers.

"I cheated on David once," she said, just as I drew a hit of rioja into my mouth. I dribbled it back into the cup, and she laughed into the canopy. "Bet you weren't expecting that."

"Do tell me all the details so I can live vicariously. Who was it?"

"Lola's father." Joni pulled the bandage tight and tucked in the end.

"No!"

"When I went home to see my mom a couple of years ago."

"No!" I watched the firelight warm her cheekbones; it lit up her eyes as she downed the last of her wine. "Don't tell me," I said, "you go home to your girlie-pink bedroom, slip on the old prom dress, and when he came a-calling in his Dodge"—I carried on talking even as she groaned at my Southern American accent—"all those loving feelings came flooding back . . ."

"Less romantic," she said. "More hormonal. I thought he might get me pregnant again. Like, maybe we're just compatible that way. I'd gotten pregnant with Lola the first time I slept with him—only time I slept with him—and you know how long I've tried with David, but no one can tell us why it doesn't work. So, I thought this was worth a try. It was kind of stupid."

"Wow! Joni Luff, you have a steely streak I've never noticed before."

"Not really, because I didn't get pregnant. We only did it the once. And I got my period the next day. I'm such a dumbass with my dates."

"Thank goodness." I watched her reaction, and when she shrugged, I added, "I mean, what were you going to tell David? And Lola?"

"That I was pregnant and happy. But now that David's not here, I can't believe I risked losing him."

"Well, holy shit. That's—" I didn't know what that was. Sad, I guess. I wanted to ask if she'd ever told David—not that it was quite the same as Julian and me; their marriage was worth saving, for starters—but Joni got up and started damping down the fire. She was done, off to bed. I gathered up the evidence of our drinking binge and took it to the food tent. When I came out, she was still there, pouring river water over the last glowing embers.

"We need to talk to the kids in the morning," I said. "With these Wild Things on the loose, we need to be more careful. It's like you said before, we've got to man up. Get some discipline. Especially the little ones."

"They're so young, they need time to adjust."

"They need to survive long enough to adjust."

Joni dropped her head back to look at the sky. "It's beautiful out here," she said, "we have shelter, and there's food all around us."

"We could look for a house?"

"What about bodies? What do you call it—the buzz?"

"At least we know this campsite is clean."

"Right. We'll be fine here until help comes."

"What help?" I asked.

"The military, I guess. If this thing is all over the country like you read, all that awful stuff going on in the cities, then it might take a while for them to reach us out here. But David'll come find us once the flights are back on." Joni stared up to the sky, and I wondered if she was looking for a sign or something more practical—a plane. "I was supposed to be there. Fly up to see Mom. We should have let Lola cut school, it was only a couple of days."

"But what if the virus has spread worldwide?"

Joni grabbed the first-aid box and clutched it to her chest. "Then we'll survive just fine on our own."

Somewhere in the forest sounded the double bark of a fox. We listened as it repeated its cry, which stopped as suddenly as it began.

"Juvenile, out hunting," said Joni.

"Like I said, we need to toughen up." Joni shook her head, but I went on. "Because we're not on our own anymore, are we?"

———

"This is so much better than glamping," Joni said the next morning, as we broke our fast on her lumpy soup and bitter tea.

"Oh, yeah, glamping is so last year," I said. "So pre-apocalypse."

But Joni kept twanging on about getting in sync with nature's rhythms and wandered off with her head in her foraging book.

"Talking about nature's rhythms," I said, handing a shovel to Charlie and Peter, "you two are going to dig a latrine." We found a private spot just outside the camp and consulted their *Survival Skills* book. I left them to it and returned to the food tent, where Maggie had mixed together the biscuits, pasta, and eggs, and was busy feeding the lot to Horatio, who was wolfing it down. As I started to yell, Lola—who was supposed to be watching the little ones—came back from the road with Billy. They both had armfuls of sunflowers.

"Look Mum-may, we found one-flowers."

"Just what we need—decorative items. Lola, you left Maggie and the Lost Boy alone, and she fed all our food to the dog." Lola petted Billy's hair with the pitying expression of a nurse tending a brave but terminal patient. She had plaited a stem of cow parsley into his side curls so that the hair pulled up, exposing the soft skin behind his ear, the spot he liked to have stroked while falling asleep. My own private spot, just between him and me.

"Come on, Billy, let's give these to Mom." As he walked past, I reached down to stroke the soft spot, but he shrugged my finger away like a gnat. I couldn't remember the last time I'd stroked him to sleep. Probably he couldn't, either.

Maggie had fled the scene of the crime, the wide-eyed Lost Boy trailing after her, and was busy sifting a pile of dirt near the cooking fire. I picked up a broken tea bag and realized the dirt was actually tea leaves, which she'd collected by ripping open every single tea bag in the box. I drew in a deep breath while I gathered all my best expletives into my frontal lobe, but before I got a chance to release them, Charlie came hurtling into the camp. "Peter's run away!"

I followed him out again.

The latrine hole was good and deep. They'd done a great job. Until Peter hit a root and tried to lever it up with the shovel, snapping off its handle.

"So then he ran away," explained Charlie, "because he thought you were going to kill him." His eyes flicked between my face and feet. "Because he broke the shovel."

"Yes, yes, I got that. My fault again." I picked up the jagged handle, which was soft and rotten inside. Threw it into the forest. "He'll come back when he's hungry." Not that we had much to give Peter once he returned; Maggie had seen to that. In the food tent, I did a stock take of the supplies I'd managed to salvage from the shop after the raid: we were good for wine, rice, and breakfast cereals. It seemed the Wild Things weren't fond of coconut water or avocados, so we had plenty of those. I'd found a sack of potatoes, but I didn't trust the unrefrigerated meat. Of course, there was always more watercress. We wouldn't starve, but there were lots of mouths to feed.

"Right, kids, sit down." My three lined up in height order—Charlie, Maggie, Billy—while Lola busied herself in the background, humming too loud to hear me. The Lost Boy squeezed his narrow frame in next to Maggie.

"You know how I said we have to stay here in the forest for a while?"

"Because of all the rotting dead bodies in the city?" said Maggie.

"Who told you about rotting—? Right, yep, because all the people caught a bug that made them really sick and now—"

"Daddy's dead, too," said Maggie.

"Yes, we can't see Daddy, I'm afraid." I repeated it in a less brusque tone. "Daddy got sick, too. I'm sorry."

"I want Daddy," cried Billy.

"I'm sorry about Daddy. We'll talk more about him soon, I promise, but now I need to talk about living in the forest—"

"Where is Daddy?"

"He's gone away."

"Where? Can we go?"

"No, we can't go there. We have to stay here in the forest because it's safe and—"

"Is Daddy coming here?"

"No. I'm afraid we can't see Daddy. Now, look, we have to talk about survival. Do you know what that word means, survival?"

"Where's Uncle David?"

"He's in America. Now, survival, we need to talk about that. It means looking after ourselves—"

"Is Daddy with Uncle David?"

"No. He's not. Now, look, listen, please. We need to talk about survival and food and we can't just waste all the tea, okay?"

"Maggie spilt the tea. Is Maggie in really, really big trouble, Mum-may?"

"No, look, forget about the tea. It was just an example. I'm talking about this . . . silliness. It has to stop." Four sets of wide-open eyes. Four wide-open mouths. "I need you to get behind me. Do you understand?"

Billy stood up and walked round behind me.

I put my hands over my face just as Joni stumped into the camp with a brace of rabbits in one hand and Peter in the other.

"Look who I found up a tree," she said.

"Be nice, Mummy," whispered Charlie.

I walked over and looked down at Peter. He met my gaze. I located the muscles that pulled my mouth upward and performed a smile. Then I squinted so that it reached my eyes. Peter's chin wobbled.

"Are you all right?" I asked.

"Yes, Mrs. Greene," he said. Charlie looked up at me, his fingers writhing together like baby snakes.

I sighed. "Don't worry about the shovel, Peter, it was old and rotten. We'll get another one." He gave a tiny nod. "And . . . you did a great job with that latrine. I'm very much looking forward to using it." His eyes squinted for a moment in confusion, and then his lips twitched up at the corners. I held his eye contact and leaned a little closer toward him. "But don't run off again. This forest is not a playground." I turned and walked away.

"See?" I heard Charlie whisper to Peter.

"Come on, everyone," I called out. "I don't trust you here on your own, we're going shopping." With Joni's help it took only a moment to shift the fuel canisters off the roof of the Beast and hide them beneath the overgrown hedgerow. Then we bundled into the car and headed back to the grocery store.

———

Lola and the big boys kept watch over the car, which I'd turned around and parked facing the road with the engine running. Peter and Charlie stood on the bonnet holding sticks. The Lost Boy stayed in the passenger seat at my insistence because he still didn't speak or react to instructions with anything approaching urgency. The rest of us ducked under the shutter into the dark interior, which a sweep of the torch showed was just as I'd left it. The Wild Things hadn't been back. Nor had anyone else. At last, some good news.

"Quick and quiet," I reminded them. "Get as much as we can while it's still here." Joni and I split up with a basket in each hand. Maggie followed Joni down the cereal aisle while I started on the fruit and veg, hoping to find something still fresh. Billy dashed over and grabbed a huge packet of crisps.

"Don't you want an apple? It's days since you've had any fresh fruit." I made to grab the bag and he whipped round, sheltering it behind his body.

"My cisps!"

"You can't just eat crisps, Billy. You need some real food."

I wrestled him for the packet, which popped open in the struggle. His desperate hand dived inside and burst back out, showering us both with oily crumbs.

"This is not the time to flip out," I hissed at him. "Just give me the crisps."

"I'm hungry!" He let out a long whine that stopped me in my tracks. Hunger does that to a mother.

"All right then, here's an apple. Eat the apple first, okay, then crisps. Yes?"

He turned, and I whipped the packet out of his hand, replacing it with an apple. He worried it with his tiny teeth.

"Too hard," he whined. "Too green."

"Just try," I said. "And stay close. Come on." He shuffled after me. I filled two baskets and left them by the entrance, picking up two more. Baskets were quieter than trolleys, less likely to alert the Wild Things that we were here.

"Keep up, Billy," I said, and he followed me to the tin aisle. I stacked up two of everything, bending my knees to haul up the baskets by the arching handles and fetch them to the entrance.

"Billy, where are you now? Bring your apple." He sidled away down another aisle, doubling back toward the crisps. Stubborn little—*Don't sweat the small stuff,* I thought, and let him go.

Lola transferred the full baskets to the car one by one, swinging them between her legs like a contestant on World's Strongest Man. Charlie and Peter watched the road, paying attention to the task. I nodded and went back in with two more baskets.

"Where are you, Billy?" I called out from the pasta aisle.

"I'm here." His voice came from the loading bay.

"Come back, would you? Right now!"

There was a suspicious silence that suggested his mouth was full of fried, salty goodness.

I staggered out once more into the light and over to the car. A bass drum in my chest thudded from carrying the heavy baskets and from the adrenaline of being nearly finished. I shouted at the boys to climb down and get inside, ready to go. "Let's make a quick getaway, kids," I said. Maggie ran past me into the car and Joni came behind her, loaded down with goodies. She had charcoal and extra-long matches, as well as a tall jar of chicken seasoning and, on the top, several packets of chocolate.

"That's more like it," I said. We grinned at each other as we passed. I trotted to the shop, picked up another two baskets.

"Billy, get into the car now, we're going," I called. "Bring your crisps!" I lifted the baskets, the heavy ones full of tins, and lurched toward the car. Joni and Lola came up on either side of me, and we shared the weight of the load.

"Are we done?" asked Joni.

"Think so. Anything we've forgotten?" I slammed the boot shut. "Billy? Get out here *now*. We are leaving."

"Don't think so." Joni muttered the items from our list and nodded, satisfied that we'd found them all. "We got a good haul."

"We did well. Jesus, Billy," I called, walking toward the store. "What are you doing? You need to come when I say come—now *come on*."

"I'll grab him," said Lola.

"No! This is what I was talking about earlier—the kids need to do *what* they're told *when* they're told. This shit is important now."

"Come on, he's only three. He doesn't understand—" Joni said.

"Then he has to learn. Let's get in the car; he'll come."

Joni and Lola got in the passenger side, sharing the front seat now that the boot was loaded. I stamped my feet to make fake footsteps.

"Bye, Billy, I'm going."

Nothing.

"Okay, then. I'm leaving." This time I really did walk toward the car.

"Bill-y?" I called in a singsong voice. I was doing it: I was negotiating with a terrorist. "It's your last chance, come now or Mummy's going." I climbed into the driver's seat, put my foot on the pedal, and revved the engine.

Nothing.

"Billy! That's your last chance, I'm going." I slammed the door and put the car into drive, rolling a few feet down the slope. Still he didn't come.

Joni looked at me with a one-sided smile. "Guess he's not coming."

"We're going to have to work on this." I pulled on the hand brake and got out of the car. "They need to follow instructions. What if something important happens?"

"They'll get it. They just need time," she said.

"We don't have time. Hold on, I'll fetch him." I strode up the slope, where the trolleys were enjoying their freedom on their sides or slumped into the drainage ditch. I jogged across the pedestrian area and ducked under the shutter into the shop. Scattered crisp crumbs crunched under my feet.

"Billy?"

I marched into the loading bay.

"This is no time for hide and seek—are you here?"

Silence.

"Billy? You're frightening me. Come out now."

Silence.

"Billy?"

Along the corridor. Out the side door. Into the street.

"Billy!"

There was no answer. There was no Billy.

Chapter Nine

It's a game, just a game. This is what I told myself as I went methodically aisle by aisle, shining my torch into unlit corners and the recesses of cleared shelves. In the gap behind cereal boxes and up on the top shelf where he could be hiding—surprise!

"Are you in here, Billy?"

My voice was so loud in my ears, I couldn't tell if I was screaming or whispering. My walking footsteps turned to running footsteps, and I went round and round the same shelves and the same aisles and ended up back at the beginning, a mouse lost in a maze. Squeak, squeak went my rubber boots on the linoleum as I turned round and down the aisles again: squeak, squeak, round and round until I forgot what I was searching for; lost in the dark tunnels of the shelves; where is he, where is it, squeak, squeak, where is my cheese? Squeak, squeak, squeak.

I forced myself to stop. Listen.

Someone was crying, and it was me.

Come out, Billy.

Please, Billy.

Try the loading area again. I pushed through the half-plastic swing doors. Not on the forklift. Not crouched, delighted by his own brilliance, behind a pallet of decaying bread. Not up the corridor, or in the office, or in the staff toilet. Not hiding behind the side door. Not in the street.

"Where are you, Billy?"

I ran the length of the railings, scanning the pavement below, but he wasn't there. Not hiding, not distracted by something gross, not fallen and bleeding and unable to answer. Not there at all.

"Where are you, Billy? Where the fuck are you?" I screamed his name up and down the street, over and over, until I couldn't stop screaming. I ran out of words and just carried on screaming, my arms raised above my head, my fingers clawing at the blank sky, which must have been able to see my boy somewhere. The echo continued to spread the message long after I ran out of breath and collapsed to the paving stones, gasping out pitiful bribes.

"I've got crisps, Billy," I whispered. "If you come back, you can have the crisps."

———

"Where's the blood coming from?" Joni said.

"I don't know."

"You're covered in it."

"Am I."

"Are you hurt?"

"I don't know."

"Jeez, Marlene—"

"Get off me, just, get off!"

Joni stepped back and held her palms up. "Okay, I'm going to look inside then."

"He's not inside."

"We should retrace our steps, Aunt Marlene, and then fan out," said Lola. They went together into the supermarket, calling Billy's name.

I cradled my left hand, which I'd somehow slashed across the underside of all four fingers right on the middle joint. I opened my fist and blood pulsed out to drip off the end of my fingertips. The boys came running, followed by Maggie. "Where's Billy?" said Charlie. I shook my head. Maggie held her hand under mine, thrilled by the drops of blood on her palm.

"He didn't come past us, so he must have gone that way or that way." Peter pointed up and down the main road. I looked at the two boys and chewed the inside of my lip. Then I dispatched them to search along the road, under strict instructions not to split up and to turn back at the brow of the hill in one direction and the pub in the other. They set off at a jog, sticks in hand. I sent Maggie to get the Lost Boy and search the car park, looking down into the drainage ditches at the sides.

With everyone busy, I stood alone, redundant. Billy had been right there. I could have picked him up and thrown him onto my hip. I could feel his hands bunching up my shirt and his strong little thighs pressing into my belly. He had been right there. And now he was gone, and the numbing pain in my gut was worse than when he'd first arrived.

"Bill-ee," called Maggie from across the car park, dragging the Lost Boy along by the neck of his shirt. His lips moved in a silent plea.

"Billy! Billy!" shouted Charlie and Peter in curt bursts that rang out down the road like a bird's warning cry.

From inside the supermarket: "Billy? Are you there, Billy? Billy?"

"Billy."

"Billy."

"Billy."

The word lost its meaning, disconnecting from the soft little boy who must be here, somewhere. Somehow not hearing us or not able to answer. I crouched down and held my head in my hands. It didn't make sense. If he were hiding, he would have come out by now. So he must be hurt. He must have run off to find a safe place to eat his crisps and fallen, and now he couldn't answer. My stomach contracted with the certainty that he was stuck or trapped, perhaps by something heavy that was squeezing the breath from him. Squeezing the life from him, even as we stood here, wasting time. Or water, he was in water, his eyes wide and startled just beneath the surface, looking up at the sky for someone to bail him out, unable to comprehend the seriousness of the situation. I could see his eyes pleading for me under the water. I could feel him in my stomach. He was here, and we couldn't hear him because we were all running about screaming his name.

"Billy."

"Bill-ee."

"Billy."

"Stop! Stop it! Stop, all of you!" I ran into the supermarket, just as Lola and Joni came round from the side door. "Shut up! Shut her up." I pointed over to Maggie and her plaintive "Bill-ee." We had to shut up and listen, and then we would hear him. He was here somewhere, and we should listen for a give-away sound, a tiny splash, maybe just his eyelids blinking underwater, that would tell us where he was. "Shut up and listen for him."

The wind carried a buzzard's cry. Sometimes when I was on the phone, Billy would creep up and fling his arms around my legs so I couldn't move. His white teeth would shine with delight at this surprise. "You made me jump," I would say, "you little tinker."

I stood still, waiting, in case that was his game. *When he comes, I thought, I can grab him and tickle him, hearing his laughter turn wild, and carry on tickling until his giggles go breathless, and when he whines that he doesn't like it anymore, my fingers slip from soft belly to hard ribs, and he begs me to stop because it's hurting a bit, but I carry on tickling him through the hysteria because I'm so relieved to have my hands back on his flesh, and I honestly don't know how to let him go.*

A buzzard rode the updraft. From the road, two sets of footsteps belonging to Peter and Charlie pattered on the wind. A gust rose in a sudden burst, and a stand of tall poplar trees on the other side of the road bent and swirled as though they'd been waiting for the opportune moment: now they thrashed back and forth like an unruly crowd, a baying mob yelling out curses of "creak-a-wish, creak-a-wish."

Burn-the-witch. Burn-the-witch.

An echo of the boy who'd stood on this spot, pale hair wild in my headlights. Holding up my axe. Taunting me.

Fat drops of rain crash-landed, helpless and winded, on the paving stones around my feet. A first foray that presaged the onslaught to come. The sky was furred with a dark underbelly of clouds. It spat in my face, glutinous drops that I tilted back my head to receive, even while Joni and Lola and the others ran squealing for the car. And then the rain fell with a sound like dustbin lids.

If Billy had crept up behind me, I couldn't have heard him. I closed my eyes and felt the water course through the gullies of my body: down my spine, between my breasts, into armpits and buttocks, running down my legs and out between the crevasses of my toes. I spread my arms to let it have its way.

The image of that boy in my headlights occupied my mind. *Where had the Wild Things appeared from so suddenly last night? Are they here now? Could Billy have spotted some children and run after them; would he do that? Or*—I opened my eyes and wiped them clear of rainwater—*they could have lured Billy away. The Wild Things have taken him. Why, I don't know, but Billy didn't wander off, that wasn't his style; someone has taken him. And the only people we know are alive are the Wild Things.*

"It's the only thing that makes sense," I told Joni moments later in the car. "They must have grabbed him."

"So we split up and go find them," she said.

"No way. You take everyone back to the camp, and I'll find them."

"But we'll find them quicker if there are more of us," said Lola.

"And what if they grab Maggie next? Or the Lost Boy?" Even as I spoke, Lola was shaking her head. "Or you?"

"All right, we go in groups," she said. "An adult in each group."

"There are only two adults." I spoke over Lola's objections. "Two. Adults. And I'll move faster on my own."

"I could stay with you, and Mom can take the kids back."

"No, Lola. I need to concentrate on finding Billy without worrying where you are."

"But that's stupid! I can help you—"

"You can help me by shutting the fuck up and doing what you're told."

Lola spun round in the seat to turn her back on me. Joni told me to calm down. I pushed the Lost Boy's feet aside so I could scrabble about in the foot well for the crowbar and torch. I opened the door and slid back out into the drenching rain.

"If you're not at the camp by nightfall, I'll pick you up here," said Joni.

"Mom!" Lola spun round in her seat to confront Joni.

Joni ignored her and pointed at me. "Can you walk that far with your leg? You should bandage your hand too."

"What the fuck?" Lola jabbed her mother in the breast.

"Don't speak to me that way, Lola," said Joni.

"It's only a mile or two to the camp. I'll be fine."

Lola shook her head and ran both hands over her dark hair to push out the water. "I always thought you humored her, Mom. Keeping the peace, like you said. But you're her doormat." As the door closed out her voice, Lola was telling her mother that she was pathetic.

I ran back to the supermarket and wrapped the torch in a plastic carrier bag. The crowbar was comforting, so I kept it in my hand. Behind the counter was a display of medicines, and I swallowed down two different painkillers and added the silver packets to the carrier bag. The wall clock told me it was past lunchtime, so I scooped some energy bars and chocolate into my bag, a packet of crisps for Billy. Outside in the car park, the Beast splashed through the puddles, and I heard it growl away down the main road.

The dark sky made it feel much later in the day, like I should be heading home to roost, not setting out on an expedition with no obvious destination and, certainly, no resting place. I had several hours to find Billy and get back here for our lift home.

I set off in the direction the Wild Things had gone with their stolen trolleys.

———

The invisible thread that remains after the umbilical cord is cut tugged at my core. I felt Billy as acutely as a contraction, a sign that I had to deliver him back again. But the empty streets and blank windows rendered me so alone that I longed to hear another human voice, anyone; there had to be someone out there who could help. I tried the police on my mobile, but the electronic voice just repeated a single word: "Sorry." I ran to a red phone box farther down the main road. It contained only a defibrillator. "Saving lives in your community." I picked up the emergency phone, which automatically dialed 999. Waited. Listened to a hollow line. Was someone listening back? "Hello? Hello?" Maybe this was an elaborate joke at my expense. A studio audience laughing at my confusion and then going "aw" at an image of Billy's kissy-lip face. Or maybe I was already dead, like in a TV program I'd watched once, and this was my own personal purgatory. An eternity of trying to reach my kids. I slammed the handset down, then picked it up and slammed it down again. Or maybe it was real, and I was alive, and Billy needed me. I shouldered open the iron door.

The village was bigger than it seemed, a web of streets stretching from the main road in arcs and squares. No rhyme or reason to the layout. I jog-crouched up the driveway to each of the houses, checking for signs of life. Some of the front doors swung open at a touch. I couldn't bring myself to enter, as though the spaces were congealed with dead air. The tangible silence told me they were uninhabited by anyone living. Some revealed the buzz, and I sprinted away. There were many cats, unperturbed. A few croupy dog barks. At every catatonic house I berated myself for wasting more time, each failure opening a new chink in my facade of determination until it crumbled altogether, and I ended up running up and down the streets, screaming Billy's name and thrashing under hydrangea bushes as though he were a strange boy in a fairy tale who might have inexplicably curled up to sleep.

At the end of one road, where the asphalt petered out in a jagged line as the village ended and the farmland started, I forced myself again to stop and breathe.

I blew out the dregs of air and tried to focus on the realities of the moment. I ran through my litany: *You cannot change the past, in the present moment you are safe, you are not in control of the aircraft.* But, for the first time, the realities of the moment were worse than my most catastrophic imaginings. Everything in this moment was worse than a nightmare. I was not safe, my baby was not safe, in fact, none of us were safe: I *was* in control, and I *was* crashing slowly to earth. Then I spotted a Haribo packet.

The blue square was tucked into the bottom of the hedge, a chubby-faced gummi bear pointing into the field. I followed the direction of its arm into the sodden grass and saw, shoved into the hedge on the other side, a shopping trolley. I reached out and fingered the severed chain that had once tethered it to the others but had been broken by an axe.

The field climbed to a stand of trees at its peak, about the size of the flattened mound where we had made our own camp, but higher and more exposed. I shifted the crowbar into a better grip and started up the path that ran along the hedge. The rain had stopped, and the earth steamed out misty specters that gathered in the hollows. The distance was deceptive: the land seemed to get steeper, and the trees higher and farther away the more I climbed. I was back in the nightmare, everything surreal and disordered. I put my head down and pushed my thighs up the hill, resisting the urge to scream Billy's name.

The peak was marked by a scraggy barbed-wire fence decorated with baubles of sheep's wool. I pushed it down to step over, and one fence-post collapsed in. A bird of prey, some kind of raptor, launched itself from the uppermost tree, making me jump. It cawed into the sky, leaving behind a silence like the one that filled the houses below. There was no discernible path between the trees, just places where the undergrowth was lower. This was no camp. I crossed the brow of the hill in a few minutes, reaching another field and another wool-webbed fence on the other side. From this vantage point I could see over the village, whose name I realized I didn't even know, and across a valley to another similar stand of trees, and then south to another field, and another and another. All of them empty and vast. A Pacific Ocean of ditches and copses and ponds and outhouses. An infinite number of spaces where a small boy could be curled up, crying for a mummy who couldn't hear him.

———

I saw no sign of the Wild Things, and eventually, the invisible thread drew me back to the last place I knew Billy had been—the supermarket. I pictured him cross-legged with a packet of crisps open on the floor, as though wanting it hard enough would make it happen. When I arrived, I lay down on the same empty spot and cuddled myself. Pain started to well up like blood rising to the surface of a deep cut. I was surprised to see the clock and find it was late afternoon already. I double-checked the time on my watch. So many hours had passed, and I had found nothing. Billy was missing. Don't they always say the first few hours are critical?

Of course, there was no *they* anymore.

Now that I'd stopped moving, I shivered in my wet clothes. Sodden fabric chaffed under my arms and between my thighs. I peeled off my soaked trousers, but stopped before I stripped altogether, not sure if it was better to wear wet clothes or be naked. But it would be night soon. It would get cold and the wet clothes wouldn't dry. And I would be lying here, freezing and useless, while Billy was—what? I closed my eyes and saw him being led away by the Wild Things, his face delighted by the attention of bigger boys, and then his eyes darkening with confusion as they turned on him, teasing and jostling, starting to push him about in the middle of their circle. "Don't like it," he says, but they laugh and jeer, and then he falls down and starts to cry, and they call him a crybaby, and one of them throws a stone at him, and this makes him call for his mummy, and they laugh harder, so one of the boys throws a bigger stone, and another, until they are all throwing stones at Billy, who stops trying to get up.

I saw it happening.

I had run off in a panic, not thinking straight, without any of the things I needed—not even a map or a coat—and sent away the car that I could be using to look for him. And I sent the others away to protect them—but for what?

What did I care about any of the others if I lost Billy?

I lay on the floor, arms bound up in the straitjacket of my half-off shirt, unable to make even the simplest decision.

"I don't know what to do," I said out loud. "I have no idea what to do."

And for the first time in my life, I cried out for someone to help me.

———

But no one replied. So I got up off the floor. I took more painkillers. I ate something. I applied another layer to my hard surface—steeling myself, like I did when I got on a plane. When the mummy guilt set me rigid enough to bear the weight.

I settled into my racing pace along the road toward camp, and everything hurt, but it was good pain, running pain. I stopped at every building to check for signs of disturbance, but as my brain focused on the problem, and a plan started to form, I was increasingly convinced that the Wild Things must have a well-hidden base and, like us, were staying away from dead bodies. If I could see Joni's map, perhaps I could narrow down the possibilities, define a search radius, and identify hideouts that would appeal to a gang of boys. Or even work out where all those kids had come from in the first place.

As I clattered over the wooden bridge that led past the ford to the camp, the sun flared low against the horizon, burnishing the underside of the few clouds that remained in the cried-out sky. Running made me brave again. I sprinted down the final slope, suddenly convinced that Billy would be there, that he had found his own way home. I turned the corner to the cars and barely heard a shout of warning before I sprawled full length into the long grass. Peter landed heavily on his feet at my side, having dropped from somewhere above, and a few seconds later Charlie arrived.

"Mum!" he panted. "You okay? Where's Billy?"

"What just happened?" I rolled onto my back.

"Sorry, Mrs. Greene." Peter managed to look both worried and delighted. "It worked, Charlie!" He scrabbled through the grass to pull free a long piece of wire.

"Yeah!" Charlie punched the air and rushed off to locate the other end of the wire, which they fixed back into place across the entrance to the camp. I pulled up to a sitting position, ignoring my newly skinned knees, which were a drop in the ocean of my soreness.

"We've secured the camp," Charlie explained as both boys carried on bustling about, "and Peter's standing sentry by the gate. If he whistles, I pull the wire up over there. Didn't realize it was you, though. Peter's going to stand here all night, even when it's dark, because he's not scared of the dark. But I'm scared of the dark, so I'm over there in the camp doing the wire. Why have you got no trousers on, Mum? Where's Billy?"

"He isn't here?" I asked.

Charlie didn't reply, so we both had our answer.

I got to my feet. Charlie was still bustling. I went over to him, crouched down on my heels, and hugged him from behind. He froze for a few seconds and then turned and folded into me. "I'm sorry I lost Billy," I said into his hair. "I'm going to get the map now and work out where he is and then find him."

"Can we help, Mum? Please. We want to help."

"It looks like you are helping," I said, getting up to inspect the trip wire. "This is brilliant."

"Peter's idea."

"Good work, Peter. You two are my knights, defending the fort." I limped up the slope to the tents, where Maggie was sitting, scratching a picture into a big round of bark with a piece of charcoal. She was telling a story to the Lost Boy. I went over and stroked her hair, but she shushed me before I could interrupt her. I sat and listened for a minute or two, watching the Lost Boy's rapt eyes move over the bark picture.

Charlie was still behind me, gnawing away at a hangnail on his thumb. The dusk seemed to rush us like a riptide, soaking the camp in darkness. I wondered why Joni didn't have the fire going.

"Where's Joni?" I asked.

"That's the thing," said Charlie. "Lola's gone, too."

Chapter Ten

Rotten Wood. Henchman's Coppice. Ashes Hollow. Torchlight across the map revealed the nature of our surroundings. As I ran my fingers over its ominous terrain, I counted up my mistakes so far. There were plenty. "Burn-the-witch, burn-the-witch," I heard in the groan of the trees. I kicked out at a log and watched the writhing underworld revealed.

My body ached when I sat still. I strode around the campfire, just to burn off some of the black acid inside me. It was building up in my stomach again, and whenever I felt Billy—the absence of him—it rose up my gorge, threatening to choke me. His name rang through my head like an alarm: I couldn't switch it off, and it wouldn't let me think of anything else. My mind filled the space where Billy should be with all the horrific fates that had befallen him. I walked in circles until my leg throbbed, and then I lay down and contorted into positions where I might get comfortable, but there was no relief, so I walked again.

Joni still wasn't back. For the umpteenth time, I followed the path to the edge of the forest, hoping she would be driving down the dirt track, ideally with Lola and Billy on board. Or at least ready to let me go out searching again. For the umpteenth time, I looked back at the tents and bit my lip over whether to leave the sleeping kids alone and go hunting for Billy. I didn't trust myself to make the right choice. There was no right choice.

The forest was going about its usual night business, indifferent to our petty human concerns over individual lives. The trees gossiped in their rustling, old-hag voices. "Welcome to our world," they were saying. There are no simple choices for us. Mother Nature can't afford favorites.

I picked up a stone and threw it into the branches. It disappeared without a sound into the black velvet. I grabbed another one and lobbed it as far into the trees as I could, throwing my whole weight behind it and grunting with the effort. I picked up a handful of stones and threw one at a time to punctuate my words: "Callous. Judgmental. Supercilious. Fucking. Bitch." The last handful of gravel pattered onto the undergrowth with the sound of water on a duck's back. I was still standing there, panting and glaring, when a light arced over the trees. Horatio gave a warning gruff and appeared by my side. A few seconds later I heard a car bumping down the dirt track.

———

I was tempted to slap her across the cheek. "Calm yourself, Jonelle," I would say, using her trashy real name. "Pull yourself together." I didn't slap her, though. I waited while she snotted on her sleeve, and I focused on the black pit in my stomach, which had started to plop and gurgle. I waited while the heat crept down my arms to my fingertips. Finally, it seethed up and flooded over me, and I jumped on board and rode the wave.

"My son"—I started with a pointed finger right in her face and a jumpy voice—"is three years old, and he's out there somewhere, and you fuck off for hours so I can't go after him and—"

"I've been out there. Looking. For them both," she whined. "Lola's missing, too."

"It's hardly the same. Billy's three—three!"

"I thought I would find them."

"And did you? Did you find them?"

She shook her head, still crying.

"Or did you just dick about wasting more time? Billy could be dying—"

Joni drew in a long shuddering breath and wiped her eyes with the heels of her hands. She sagged for a moment and then looked up at me. "You left him behind to make a point. This is on you, Marlene."

The trees rustled.

When I didn't reply, Joni heaved herself to her feet. "I thought she would be here when I got back. I was sure."

"She's not here," I managed.

"I've looked everywhere. What am I going to tell David? I wish he was here." Joni drove both hands through her hair and wrenched her head back. "I've lost both of them." Her face clenched as a scream got trapped behind her teeth.

I'd felt the same draining of hope, the same free fall into the void it leaves behind. But my hollow insides echoed now with a clanging urge to fight. The din was too great to find words for Joni. The only word in me was *Billy*.

Joni barely noticed my hand on her back, pushing her toward the yurt, into bed. Rest. She hardly heard me promise that I'd find them, whatever it took, both of them. I ushered Horatio into the boot of the car and raced off up the dirt track to find my boy.

———

Lola had gone out from the camp and simply not returned. Billy disappeared in the village. On the map, I had drawn a circle between the two sites that took in a number of remote farms. As the Beast rolled down the driveway of the next farm on the short list, there was no sign of the Wild Things. Only gangrene hanging in the air from the cowshed and the claggy sound of the cows' labored breathing. The beam from my headlights bounced over a dirt-encrusted road that offered no telltale tire marks or footprints. Just a smooth sheen of mud that the rainstorm had washed from the verge like an incoming tide. In another few days, the road surface would disappear altogether from view.

My eyes watered with tiredness as I checked the map for the next destination—a stand of trees marked with the symbol denoting a ruin. It was a possibility. All the locations I had identified lay within a modest radius of our camp and the supermarket. I would have to make the final approach to the ruin on foot, and the contours on the map suggested it was steep. I thunked the car into drive, and the Beast found its grip on the muddy surface.

The radio was scrolling through dead air again, an electronic pip followed by white noise. I hummed along with the monotonous tune. It sounded like a car braking heavily, and then I was braking heavily as I spotted the silhouetted crenellations of a tower up on the hill. I had to squint to focus on the map. It seemed like the right place. The red light of the clock said 3:14 a.m., and I didn't have enough memories to account for the hours I'd been searching. I wondered how many nights I'd been without proper sleep. It must be Wednesday by now; five nights we'd spent in the woods. But then sleep didn't matter anymore: I couldn't stop if I wanted to.

Ahead of me, the hedge broke for a wooden gate. I drove up to it and jumped out, leaving the engine running. The crowbar made short shrift of its chain, and I drove into the field, stopping to engage the four-wheel drive, before heading in a direct line for the ruin. The Beast ate up the slope. The dense grass gave us traction, and we powered up to the tree line. I pulled on the hand brake and turned off the engine. Silence dropped around us like settling flies.

The shattered turret loomed over us, a black rent in the sky, its corners collapsed into the shape of an eyetooth. I knew at once this wasn't the place. Even the most brazen of children wouldn't dare. I didn't dare. But I slid out of the car, leaving the driver's door open and the headlight warning alarm binging, and forced myself up the rest of the slope. I had to be brave for Billy. I had to turn over every last stone if I were ever to sleep again. Horatio was close behind me as we entered the wood, his paws padding lightly as though he, too, were on tiptoes.

The torchlight threw the trees into Gothic shapes. I recoiled from a fox that seemed about to spring from the undergrowth, but saw it was a root. I gulped air, and my breath clung heavily around my head as though I were breathing inside a helmet, the atmosphere crushing me as surely as water or space. *It is just fatigue,* I told myself, *tiredness letting my brain lower its defenses so the demons could sneak out to play tricks on me.* I laid a hand on Horatio's shoulder and put one foot before the other until I reached the hole in the side of the tower that passed for an entrance.

The space inside the ruin was so black that it seemed all the fearful dark that surrounded me had gushed from its depths. The darkness repelled me like a magnet. Even the light of the torch was swallowed, revealing nothing but more darkness. Behind me, Horatio shifted his weight and gruffed. It was too much. My legs took control and carried my senseless body back down the path, covering the distance with uncanny speed, and I was back inside the car, fumbling the door closed and locked, punching the button to start the engine, and pulling the gear stick into reverse. The Beast shot backward down the hill, and I screamed when a dark shape passed through my headlights—Horatio. I swerved to avoid him as he came round to my flank, and the steering wheel wrenched out of my hand as the car jackknifed into a violent right angle.

We hung, the Beast and I, for teetering seconds, suspended on two side wheels over the steep slope. Horatio galloped away into the dark space beyond the headlights. The car gave a furious roar as my foot slipped and over-revved the engine. The two wheels that now grasped for traction in thin air gave a bitter whine. *How do I stop the car rolling?* I thought. *Steer into it? Or is that a skid? I'm so very tired.* And then the grass retreated from my driver's-side window and was replaced by the starry night sky.

———

From far away, a voice wakes me. "You're lost," it says. My mother is walking away across the savannah, not looking back. I run to catch her, red grass stinging my cheeks. Exhausted, I fall back, my eyes blurring with dots and darkness.

Red grass whips me awake. My mother is far now. But she is dead; she can't be here. On the horizon, she turns and says, "You're lost," and steps off.

I see only dots and darkness.

Find yourself.

Dots. The dots are in the car, on the ceiling. I'm in the car.

Open your eyes.

The air burst with screaming—crows or rooks, big black birds with ragged witch-cloak wings, bickering over carrion. The world was too bright. I could only open one eye; the other was glued closed. I scratched my eyelashes out to free it and shivered in a dawn chill that came straight out of the earth. I was lying across the front seats, my head bent to the side against the passenger door. When I moved my shoulders to sit up, pain shot down my neck. I capitulated and stayed down.

The Beast had rolled down the hill. The sky was in the right place, though, so we'd landed on our feet. I hauled my legs up to my chest, and everything seemed in order, so I rolled onto my side and pushed up with my arms, sliding back into the driver's seat. A loud thud was my Burmese Nat, the heavy silver figurine that I'd picked up as I left my house, slipping from my legs to the floor. I wondered if he was responsible for the egg rising on my forehead. I pushed him back under the front seat with my foot. Outside, Horatio gruffed. I got out, carefully stretching my head side to side, and rubbed both our necks as we walked round the car.

The Beast hunkered at the base of the steep slope. As well as a broken window, the bonnet and roof were crushed, and both sides were concave, bent to the contours of the land. One headlight drooped on wires from an empty eye socket, like a pair of comedy glasses. I lifted the light and inspected it; I hadn't realized in the brightness of the morning, but the lamps were still on. I slotted the unit back into the eye socket and shoved. It clicked into place, fixed.

I put my head back and let out a whoop into the sky—*The Beast lives!*—a loud "fuck-you" to the universe. The crows or rooks or whatever they were joined in.

Up on the hill, the ruin looked much reduced against the bone-white sky. I realized it wasn't a tower or a turret or anything so mysterious, just a squat brick building: some kind of abandoned industrial relic, perhaps an old mine head, whose roof had long since fallen in and no one cared enough to clear it up. Even the trees around it looked scrubby and juvenile in the cold morning light.

I turned my attention to my injuries. In the glove compartment, I found wet wipes and cleaned my forehead, which was cut open as well as swollen. The blood had gummed up the one eye, and I already had a blue bruise that would spread nicely. But I'd escaped quite lightly, all things considered. The Beast growled back to life with an emphysemic rattle, and the clock showed it was just after 6:00 a.m. My mouth was parched, and I could smell myself. I loaded up Horatio and headed for the next place on the map.

———

I clicked the radio on and hummed along even though the white noise shushed me. "Peep, shush, peep, shush" went the radio, flailing around for stations that didn't exist. At the top of the dial, it fixed on a frequency, and the car filled with pips. It was more irritating than the white noise—insistent, nagging—so I switched it off.

I was lost. The map showed that I'd missed a turn, but I could follow this lane down via a watermill and pick up the trunk road. The hamlet around the mill was on my list of sites to check, so I decided to go there first. I turned left onto a one-car lane that you'd normally drive slowly for fear of meeting another vehicle, but I sped along between high hedges. A mile or so farther on, I passed a couple of ramshackle cottages, both with vans parked outside. Buzz-infested, for sure. I didn't even brake.

Down a hill and over a stone bridge, the road turned sharply left in front of a gate and into a field. I struggled to make the turn and, as I flashed by the gate, I saw a small figure streak behind the hedge. I hit the brakes. Backed up.

There. Way across the field, a boy was scrambling over a fence toward an old barn. I grabbed the map: the barn lay at the end of a track that joined the road a few hundred yards ahead. I slammed the car into gear and raced down the lane, spinning the steering wheel into the turn, so that the wheels scrambled for grip before we picked up speed again and came to a skidding halt moments later outside a hay shed. I jumped out.

Water gushed from a tap against the wall of the barn, and I stepped forward to turn it off. The ground was littered with empty cans of pop. The air was still.

My heart gave a loud thud, as though I'd come back to life, and then I was running into the barn, clambering over the bales, shouting Billy's name and throwing aside a pile of sleeping bags that lay on top of the hay, screaming for whoever was there to come out, show themselves, tell me where my son was. No one was there, just a half-dozen sleeping bags and a few grubby clothes.

"Billy? Billy!"

I stopped to listen for a reply. Outside the barn, farther down the dirt track, I heard the crackle of bicycle tires over gravel.

I jumped down from the hay, landing heavily in the dirt, and just caught the movement of the bikes as they turned out onto the lane. I ran to the car and spun round after them.

Way ahead of me, the hunched figures weaved across the road with blurred legs. I wrenched the gear stick into manual and forced the car into second, the engine furious as it engaged. I gained on the boys in seconds: there were five of them, the smallest one at the rear careering across the lane as he looked back over his shoulder to check on me. He went up onto the verge and righted himself, pushing ahead again down the center of the road. I revved up right behind them, snapping at their tails, and slid my window down.

"Stop!" I screamed at them. "Tell me where Billy is."

The boy in front waved one arm round in a circle, and the little peloton broke into two halves, a couple of boys veering off into a field and the others turning down a side lane hidden by the high hedge. I shot past, braked, fishtailed to a stop. In reverse, the car weaved and whined until I had enough room to make the turn. I forced the gear stick back into first and the car jumped forward, its great haunches bunching up to thrust us round the corner into the narrow lane, where I only saw the small boy who had come off his bike and was lying in the middle of the road as I ploughed right over him.

Chapter Eleven

The crows followed us home. Or at least there were black birds keening in the sky as I drove to the camp. I left the car on the dirt track and walked the final stretch. By the gate, an oil lamp stood on the dirt-packed ground, encircled by dead moths. I bent to turn the dial and extinguish the spasming flame. Under the hedge next to the lamp, hidden in a little hollow of branches, slept Peter in a blanket. Our sentry had still not abandoned his post.

He was much sturdier and heavier than Charlie, but I scrambled him out of the hole and into my arms. His head lolled against my shoulder, face turned to mine with his lips tight: still defiant. The kid was a good friend to Charlie. Maybe one day, when all this was over, he would be his best man, and we would all laugh and shake our heads in disbelief at his humorous tale of how we survived by hiding out in the forest: a band of thieves. I carried him up the short slope to the yurt and laid him down on my mattress. He rolled onto his side, and I tucked the blanket back around his legs.

Then I went to my own tent, looking for a spare sheet or a sleeping bag: a shroud to cover the dead boy on the back seat of my car.

———

Joni was talking to me. I could see her mouth moving. It was possible I was going to vomit, because my mouth kept filling with saliva, and my skin spiked with sweat. That was it, I had car sickness. It would be okay if I could focus on the horizon, but I couldn't see that far, trapped here inside the wood. I kept very still and tried to slow my pulse by concentrating on it, the way I had when I was a child, lying alone in a dark room with fruit bats darting outside the window grille.

The kids ate their breakfast. Peter and Charlie on one log, Maggie and the Lost Boy on another. No Billy. No Lola. They chewed in slow motion, as if the food were very dry. And they watched me without looking my way. I had an urge to lie down right there in the dirt, but it didn't seem appropriate. Joni was talking to me again.

"Marlene?"

"It looks worse than it is. I'll be okay after a cup of tea."

"What?" She stopped in front of me, holding tissues in one hand and disinfectant in the other. "I told you to stop your humming. It's freaking the kids out." She pushed my head back and started wiping blood out of the cut on my forehead. It hurt, the way she did it.

After a while, the kids got up and dropped their bowls into the washing bucket and whispered between themselves about who would take it down to the stream. Peter picked up the sponge and went. The others filed to the tent to get dressed. Maggie tried to sneak down to the car, presumably to peek at the dead boy, and for once the Lost Boy let her go. A word from Joni stopped her short, and she scuttled into the trees.

"Did you see Billy or Lola?" asked Joni.

I shook my head.

"Are they the same kids you saw at the store?"

I supposed so.

"Did you recognize them, though?"

I shrugged. *How many gangs of feral scouts can there be?*

Her eyes bloated with tears. "They're just little kids, Marlene."
Here we go, I thought, *the floodgates are open.*

———

I took the pickax and a garden fork a little way into the field and started
to dig a grave. The quicker I got it done, the quicker I could get back
in the car and look for Billy. My digging the grave was supposed to
make amends for not helping Joni prepare a funeral. We were having
a funeral, even though we didn't know the boy's name or anything
about him. And our own two kids were still missing. There would be a
trail of ashes to the grave and a natural shroud for the body and some
kind of poetry. Joni didn't need me—spiritual welfare was her racket,
not mine—but she insisted on my attendance. I couldn't tell if it was
intended to be therapy or punishment.

If Joni was right, and the Wild Things would run away now and
take Billy and Lola with them, or punish them in revenge, or come
after us at the camp—if, basically, I had fucked up to an even greater
degree than a kid's dead body in my car would already suggest—then
I had to get back out there and find them. Joni could stay here if she
liked, weeping over Lola and David, consoling herself with rituals,
but I would dig this grave and go out searching again. I knew in that
moment, I would never stop searching. The idea made me feel better
and infinitely worse.

Charlie came out from the forest and picked up the fork.

"Mummy?"

I thunked the pickax into the rain-soaked sod and stopped.

"What was the boy's name, Mummy?"

I didn't know. I had never met him before.

"Did he take Billy?"

I didn't know. Maybe. No.

"Oh." Charlie looked confused.

I seesawed the pickax out of the earth, swung it once more, and very nearly put it through my own foot. I stopped again and crouched down. Charlie backed up and tried to sit on my lap, sending us both sprawling to the ground. I put my arms around him and pressed my face into the back of his neck as the wet grass swabbed my skin.

"It was an accident, Charlie."

"I know, Mummy. It's okay."

His hair smelled of oxygen, and I took a deep breath. "It's not, though, is it?"

"No, not really. The boy's dead because you ran over him with your big car." Charlie dabbed his fingers over the bruise on my head. "Does it hurt?"

I nodded.

"What will happen to the boy?" he asked.

"Which boy?"

"The one who's dead."

"Nothing. He's dead. Nothing happens to him now. That's the point."

"But where will he go?"

I took a deep breath. "Well, Charlie, some people think that when we die we go to heaven. Where people are always happy."

"Joni says there's no such thing as heaven. We just go back into nature, she said. Like molecules and that."

"Oh. Well. That's probably true."

"I think so." Charlie got back to his feet and started pulling the broken turf away from the grave with the fork, exposing the rich earth beneath.

When the grave was finished—a pitifully small gash of humid darkness amid the late-summer green pasture, as though we were planting a tree, not burying a life that had never been lived—I packed a bag with all the things I needed to return to the hunt. Peter and Charlie were

coming with me. I promised to be back in time for the funeral. I promised to find Billy and Lola. I promised not to lose Charlie and Peter in
the process. I intended to keep the second two promises.

"Come on, boys," I called. "Get in the car; time to go."

But Peter was missing from his sentry post. I heard him shouting
farther up the dirt track. "Charlie! Mrs. Greene! Charlie!"

"Now what . . ." I trudged down to the gate to see what he was
up to.

Peter was racing toward a small figure who was trotting down the
path on a little cloud of dust: a boy, singing to himself as he made his
way home. It was Billy.

———

"Mum-may?" Billy touched the purple-black rings of exhaustion and
damage on my face. His hand came away wet with watery grime and
blood, and his smile faded as the world wobbled with the realization
that Mummy was not in a state of authoritative perfection.

"It's okay, everything's okay." I kissed my muck off his hand and
tried for a laugh, but hysteria wrestled it into a grotesque, damp sob. I
held Billy tight against me with one arm, while my other hand groped
his body, feeling for evidence of harm. He laughed into my neck when
my fingers found the ticklish spots.

I pushed him to arm's length and looked hard into his eyes.

"Did someone hurt you, Billy?"

His mouth twitched into a nervous smile, but his eyebrows bunched
together. *Confusion? Fear? Trauma?* I always thought I could translate
every nuance of his body language. But this left me dumb.

"Billy? Where have you been?"

He tried to shrug, but I was holding his shoulders too tight.

"You're scaring him," said Joni. She glanced up the track, looking
out for Lola, and I felt a pang of guilt that only *my* nightmare was over.

But not enough to keep my attention from Billy. I looked into his eyes for a few more seconds, and his blue gaze tried to make sense of this curious turn of events. Then I began tearing off his clothes: first his jacket and shirt, turning him round and stroking a flat palm over the bum-fluff of his back, lifting and lowering his unresisting arms; then his trousers and underpants, running my hands down the length of his legs from hip to ankle, which had no more than the usual toddler grazes. Then I pulled off his shoes and socks, and he stood naked in the morning chill.

"Marlene, he's okay." Joni's hand was on my shoulder now, as though I were the one who needed to be consoled. "He's not hurt."

I whipped Billy into the air and laid him flat on the stony dirt, pulling his legs apart to check between and behind. He giggled and moved his hands to cover himself. I pulled him up to his feet again.

"Did anyone touch you, Billy? You can tell me. Even if they told you not to tell me, you can tell me anything. I won't be angry. You're not in trouble." I took my hands off his shoulders and placed them flat on my own thighs, because I was shaking him. "Just tell us what happened, Billy."

"Ice cream."

"What?"

"Yummy, yummy, in my tummy." Billy looked from my face to Joni's and then, with an air of triumph, settled on his great rival, Maggie. "The man gave me ice cream. And there's none left for you."

———

The dead boy had been washed and laid out. Joni carried him from the river, hidden inside my sleeping bag, which she'd agreed to use as his shroud after a protracted row. If she really thought that giving up a warm sleeping bag was designed to assuage my guilt, then she failed to understand the depth of feeling that is churned up by running over and killing a small boy, and then scraping him off the road and pressing my face to what remained of him so I could listen for breath, and then lifting his mangled body into the car and coming home to explain to my children that the stains on the leather are from another child's blood. Call me soft, but I just thought the sleeping bag would keep him warm in the earth. Symbolically speaking.

Peter and Charlie had raked up all the ashes from the fire and were scattering them in a thin line from the tents to the grave in the field. This would stop the ghost from returning, Joni said. Maggie and the Lost Boy were crayoning pictures of food and other useful household objects onto leaves. These were his grave goods. What the archaeologists of the future might make of our burial rituals, I could hardly imagine. Apparently, it was all authentic. And I was assured it would bring us closure. Joni seemed to have shut out the fact that Lola was still missing, and we had no idea who had taken Billy; the matter was anything but closed.

Still, the preparations kept the kids busy so I could concentrate on Billy. We were ostensibly fashioning half-arsed decorations out of grass, but really I was questioning him. I tried to make it light, keep smiling, not grind my teeth. But the fever was brewing in my belly again, and I fed it a slow-drip stimulant of information gleaned from Billy's unreliable memory.

There was, without doubt, a man. No kids, just a man. Definitely no Lola.

There was a building. But there were also trees.

And there were steps: aloney steps.

"Aloney steps?"

"Yep."

"Do you mean stony steps?"

"Nope. *Aloney.* Aloney steps."

"I don't understand, Billy. What are aloney steps?"

Shrug. His head bent lower over his knotted grass. His lips pursed with feigned concentration. I backed off and moved on.

"So tell me about the ice cream. Yummy!"

It was raspberry ice cream, of that we were certain. It was served in a blue bowl, which was a shame because Billy's favorite color was yellow, but he overcame that disappointment to eat the ice cream with a spoon. The spoon had a horse's head on the end of the handle. There was a second serving of ice cream, but then it was finished. He was allowed to lick the bowl. He was allowed to lick the carton that the ice cream came from. And he was allowed to sleep with the spoon because he didn't have his toy, Rabbity, who was waiting for Billy here in the tent. The ice cream was yummy, yummy, in his tummy.

He couldn't remember how he had gotten from the supermarket to the ice cream, or what the building that housed the ice cream looked like, or what the man with the ice cream was called.

"The trouble is," said Charlie, when he came over to criticize our craft skills, "Billy has a rubbish remembery. All we know is, there's a man with ice cream and stony steps."

"*Aloney* steps."

"What does that mean?"

Indeed. But the fact remained, this man with ice cream had kept my son for a whole night. Why? I had no idea if he was Fagin or Father Christmas, but he needed to be found and taught a swift lesson about boundaries.

———

"You need to sit with him." Joni pointed toward my tent, where the dead child was crumpled inside my sleeping bag with all the dignity of a pile of laundry. "He should have someone sit with him." She stood for a while with her arm out, and then dropped it. She stumped off down the track that led out of the camp, but after a few minutes returned and dived into the yurt. Then across into the food tent.

I'd offered to go out in the car again and just drive. Or Joni could go, and I'd stay with the kids. I didn't want to scare her, but the only explanation I could find for Billy's disappearance was that this man had used Billy to lure Lola into the open. Find this man with the ice cream and we'd find her. Plus, I had a few choice words to say to him about taking my son.

"We should be out looking for Lola," I said. "This funeral can wait."

"Where?" Joni asked. She waved at the trees, the empty fields, the track that curved up to the road in the shape of a question mark. "I don't know where else to look," she said, her voice moony, as though she were missing a shoe. She drifted for a moment toward the camp-fire, like she was floating from the shore. Then she seemed to surface; she spun round and started on about the vigil. Our new rituals, as she saw it. The privilege we had been given to restart society. The responsibility that came with it: we must show our children how to interpret our lives. And deaths. Get it right this time, not like before, everything twisted and masculine, all messed up. We must show the new generation how to grieve. How to take time to feel. How to honor ourselves.

Not that I disagreed with her, but what about science? If I could choose between a new religion or vaccines that would prevent deaths, machinery that would harvest food, a GPS that could locate Lola—I wasn't ready to give up on civilization just yet.

Billy pulled away the map I was trying to study. This man must be nearby—otherwise how had Billy gotten back? But a three-year-old couldn't explain, and the map didn't help. It told me nothing. The longer I waited, the more questions flapped like black birds inside my head. About this man. And the Wild Things. Where they both were, how they connected, if either of them had Lola, what they wanted with her. There were no shortcuts to the answers. Siri couldn't tell me. I would have to find out by old-fashioned legwork. But right now, Joni was fixated on the funeral. "A vigil, Marlene. You can do the first sitting. I'll come when I'm done with the food."

"Are we having a wake now? Will there be Guinness and a ceilidh band? Should we send out invites to the rest of the Wild Things? You never know, they might bring Lola back with them, as we're not out looking for her."

"Eating unites us. David said that once, during our wedding dinner at Mom's place. She asked him to say grace, and he said that Pennsylvania would always be home for him now that our families were united, and we would celebrate that bond every time we broke bread, wherever we were in the world, even when we were apart. Because eating unites us. He made Mom cry, and I think she kind of fell in love with him, too, at that moment, because she never cries. It must have skipped a generation: I cry all the time. Lola never does." Joni looked heavy, bloated, as though she were swollen by emotions held, for once, on the inside. She stamped over to the food tent but turned before she ducked inside. "Maybe if we give this boy back properly, the universe will give us Lola in return. Do the vigil, Marlene."

I saw more logic in being out there, searching the lanes, but it was her daughter.

I got myself a cup of tea and walked over to my tent. The entrance curved like a cave. The inside eked out what was left of the tree-filtered sun. There was something unnatural about being inside a tent during the day. However generous the proportions, it was cramped and awkward, like being forced underground. I picked my way across to the lumpy blue bag and stood over it. I closed my eyes and tried to focus on the breath entering my body, but all I could feel was the space between my feet and the sleeping bag, as if the air had grown tendrils that were reaching out toward my legs. Its strands fused me and the boy so that we were forever linked by this inverse umbilical cord, death replacing birth.

In my mind, I saw the boy's narrowed eyes as he turned his head to watch me bearing down on him. His foot slipping from the pedal, the leg still pumping the air. His sandy hair whipping in the wind. The same hair clogged and sticky as I turned his face from the road. His legs pumping out blood as I lifted him up. His eyes narrowing to a close.

I stepped away from the sleeping bag, out of the tent, past Billy, and into the trees to the latrine. I kicked aside the log seat and sunk to my knees over the deep hole in the earth, and let my mouth fill with bile. There was little to come up—I hadn't eaten properly for days—but I let myself retch and retch until my stomach muscles burnt with the effort. When it finished, I took two fingers and pushed them deep down my throat, stirring my guts to buck beneath me again. Sure enough, there was more, more bile that I spat down the hole. Again and again I forced it out until there was nothing left but rude air. I kicked dirt into the latrine to bury it and pushed the log back into place.

As I came through the trees to the camp, I heard Maggie's spindly voice rise into a slow song, which was soon accompanied by Billy's:

Ring-a-ring o' roses, pocket full of posies.

They were standing under the awning of my tent, holding hands in a circle with the Lost Boy, who joined them to silently mouth the words. The three of them shuffled round in the dirt singing in flat tones:

A-tishoo. A-tishoo. We all fall down.

Joni appeared in the doorway of the food tent, her hand over her mouth. The kids didn't fall down, but kept on turning and singing: a vigil for the dead boy.

The cows are in the meadow, eating buttercups.

A-tishoo. A-tishoo. We all jump up.

My keys were in the car, ready to go. I couldn't sit and wait for the universe to intervene. We had to find Lola and move somewhere safer—somewhere with windows and doors—before this *man* or the Wild Things came back for more. I turned into the trees and down the short slope. The kids' voices followed me as I slid behind the steering wheel and, even after I slammed the door, they seeped through the shattered quarter light.

Ashes on the water, Ashes on the sea. We all jump in, with a one-two-three.

Chapter Twelve

Ashes on the water. Ashes on the sea. The tune played through my head as though it came from a tinny pair of speakers. The cool river harried my feet, and I spread my toes to let it through. *We all jump in with a one-two-three.* An iridescent dragonfly rested for a moment before skimming away over a foamy swirl on the surface. Joni would probably know what kind it was, but I had no clue.

How strange, I thought, *if these names die out. If this knowledge is lost by people like me who don't speak the language, and then the library books crumble and the contents of the Internet evaporate into the ether. Someone else will get to name the animals and plants all over again. Maybe in Chinese: surely the Chinese are still alive, some of them at least? But their exotic words would be all wrong for our plain English creatures. All wrong!* A few drops of water fell into the river beside my pale feet. How ridiculous, crying over words. I bent down and splashed water over my face. How ridiculous. I'd have to put the kids onto it. It was the sort of thing Lola and Maggie would be good at. I could imagine Maggie saying the dragonfly looked stuck-up, and Lola would call it an ice queen. "Let's name it a *Haughty Ice Queen*," they'd squeal. And so it would be.

If Lola were here.

A sharp rustle from downstream startled me. A heron on a branch over the water. Its poise was mesmerizing: taut muscles, actively still, unblinking eyes, its tiny little brain free of the encumbrance of intellect.

The bird would get a fish because that was all it ever did. I stripped off my filthy jeans and shirt and knelt in the shallow water to wash myself with a cloth. When I was finished, the heron had gone.

I gathered the dirty jeans into one hand, ready to throw them away over the hedge, when I felt something hard inside the pockets. I pulled out the fabric jewelry pouch. Inside, my mother's jade brooch, smooth as a river stone. It came to me after she died in the crash, taken from her body in the wreckage of the light aircraft piloted by my father. A sunset joyride. Her will stipulated that I "mind it for the next generation" as though I were just a stepping stone to her genetic immortality. And I'd very nearly thrown it away. That was a habit of mine: not paying attention to the things entrusted to my care.

I put on a less dirty pair of jeans. They smelled of Horatio, but were an improvement on the blood-soaked pair. The fabric jewelry bag slipped into my pocket again. As I pulled down the Beast's rear door, I spotted Billy's toy gun stuffed behind the seat. It was surprisingly heavy. Quite convincing. I slipped it inside my waistband. Of course, a real weapon would be gold dust. *Maybe in one of these farmhouses, if I can brave the buzz?*

I sat on a rock to get my socks on. The water bustled past. I noticed again the foam that made a galaxy around the rocks. It didn't look natural. It wasn't like the scum you get on the sea. If someone were to wash themselves in the river, like I just did, the soap would come this way. Someone must be upstream.

I forced my boots inside my backpack and got my wellingtons from the car. Rolling my trouser legs up over my knees to stay dry, I stepped into the river. Across the field, a thin column of smoke rose from our camp. I'd made sitting ducks of us when I decided to come back here. Part of me wanted to rush back and bundle my three in the car and go somewhere I could just close the door on the world and hold them close. But we weren't going anywhere without Lola. The quicker I found her, the quicker I could get back to Billy. I followed the river upstream.

After wading around the first bend, I stopped dead in the middle of the water. I hadn't come all that far from the camp as the crow flies—a toddler would make quicker progress over land. But I was a goo ' from the safety of the car. And I was exposed. What would I do ʜ ᴧ did find this man? Splash him? At least he wouldn't be expecting me to come up the river. If nothing else, I had an element of surprise. And a toy gun that looked real from a distance.

Farther upstream, the water slid out from under a squat arch of bricks. The tangle of thicket above the tunnel prevented me from going over. There was only one way through. I put my hands down into the water and crabbed forward, my wellies filling with water amid great echoing footsteps. So much for an ambush. I crept along, my backpack dislodging masonry that plopped into the water behind me. The exit was covered in a gauze of branches, which grasped at me as I broke through.

Ahead, the landscape was sliced in two by the watercourse, as definitively as a tear through a piece of paper. To the left, a copse grasped across the stream. To the right, lush parkland was decorated with ornamental trees. In the distance, probably a mile back, stood a honey-colored mansion with a flat front and a long stone portico. *This must be Moton Hall*, I thought, *a minor National Trust property that's marked on the map.* I'd poked my nose down the drive the night before, but there'd been no signs of life despite a number of parked cars: buzz. I'd retreated.

I stepped up onto the grassy bank toward the stately home, but instinctively turned to check the dark wood behind me on the other side of the river. And there, at a muddy spot where a path through the trees reached the water, stood a fishing rod. My insides recoiled from what I was looking for: human activity. I slid my backpack to the ground, pulling out the crowbar and Maglite. I changed the wellies for the big boots in case I needed some heft. I stepped into the water and picked my way across the rocks before slipping into the trees.

Just a few paces from the river, the forest turned Grimm. A wide-girthed tree marked the way, its spiraling torso pocked with bulbous lumps like an old woman's swollen knees. I almost tripped over a walking stick with a handle of natural knotted wood that lay on the ground. It felt good in my hand, heavy but deft. It swung in time with my strides.

The trail led me around a dogleg into an avenue of enormous shade trees. It was overgrown and unkempt. A road to nowhere. I'd stopped to see if I could make out the path, when a snapping twig to my left spun me round.

"Are you lost?" An old man stood a few yards back. He was smaller than I, but hardy-looking, sinewy, like the forest. "You have returned my stick. I am forever in your debt." He came through the trees with his hand out. Automatically, I offered the cane to him. He reached slowly forward, eye contact all the while, and plucked away the stick. As soon as it left my grip, I felt vulnerable, even though the crowbar hung down from my other hand.

"By way of thanks, may I offer you tea?" he said. "I even have milk. I suppose you have run out of milk by now?"

The underwood twined my feet as firmly as hands rising up from the earth. I would make little headway by running.

"You live at the house?" I nodded my head toward the stately home.

"Moton Hall? No such illusions. No, I'm this way." He turned into the trees, and I used the crowbar to hold aside an overladen branch to follow behind. There was no obvious path, but bent twigs and broken flower heads suggested that he often passed this way. As we walked, he rabbited on about the trees—something about chestnuts—seemingly unconcerned about my reply, because I said nothing to encourage him. With each stride, his stick inflicted a fleshy jab into the soil. *This could be my man. The one who'd held Billy. Who could still have Lola. Who was now leading me deeper into the woods. What was I thinking, coming out here, all invincible with a pair of heavy boots and a toy gun, like a kid playing dress up?* I felt not just vulnerable, but worse: naive. Out of my depth. It made no sense that someone had taken Billy, and then returned him, unharmed; I saw that now. Billy must have been bait. My stomach crawled within my body as I realized how smoothly this man had lured me here. *Maybe he already has Lola; now, me. Then what? Joni? Christ, would he take Maggie—what would he do to her?* My hands gripped both ends of the crowbar, and I stepped closer behind him. He half glanced round, still walking and talking—"the Spanish Armada, would you believe!"—gesturing up into the umbrella of a vast tree. My footsteps muted on the bare ground under the canopy; I caught up to an arm's length from his shoulder, focused on the leathery patch of skin behind his ear. I raised the crowbar, but as I did so he swung up his stick. I jumped aside and stumbled over a root, but he was only reaching up to hook a tree branch.

"Watch your step, dear."

His voice was as waxy as the leaves he held in his straining grasp. I scooped up my crowbar from the forest floor. When he finally released the branch, it freed itself with a shudder, leaving on the end of his stick a perfect pair of chlorophyll-green chestnut cases. He held them out for me to take. "They're early this year. It's been so warm. We'll have a bumper crop of conkers." The spiked cases sat on my palm like some medieval weapon. "As I was saying, quite different from Spanish chestnuts. Anyway, here I am." He indicated the end of the tree line, where a small field lay like an island inside the forest. It was neat, as though freshly swept. To one side was a small wooden building, little more than a garden shed, with a tin roof and shelves on the outside wall where tools and cleaning products were covered by an overhang.

The man crossed the grass to undo the padlocked door, then sat on the step to remove his boots, placing them upside down onto two sticks that were fixed to the inside of the door for that purpose. His fussing gave me a chance to glance into the sparse room. Bunk beds, with the bottom layer given over to a kind of work space. A sink unit with a single hob. Plates and a mug tree on a high shelf. I couldn't see under the bed, but that appeared to be it. Spartan. Nowhere to hide.

"Sugar?" He waited in the doorway.

Beyond the hut, the land sloped steeply down to rejoin the forest. A set of three shallow steps, their honey-colored stone stained green with age, was stranded in the middle of the grass. A trail of heat tiptoed up my neck and onto my cheeks.

"Sugar, dear?"

I walked past him to the secluded steps. A carved stone acorn lay on the ground. One soft footstep, and he was next to me, barefoot in the wet grass. His head barely reached my shoulder, but his feet twitched with wiry tendons.

"Curious, aren't they? The Lonely Steps, as they're known. A clue to the illustrious past of this dingy dell."

The Lonely Steps. *Aloney steps.* Heat zipped down my arms, and my fingertips tingled around the crowbar.

"They're rather charming, don't you think?" He waved his arms to take in the scene. "Very Narnia."

Billy had been here. This was the man. Flapping birds wheeled through my mind, all the questions I wanted to ask cawing from their beaks. I could have swung my crowbar and smashed it down on his hammy face. I could already feel the shattering bones reverberate through the metal into my fingers. But I mustn't. I mustn't do that. It wouldn't help find Lola. I hooked the clawed end of the crowbar around my boot laces and hauled them tighter, one by one. *Billy's okay,* I told myself, *he's safe with Joni. Lola is the priority now. And I won't find her by putting a crowbar through this fucker's face.* But I couldn't look at him; I couldn't listen to his pontificating voice and keep control. As the leather cut into my ankles, the black birds settled. Billy hadn't seen Lola here. She could be nearby, though. At Moton Hall. While the man prattled on about *The Lion, the Witch and the Wardrobe,* I sized up his "dingy dell."

"But much as I'd like to see myself as Mr. Tumnus in this delightful fantasy, I have to concede I'm a little old to be considered puckish." He turned to smile at me, as though I might humor him. The man thought he was a fucking faun. My hand found my waistband and settled on the toy gun.

"What about that tea?" I asked.

"Yes! My apologies, I don't get many visitors." He moved toward the shed. I matched his stride, one pace behind. The toy gun was in my right hand, the crowbar hanging from the left. He stepped up onto the porch, into the doorway. When he made as if to turn back, I jammed the metal barrel into the muscle behind his ear.

"Get inside."

"What?"

"Inside." I shoved him hard, and he stumbled over the threshold into the shed, leaving me on the porch. The gun fell from my hand with a clatter as I slammed the door shut and closed the padlock. A metal hook released a shutter, which swung round to cover the only window, and I slotted the crowbar through the lock to hold it fast. He was trapped. I bent over double, hands on my knees, letting a rush of adrenaline claim me. When I stood upright, I was still shaking. Around the clearing, nothing stirred. Nothing cared.

"Are you still there?" His disembodied voice sounded older.

I balled my hands into fists, and the pain of my nails digging into my own flesh focused me.

"Why did you bring my son here?"

Nothing. I wondered if he had heard me through the shutter. But I waited. I had made the opening gambit. I had taken control.

"He darted out the back door of the supermarket and right into the road. Goodness knows where he might have ended up. So I rather think I rescued him, *Marlene*."

He knew my name. *How?* All the implications—*how long has he been watching us?*—made a salvo into my mind. I mentally swiped them off the playing board. He wanted to rattle me. I had to focus.

"Billy didn't need to be rescued. I was looking for him," I said.

"You were trying to scare him."

A flush betrayed me. I was glad he couldn't see.

"I only drove a few feet across the car park, that's all! It doesn't give you the fucking right—"

"Gutter language!"

"It doesn't give you the *fucking* right to kidnap him."

"You frightened him. I looked after him," the man said.

"You *kidnapped* him."

I stopped myself. He was goading me, and I was making it easy for him. I had to keep the upper hand. Negotiate. I was a good negotiator. I knew what I wanted—Lola. So now I had to find his side of the bargain.

"What do you want?" I asked.

"What an excellent question. I'm making tea, by the way." Teacups rattled. When he didn't answer my excellent question, I walked round the shed. A tiny generator meant he had power—there was a canister of fuel—and a long wire of some kind was rigged up across several poles. The shed was entirely encircled by trees. The place was weird and forlorn and beautiful. I got down on my knees and inspected the base: concrete, not likely to be a cellar. The only place Lola could be—if she was here at all—was inside. But she would have heard me, surely. And even if she was bundled up, the shed was so small, I would have heard the slightest knock or scuffle or gagged shout. Unless she was drugged. I had to check inside. Under the bed.

I came full circle and stood on the porch by the door. I could hear him moving about on the other side. A scraping side step. Slop of tea bags into the sink—one of my husband's habits, leaving the dank remnants behind like a dead mouse for me to scrape into the bin, bleach away the tannin stains. A creak, and the floorboard beneath my feet dipped. I jumped back, but of course he was locked inside.

"Do you want this tea?" he said. "I made one for you."

"I'm not opening the door," I said.

"But the milk—terrible waste," he said, outraged. I pictured the room behind him. Sink. Camping stove. Bed. But no fridge.

"Where did you get the ice cream for Billy?"

He started talking about an icehouse at Moton Hall. Kept in working order for the tourists. He was awfully garrulous for a man who lived in isolation. And remarkably calm for someone who'd been locked inside a shed by a stranger. It was belittling somehow. Like he didn't appreciate what I was capable of.

"Did you touch Billy?" I spoke over him. There was a pause. "Did you touch him?" I laid my hand on the door: rough, knotted wood under my fingernails.

"'What but design of darkness to appall?'" There was another silence, and then he continued in a tone that suggested the conversation was tedious. "Our children's lives are safer than they've ever been, and yet we find menace all around us. I do wonder sometimes if we want to see evil? The simple fact is, not every male is a *pederast*. Your son was quite safe with me."

"If you're not a pervert, why did you take him?"

He tutted. "Let's go back to *what do you want?* Such a simple question, but could you answer it?"

"I don't need to," I said. "I'm out here. Free to go. But you are locked in, and I will cut off your water when I leave, and you will die. So you answer the questions, okay?"

"As you wish."

"What's your story?" I said.

"My story?"

"Yeah. Why do you live out here?"

"It's my home."

"It's not normal, though, is it? Living like a hermit. In the forest. In a shed."

"Is that all that you hold dear? Being normal?" he said.

Splinter in the pad of my hand. Stinging. Pain is just an alarm bell. You can switch it off. "I'm just looking for answers for why you took my son. If you're not a pervert, what other reason could you possibly—"

"Maybe you should look closer to home, Marlene. Can you think of a reason why someone might take a child away from you when you use abandonment as a form of discipline?"

"Have you been watching us? At the camp?"

"I saw quite enough at the shop when I was going about my own business. I saw a mother trying to scare a child into submission."

Beyond rage—a cold, precise clarity. The black birds flitted from my mind, and my voice pealed through clear air. "All right, you know what I want?" I said. "I want to find Lola. I assume you've worked out who she is while you've been *going about your own business*. When I've found her, I want to find somewhere safe to live. I want food and shelter. Caveman stuff. I want to find out what the fuck is going on. And I want you to leave us alone."

"Well, I can help you with one of those."

"I don't need your help—"

"More than one actually. I can tell you what's going on. There's chatter on the radio."

I picked at the splinter. Drove it in deeper.

"And I can tell you where I saw the young lady," he said.

"Tell me then."

"Open the door. Drink your tea. And we can talk like adults."

"Just tell me."

"As you wish. They're calling it the English Plague. Just when we thought civilization would be toppled by a virtual virus, they hit us with an old-fashioned bubonic. Mutated, of course, to be more virulent. Scientifically *fascinating*. Carried by carbon monoxide, they believe, hence the rapid spread in the cities—" he went on with some enthusiasm.

"I know this already. Terrorist attack, man-made virus. What I want to know is—are they sending help? Where can we go that's safe?"

Silence. The floorboard bent under my feet as though he had shifted his weight. I could picture the flexing tendons of his gray feet.

"The stories are rather conflicting, depending on the source." His voice was lower, less animated. Breaking bad news. "There's rather a lot of conspiracy and speculation flying about. Hard to know which voice to trust—"

"Just tell me," I said.

"There's not much in the way of help. We're under quarantine."

"Who's under quarantine?"

"*Britain.* The British Isles are under quarantine. We've been left to die."

I picked up Billy's toy gun from the floor, pointed it with a straightened arm at a single buzzard circling in the sky. With one eye closed, I got the bird in my sight. *Click.* As I lowered the gun, the bird soared ever higher.

"Why would they do that?" I asked. "Leave us to die?"

"Because as far as they're concerned, we're not survivors, only carriers. If we die, the virus dies too." He sniffed. "I blame Brussels."

All at once I heard the flapping of black wings. *No help. No rescue.* The world lurched and realigned, like a train jumping the points. It was a familiar, if unpleasant, sensation that came at moments when I realized I was alone: the tracks fell out from under my feet, until I found my footing again and forged ahead into the dark. With the clarity of a bell I saw a memory of the day my parents came into my bedroom in Kenya—both of them, *is it my birthday?*—and said I would go to England, alone, to boarding school. We'll see you at Christmas and for the whole summer! Jump, shift, forge ahead into the dark. Then a decade later at university, dashing through rainy puddles with a soggy message from the chancellor's office. Ashen faces, terrible accident— both parents! Alone again. Jump, shift, forge ahead. And now this.

133

We've been quarantined. Jump. No one's coming to help us. Shift. This was the point where I should get back on track. That's what I do. But this time, I struggled to find my footing.

"Are you still there?" he asked.

"I'm here."

I looked around the clearing with fresh eyes. Stately trees. Leaves on the turn. Decay setting in. The buzzard was gone. "Best to sit tight," he was saying. "You don't want to end up in the isolation camps. There've been eyewitness accounts—ghastly—"

A click of the padlock, and I flicked open the lock. The door swung back. He was sitting on the bottom bunk, knees together like a child.

"Tell me where to find Lola, and I'll be on my way."

He shrugged. "Hard to say. I saw her once with those young chaps near the Hoar Wood. Making quite a go of it, they are. I glance in on them when I'm doing my rounds. But I haven't been out today, so—"

I crouched down to look under the bed: clear space. Not even a dust ball. The man was fastidious.

"You don't believe me?" he asked. "You think she's here somewhere?" A wave of his teacup indicated the lack of hiding places.

"What do you expect?" I said. "Whatever trumped-up excuse you've made for yourself, you took my son and kept him all night."

He tried to speak over me—"If you would just let me explain"—but I raised my voice and barged on.

"I'm his mother, for fuck's sake, his *mother*. I was beside myself. And there's no one out there to help anymore. No one to call. Have you any idea how terrifying this is—" My rage flickered, but didn't catch. He raised his eyebrows once, quickly, as though conceding the point. I felt empty somehow. Spent. Like you might after a good cry. My eyes slid off his and settled on a small table that was wedged between the end of the bunk and the outside wall. Half-hidden behind the door. Several framed pictures of the same child, a baby, an unfocused shot of a toddler on a rocking horse, a boy in a wheelchair. A toy car perched on one of the frames. A candle stub on a saucer. When I looked back, he was watching me. Defiant, as though waiting to see if I would dare mention it. But I turned away, onto the porch. Away from the shrine. Another dead boy. It was uncanny, as though he'd magicked it up. Just as I was talking about Billy. His son, I assumed.

I walked rapidly toward the Lonely Steps, reached down to touch the sandstone acorn, which was as warm as a newly laid egg. There was no mother in any of his photos. Footsteps came up behind me. I turned to face him.

"When you're out *doing your rounds*, just stay away from our camp, okay?" I said.

He dismissed my hostility with a wave. "About Billy . . ." He made a show of considering his next words. "When he came running out of the store onto the road—I thought it might be a lesson for you. A short, sharp shock, you know. You were being so severe."

He had that evangelical look in the eye, as though he were doing me a favor. Like the attachment mums at the school gate, beseeching me to reconsider my wicked working ways. Hearts bleeding for all the little children.

"Things have changed," he said. I fixed my gaze on his bony feet, as one slid over the other. "There is no one to help, but also no one to interfere. We can't call in the psychologists—which is, quite frankly, a blessing in disguise—but the children *are* traumatized, and we have to show them the way back from this dark place. Do you see? We have to raise them on bedrock now. At a time like this, they need bedrock. Not quicksand."

"You should write a book," I said. It was satisfying, in a fleeting way, to see him tut and turn away. But at the same time, I felt a dull jolt of recognition, a lurching flash of my train leaving the tracks. A yearning for sound footing. Roots. Bedrock.

"I tried to return Billy straight away," he went on. "But you and your friend were both out, and I couldn't leave him in the camp alone with the other children. It wouldn't be fair on them to be responsible for such a little one. So it was unfortunate that it went on rather longer than I intended." He let out a cleansing breath, as though this counted as a heartfelt apology.

Unfortunate. It was all most unfortunate. The scab behind my ear gave with a pleasing sting. I rubbed blood between my fingertips until it turned to rubbery grime that I flicked into the trees. Even if it was true that the kids had been left alone in the camp while Joni went out looking for Lola and I was hunting for Billy, every condescending word from this man's lips seeded indignation that spread like a weed until I was too overrun to speak. I tucked the crowbar under my armpit and walked down the stone steps. Along a path through the trees, I could see straight down to a wide stubble field and across to our campsite. But he wasn't finished with me.

"He's a delightful child, Billy. A credit to you. In my day, we would have corrected him to the right hand, of course, but that is considered old-fashioned now."

I carried on walking.

"I was a headmaster once. A minor preparatory school, so—" He paused to allow time for me to be impressed. Almost as I got out of range, he said, "I had a son, too."

I stopped at the end of the path. *Is this another excuse? "I miss my child—so I took yours?"*

"I'm sorry your son died," I said.

He stood at the top of the Lonely Steps, rolling the acorn beneath a bare foot. He kept three photos of his boy, but none of the mother. Perhaps any normal person would have been curious. Perhaps in normal circumstances, I would have felt a pang of sympathy. But I couldn't shoulder his despair alongside my own. I couldn't carry any more guilt than I already lugged with me from moment to regretful moment. And weren't they all dead now, anyway—all the sons? Apart from mine. My children were alive, and I intended to keep them that way.

"Where's the Hoar Wood?" I called to him.

He explained how to find the pathway from the Bury Ditches.

"Remember what I said, Mr. Tumnus," I shouted over my shoulder, and gave Billy's toy gun a wave in the air as a general reminder of its existence. "Stay out of our camp."

"And remember what I said, Marlene. Those children need bedrock."

I gave him a one-finger salute above my head and heard him tutting as I strode away.

Chapter Thirteen

The sun dipped below the ridge of the Long Mynd as I strode back across the field to collect the car. Dusk leached out of the forest and spread over the fields. A sharp cry from high above alerted me to an arrow of geese, their beaks aimed south, and their wings thrumming the evening air. Their faces were rapt like pilgrims, leading the peloton to a better place. My mind filled with an image of another peloton. Boys flying along together, wheel spokes thrumming the air, the wind in their faces. *Don't look back,* I thought. And then I shouted it as the geese powered overhead.

"Don't look back!"

I ran a few steps after them, my legs heavy on the land and the backpack clattering against my spine, but their pumping wings soon became silhouettes, and then dots, and then clear air. They never looked back.

At the camp, I slid down from the Beast and squinted through the darkness to make out Peter and Charlie's booby trap. At just the right height, the sunset glow caught the thin wire, and I was able to step cleanly over it. I smiled at their ingenuity.

As I came up the steep slope, I heard Joni's low drawl, taming the kids with a story. One of their favorites, *Where the Wild Things Are*. Billy was sitting between her outspread legs beside a plump campfire. The light flickered across his face, warming the soft skin behind his ear. Maggie was chewing a marshmallow off a stick, which she then passed to the Lost Boy, who sat close beside her. Peter and Charlie silently role-played staring into one another's monstrous eyes.

"It's rumpus time!" announced Joni.

She leapt up, and all the kids joined her as they circled the campfire, performing war cries and tribal chants and ululating songs. "Hookah-lakah, hookah-lakah. Wokah-wokah-wokah-wokah. Ah-yee!"

"And sit down!" Joni's deep whisper cut through the ruckus, and they scurried back to their places. Somehow, they knew exactly what to do. Sure-footed on her bedrock. She folded herself down in the middle of their circle and picked up the story. I walked into the camp just as the lost child got home.

Billy saw me first, and the spell was broken.

"Mum-may!" He clamped on to my knees.

"It's past our bedtime!" said Maggie.

"Quick, get to bed!" said Charlie.

They scattered like mice, leaving just Joni. "Lola?"

I brought home disruption and disappointment. Quicksand. As soon as I told Joni about the Hoar Wood, she snatched up her car keys and faded into the night.

I carried Billy to his sleeping bag and stroked his soft spot with a curling finger as though I was stealing icing from a cake, like I might actually be able to eat him all up. I thought of the times I'd chased him around the house, threatening to bite his bum. The times I pretended to chow down on his soft tummy. Put him between two slices of buttered bread and have him for my tea. How his joyous laughter—she loves me *so* much—was tinged with a juicy tang of fear—she's *wild* with love. I thought about the story Joni had just told, of a fierce love, the kind that devours.

Billy turned his head and slept. I went to settle Maggie, who was top to tail with the Lost Boy. Her hair was knotted around a sticky burr, and I untangled it, pulling it out strand by strand until it was free. By the time I'd finished, she, too, was asleep. The Lost Boy stared off into the darkness, and I patted his knee under the cover and let him be. Peter and Charlie took longer, as they needed to hear all about the man and his aloney steps and the strange house. "No, he didn't say why he lived alone in the forest." "No, he isn't an outlaw." "No, he doesn't want to hurt us, at least I don't think so." "Why not? Gut feeling." "Yes, I know I sound like Joni." I stood up to leave: "But you boys must never go there by yourself, understood?"

"Understood."

Afterward, I sat by the fire and rubbed my index finger across the underside of my wrist. It was the closest I could get to Billy's silken ear. I rubbed it and settled down to wait for Joni to come back from the Hoar Wood. Later, a rumble of tires woke me, and I sprang to my feet in time to hear one set of footsteps climbing the granite path. I went to the food tent and brought Joni a bowl of her own hot soup.

———

I was desperate for sleep, weepingly tired, but my legs twitched me awake again and again. Random spots on my body pricked with itches that I slapped at like mosquitoes. Every time I rolled over, the air mattress made a noise like I felt. In the end, I grabbed a blanket and left the yurt before I woke everyone up. I looked over to my own tent, but the silence left behind by the dead boy echoed in the negative space. So much for the trail of ashes. His ghost rode my wake. I walked the opposite way, past the latrine and through the trees to where his grave lay, a black mound on the flat landscape of the field.

I stepped out from under the tree canopy like quarry, checking around with twitchy-rabbit glances. The light from the stars messed up my perception, so that I stumbled over the grave, surprised by its real contours when they rose from the depthless backdrop.

"Sorry," I whispered. I hunkered down next to the freshly turned soil. The clods of mud were claggy in my fingers. Nothing could grow in this suffocating earth. It was no place for a young boy. "I'll stay with you," I whispered. "The first night is always the hardest." I unrolled my blanket next to the grave and lay down. There were so many stars, it seemed their combined weight had pushed the sky lower. I reached up a hand to the Milky Way, which arched across the sky like an exploding rainbow, thinking I might actually touch it. And that was how I lay for a long time, one hand on the grave and the other on the sky.

Then there were footsteps in the grass.

"Are you sleeping out here?" Joni was incredulous. She stood over me for a moment, looked up, then sat cross-legged at my feet. She released a husky moan, like someone's last breath after a long fight.

"I'm sorry I didn't come to the funeral," I said. "Couldn't face it."

"It was awful. The kids got ornery, so I sent them away. By the end, it was just me and Peter."

More deadened footsteps, and Horatio arrived. He sniffed at the grass with some disdain, turned a couple of circles, and managed to squeeze most of his bulk onto my legs. His body swelled and deflated as he let out an enormous put-upon sigh, and then we were still again.

"Do the stars make you feel safe?" Joni said. "Like nothing bad could happen under their watch?"

"More like detached. If someone came up and throttled me now— it doesn't matter, does it, in the scheme of things?"

"That's horseshit. It's never mattered more." Joni's voice was tight. "You know how people say they would die for their kids? I never got that. What good are we dead? What's hard is living for your kids. We only matter because we matter to them. It's doubly true now."

We both fell silent until Joni spotted a satellite. We watched it like two shipwrecked sailors on the shore, catching sight of a boat on the horizon. I had an urge to wave my arms and shout. But the satellite wasn't even life. Just another relic moving through space on autopilot. Like us.

"It's hard to imagine there are people out there," said Joni.

"So many stars. There must be life on other planets."

"Not aliens. I mean here. On Earth. It's hard to imagine there are people out there—and the fuckers have quarantined us on this shitty island. Are they just carrying on? Eating and drinking and going to the movies, while we're fricking dying? Who's in charge anyway? Like Europe? NATO?"

"Wish I knew. We need to get a shortwave radio somehow." I shoved Horatio aside so I could sit up, and he trudged back to the comfort of the camp. "Maybe it's bedlam out there, who knows? Even if we've got the worst of it, like the hermit said—if we're at the epicenter, in the eye of the storm or whatever—it must have spread to other countries to a degree. Maybe there's proper apocalypse stuff going on—looting, fighting, killing each other for a loaf of bread."

"But David is out there somewhere." Her throat was thick. "I don't even know what day it is."

"Wednesday." I looked at my watch. "Almost Thursday." In the past few days, I'd not thought much about David or the fact that Joni had had no news of him. Any grief I had for Julian was so tied up in a rat's nest of him leaving me and the plague and his affair that it was too tangled to unravel. I had simply laid it aside to pick at later. I was good at prioritizing.

"Or maybe they're fine," I said. "Maybe they're still going to work, to school, to the movies. And we're just another slot on the evening news."

Joni cried for a long time without a word of explanation or apology. I kind of envied her that.

—

While Joni cried, I thought about my mother. Deep in my pocket, I still carried her jade brooch. The stars led me back to a safari when I'd been about Charlie's age. One night, the nurse woke me and took me outside to see the sky. The air was filled with stars and also laughter from the bar: an equal source of wonder. But my mother spotted us and escorted me to bed. She stalked away through the savannah to the party without spilling a drop from her champagne flute. I'd cried because her dress was getting snagged in the red grass. *Why did she never look after her beautiful things?*

I told Joni the story once she calmed down.

"Did you love your mother?" she asked.

"She was perfect," I said. "Of course I loved her."

High clouds unfurled a veil across the stars, as though our time were up. The jade brooch dug into my hip when I got to my feet.

"I think we should leave," I said, as we headed to the camp to get warm.

"We need to find Lola first."

"Of course, no question. The Hoar Wood surrounds the hill fort: it's not that big. We'll go back again tomorrow. Keep looking until we find her. Then get out of here."

"I drove all around it earlier. Ran up to the summit, even. Shit." Joni stopped to unhook her trousers where they'd snagged on a thorn bush. She fiddled and swore in the dark.

"They could be holding her inside the wood—" I said.

"Holding her? Is that what the hermit guy said?"

"No, I told you, he just said he'd seen her at a boys' camp. But why would she stay away?"

"She's pissed at us. Both of us. Fricking thing, get off me!" Joni pulled her trousers from the thorns, and there was an inauspicious rip.

"You all right?" I could see only her hunched shape in the darkness.

"Awesome. My kid's missing and my ass is hanging out."

The Lady Lola had never struck me as a rebel. A bit enigmatic, perhaps—the Mona Lisa in Doc Martens—but she was no hothead, not the type to sniff glue or come home pregnant. Or run away and scare the bejesus out of her mother. And she had been so intent on finding Billy, her cousin. But I also had no idea if teenage girls' tantrums lasted for two hours or two weeks. And, of course, it was comforting for Joni to hold on to the idea that she had chosen to stay away.

"I'm going out again now," Joni said. "She must be somewhere. Maybe I missed some roads—"

"Why don't we go in the morning," I said. "All together?"

"I have to go now."

I recognized the compulsion in her voice. It was pointless to fight it. "Fine," I said. "And then what?"

"I want to get as far away from here as possible."

For once, we were on the same wavelength.

———

The kids were hiding inside a tree, a hollow oak with a bed of soft leaves. They wanted it to be our new home, even though they all had to stand up to fit inside. We let them play to give us a moment to consult the scribbled-up map.

"Here's the wood. I went all around here last night." Joni traced a large green patch, crisscrossed by blue waterways and surrounded by gray square symbols. "They must be someplace else."

"We'll widen the search area," I said in a tone that would steady a horse. I started marking each gray square building with a number in a route that brought us in a large circle back to where we stood now, at the foot of the Bury Ditches.

Buried witches.

"We can get round these wooded areas and all the buildings in a day," I said. But it had already cost us half the morning getting the small people mobilized. And then we had wasted time at Moton Hall, checking out the icehouse that the hermit had mentioned in such loving detail. We found nothing but buzz. Now we were finally at the Hoar Wood; it would make most sense to split up, but Joni had been out all night. The last thing we needed was another crash.

"Maybe we should ask the hermit guy to show us exactly where he saw her?" Joni was looking over the wooded knoll that rose 365 meters, the map told me, like a man's hairy beer gut. The search area did seem big. I was trying to formulate an answer when the kids all rushed out of the tree and started shouting.

Mummy! Mrs. Greene! Mummy!

"What now—"

"Can't you hear it?" Charlie shouted. They all shouted. I looked at Joni. She shrugged. The kids turned round and round, looking up into the sky, their mouths moving, like they were dancing to some celestial music.

"What is it?" I said.

"Wait!" said Joni, holding up a hand. "I *can* hear it."

"What?"

"Chunka-chunka," said Charlie, shouting right into my face, his mouth wide with joy. "Chunka-chunka!"

And then I could hear it too. The thudding of a helicopter. I closed my eyes until the sound stepped out from the crowd of wind and leaf noise. Its rhythm throbbed steadier than my heartbeat. The volume swelled, and then a machine burst over the wooded knoll in a blizzard of leaves and noise. We instinctively cowered. Billy sprang into my arms, and the others clung to my thighs as though they might be swept away by the tide. The helicopter powered over our heads and then turned in a steep circle, dipping toward us like a giant turning its gaze on an ant.

"What kind is it?" yelled Joni.

"A big one," I shouted back. It wasn't a police chopper, and it wasn't military green. "It's like one of those sea-rescue things."

"Rescue! We're rescued!" Peter and Charlie leapt up and down, screaming for the machine's attention. Billy buried his face in my chest, and I put my hands over his ears. As the kids streamed away across the field, the helicopter completed its loop, dipped its nose, and thwacked off toward the hills. We watched it leave us. Somewhere over the Long Mynd it turned into just another pixel that made up the sky.

———

The trouble with the Wikipedia generation is that they cannot tolerate ignorance.

"I know fuck all about helicopters," I pointed out for the umpteenth time. "I don't know what type it was. I don't know who was flying it. I don't know what it was doing. I just don't know." With one hand on the steering wheel, I punctuated that final statement with jabs in the air.

Joni shushed me under her breath. I sucked in a lot of air and braked hard, because I had nearly missed the turn into a farm driveway.

"What fuck-all color was it?" asked Billy.

I pulled up outside a house with a wide stackyard, strewn with vehicles, and several long outhouses. I switched off the engine, and it tutted in the silence.

"Stay in the car."

"But, Mum!" Charlie said. "You said Peter and I could help."

"Charlie . . ."

"Please!"

The kids would fight if I left them alone in the car.

"All right, but you little ones stay here."

Maggie set up howling.

"Maggie?" I laid a hand on her knee, and she stopped. "Can you please be in charge of Billy and the Lost Boy? It's important that they stay in the car."

Her eyes narrowed. "I think you should lock the doors, Mummy," she said, "and leave my window open a bit so I can shout if they try to escape."

"Good idea," I said.

Joni headed off to circle the house. Charlie, Peter, and I turned the other way toward the barns.

"If you hear a kind of buzzing, back away, do you hear? There could be bodies."

"We don't look, we definitely don't touch," Charlie parroted the rules back to me.

"Right. And no climbing, Peter."

"Yes, Mrs. Greene."

"Just look for signs of life: empty drink cans or rubbish or sleeping bags. A quick look and we move on, okay?"

"Okay."

We stopped beside the towering doors of a shed. It reeked of diesel fumes that must have built up over the past few days, so I pulled aside the doors to let it air for a moment. Beside the shed was a low concrete building. It looked as though some kind of animal stalls, an old dairy perhaps, had been converted into a squat row of lockup-style garages.

"Just check down there," I told the boys before the lure of tractors and combine harvesters could tempt their immature lungs into the noxious shed. They trotted off toward the garages, and I held my sleeve over my nose and mouth and entered. The fumes made my head woozy, but the shed was otherwise immaculate. The concrete floor squeaked under my rubber boots. The blades of a plough glinted like razors in the light. I heard Charlie calling me from outside, and I scanned quickly under the vehicles, but there was no sign of a hideout. I slid the doors closed behind me.

Charlie ran out from the garages. "Mummy, see this." He held an empty canister. It was white with a nozzle hanging from a piece of dirty string, its spout stained yellow. Charlie wrinkled his nose against the smell. From inside the garages, I heard the fingernails-down-a-blackboard friction of metal on metal as one of the shutters rolled up. Peter's footsteps stumbled about inside. I took the petrol can from Charlie's hand.

"There are loads more, Mummy." He wiped at his eyes, which were pink and weeping from the pent-up vapors. "And gas bottles, like Daddy uses for the barbecue. Come and see."

He turned back toward the outbuilding. My hand missed his collar and grasped air as Charlie sprang into his stride away from me.

No!

I didn't know if I said the word or only thought it.

The shriek of another shutter grating through its metal slats was followed by a muted wallop. A single flash of light issued from the garages and evaporated into the daylight outside. My feet slid out from under me, and I was falling as an ice-blue flare roared from the low entrance. Then orange fire mushroomed out and broke apart to dance in eddies up to the sky.

As I scrambled up, reaching for Charlie, whose mouth was already shouting, I dragged him backward across the gravel by his shirt, cannon booms echoing inside my ears, and saw his lips press together and apart as he yelled, *"Pe-ter!"*

I crashed onto my backside and pressed my hands over my face. Through my filthy fingers I watched a broiling torch dart from the low entrance and run, shrieking, straight toward us.

Chapter Fourteen

Buzzing. Somewhere nearby there was the buzz. I had my hand under Peter's head as he lay, limp and submerged, in a claw-footed cast-iron bath, the cows' drinking trough in the field next to the shed. I tried not to disturb him as I cast around to see where the body lay, where the buzz was coming from. I screamed at Charlie to get back to the car, but he didn't seem to hear me. Joni came running across the stackyard, and I screamed at her to find the buzz. "It's near here," I screamed. "It's right here somewhere." Joni reached us and stopped a few feet away, staring down into the bath. She raised her shoulders to her ears and folded her arms across her breasts. Shaking her head, she turned away. "No," I saw her mouth saying, "no, no."

"The buzz, Joni!" I screamed again. "There's a body here; where is it?" I was possessed with the idea that it was hidden on the other side of the bath, that I'd failed to notice it when I ran behind Charlie with Peter in my arms and flung him into the cold water. *Charlie must be right by it, he might touch it, and the plague will get him.* But I couldn't reach him, and I couldn't let Peter go or he would sink under the water. "Joni! Joni, for fuck's sake, is it there? Is the body there? There's buzz every-fucking-where." It was loud, so loud in my ears.

Joni was still shaking her head and clutching herself, but she seemed to come to. She took a couple of steps around the bath before inching closer, looking at Peter all the time.

There's no body, she said. There's no buzz.

"There's buzz!"

"It's in your ears." She pointed at her ears. I realized I was lipreading. The buzz was in my ears. It pulsed in time with my rabid heartbeat. I lifted my free hand to my right ear, but when it came away I couldn't tell if the fingers were bloody from me or from Peter's burnt skin. In the bath, his body tensed rigid, his eyes opened, and he began to shriek again.

———

Make it stop. Make it stop. Make it stop. In the twilight of the yurt, I pulled Charlie close to me as his muscles contracted in response to his friend's screaming. Billy seemed to have opted into a fitful sleep. Maggie was hiding under her hair, scribbling with crayons on a piece of paper alongside the Lost Boy. The yurt offered no escape from the sounds of pain. Peter's fit went on until our muscles reached exhaustion. Charlie let out a sob, and I kissed his head over and over, as though I could suck up his anguish and swallow it with my own. *Make it stop. Make it stop. Make it stop.* Peter stopped, but only for a few minutes. Then he started screaming again.

"Enough," I said, out loud. My voice still sounded far away, though the buzzing had faded. I almost wished for it back.

Inside the food tent, we had covered the trestle table with cling film and laid Peter on it. He writhed when the fits came, presumably from the discomfort of lying on his burnt back. The slightest movement hurt him so much, it was impossible to imagine driving him around to look for a hospital: that much pain would surely kill him. Besides, what state would the hospitals be in?

So we stayed put. I feared he could slip off the cling film table, but Joni said we had to stop the burns from getting dirty as he had no protection against infection. Already, the skin where we had cut away his clothes was raw and glistening. His limbs were a butcher's counter of pink flesh.

My hand hung in the air over his body. I thought I could look at him, that I could bear it—that I must bear it—but like I had when we stripped him earlier, I turned away. I stood close by, to catch him if he should fall, but I turned away from the sight of him.

He stopped screaming, but he tried to raise his head, as though looking for me.

"Mama?" he said, his voice soot dry. "Sorry, Mama. I hurt myself."

He raised his drooling hand toward me.

Make it stop. Make it stop.

I took the hand as gently as I could, letting the less-burnt palm rest in mine, without touching the raw back.

"Mama's here, Peter," I lied. "Mama loves you. Sleep now."

Make it stop.

Joni sat on the cooler beside his head. She hadn't looked at me even once since I came into the tent. She had on a pair of latex gloves from the first-aid kit. Next to her on the trestle table was a tube of calendula cream, unopened. It didn't look like she had done anything but sit there since I left her, as she had requested, to see to him. Peter fell still, and even his eyelids stopped moving. I bent to check the slight rise and fall of his chest that showed he was breathing, then I laid his ruined hand back onto the table.

"What do we need, Joni?"

She rotated her head up to me, as though she were the one having trouble hearing.

"What do we need to treat Peter, Joni?"

"Help," she said. "We need help." She dropped her gaze to the table, to a spot off to the side of Peter's head where the cling film was smeared with a runny yellow mucus.

"And failing that? What do we need to treat him ourselves?"

She held up the tube of cream. "I only know calendula," she said. "'A topical herbal remedy for the symptomatic relief of sore and rough skin, including light abrasions, chafing, minor burns, or sunburn.' That's what it says right here." She waved the tube at me. "What do you reckon, Marlene, should I rub it into his sunburn, huh? Apply three times a day and hope he doesn't die of shock first?"

Peter still had his shoes on. The synthetic fabric of his socks had so burnt into the skin around his ankles that we dared not pull them off. But I could see that his legs were swelling, so I reached down to release the Velcro tabs to ease the pressure. Even that slight movement set him off, turning his head and moaning, and I knew it would be just seconds before he started screaming again.

"He needs something for the pain, Joni. Where will I find morphine? Would a GP stock morphine, do you think?"

She didn't answer but just leaned close by Peter's ear and started humming a low tune.

"I'm going to take the kids and try to find something. Okay? Joni, do you hear me? The kids are coming with me, okay?"

As I left the tent and gulped down fresh air, Peter threw back his head, and Joni's song was swept away by the torrent of his pain.

———

Standing on a plant pot to reach the window, I could see the black shape of a body slumped across the reception desk in the waiting room. The telephone hung on its curly cable in front of a poster urging the elderly to get a flu shot. Before I could tell him to stop, Charlie flung himself in a shoulder charge against the surgery door. It withstood his scrawny assault. The double glazing kept the buzz inside, but the onyx blanket that stretched over the body shimmered as the lock clattered, bringing back the taste of bile, the memory of plump flies spattering my skin.

"Round the back," I said. We gathered our tools and found a window at the rear of the clinic. I slammed the sharp end of the crowbar into the glass, but it bounced off the surface, ricocheting out of my hands. The clangor of echoing metal joined the din in my head.

"Let me try," said Charlie, his voice even higher than usual, but he could barely lift the sledgehammer. I took it from him, and his hands flopped down and resumed twisting his jogging bottoms into knots. The sledgehammer bounced away, too.

I knew what I would have to do. We went back to the car.

"Get in, Charlie." I opened the passenger-side door and waved him in. He stepped away and started banging the heels of his clenched hands against his thighs.

"No."

"You have to wait here."

"No." His arms were a blur as he beat his fists on his legs.

"I'll only be a moment."

"Don't go inside with the buzz!"

"I'll be quiet so the flies don't get me. That's why I have to go on my own."

"You'll die, just like Peter!" His eyes were glazed with panic. "And then I'll die too."

"Charlie." I crouched down and held both his hands to stop him from beating his own legs. "Look at me, Charlie, look at me with your eyes into my eyes. That's it. Peter's not dead. But he's hurting, and I need to get him some medicine. I'll be really careful. Now please stay here."

Before he started up again, I stepped quickly over to the surgery door and busted the lock with the crowbar.

The buzz rose, more languid than I'd seen it before, and settled again without bothering me. But the smell was like nothing I'd known. Instinctively, I turned to run back outside, but Charlie was there on the pavement, twisting his trousers around his fingers and waiting to pounce. So I forced my gorge down and gave him a small wave to show that I was still alive, not overwhelmed by flies. Then I clamped my hand over my mouth and nose, and edged round the waiting room as far away from the body as possible.

The first closed door revealed a consulting room. I went inside and shut it behind me. In a cupboard over the small sink, I found some cotton wool balls, which I dabbed with hand sanitizer and shoved up my nose. I stowed some basic supplies in my backpack and managed to get into the next room through an interconnecting door. It was a mirror image of the first, except with a stethoscope, which I swiped. I cracked open the door into the hallway and, as expected, faced straight into the reception booth.

The woman's swollen foot dangled an inch from the ground, a court shoe fallen away and a hole in the flesh-colored tights revealing gaudy orangey-red nails against blackened toes. I wondered if she'd just had them done to go on holiday. *Had she missed salvation by a day?* I fixed the elastic sides of a mask behind my ears and moved down the hallway.

There was a second waiting room at the rear. It opened into another consultation room that was kitted out with surgical equipment, giant insect-eye lights, and a store of scalpels and syringes. My backpack was getting full, but none of this was what I had really come for. Back out in the smaller seating area, though, I realized what people had waited for here: the dispensary.

The counter was shuttered, and the door, bolted, but my crowbar made short shrift of the security measures. I stepped inside. The walls were lined with cubbies and shelves, the piles of mostly white boxes and jars ordered but not labeled. I turned to the nearest pile: Epilim. Stacks of the stuff—Epilim syrup, Epilim tablets, Epilim coated tablets, Epilim controlled-release tablets in 200s, 300s, 500s. So much Epilim. I picked up a box, turned it round and round, but none of the several printed languages told me what it was for. I ripped the cardboard flap and dragged out the folded paper instructions: *Epilim is a medicine used for the treatment of epilepsy in adults and children.* Epilim: epilepsy. Of course. I stuffed the box and the instruction sheet back into the cubby.

There were dozens—no, hundreds—of other names, all as strange and exotic and meaningless as Epilim. I ran my hand over the boxes, like a blind person who never learned braille. I muttered their names aloud but still didn't understand. When I turned, my backpack swept a row of glass bottles to the ground, where one smashed and scattered golden-yellow capsules across the floor. A wet pop beneath my boot, and I tasted a familiar tang on the air: cod-liver oil.

I'd wasted all this time and found cotton wool and cod-liver oil. My heart flipped in my chest, dragging the air from my lungs with it, and I grasped the counter for support. It was stiflingly hot in this tiny room. The green mask blew in and out with my panting. I flung it away so I could breathe.

I had to focus. Focus on pain relief, just pain relief. A pile of little plastic pots stood on the counter, the kind that nurses use to dole out pills. I picked one up, and it took me back to my first C-section, asking for pain relief and being handed a little pot of pink pills. "Hope it's the strong stuff," I had said to the nurse, who smiled her seen-it-all-before smile. "Ibuprofen," she said. I felt belittled.

But it had done the job. Even now, it would be better than nothing. I focused my eyes on the shelves and my mind on the few words of this foreign language that I did speak: ibuprofen, paracetamol, codeine, pethidine. After a few minutes, I found bottles of pink liquid, as well as suppositories. *Good, better,* I coached myself as I packed them into my backpack. *We can do this. Now for the strong stuff.*

I scanned the shelves for any names similar to morphine. Nothing. Why didn't they arrange the drugs in types—painkillers with other painkillers? It made no sense. I stepped round and round until the cod-liver oil was a slick under my feet. I turned once more and noticed a cupboard under the counter. Inside was a large safe. A printed and laminated sign stuck to the outside read, "All opiates locked in safe. Safe is alarmed at night."

So that was that. At least the drug addicts were protected.

———

Joni was right: we needed help. Peter needed help.

We drove alongside a cricket ground, and I realized we were about to pass the high street in Wodebury, the village where I had first seen the bodies. It was ages—eons—since I was last here. It was all I could remember. Everything from *before* had simply dropped away, like rocks down a chasm. I had left Marlene Greene behind on this high street and driven away. Now I was just borrowing her body, wearing her boots.

I sped past the junction, trying to prevent the children from seeing the bodies. Trying not to look myself. The kids were too busy bickering and elbowing each other. But my eyes darted across, drawn like flies, and there were the three corpses. Only now two were on the pavement and one lay in the street. How is that possible? I thought, *Animals? What kind of animal could haul a whole body along the pavement? Dogs?* I didn't stop to work it out, but pulled up instead on the stone bridge, just out of sight of the pub, and squeezed the top of my nose until I felt pain in my teeth. *Make it stop.*

I dropped the hand brake again, and we sped off, the high hedges blurring past my window.

"That helicopter could save Peter." Charlie didn't look up from studying his hands in his lap.

"That's a good idea, but I don't know where it came from."

"Maybe it'll come back?"

"I'm not sure we can wait that long."

"What are we going to do, Mummy?"

"We're going to ask for help."

I pulled in to the camp to pass Joni the liquid paracetamol and suppositories.

"The morphine was locked in a safe. I'm sorry."

She took the two white boxes and sat with one in each hand. Peter had passed out again, but Joni shook her head when I offered to help give him the drugs.

"I'll make it right," she said.

I took a few steps toward the car, but stopped and turned.

"Why do you have to make it right, Joni?"

She opened the boxes and lined up the bottle and packet beside Peter's head, taking out the instruction sheets and ironing them flat across her thigh with her palm, humming all the time.

"This isn't our fault," I said. "We never could have known—"

She turned over the sheet to read the other side. Peter gave a moan and shifted his head. The onslaught was coming. Joni closed her eyes and hummed louder.

"Do you want me to stay with Peter for a while?"

I waited.

"Joni?"

When she didn't answer, I turned and ran back to the car. I had to find help somehow. We raced up the farm track to the far side of the field where the hermit's shed hid in the trees.

———

He was out. I hammered on the door hard enough for the rattling padlock to scare away the roosting pigeons. He must be "doing his rounds."

"Mr. Tumnus is the world's worst hermit," I told the kids.

The creeping sense of unease that I got from the forlorn clearing twisted my gut between its bramble fingers. But as I watched Billy sitting on the sloping stone parapet of the Lonely Steps, bucking his hips to try to get himself to slide, I shook my head. Billy wasn't scared here. And there was no rational reason why I was.

"Mummy? I said, 'what's a hermit?'" asked Charlie, tugging my sleeve.

"A loner. An oddball. Someone who hides from the rest of the world." And maybe that's all my disquiet amounted to: a curtain-twitching suspicion of the stranger in our midst.

"So are we hermits?" said Maggie, with her usual scalpel logic.

"No, love, we're perfectly normal. Get the Lost Boy in the car."

As I slammed the door behind them, a wraith cry floated across the field. Peter was awake again.

I got in and started the engine, just for the background noise. The kids all looked at me, on tenterhooks for a solution. I bounced my palms gently on the steering wheel.

"Mummy?" said Charlie.

"What?"

He shook his head and gave a tiny shrug. It was bad enough not knowing the answer, but these poor kids didn't even know the question. I reached over and took his hand.

"We'll find help," I said. And I turned the car onto the road to Moton Hall.

Gravel swarmed up from beneath my wheels and stung the flanks of the car. The stately home looked much larger from the side where the mismatched domestic extensions and over-the-centuries additions huddled in the background, trying not to let down the symmetrical perfection of the facade. The layout was as tangled as undergrowth. It was as though every place in the countryside were as densely layered as the forest.

"He could be anywhere." I was bouncing my palms on the steering wheel again, harder now, so that I accidentally pipped the car horn and made myself jump.

"Ha-llo," called Billy, waving toward the front part of the house. Framed in one square pane of a sash window floated a white face. It faded back into the darkness.

I was out of the car and across the gravel in a moment. The kids scrambled after me. I held one hand above my eyes to peer through the glass, which was enameled orange by the lowering sun. I glimpsed a hallway filled with serious antiques, and a wide doorway that opened to the next room. I moved along one window. Inside a vast library and music room sat the hermit in a high-backed chair, pretending to read a book. One of his willow-pattern teacups stood on the glossy wood of an ornate side table.

I banged on the glass. He looked up and pulled his glasses down onto the tip of his nose, peering at me over the top.

"I need your help," I shouted.

He cupped a hand around his ear.

I licked my finger and wrote backward onto the glass, one letter in each of the small panes: HELP.

He folded down the corner of his book and slipped it underneath the teacup. Then he came over and jiggled the lock until it released, letting the massive window roll up on its pulley.

"What happened?" he asked.

"One of the kids got burnt. Badly. He's in pain, and I can't find any morphine."

"I don't have any morphine."

"Of course not. But you mentioned a radio. Can you contact anyone? Can you call out?"

He was already shaking his head.

"What about these broadcasts then? Do they say anything about helicopters? Because we saw one earlier over the hill fort. If I could get them to come back for Peter, he might have a chance."

Now he was at the chair, slipping the book into one pocket and wiping the teacup on his handkerchief before dropping it into the other. I carried on talking to his back.

"Any idea where they might be based? If I could drive to them? Or anyone else I might find who could treat Peter?" I glanced behind me to see if the kids were in earshot. Charlie was there, his fingers twisting his trousers again. I leaned in through the window and lowered my voice. "The boy's going to die if we don't get help."

He waved at me to move back so he could climb up and out of the window.

"If this helicopter has seen you, I rather think we're all going to die."

———

I cut the engine and we freewheeled down to the camp. The tires thrummed over the hard-packed dirt like a hearty soup plopping on the stove. But there would be no home comfort for us. The sun shattered into rictus fingers as it slumped behind the hills. If the hermit was correct, the helicopter that circled right over us had "nefarious intentions." "Otherwise," he had said, "why didn't it land and pick you up?"

The old man was paranoid, ranting and raving about long-past wars—neighbor against neighbor—and how Europe had been waiting for a chance to turn on the outcasts. As the hermit had scurried away from Moton Hall with his teacup in his pocket, Charlie had tugged at my elbow—"What about Peter, Mummy?"—so I'd let the old man go. He was a nut. Even so, I couldn't stop asking myself: *Why didn't that helicopter land?*

"Look," said Billy. An owl sat on a fence-post, its feathers backlit to form a white aura, and watched us with sunset eyes as we passed. "Buh-bye, little owl," called Billy. "Buh-bye," we echoed around the car.

The camp was mercifully quiet. Even the kids hushed as we stepped up the slope to the tents. Charlie slipped his hand into mine, and I squeezed it three times. He squeezed back.

Joni sat by the empty firepit. She stood as we reached her, forcing her torso up from the ground by pressing down on her thighs. She said something as she turned toward the yurt, as stiff and flat as a figure in a cave painting.

"Joni?"

"I'm done."

My legs carried me into the food tent where Peter lay on the trestle table, covered with a thick sleeping bag. Joni's sleeping bag. I laid my hand on his chest, but there was no rise and fall. His stillness spread up my arm like creeping anesthetic, until we were suspended in silence, stuck in the pause between breaths. A long groan rose from inside me, as though my last breath were also being sucked away. I snatched my hand from the body and hugged it to my chest, spinning round to see a row of questioning eyes behind me.

"Go," I said to the kids, pointing in the direction of the stream. "Get some water."

Billy and Maggie shot away in obvious relief, dragging the Lost Boy with them. Charlie dithered, building up to saying something.

"Sit down, Charlie." In the dirt beside the log where Joni had been sitting was a pillow. We both sat down, and I laid the pillow over my knees, letting Charlie's head rest on top. My hand settled into the cool hair of his nape. Up close, my parched skin stretched in a fine web of triangles across my knuckles. Like toughened glass under pressure, it had shattered. Charlie was tracing the pillow with his fingertips, the butterfly-wing shapes of brown stains. I finally let myself focus on the blood and mucus that smeared the white cotton.

"Is this Peter's blood, Mummy?"

I agreed that it was Peter's blood on the pillow.

Joni. What have you done?

For a second I thought I might cry.

That must have hurt, Joni. It must have hurt you so much.

But like a lost sneeze, nothing came.

Chapter Fifteen

"Once upon a time, long ago, people didn't die but instead they shed their skin, like a snake."

"What's a shed of skin?" asked Billy.

"It means the skin peels off," I said.

"Urgh! Why?"

"A snake sheds his skin so he can grow a new one."

"Don't want a snake story!"

"Hold my hand if you're scared."

"So one day, a long time ago, when people didn't die but shed their skin like snakes, a mother told her children that soon she would shed her skin. But the children started crying. Children don't like things to change, you see. They get frightened. And these children cried and cried so much that their tears kept their mother's skin moist so it didn't shed. And every time her skin started peeling, they all cried over it. This went on for many years. But one day, the sun saw what this mummy was doing. The sun got very angry, because she has to be brave and leave her children of the earth all alone every night. She thought this mummy was cheating. So the sun shone as hard as she could on the mother's skin, and this time, when her skin parched and cracked, the children's tears made no difference. This time, her skin didn't just shed—it wrinkled up like a walnut, and she died. And ever since then, people have to die and can't come back to the earth ever again."

There was a long silence in the tent.

I probably should have stuck to *The Gruffalo*. But I wasn't sure they would have swallowed a plucky-little-underdog story. I was swaddled in the limbs of my three children. Maggie's face brushed hot and soft against my shoulder as she turned it up to me.

"Is that story true, Mummy?"

"No. It's a myth. My nanny told me that story a long time ago when I was feeling sad. Because my friend died."

"Why did your friend die?" Charlie, of course, wanted hard details.

"He caught a disease called malaria." I said. "You get it from—"

"Mosquitoes."

"That's right. But let's not talk about that now."

"Are you feeling sad?" Maggie asked.

"Very sad. What about you?"

"I'm very sad, too. And so are Billy and Charlie. And him."

The Lost Boy gave a little moan of agreement, no louder than a bird's sigh. But we all turned to him: it felt like a breakthrough.

"Do you want to come and sit with us?" I asked.

When he didn't answer, I disentangled myself and scooted across the tent on my bottom.

"You can come and sit closer if you like. You must be very scared."

He faced the back of the tent. His take-everything-in eyes were almost covered by a sweep of glossy hair. I scooted closer.

"Why don't you tell us your name, hey? Can you tell us?"

He braced his shoulders up round his ears.

"It's okay. We just want to help—" I laid a hand on his arm; with a swinish cry, he writhed out of my grip and clamped his teeth down on my wrist. Then he was up and floundering over mattresses to escape the tent into the dark. Maggie seized his gray blanket and raced after him. In the torchlight, I saw a perfect red crescent embossed on my skin.

I followed. As though she could follow his scent, Maggie dashed through the darkness toward the yurt and almost collided with the Lost Boy as he shot back out again, still making the same piglet noise, and we all chased him down the slope, where he scurried on his belly under Joni's car. Maggie bent down and held out his blanket. A skinny wrist emerged and drew it out of her hand.

She nodded once, satisfied. "He just needs his blankie." And they all turned back to the camp, leaving me in the dark, alone once more with the muttering trees.

———

The second grave was tougher than the first. The ground was too wet. It rained just enough for pools to form as I dug, but not so hard that I could be excused. I lifted my head to let the water wash mud from my eyes. When I looked back down, the hole was full of leaves, floating like empty lifeboats.

Where is Lola? I closed my eyes for a moment and hoped that she at least had shelter from this rain. That it had driven her into one of the barns along Joni's latest route, so she would find her this time.

The kids sat on the tree line beneath a tarpaulin bivouac that Charlie had mastered from his survival manual. Huddled in the glow of an oil lamp, they fed themselves beans from the tin and drank cans of sticky pop. As I worked, I glanced up to check on them. Each glimpse of my children gave me a frisson of angst in the gut, like passing a shrine on a mountain road. This grave could have been for one of them.

I hauled sodden soil until the hole was almost knee-deep. But it wasn't enough. I brought the pickax down again and again, and every movement cauterized my aching shoulders. Sometime later the grave was thigh-deep. I scooped loose soil away with the metal bowl I was using in lieu of the broken shovel, throwing it onto the grass, sitting for a moment to rest my thighs while bailing out. The hole still wasn't deep enough, but my wrists were so weakened, I could hardly lift a full bowl of earth. A sob broke over me as I stood on burning legs to prize the pickax out of the mud again and haul it onto my shoulder. I spread my feet apart for balance, and they slapped into water. No, not yet—I had to go deeper. It wasn't deep enough. Above me, yellow lightning strobed inside the clouds. The sky growled an immediate response. The pickax slipped from my numbing hands and slapped into the wet mud. Maybe I had done enough. "Thank you," I whispered to the storm. And gathered my tools from the grave.

I carried the sleeping children one by one in juddering arms to the camp. The treetops thrashed in ecstasy at the high wind, and moments later a wall of water fell from the sky. Horatio darted inside our tent for cover. I ripped off my wet clothes and zipped us inside our cave, then reached up to extinguish the hanging lamp. My fingers fluttered around the dial like a moth. I stopped. The darkness was a hot breath against the scorched muscles of my neck.

I unhooked the lamp and unzipped the door again, stepping back out into cold rain. My bare feet splashed across to the food tent. I adjusted the light so it would burn for as long as possible, stood it on a chair next to Peter. He couldn't lie alone in the dark.

———

In the steaming light of morning, I inspected a food parcel that had been left outside our tent. A sprawling note informed me that our benefactor intended to "clear out before the end of the day following the sighting of individuals in a helicopter who failed to identify themselves." He said he thought we could make use of the perishable food items he'd delivered. Plus he had additional news, he'd written in an enigmatic postscript, which he could explain if I'd come to his dell.

If he'd found out where the helicopters came from or where we should go for help, why didn't he just write it down? I cursed the prissy old fart, but knew I'd be too intrigued to let it go.

First things first, though: we needed food, and then Lola. He'd left us a dozen eggs, fresh tomatoes, and newly baked buns, as well as some tins of food. I sniffed the buns, checking for any whiff of contaminant, but my stomach grumbled at my cynicism. I broke one open and breathed in its warmth. The kids piled out of the tent and fell on the bread. Charlie sunk his teeth into a tomato and chewed with his eyes closed and red juice on his chin. It must have been days since we'd eaten anything fresh. Even Joni's watercress might have tempted me now. I lit the stove to cook up the eggs.

While I cooked and we ate, I started a game to forestall the inevitable onslaught of questions. "We went to the supermarket and we bought . . . smoked salmon and gravlax sauce."

Charlie picked up the thread: "We went to the supermarket and we bought smoked salmon and Galaxy sauce and big juicy sausages."

"Smokey Simon and Galaxy sauce and big juicy sausages and Oreos," said Billy.

"Smokey salmon and Galaxy sauce and big juicy sausages and no Oreos because we've already got some so that's just stupid and chicken nuggets," said Maggie. We waited for the Lost Boy, but all that passed his lips was scrambled egg.

"We'll get all those things," I said after a while, "and he can pick something yummy for himself."

"And Peter," said Maggie, "can we get something yummy for Peter, too?"

I was saved from answering because the flap of the yurt opened, and Joni slipped out. She must have been out most of the night; I never heard her get back.

"Good morning, Auntie Joni," the kids chorused.

Without looking our way, she ducked behind the tent toward the latrine.

"What's the matter with Auntie Joni?" asked Charlie. "Is she impressed?"

"Depressed." I dished up more eggs. "She's feeling bad about Peter. And she's very tired. Eat up, we've got a big day today."

"Why?"

"We're going to get Lola and then find somewhere nice to live."

I took Joni's plate and carried it into the yurt. The place seemed massive now that we had all cleared out, leaving only Joni's jumble in the corner, which was heaped up as though she were still hunched inside. I made the bed, straightening the blankets and putting her pillow back together: a bundle of Lola's T-shirts wrapped inside Lola's black jumper. I pressed it to my face, but it only smelled of forest. The canvas flap moved behind me, and I dropped the pillow onto the mattress, bending to fiddle with the plate and mug instead.

Joni brushed past me and flopped onto the mattress, rolling away to the side, her limbs folded together like the fingers in a fist.

"I brought you some breakfast. There's eggs and tomatoes and fresh bread."

She drew her knees to her chest, fetal.

"Are you hungry? You must be hungry."

Her neglected hair spread off the mattress. I hunkered down and picked up a chunk that was twisting around itself, starting to dreadlock. It was messy-beautiful, like the undergrowth that coated the huge tree Peter had climbed in the forest on the first day.

"I wish I'd believed Peter when he saw those fires," I said. "Given him the benefit of the doubt. It wouldn't have killed me to listen to him."

Joni humphed.

"What?"

"It would have killed you. We would have gone out and got infected. That's what kills me about you, Marlene. Even when you're acting like a piece a shit, you still come out smelling like a rose."

"I'm sorry, Joni. I just came in to give you some breakfast. And say that we're having a funeral for Peter today. You were right about that: it's an important ritual. We need to do it."

She didn't reply.

"And I also wanted to say, for the record—you did the right thing. For Peter. There was nothing we could have done for him. Except . . . wait. I can't begin to imagine how awful it must have been, Joni, but it was brave. Merciful, even."

Joni heaved herself over to face my way. I reached out to deliver a gesture, a hand on the shoulder or some other expression of support like she might offer. But her eyes burnt red, and my hand hung in the air between us.

"The angel of death," she said, her voice bumping along the ground to reach me. "Get out of my tent and keep your fricking kids out, too."

———

The ashes were sodden from the downpour. We dropped them in sloppy, gray lumps as we trod the path from the camp to the field. The sun streamed down. For a second, it graced our heads while the green grass washed our feet. But then the tender moment passed, and we trudged to the hole in the earth, next to the lumpy soil of the first grave, which had been washed away into a cowpatty mess. The new grave was knee-deep in rainwater.

I stood and stared into it. Lifted my hand to Charlie, his grip in mine.

"We can't use that," I said at last.

We walked back to the camp, with Billy lying, at his own request, like a baby in my throbbing arms. Wracked and tender. His eyes were fixed on the backlit leaves of the canopy, as he used to do as a baby in the pram. "What the hell does he see?" Julian had asked me once on a park bench. "What's he thinking?" The blue gaze had been unrelenting. The leaves danced for him. *Do they still dance? Is that what he sees now?* I studied his passive face, inches below mine. His eyes were different now, though: glassy and rigid, like a fish's. I hoisted him into a different hold and pressed him flat against my chest, his legs instinctively clamping my waist. I turned his head on my shoulder so his face tucked under my chin. While we walked, Charlie outlined the details of a Viking funeral. It was all burning boats and floating pyres and sacrificial maidens.

"But it was raining all night, Charlie. We won't find enough wood for a fire."

"We could use the charcoal?"

"It won't burn long enough."

He chewed on his finger. "It would burn inside that tree. The hollow one at the Bury Ditches? All the leaves inside would still be dry, and there were bits of wood and sticks and that. It would be like an upside-down boat." He looked up at me with hopeful eyes. "Peter loved Vikings."

"No fires," I said, "no way." But we had to do something with him. And there wasn't time to waste. We had to take care of Peter, but there were also the living to think about: Lola, Joni. "No fires, Charlie. But we could use that tree."

My early childhood didn't include funerals. People died, of course. There were parental tears behind closed doors, hushed outbursts. But I never attended church. "Too upsetting," they said. "You wouldn't understand." Instead, I stayed home with the nanny, eating cake, and when everyone got back from the funeral they kissed me too hard and pressed coins into my hand. As is so often the case with parenting matters, I'd only realized my mother's true motivations once I had children of my own: she didn't want me at the funeral because she didn't want to be constrained by my presence. She didn't want to hold back her emotions to avoid upsetting her child. But times change. As Joni had said, we make the rituals now. Not that I had a lot of choice; I couldn't leave the kids with an aunt who had put herself into a voluntary coma. So they had to come with me. But I could also see that it was best for them. To learn how to grieve, to honor a friend. Pay their respects. I had to show them how to take care of themselves, and not just their physical requirements.

So I made the kids get in the car and not look back while I carried Peter's body down the slope. I had already searched the tent, trying to find a favorite object, something to leave beside him in the grave. But he had nothing. Even his shoes were still on his feet. As I laid him onto the filthy carpet of the Beast's boot, I remembered that back in the city I had promised to check on his mother and get his Star Wars Lego. But I never did. I never did anything for him. I never even spoke to him about his mother. I just assumed Joni had taken care of all that emotional stuff.

Shame sideswiped me, and I sunk to my haunches behind the car. I laid my palms on the ground and pressed my forehead down, too, grinding my face into the sticks and stones. A feral cry burst from me like vomit. All the things I had never felt, buried in the deep, seemed to surge up, catching me in the barrel of the wave. Squeezing the air out of me. Leaving me gasping. I pushed myself up from the ground and drew in a long breath, the sound of waves retreating over riprap, and slumped again. Then I thought of the silver Burmese Nat, my house guardian, one of the few things I had salvaged from home. I got up and dug him out from under the driver's seat, placing him next to Peter before we set off.

———

There was little dignity for Peter while he was being shoved inside a tree. None of the formality and solemnity I had imagined. I still felt washed out, as though by salt water, flushed and stinging. Empty. The kids were restless, nervy. I pushed on with the plan. The fronds I wanted to lay across Peter's body clung with every resolute fiber to their branches, refusing to be torn or twisted away. I left them broken, hanging from moist gashes. Sharp tang of sap. The sense of waste angered me. *The tree will die now!* I stamped at the mud that clagged my boots. We gathered fallen branches instead. Thick as antlers, dried leaves curled fetal. Back at the hollow tree, I tried to arrange Peter in a ceremonial way under the cover of the wood. But Maggie kept throwing in handfuls of grass, and Billy contributed bits of rubbish that he'd found in the field—a polystyrene cup, a miniature plastic horseshoe, a bent feather—and I lost my temper and told them they were being disrespectful. They wheeled away, pushing and pinching, taking it out on each other.

Above me, a buzzard screeched. I stopped and looked around for Charlie. Over toward the bulk of the hill fort, he was trudging back from the car park, holding out the bottom of his shirt to carry stones. The Lost Boy did the same. I captured the other two with a firm hand on the shoulder and directed them to gather more rocks. While they were busy, I settled Peter and placed the silver Burmese Nat at his feet. Facing out, spear high. I loved its fierce gaze, the way its back arched in an ecstasy of sacrifice. Defender of home and hearth. "Look after him," I pleaded, and had one last stroke of its smooth back.

The children piled their stones around the entrance to the tree. Nothing elaborate—there weren't enough rocks for a wall—but we made a little threshold that sort of defined the place as his. Once we were finished, we stepped back and looked at the overall effect in silence. I put my hand on Charlie's shoulder, but he was too mesmerized to notice.

It was time. I had to push us through this memorial. "It's normal at funerals to tell stories about the person who died. To remember them. If you want to say anything about Peter, you can."

There was a long pause. One of the stones shifted with a sharp click, and we all jumped.

"All right, I'll go first," I said. "Um, Peter had a lot of energy. He was a curious boy, and he loved to try new things."

I sounded like a school report. All wrong. My thoughts were too slippery. I steepled my hands over my face as though I might catch them. And then I saw Peter's face clearly in my mind: the moment when Joni brought him back after he'd run away from the broken shovel, his willing smile, the direct look in his round eyes. Like my Nat.

"Peter was brave. I used to think he played the fool to get attention, but I underestimated him. When he tested Charlie's mad inventions—like that skateboard with only one wheel, do you remember that?—he did it to help. He was glad to be your friend, Charlie. And who could ask for more than that? And he climbed that big tree on the first day because he sensed something was wrong—he had good instincts. He was looking for his mother—" This fact only occurred to me as it came out of my mouth so that I almost choked on it. "And again, when he sat all night by the gate, he wanted to protect us. Peter knew his own strengths. Which is more than most adults can say. He was a brave boy—"

My voice pulled too tight to speak. Thoughts and feelings slipped away, and I gripped myself to hold on. We had to get through this; I was the only one who could navigate us through. Charlie squeezed my hand, but he still didn't say anything, and there was another long silence.

Billy stepped forward and pulled from his pocket a shiny blue packet. He held it between two hands, his eyes moving between the packet and the tree. His mouth bent up with confusion, and he started to cry. I eased his fingers apart. Inside was a crushed Oreo still in the wrapper.

"Do you want to give this to Peter?" I asked.

"Sharing is caring," he said, but closed his fingers over his last biscuit. A moral dilemma too onerous for three-year-old shoulders. I bent down and kissed the tears off his cheeks. His skin was flawless. I hissed a fierce wish inside my head—my first prayer since all this happened: *Let Billy forget. He is surely young enough. Let him forget the fear, the hunger, the screams of other children. If one of us can come out of this unscathed, let it be him. Let it stop, and let him forget.*

When I released him, he wiped his runny nose on my shoulder and held the biscuit up to me. I leaned into the tree and dropped it through the branches. Billy took a wobbly breath and smiled with relief—he'd found the strength to do the right thing. He stepped back into the line.

"I didn't like it when Peter scared my rabbit," said Maggie.

I waited to see if there was more, but apparently there wasn't. She was truly her mother's daughter.

The Lost Boy delved into his pocket and held out a single Lego brick.

"Thank you. Peter loved Lego, did you know that?"

The Lost Boy nodded. I placed the brick in the tree. We waited in line again. Buzzards drifted overhead.

"Charlie? Anything to say?"

Charlie stood ramrod straight, fists clenched by his sides. He shook his head.

"Sure?"

He closed his eyes, and tears surged down his face. I dropped to my knees in front of him and held his tight body. His tears ran down my neck and formed a rivulet along my spine. They seemed to carry all his words in perfect eloquence. I kept my palm flat on his back as though I could soothe his pounding heart through the skin. Charlie would never forget. Of that I was certain. He was older, and this experience was too intense. And a thought dropped into my mind like a brick: *What if this is our life now? Any hope of forgetting presupposes change, that the horror will stop. We go back to normal, and this becomes some traumatic event that we survived, like a plane crash. But maybe this is it.* Charlie and I clung together in the wet grass. Eventually, our heartbeats slowed, and Charlie's muscles softened. He folded into me, and I gathered up his long limbs in my arms.

"Say good-bye," I whispered as we walked away.

"Good-bye, Peter," he said. "You're my best friend."

———

As we pulled into the camp, I heard screaming from the tents. I raced up the slope to find Joni tearing down the yurt, bellowing like a pierced bull. Standing nearby, with one hand spread over her mouth, was Lola.

Maggie and Billy flung themselves around their cousin's legs. Charlie followed, more subdued. I put my arms around Lola, as best I could with all the kids in the way, and crushed her slender shoulders into a hug. When I released her, ready to ask a dozen questions, she got in first.

"Mom's incensed."

Joni wrenched the canvas from the poles, and a loud rip came from one of the seams.

"So I see. Can I assume, then, that you weren't kidnapped and held against your will?"

"I met a boy."

I put my hand over my face to hide a snort of laughter.

"A whole group of boys, actually. After Billy disappeared, when you went off by yourself, we drove around for a long time. I found a bike by the side of the road, and Mom let me cycle up to the Bury Ditches, to check if Billy was there, while she brought the young ones back for dinner."

Joni hadn't mentioned that she let Lola go out alone.

"I met some little kids behind the hill, and they took me to the Hoar Wood. And that's where I met Jack."

"Seriously?"

"Seriously. He's looking after those boys all alone. Trying to."

"You were gone for two days, Lola. Three nights."

"I know. I'm sorry, it's just that—"

"Your mum's been crazy with worry. We all have."

"I'm sorry, I am. But the first night I was kind of mad with her. With both of you. You told me to fuck off!"

"Lola, I was—"

"I get it. You were scared about Billy. Just listen, please."

I folded my arms across my chest.

"So right after the first night, I meant to come back, but then when we woke up in the morning—"

"*We* woke up?"

"It's not what you think. We didn't—look, when we *all* woke up, some of the boys had run off, and Jack asked me to stay with the younger ones while he found them. And then we saw these helicopters, and Jack said we needed to get under cover. So I helped him move everyone to another camp. And then it just got crazy with all the little kids. God, just feeding them and keeping them out of harm's way. Surely you of all people understand how it gets. Time just goes." She snapped her fingers in the air. The way Lola stood, hands on hips, flicking her hair away from her face with the back of a hand, she reminded me of every mum I'd ever met at the school drop-off. Harried. Exhausted. Furious at the day for having so few hours in it.

"I do understand. But you could have sent someone with a message."

"The new camp is quite far—"

"We've been out looking for you the whole time. If we'd known—" I stopped myself, but the implication hung in the air.

"That's what Mom said. Because you were looking for me, Peter died." She raised her chin a fraction, but blinked back tears.

"It's not your fault."

Lola nodded rapidly. "But if I'd been here—"

"It's not your fault." I pulled her against me, and she kept her arms folded across her chest, but let her head drop onto my shoulder.

"He really died?" she whispered.

"Seriously, Lola. That wasn't the worst of it."

Joni seemed to have disappeared, leaving the yurt in a pile of string and fabric, as if a parachute had descended in the middle of our camp. The kids were busy scaling its peak. I gave Lola a we-have-not-finished look and followed the path into the forest. It took a few minutes to find Joni. She sat against a tree, her head slumped forward to rest on her bent knees. I sat in the leaves next to her.

"Thank God Lola's safe."

Joni didn't say anything, and I realized that she wasn't resting her head on her knees: she was looking down between them at her phone, which she cradled in her hands. She was flicking through photographs.

"You all right there, Joni?"

She pressed the switch and the phone went blank. She slipped it down her top inside her bra.

"You're lucky," she said. "Everybody you care about is either here or dead."

"Well, that's one way to look at it."

She shifted her hips so she could look up the long trunk of the tree to the canopy and the blue sky beyond. I watched scudding clouds until she spoke again.

"I can't stop looking at this damn phone. I keep thinking it might ring. David might call. I've been keeping it charged in the car just in case. Even though I know it's stupid."

"It's not stupid—"

"And there's all these photos of home. I don't know if it makes me feel better or worse. It's not so bad at night. If I can see the stars, then I convince myself I'm home."

"Let's go home then, if that's all it is. We'll go back to your place, regroup, and work out what to do next."

She snorted. "I don't give a fuck about that shitty house. You think I like that dump? The rattling windows and the shitty cars outside and the fricking warped doors that won't even close. Why do you think I didn't fix it up, huh?"

"Cos you were busy with more important things?"

She guffawed into the treetops. "How generous of you. You thought I was a slob. But it was my little rebellion against this shitty country. Fucked if I'd put my energy into that hole. David promised we'd come to England for two years, tops. It's been a decade. And now he's home and I'm stuck here? That piece of shit."

"I always thought you were settled here."

"Well, now I want to go home. To Mom's place. Pennsylvania."

"David's in New York."

"But he could get there. He could walk if he had to, if it's that bad. He could just walk for however long it would take. But how can I get there? I'm stuck here. Marooned." Joni grappled her phone out of her top and scrolled rapidly through to an image, which she held out to me. Corner of a picnic table in the foreground before a long view over mown fields, forest, huge sky. But strangely familiar, bucolic. It could be right here in Shropshire. "We could really live there. Thrive. We did it before, my mom and me, when Lola was born. After my father left and then my brothers, both of them one after the other. And I promised I wouldn't leave her, but of course I did, soon as I met David. I left and took her only grandchild away."

"You'll see her again," I said. *Unless this is all that's left.* I didn't dare say it out loud. Might come true. I shooed the thought into a corner.

"All her children left her," Joni said.

"That's what children do. We know that when we sign up."

"I'm not ready."

"You don't have to be. Lola's right here. She's fine."

Joni shook her head, scrolling through pictures, the images flashing by too fast to take them in. "I thought I could do it all again," she said. "Raise another child. But I can't."

I picked up some sticks and a strip of thin bark. I tore away a long shiny ribbon and fiddled with the sticks until I'd made a wonky sort of cross. Then I made another. One for the boy's grave and one for Peter's.

"We need you, Joni. I know it feels like it's all going wrong, what happened with Peter, but we need you."

"I'm done."

"You can't be *done*. We're only just starting."

She didn't answer, just sat with bucolic images flashing past her eyes. At least she was up, out of the tent. And now that Lola was back, we could leave. I picked up my crosses and set off to find out where to go next.

Chapter Sixteen

The hermit sat on his porch, wrapping an extensive willow-pattern dinner service in newspaper and loading it into a wheelbarrow. He startled to his feet as Horatio ran up the Lonely Steps, but lowered himself back down and continued his packing when he recognized the dog. He greeted me with a lift of the chin.

"Going somewhere?" I asked.

"As I explained in the letter, I'm clearing out. Take my advice and do the same—just friendly advice, mind you, I know how you begrudge interference." When I didn't rise to the bait, he carried on talking. "It's not safe here now those helicopters have spotted us. Well, spotted you." He looked up into the blue circle of empty sky that split the canopy above the clearing like a child's drawing of a duck pond. "I thought they would take longer to find us out here. They're organized, I'll give them that."

"Who? Who are you talking about? Why are you so worried about this helicopter? There was only one, and it just flew overheard, doing a recce, perhaps. Granted, I don't understand why it didn't pick us up, but it didn't threaten us, either—"

"That's what I wanted to tell you. Chatter suggests Johnny English hasn't been made entirely welcome on the Continent. Treated rather poorly, in fact. The problem is, they were homegrown terrorists, and opinion seems to be that we should keep our homemade virus to ourselves."

"I know they were homegrown terrorists, but that's not our fault, is it? Surely the world has a duty to protect us?"

"The world is protecting itself."

I looked away from him, away from the truth of it. "Well, even so, couldn't the helicopter have been from the Red Cross?"

"Was it a Red Cross helicopter?"

"No, it was black, but—"

He closed his eyelids for a long second, as though praying for patience with an exceptionally dimwitted child.

"That doesn't mean anything," I said. "The humanitarian effort must be huge, bigger than anything they've ever dealt with before. They could be using whatever they can get their hands on—private helicopters, like the little ships at Dunkirk."

"No, I rather think we're on the other side of history this time, the wrong side. The world doesn't want a plague. They'll do anything to stop it."

"I find it hard to believe they're going to exterminate us. You're talking about genocide."

"Have you forgotten Hiroshima? Nagasaki? And why did we sanction the extermination of hundreds of thousands of people in Japan? To prevent loss of life. To save ourselves. So don't underestimate what fear can do to the human mind." He stopped and looked down at the pile of crockery, lying forgotten at his feet. A dinner plate shook in his hand as he picked it up, and he steadied it as he resumed polishing. "Are you one of those people, Marlene, who believes in the power of positive thinking? My wife used to say that if she visualized a parking space, she would always find one." He placed the plate into the wheelbarrow with an under-the-breath "there." "But she didn't always get what she wanted." Wife in the past tense, fussing over her china. So this is what happens when death cuts you adrift from your family, when there is no weight of responsibility to anchor you down. You just float until you're lost. After my parents had died, when I found myself alone, I hooked on to Julian; for better or for worse, he was ballast. And then the family came and there was something to work for, and I stayed on course. They set my course. If nothing else—if Julian resolutely failed to ever support me in even the smallest way—at least he gave me the solidity of supporting him. Now, watching the hermit adrift among his dead wife's belongings, haunted by past horrors, I thanked Julian for the first time.

"I never really understood positive thinking," I said. "We'd all just be fabulously wealthy and thin. I guess I believe in luck."

"And are you a lucky person?"

"I've survived this far. As have you."

"More luck than judgment, if I may say so. On both our parts." He bustled off into the shed, and whatever he said next was obliterated by tap water pounding into the sink. I stepped onto the porch. He was drying his hands on a tea towel, rubbing it over each fingernail as if polishing them.

"Thank you for the food parcel."

"Oh, yes, yes. Welcome. The Aga up at the house runs on oil, most convenient in the circumstances. I wanted some rations for my long march. Dead bodies in the kitchen, unfortunately, but that's a necessary evil. Excuse me." He blustered past and added an old-fashioned leather suitcase to the wheelbarrow. Then he went back inside and set about putting on his socks and boots.

"You baked the bread in a kitchen with corpses in it?" I said.

"It's a big kitchen."

"But the virus—"

"Doesn't seem to have killed me yet. So I rather think the bodies are little more than an inconvenience. Needs must."

Inconvenience. The thought of eating those buns—the kids eating those buns—filled my stomach with a buzz of disgust. And yet we were still here. Maybe it was time for *needs must*?

"So is that the 'news' you mentioned in the letter—this chatter?"

"There wasn't a lot of detail. And some of the messages went too fast to decipher."

"Decipher?"

"Some of it's in Morse code. I learned Morse as a boy, of course, but I'm woefully rusty, only got the gist. And many of the shortwave channels are foreign—Radio Moscow and the like. Do you speak Russian?"

"No."

"No. Shame, that. They're coming through strong. Can't understand a damn thing. Apart from 'Angliyskiy.' Seems to be every other word." He prattled on about the vagaries of foreign broadcasts, but I had a hard time concentrating; his voice sunk away, and only the odd phrase surfaced into my consciousness. "Quarantine." "Atrocities." But inside my body, a giddy sparkle spread from my extremities to the core. Only once it reached and gripped my heart did I realize that it was euphoria. People living, people talking. Politics and religion. All the usual shameful human behavior. But life, nonetheless: not this paltry survival, but actual living. Terrorism, murder, state-sponsored inhumanity, I'd take it all, so long as I didn't have to watch my children suffer one more day in this bloody awful Eden. Something like the relief of aircraft wheels squealing onto tarmac—only magnified beyond tolerance—sent a punch of adrenaline through me. *So what if we are under quarantine? If they won't come to us, we can go to them. Joni can go home. Billy can forget. All of us can heal.*

"So what exactly are they saying?" I needed him to get to the point.

"Picked up some Arabic, Chinese. Scandinavians broadcasting in English, but keeps getting interference. The raving Christians would be quite amusing if they weren't such"—he ground his fist against his ear in a toddler-like movement—"dreadful, dreadful people. But shortwave is not your simple car radio, you can't—"

"The signal's better at dawn and dusk. Okay, then I'm going to pack up the camp, and I'll come back later," I said, and in reaction to his undisguised surprise at my old-school knowledge, I added, "I grew up with shortwave. Expat kid. You said you caught the gist of the Morse code messages? Any clues to where exactly we should go? There must be someone offering help. For the kids at least."

"'Quarantine'—they repeat that word a lot—'quarantine.' And don't go south."

Don't go south. So much for a gentle new life on the Mediterranean.

"And the rest is much as I told you before," he said. "The scale of it has taken them by surprise. They've come down hard on the Continent—whole villages sequestered, refugees in isolation camps, some say mass exterminations." He stopped, and the horrific images seemed to wraith around the clearing for a few seconds before evaporating.

"Whatever happened to 'women and children first'?" I said.

"That seems to have been replaced with 'each man for himself.'"

"So where are you going?" I asked.

"I'm going to hide in a cave, and when I come out the land will be cleansed. And then I can return to this corner I call home. The humble Mr. Mole after his adventures on the river."

He turned and surveyed his domain. Whatever he saw added up to more than the sum of scrawny trees, three stone steps, and a shed. It was time to go and get packed up, but I lingered, sure there were more answers if I could only find the right question.

"What is this place?" I asked.

He smiled. For the first time, I saw his neat teeth, oddly childlike in his elderly face. "These are my ancestral lands." He waved his arm in a wide circle and turned back to the wheelbarrow, picking up the handles. "The Lonely Steps are all that's left of the ornamental gardens. In medieval times, the hall was over there. The woodland fought back, but nature can't obliterate the family tree, eh?" He looked pleased with himself, despite the tears in his eyes. "Of course, my ancestors managed to lose the lot."

"Every tree has a few bad apples."

"Indeed. But now the apparatchiks at the county council are no longer with us, I will rebuild it. One more winter, perhaps." He pointed up to the sky. "Patience, William Moton, have patience." He grinned at me and pushed off toward the path that led to Moton Hall.

Horatio came gamboling out of the wood and stood alert on the grass. I followed his gaze into the trees, but everything was listless and undisturbed. Then I picked out a high drone.

"Farewell, Marlene," the hermit's voice floated over the strangled squeak of the wheelbarrow wheel.

"Can you hear that?"

"I can barely hear a thing at my age."

"Helicopter."

He let the wheelbarrow thunk to the ground and dashed back to the shed, scrambling underneath the bottom bunk and pulling out a silver heat blanket, which he wrapped around himself as he folded his limbs down onto the floor.

"Get inside! Otherwise they'll see you; the cameras will pick up your heat signature," he yelled.

I stepped backward under the green canopy, watching the circle of sky. It was hard to place from which direction the sound was approaching until the tops of the trees bent in submission, and the upsurge of noise told me the helicopter was close and low. It must have skirted the clearing on the side of Moton Hall. The thrumming receded as quickly as it had appeared.

William Moton shot out of the shed, trailing the blanket as though he'd just finished a marathon.

"They'll be back! Get away from here." In his panic, he let the silver blanket go, and it floated for a moment in the air behind him, still bent to his form, and then crumpled to the ground. He snatched up the wheelbarrow and jostled off down the path.

"Good-bye, William Moton," I called after him, "and good luck."

"Get away from here," he yelled. "And don't go south."

As the hermit fled into the trees, I hauled Horatio inside the shed and pulled the door closed. Of course the outside world would do anything to prevent the spread of the virus—wouldn't we do anything to protect our own? Hadn't I done exactly that? But if I was going to rally my troops, I needed a plan—a better one than "hide in a cave." Part of me wanted to run like William Moton, but I also had to hear for myself the outside world that had turned against us. A tremor of fear made me fumble and drop the headset that was attached to the radio equipment. I'd expected a transistor handset, like the Roberts I had stupidly left behind in my house along with all the other lifesaving items. But this was more complicated. He must have built it out of scraps: coils and diodes brought to life by red-wire veins. I flicked a switch, and the shed filled with a crazy oscillating wail. I changed the channel to heavy interference, changed again to a mournful foghorn. I needed a hint of where to go next. Anything. The Bakelite dial clunked between electrical howls and sniveling static. The sound of mayhem.

I switched it off and let the quiet settle back into place. The lilt of birds bickering over the life or death of a worm. Reception was best at night; we needed to get away, but if we packed up the camp now, I could come back and get some sort of steer before we set off. I exited the shed and scooped up the silver heat blanket. Horatio froze on the grass, facing the trees with his head tipped to one side.

"What is it, von Drool?" I called to him, walking toward the stone steps. He tipped his head to the other side. "Let's go—"

Then I heard a noise like whooshing radio static. But it wasn't coming from the shed: it was the slap of rotor blades spanking the air. Out of sight, the engine whined as the helicopter came in to land, and then steadied to a violent buzz. The sound had such physicality it seemed to crane over the trees to grasp at me. I could imagine it hunkering on the grassy lawn, its brutality crashing the elegant facade of Moton Hall.

Horatio gave a gruff and scuttled past me, jumped down the Lonely Steps in one bound and onto the path through the trees in the direction of our camp. A rapid clattering made me turn back to face the clearing. William Moton appeared, still pushing the wheelbarrow, its cargo of porcelain bucking over the bumps. He pushed it right up to the door of the shed before he noticed me standing on the steps and hissed, "Run, you idiot woman!" As he turned to look behind him, the wheelbarrow tipped and the contents slid across the grass. He bent to try to lever the stack of plates back upright, but gave a cry of anguish as footsteps crashed through the woodland, the heavy tread audible over the distant buffeting of the helicopter. He left the plates and scooted behind the shed, where he leaned up against his home, peeping round the corner once before sliding to the ground. His despair startled me into action, and I leapt down the stone steps and slipped into the trees just as the first figure emerged from the path into the clearing.

It strode forward on stiff legs, rendered into gigantic proportions by the bulk of a biohazard suit. The impact of every footfall juddered aftershocks through the rigid uniform, starchy-white in the sunlight. It stopped, and the wasp eye mesh of its helmet whipped from side to side, the jerky movements belying the menace of its intense focus. It raised its legs and descended on the shed, as two more suits appeared from the dark hole of the wood.

"He's here."

The deep voice was so human it jolted me. I couldn't tell which one had said it, but it must have been the one who was pointing an arm at the stricken wheelbarrow. The first figure moved toward the shed, toward the hermit who was slumped behind it, toward the steps, toward me. My legs wanted to run, as though they possessed instincts superior to my own, but the route to the farm track was too open, too exposed. I shrank into the undergrowth. My hands weren't even shaking anymore. My body was thick and numb and helpless, disabled by a fear as powerful as an epidural.

The white figure ate up the ground. He slapped the door open and glanced inside, then rounded the shed and stopped when he saw William Moton, turning his wasp face back to the others.

"Target."

"Go ahead."

The white figure reached into a deep pocket in his trouser leg—as coolly fastidious as the man prone before him had once been—and withdrew the dark shape of a weapon. His arm scissored up, and he fired a single shot into William Moton's forehead. The hermit flopped with his head lolling to one side, like a child playing dead.

"Clean?"

"All clean."

The white figure pocketed the gun and moved back to the others. They said a few words I couldn't hear, their voices too low against the background drone of the idling helicopter. Two of the soldiers cast a final look around the clearing and moved toward the trees. A soft rustle behind me and I whipped my head round, expecting to see Horatio. Instead, peeping round a tree on the verge of the farm track, was Charlie. Some twenty yards away. Nothing between him and these killers but a few trees. His eyes locked on mine and his composure chilled me to a steely focus: I made a zip motion across my lips, then raised both hands and held them over my eyes: *hide*. He slipped behind the foliage. A voice from the clearing drew me back round again. The third suit brought a tablet computer close to his wasp face and finger-pinched the screen.

"Wait."

The white figures turned from the tree line.

"There are two here."

They accepted the information with robotic indifference. The one with the tablet held out the computer as they came back onto the grass, gesturing to details on the screen. He pulled out a walkie-talkie and muttered into it. I turned to check on Charlie. No sign. My legs twitched to go to him, but the path was too open, and the undergrowth too noisy. *Stay behind the tree,* I willed Charlie telepathically. *For God's sake, don't come to me.*

"Let me see." Back in the clearing, the shooter took the tablet and zoomed further in, turning it this way and that to get his bearings. Then he handed it back and pointed down the path that passed right beside me. He crossed the grass, past the overturned wheelbarrow, to the top of the steps. Just three stone steps and he'd be on the path. At least he would see me before he got to Charlie. I wanted to look back again, but I couldn't take my eyes off the white figure, so close now. He stopped and looked around him, computing the strangeness of the Lonely Steps. His boot made contact with the stone acorn, a steel toe cap sending it arching down the slope to rest just ahead of me, where the undergrowth of the copse gripped the edge of the pasture. One starchy stride onto the middle step. He turned to the others and waved his arm at the dead man.

"Look at this place. The guy's a loner. Are you sure there are two?"

"There's two on the screen. We got two."

The shooter shrugged and stepped onto the path. A few strides and he would be parallel with me. Then just one glance to his left—if I moved, he would hear me. If I didn't move, he would see me. If Charlie moved—I would have to stand up, deflect the attention. Mother bird, lead them away from the nest. I could run. The biohazard suit might slow the soldier down, but I had nowhere to go. The undergrowth was too thick. The path led toward Charlie. And my legs were numb.

But how can I just stand there and die? What sort of mother leaves her children? Even to die. I put my hands on the ground and pushed myself into a crouch. If I ran to the right, the trees would provide some kind of cover—I could lead him away from Charlie and reach the farm track farther down toward the ford. If I could distract him, it would give me a head start. I picked up a hard twig knuckle. If I threw it behind him, made him turn away for just a moment—

"Target!" The voice from the clearing called out the warning. The soldier on the path took two steps forward. I dropped chest down onto the ground again. His arm levered up, gun pointing not at me, but farther down the track. I craned my head up as instinct shouted in my head—*Charlie!*—but Horatio was on the path, standing with his head to one side. He had come back for me.

"Just a dog," the suit called. His wasp face bore down on Horatio.

Heavy footfall, and the white figure holding the tablet appeared at the top of the steps.

"Big dog, though," it said, examining the screen, considering.

I heard Horatio's tail bat the ground once as he looked up into the gun, confused by the featureless mesh of the face: the single eye of the barrel that watched him.

The white figure on the steps slid the tablet into his pocket, turning away.

"Yah, looks like our target. Clean it up."

The suit fired a single shot into Horatio's muzzle: the dog gave a low gruff, his long legs tried to steady the load, his claws gripping at dust. The suit turned away before Horatio even hit the ground. He pocketed his gun and followed the other white figures back up the Lonely Steps toward Moton Hall, crushing the dead wife's plates underfoot as he went.

———

Corn stubble clattered against my boots as I ran. I left stealth behind in the wood and gave in to a blind urge to run, towing Charlie behind me like a balloon on a string. I careered to the bottom of the field and scrambled a fence to get to the camp. The buzz of the helicopter had receded, but I knew we would hear it again before too long. I gave Charlie the car keys and told him to start the engine. I didn't want him to launch into a story about Horatio, or we'd have all that to deal with, too. No time.

I was calling their names as I reached the tents. They were all there—bar Joni—sitting on logs around the campfire. For a second, it was like the first day we arrived. The scene was everything I had been looking for back then: the team, together, collected and calm. But their expressions were inhuman. Like gazelles on the plain, heads snapped up as I ran in.

"We need to go. Now!"

Lola flitted off to find her mother while I stuffed some supplies inside sleeping bags. I shepherded the children toward the car, taking advantage of their compliant bewilderment to hurry them along. We stopped in a huddle beside the Beast, and I didn't know whether to get in or not. Any second now, one of the little faces would split open and ask, "What are we going to do, Mummy?" and the question would burst the dam of my inundated mind, and I would scream, "Run or hide, take your pick!" Laughing hysteria into their startled faces. "Because you think I know what to do, don't you? But that's the big secret adults keep: we have no idea what to do. So your guess is as good as mine. Run or hide, kids? Run or hide?"

"You decide," I would tell them, "because I don't know how to help you. I just don't know." I slapped my hand over my mouth to hold it all in.

A grip on my shoulder made me jump. Lola.

"We should take Mom's car. Yours is knackered."

I looked at the Beast: battered and filthy, windows missing, the smashed headlamp slipped from its socket again. But that car had never let me down; it never stopped going. It felt disloyal to leave it.

Lola was asking, "What do we do, Aunt Marlene?"

The Beast's engine was running. I put my hand on the bonnet. *Warm. Leave it running. If the helicopter picks up its heat signature, the Beast can do one last thing for me and distract them for a few minutes.*

"We go. Now."

Lola started lifting the kids into the back seat of Joni's car. Billy was fighting to get out, shouting something.

Wabbity.

"I can't get Rabbity, Billy. We don't have time." I wrestled him into his seat belt, pressing my head into his stomach to hold him down.

"Effie Elephant!" Now Maggie joined in, taking her belt off and scrambling back out. I held up my palms like two white flags: I would have to surrender this battle to win the war.

"Stay in the car!"

I ran back into our tent. Scrambling among the bedding, I found the various soft toys, their beady eyes looking alarmed by the turn of events. Outside, Joni moved toward the car in slow motion, as though getting accustomed to sea legs. I pushed her into the boot on top of whatever belongings and food we'd grabbed in the rush, and ran to the front seat. Lola climbed up next to me.

"What are we running from?"

"Guys in a helicopter. Tracking us with a heat camera, I think. They killed the hermit." I hissed: "And Horatio."

"The boys heard that helicopter a couple of times. No one could agree whether to trust it or not. Jack thought it might be mercenaries."

"We can't trust it, believe me." I pulled the car round so that we faced the dirt track, but stayed under cover of the trees. "It landed at Moton Hall, which is beyond that woodland." I pointed up the path to the left. "The main road goes past it. So we need to go the other way and hope they don't fly overhead. But that lane is narrower, slower, and I don't know where—"

"I know a place to hide," said Lola. "We won't be on the road for long."

"Where are we going?"

"To the railway. To find the boys."

The Wild Things. I closed my eyes for a moment. Maybe Lola didn't know about the first boy, the one I'd run over. Maybe Joni hadn't had time to tell her. Would these boys know it was me? Would they give us shelter if they did?

"What are we waiting for?" Lola shouted. I grappled with the unfamiliar gear stick, and the car lurched down the dirt track toward the railway.

Chapter Seventeen

"The younger boys are hopeless, though. They keep touching things they shouldn't—like fire!—and they're always fighting and stealing each other's stuff. It's like"—Lola searched for the right phrase—"it's like *Lord of the Flies*. Jack said he half expects to find a pig's head on a stick."

"Sounds like every Saturday morning in my house." The hedgerows blurred past my window.

"You have to tell Mom they needed me." She glanced toward the boot, where Joni was wrapped up amid the sleeping bags. "I thought she'd understand."

"Where's this turn, Lola?" In the wing mirror, I scanned the sky, but there was no movement, nothing to stir up the dense clouds that hung above us like the thick globs of ash we'd dropped on the path to Peter's grave.

"We're going so fast, it's hard to—no, it's further down. I've never seen Mom this bad before. Oh, it's here—right, right!"

Lola gripped the dashboard as I swerved into a narrow lane, where a line of grass down the middle had grown so high I could feel it scraping the underside of the car. The hedgerows had shot up, too, and provided a degree of cover. Still, I kept up the pace. Better to get off the road. "Your mum's had a rough few days," I said. Inadequate words, as though she'd had a run-in with her boss or a marital dispute. Some first-world problem. I took a bend too fast, heavy braking, someone's head bopping against the glass behind me. I dropped two gears to get back up to speed. Rev counter fingering the red.

"We need to go all the way to the far side." Lola pointed to a gateway into a field, and we turned in and rattled onto the pitted ground. Her juddery robot voice would normally have caused hilarity among the kids, but our sudden departure had muted them. They held themselves steady on the back seat as though good behavior might help them. I followed the lay of the land until the field ended in a scrubby open space. The car was well hidden from the road, but I pulled up close to the tree line to shield it from the air and then scrabbled the hermit's silver heat blanket over the bonnet. No idea if it would make much difference.

"Where are we?" I asked Lola. We stood on shattered concrete that was covered with a cargo net of brambles.

"This is the old railway line. It was decommissioned in the nineteen sixties by a man called Beeching, who closed over two thousand train stations across the country."

Lola was shiny-eyed with her new knowledge, and I knew right away that Jack must have taught her this fact. Along with goodness knows what else.

"Look, this is the old train station," she said, high-stepping to the far side of a boggy pond, where a stone arch rose in a sea-monster hump from the ground. Lola scrambled onto the hard-packed earth of the platform, where passengers holding parcels must once have stood and peered down the line waiting for loved ones, or for escape. Any buildings or signals or rails were long gone. But the wind flailed across the scarred landscape, as though it were being dragged along invisible tracks.

The kids opened their doors and climbed down from the car. Billy came over to be picked up. I grappled him onto my back to leave my hands free to carry bags.

"So where is it?" I called to Lola, who was beckoning us onto the railway platform.

"We have to walk about two miles north."

"Two miles?" I could run it in less than twenty minutes, but at toddler pace it was too far to walk.

"The railway leads us to an old lead mine. That's where the boys have their camp."

Very secure hideout. Good plan. But I hadn't forgotten them raiding and hacking my car outside the supermarket. And what if they recognized me? We needed to keep mobile, just in case.

"We're too vulnerable on foot," I said. "We'll drive."

Lola held out one palm like a traffic policeman.

"Jack wants the site to look unused from the air. Because of the helicopters. We leave nothing outside that suggests habitation. No bikes, no rubbish, nothing."

"We'll hide the car when we get there."

"We can come back for it if we need it," she said.

"Do you have any idea how long it will take four children to walk two miles?" I started ushering the kids back toward the car. "We have to drive." I turned around to see if Lola was coming, but she was on the far side of the platform, pulling a bike out of the trees. She ran a few steps and hopped on, her black top billowing out behind her straight back like Mary Poppins's umbrella.

———

We rumbled along the path of the former railway, which carved through the land like an ancient riverbed. After a mile, a few buildings cropped up, their slate roofs burst open by saplings. Farther on, another stone platform surfaced. I followed Lola's dust cloud around a wide bend to where two stretches of rusted track started, one traveling a few pointless yards into a pile of dirt, while the other curved round and disappeared into a hole in the side of a hill. The entrance was a stone arch and an iron gate, as solid as a portcullis.

A shrill whistle sounded, and Lola appeared from wherever she'd stashed the bike.

"You can't leave the car out there," she said.

"I don't know if we're staying yet."

"It's a lead mine, Aunt Marlene. Are you going to find a better refuge from helicopters with heat-seeking cameras?" She turned toward the portcullis with a shake of the head. "I mean, do the math."

I did the math and calculated that I would move the car under the cover of one of the least tumbled-down outbuildings. I pulled as deep inside as I dared, wincing as the tires popped and crunched over broken debris. There were gaping holes in the slate roof that a heat camera could presumably see through, so I fixed the heat blanket over the bonnet again and emptied the sleeping bags to drape them on top. It was the best I could do, and when the kids started to get down, stumbling over half bricks and rusted nails, I diverted myself to help them. We dragged our belongings to the iron gate, where we stood in an anxious group like evacuees waiting to board a train. We just needed cardboard tags slung round our necks. Joni lumbered across the clearing to join us, standing with her arms held in front of her chest as though something might strike her at any moment. Maggie, Billy, and the Lost Boy were holding hands. Charlie stood alone, twisting his trousers into buds.

With a deep groan, the iron gate swung open, and Lola motioned us inside. I tried to usher the kids ahead, but they balked at the darkness, so I bent my head and knees and led the way into the narrow tunnel. They trailed behind me, and we stopped to let our eyes adjust. I told them to watch their heads and not trip over the railway tracks. Charlie asked why the hill didn't fall down on our heads. He ran his hand over the stone walls and seemed reassured that it had stood here for more than 150 years, so there was no reason why it would collapse today. Joni finally shuffled in but failed to shut the gate behind her, so Lola tutted and squeezed back past us all to do it. We followed the tunnel—me stooped and awkward—toward an orange glow up ahead.

As we moved farther inside the hill, the crisp tang of minerals was overwhelmed by the pall of oil lamps. My boots crackled over sharp pebbles, and I didn't need to check that the kids were keeping up because I could make out their crunchy footsteps bunched up behind me. Charlie gave a whimper, and I twisted my bent neck up to see a grinning skull, sprayed in glow-in-the-dark paint onto the stones, beside a slogan that declared, "Keep Calm, It's Already Happened." I shifted my load onto one arm and used the other to scoop Charlie along beside me. Joni brought up the rear, her wild hair silhouetted against the bright sunlight like a yeti.

A burst of tinny recorded laughter drew my attention down the tunnel, followed by a real outburst of hilarity that echoed toward us. We crept forward to a soundtrack of more laughter and a car engine. The passage expanded until I could stand upright, and then the orange glow spread out to reveal a mucky cavern, where a group of equally mucky boys were watching an old TV show on an iPad that had been hot-wired to a car battery: my car battery, I couldn't help but notice, the one I had requisitioned.

The rippling lights illuminated half a dozen enthralled faces. The soundtrack pealed around the cavern. A quiver of anticipation ran through the rapt boys, who tensed for the opportune moment, and then shouted as one:

"Can we please stop talking about my mother's vagina!"

I exited the tunnel into their midst. One by one, their laughing faces startled to stone, but their outburst lingered in the air, bouncing around us like a mischievous imp. Boys of various ages littered the floor. Several of the smaller ones scurried into dark recesses. The older ones gathered themselves up more deliberately, saving face. One glanced at another, the crumbs of a smile stuck to his lips, to see if his friend might be up for some rebellious smirking. But the friend looked ashen.

"Hello," I said. "I'm looking for Jack."

By the time they worked out who was best able to reply, Joni and our kids had materialized behind me and were blinking around the cavern. Lola strode across and flicked off the iPad, muttering under her breath about it. Most of the boys got to their feet, and I estimated that the oldest was maybe fourteen, while the youngest wasn't much older than Charlie. There was a lot of shuffling.

"I'll find him," said Lola, and disappeared farther into the cavern.

I stashed our luggage on a pile of rocks against a slimy wall. When I turned, the boys dropped their eyes from my face. I glanced over them but couldn't see the electric filament hair of the one who'd slashed my tire.

"Are you boys all right?" I asked. There was lots of nodding.

"How long have you been here?"

Some shrugging, looking at each other for confirmation: "A few days, yes, a few days." A couple of the smaller boys shuffled forward and looked up at me with Oliver Twist eyes.

"Is anyone hurt?" Hands pointing to the back of the cavern: "Him, Harry Berman, he burnt his fingers."

"Have you got anything to eat?" They indicated a mess of crisp packets and biscuit wrappers.

"Any proper food?" Heads shaking.

I sighed and looked around their dank home before leaning down to their height.

"Are you really all right?"

"Yeah," said the one who'd wanted to smirk. He pulled rapidly at the end of his nose, tugging the septum between finger and thumb in a ferrety gesture. But another little boy stepped forward, and I put my hand on the back of his head, and he stepped forward again and pressed his face into my hip. His body shook against mine.

"Don't cry, you wuss!" said the ferrety one, but no one else laughed.

A stream of white torchlight appeared in the second tunnel, bounding around the stones, followed by two sets of crunching footsteps. Lola emerged first, flanked by a youth who unfolded himself to my height, though a great, bohemian forelock of curly hair made him look even taller. He occupied that boy-man space whereby his scaffolding held up his T-shirt, but the rest of the structure was yet to be filled in. The pair crossed the cavern, his palm beneath the Lady Lola's elbow as they stepped in time over strewn rocks and small boys, then Jack overtook his consort in two long strides and held out a hand.

"Hello, Mrs. Greene," he said, with a firm grip and brisk nod. "I'm Jack Ingram. Sorry this place is so rubbish." He stepped over to Joni. "And you must be Mrs. Luff." But Joni seemed to have traded places with the teenager and was leaning, surly and pock-skinned, against the wall. She didn't respond. Both Lola and I stepped in to bustle Jack away, though I couldn't be sure which one of them I was trying to protect.

"Lola tells me you had a close call with the helicopter?" he said. "We thought they might be humanitarians or peacekeepers at first, but when it failed to land or show a standard—"

"What's a standard?" asked Lola.

"A flag," Jack and I both said at the same time. The boy shrugged. "My father was in Afghanistan and Iraq. He was offered a job with one of those private military companies once. Good money, but he didn't want to be called a mercenary." Jack had excellent manners, straight back, neat clothes amid the dishevelment around him. I recognized the type from my time at boarding school. Jack had all the military bearing of a forces kid.

I explained how the biohazard-suited mercenaries—as he had no doubt correctly identified them—hunted down each person they detected with the heat camera for extermination.

"The flyover must have been a recce," he said. "Then they came back to carry out the op. Clean up."

As I saw the scene play out again in my head, I noticed for the first time the accents of the voices saying, "Clean?" and "All clean." Two different accents I couldn't precisely place, though one I recognized as a twangy white African. Maybe Rhodesian? The other, Eastern European? Hired guns, most likely, covertly paid by some foreign government that was too impatient to wait for the official wheels to turn because by then it would be too late; the epidemic would be a pandemic. William Moton's phrase came back to me: they don't see us as survivors, only carriers.

"Well, the Cleaners won't find us in here," Jack concluded, though his voice pulled up the end of the sentence to leave it hanging from a string between us. A tiny chink in his confident armor.

I offered Lola some cream for the injured kid's fingers, but Joni intercepted it and ducked off into the dark to see to him herself. Lola and I exchanged significant looks about this new burst of activity, while Jack gave us a roll call. I lost track after the second Harry and third George. It didn't help that their faces all looked the same, mono-chromed by the torchlight, all round eyes and upside-down mouths, as though they'd sketched unhappy faces and stuck them on. The appear-ance of an adult had popped the balloon of their bravado, and only one of them had any puff left in him: the ferret, who produced a school tie and fixed it around his head to cover one eye. I lifted the dangling end to inspect the insignia.

"St. Govan's College," said Jack.

Posh boys. And I'd taken them for a bunch of hoodie hoodlums. Jack had the same emblem on his polo shirt.

"I'm head of house." He tapped his chest. "We were on this orien-teering course when Mr. Holden got a call, and he went down to the village, but then he never came back, so Mr. Thomas left me in charge and went to check what was happening, and that was the last we saw of him, too."

"And you've been here ever since?"

"Just the last couple of days, after we saw the helicopter. Some of them ran out and tried to flag it down." He indicated the smaller boys with his chin, and they lowered their own in shame. I remembered standing in the field beside the Bury Ditches, screaming and laughing that we were being rescued, while all the time the Cleaners were totting us up into a head count: collateral damage. "So we decided to leave the Hoar Wood," Jack went on, "but then we had to get everyone back together after the schism—"

"Schism?"

"It's like a splinter group."

"I know what a schism is."

"Of course. So this one fifth-former who's a total—" He pulled up short, seeking a replacement for a rude word.

"Botheration?" I offered.

"Right. He went off with some of the younger ones for a couple of nights, said they were going back to school, but ended up sleeping in some hay barn—"

He broke off, and we both spun round in response to the honking din of a car alarm. Jack ducked down the tunnel, and I crabbed along after him, through the iron gate, back out into the white glare of the day. He was racing across the clearing toward my poorly concealed car, where the sun streaming through the broken roof revealed a lanky boy bent into the effort of breaking the door open with a crowbar. His hair flashed in the beams of sunlight, glowing white like an electric filament.

It was the same feral little shit who'd slashed my tire at the supermarket.

Jack tackled the boy from the side, grabbing the crowbar with both hands, forcing the younger one to stagger back. They squared up to each other, the lanky kid shouting and gesticulating at my car, but his words were carried away by the whooping alarm. Jack threw the crowbar out of harm's way. I dragged the key fob out of my pocket and popped the car doors to silence it.

"—the heat from the engine!" The kid was yelling and jabbing Jack in the chest with a pointed finger. "Just *think* about it!"

Jack glanced over his shoulder toward us with the drowning look of someone who'd gotten into a debate and only then realized they're wrong. He took us all in—me standing next to Lola, surrounded by the other amassed children—and snapped his head back.

"Agreed. We have to hide the car better than this. Can you deal with that, Woody? Get it covered over?" He said the last part for my benefit: "But don't wreck it, yeah? We might need it."

Jack held the boy's eye for another couple of seconds before walking back toward us.

The younger kid swaggered along behind him, followed by a gang of smaller boys who cruised in his slipstream. "All right, Boy Scout. Don't get your woggle in a knot." The gang sniggered at this witticism.

Jack didn't react, but his shoulders sagged under the tension, and even his hair slumped a bit. Lola held out one hand as he passed, and her fingers trailed the length of his arm. Several boys wolf-whistled.

"Oo-oo, let's hope the Boy Scout came prepared," the lanky boy brayed, to the mirth of his minions.

"Your name is very appropriate, Woody," Lola scolded him. "Peck, peck, peck with your little pecker." And she turned to follow Jack.

Woody forced himself to laugh, looking round the group until his eyes rested on mine. He glanced back to the car and returned to me, visibly working to put it all together until his face crumpled into a frown and his lips wrenched down further into a furious snarl.

"That's that witch!" he yelled, shooting his pointed finger toward my throat. "She's that witch who took my brother."

Chapter Eighteen

I sincerely hoped the lead mine was a long way off the helicopter's radar, because the heat was rising. We stood outside in the clearing, a massed group of sitting ducks, flapping and honking to draw attention to ourselves. I glanced at the sky and saw a pop of light in the gray depths. A storm could work in our favor, assuming the helicopter couldn't fly in a storm. Or maybe it could, one of those big rescue helicopters. We needed to get back under cover, but Woody was still railing against me.

"Is it true?" Lola cut Woody off. My own niece clarifying if I had, in fact, killed a child. I had to drag the air into my lungs so I could draw enough breath to answer.

"There was an accident when I was out looking for Billy. The first night you were away. A boy fell off his bike, and I ran him over."

Woody started shouting again. His earlier faux-gangster posturing was gone, replaced by genuine apelike arm swings and lunges. I could see him riding the fumes of his anger, avoiding the loss of face that crying in front of his friends would entail.

"Can I call you 'Woody'?" I asked, when he ran out of steam. Lightning skittered through the clouds; we needed to get under cover soon, but if this scene was going to turn nasty, I'd prefer to be within reach of the car.

"It's my fucking name."

"Thought it might be a nickname. Boarding school kids always have nicknames, don't they? Mine was Bogey Greene for a while, and then Stick. Because I was tall."

"Woody's my real name. I guess my parents gave me a stupid name. My stupid *dead* parents."

Smooth, Marlene. Smooth.

"Can we talk by ourselves?" I pressed on. "So I can explain what happened to your brother—Lenny, is it?"

"Lennon. Just tell me now." His face flinched for the blow. I saw then that he still had hope. Woody must have come back looking for his brother, maybe finding blood on the road. But, just as I had when Billy vanished, he refused to believe the worst. I turned my back on the rest of the group so they couldn't hear me.

"It's going to be upsetting, Woody. You don't want to do this in front of everyone."

His eyes darted between me and his minions, whirling like a slot machine. I waited to see which instinct would hit the jackpot: his innate deference to an adult or his bullyboy's need to keep up appearances. Or maybe another spinning reel would win out: his simple desire to find out what had happened to his brother.

"Lola?" I said, and she gave a rabbit-like nod. "We need everyone under cover and some food inside them."

Lola regained the use of the arms that hung by her sides and marionetted away. The kids edged back toward the tunnel, still shooting me under-the-eyelashes looks, leaving Woody and me alone in the clearing.

"Is there somewhere under cover we could go to talk about Lennon?" I asked him. "Somewhere private?" The storm was sweeping black shadows across the land, and the sky spooled through a time-lapse movie of itself. Woody hesitated long enough to show that it was his choice, he was in charge, then he slunk off toward a deep railway tunnel on the other side of the clearing, and I followed, rehearsing in my mind how I might tell someone that his baby brother was dead. And I was the one who had killed him.

———

He didn't ask a single question. I inched my way through it—from Billy's disappearance to the all-night search, my crash and the chase to the accident, and the funeral to Billy's reappearance. I explained about the vigil and the ashes and how I marked the grave with a small cross. I admitted that I couldn't face the burial, but it sounded like I felt sorry for myself. Poor, traumatized me. I stopped talking. Outside the tunnel, the wind toyed with a tree branch that it had broken off and was pushing around the yard.

I sat with my back to the wall and waited for Woody to speak. He sat opposite me for a long time, fiddling with his fingers, biting off hangnails. Then one of his index fingers slipped in and out of his mouth in a compulsive way that made me want to tell him to stop, but of course I couldn't, so I looked away and tried not to hear the sound of his teeth grating over his knuckle bone. He pulled the finger out of his cheek with a soft pop.

"I should've—" he began.

There was a flash of lightning outside, and we both counted under our breath until the sullen rumble arrived. Ten miles away. But closer than the last. As I waited for Woody to speak again, I counted the railway sleepers as they merged into the darkness.

"I told my mum I'd look after him," he whispered.

Woody's guilt acted like a catalyst for my own, and I had that same desire I'd had before—after Peter died—to grind myself into the earth. The shame crawling out from under my skin. I was supposed to be the adult here, the one most able to take the high ground. But instead I was wallowing at a grieving boy's feet, awaiting forgiveness. Because, being honest, that's why I was hunkering in this dank, dark place. No high ground here.

"How old are you, Woody?"

"Fourteen. Lennon was only nine. It was his first term."

"I used to ask Charlie—he's my oldest—to look out for the younger ones. In the back garden. Or the playground. But I just meant for him to keep an eye on them. Shout if they were wandering off, that sort of thing." I leaned forward to catch Woody's eye. "Your mother didn't expect you to save Lennon from all this." I waved outside. "You can't hold yourself responsible—"

"Nobody's perfect, yeah? We all make mistakes. Learn from it and move on." His lip curled as he spoke. "You sound like my mum."

"She's right, though."

"She didn't know what I'm like." He was gnawing on his knuckle again.

"Were you mean to your brother? Did you tease him, hurt him sometimes, let the big boys steal his comics?"

He nodded.

"And now you feel guilty?" I said.

He nodded.

"But that's what people do, Woody. People are just walking bags of impulses. Not just teenagers—all of us. We do shitty things because we think we have time to make amends. But sometimes we run out of time." A flash of lightning jolted me out of my rant. It lit up Woody's sharp features, his electric hair and keen eyes. "And just because we survived this virus, I'm afraid it doesn't mean we've been reborn, all perfect. We're still just shitty humans. We can try to imagine that we're going to forge a new civilization with better values. But we won't, will we? Because it's never happened before."

"Like the Romans and that."

"We just live with the guilt. We survive and live with the guilt."

Woody's finger went to his mouth, and he gave a soft pop as it slid from his cheek.

"But how come Lennon died? When he was the good one?"

"I'm sorry, Woody, I can't answer that. And I'm sorry about Lennon. I'm sorry about your parents and all of this. I'm sorry I can't make you feel better, but I can't make myself feel better, either. I don't know how."

He got to his feet. I did the same.

"I'm hungry," he said.

"We brought pasta. There should be some left."

He stood there while we counted another rumble of thunder: five miles. Then he gave a final pop and walked into the wind toward the hill.

I went the other way to the car. They were right about the helicopter picking up the heat from the bonnet; it would still be warm. I reversed out of the overgrown building, revving the engine to force the wheels over some rubble. A yellow light lit up the console: the petrol gauge was on empty. I slapped both palms against the steering wheel; we had left the fuel canisters under the hedge at the camp. It was only a couple of miles—the remaining fuel would get me that far—but it meant breaking cover again. I cursed my easily distracted mind. The railway tunnel swallowed the car beneath several yards of earth and stones where it could surely not be detected from above. As I trudged back out of the darkness, a querulous cry pealed through the air. I thought I knew all my children's noises, penguin-like, but here were Charlie and Billy hugging each other in the mouth of the hill, dissolving in snotty tears, making sounds I had never experienced. They mewled again as I reached them.

"Don't go," Charlie managed. Billy contributed a vast mucous bubble that burst wetly into the air.

"I'm not going anywhere. I just moved the car," I said, gathering them to me.

"I thought they made you go away." Charlie gulped at the air. "And I had to stay here and be awful."

"Orphan." I herded them inside for pasta and platitudes. "You don't have to be an orphan, not today anyway."

———

The storm passed, but the children were rattled, and, though it was late, only the youngest slept. I gathered that the Wild Things had grown seminocturnal, larking about late into the night, keeping their spirits up to cover their fear. Joni had helped Lola to cook dinner and was now telling them a story. She was still heavy and dull, like a sedated version of herself, but it was a start. She got them settled down. But little surges of giggling would set them off again; it would be a long night.

"Madrid," said Charlie. "Too easy."

"Croatia?" I said.

"Zagreb. Still too easy."

"Malta?"

"Valletta."

"Nice one," said another voice in the orangey darkness off to our right.

Charlie shifted position to curl up against my chest like a shell. As well as all the other things he liked to hoard, Charlie collected capital cities, and his favorite game proved to be soothing.

"All right: Slovenia?" I said.

"I don't know how to say it, but I can spell it: L-J-U-B—"

The ferrety boy, George the First, as he was now known, shuffled closer and cut in over Charlie to pronounce "Ljubljana" perfectly.

"Slovakia?"

"Bratislava," they both said at once.

"Sounds like a cake," added Charlie.

"I'll have a cup of Earl Grey and a large slice of Bratislava, please," I said. It was a relief to hear a smile in their voices as they went off on a tangent, ordering outlandish fantasy food items.

Two shapes loomed up, and I warned Jack and Lola not to step on Billy, who was asleep next to me. Maggie was curled there too, gnawing on her thumb, next to the Lost Boy. The teenagers folded themselves cross-legged beside me.

"We've been wondering," Jack started. "If you have a plan?"

Between us, we decided to wait in the mine until there was no sign of the helicopter for long enough that we could assume it had given up trying to trace us and moved on to another area. Then we would go back and get the hermit's radio, find out where it was safe to go, and head there after stealing a second car from Moton Hall. But our fuel supply would only get us so far. Sooner or later, I realized, we'd be forced to stop running.

"All right," I said. "Bright and early tomorrow morning, we start waiting."

A crunching footstep, and another small face appeared in our circle of lamplight. One of Woody's boys. His eyes darted over mine but rested on Jack's.

"Is Woody here?" he asked.

"Thought he'd be with you lot."

"Nope."

In my head, I heard the soft pop of footsteps across soggy ground: searching, I assumed, for a muddy grave in the night.

———

Our camp stank of foxes. I could smell it from the car when I stopped next to a bike that looked the same as the one Lola had ridden earlier to the mine. I switched off the engine—the car was already running on fumes, and I didn't want to get stranded in the middle of nowhere—but let the headlights roar through the dark trees. I followed shadows of myself up the slope to the tents. We had left it in disarray, but animals had obviously been through too. Food scraps, rain puddles collected in the white canvas of the yurt, muddy paw prints stamped all over. The place didn't belong to me anymore, and I had an uncomfortable sense of being oversized and conspicuous, lit up like a beacon. I rushed through the camp toward Lennon's grave. The darkness between the trees was no more comfortable than the light, though. I shrank and crept along behind the will-o'-the-wisp trail of my torch, every step forced by the pure desperation to get it over with. In the moonlit field, Woody was crouched beside the small cross.

"You found it," I whispered.

"Lola already told us where your camp was."

"Aren't you scared of the dark?"

"Shitting myself."

A shrill fox bark carried across the field. Eerie in the fog that followed the rain.

"Let me know when you've said good-bye, and I'll drive you back," I said.

"I got a lot to say. I'll get back all right."

"I'll wait in the camp, give you some privacy."

"Just go!" His shout lacked punch in the wide-open space. He felt it and got up, turning to face me. "Why are you following me? Do you want to kill me, too?"

I handed him the torch from my key ring. "I've got something to do near here," I said, "which will take about ten minutes. Then I'll come back and pick you up. It's not safe out here."

He didn't reply, and I walked—scurried—back into the white shards of the headlights. The Beast's engine was no longer running, its final mission accomplished. Under the hedgerow, I found the remaining fuel canisters. I needed to top up Joni's car, but darkness slithered out from between the trees, so after spilling more fuel than I got in the tank, I gave up and hauled the cans into the trunk. I'd have enough to get me where I needed to go and back to the mine.

I drove up the path toward the ford, turning off to the hermit's shed. This time I killed the lights. In the glove compartment, the heavy Maglite. From the back seat, a plastic carrier bag. I started into the trees. Almost immediately, my torchlight picked out the dark form of Horatio. I angled it away; I didn't want to see him, not now. Not when I wanted to be in and out, no messing around. No Horatio, no William Moton; that was the plan. Just the radio. I kept to the edge of the path, one foot skidding on blood, iron tang in the air, then three quiet, scuffing Lonely Steps, and I was in the moonlit clearing, everything silvered and flattened like a stage set. I couldn't resist darting the torch across to the hermit's body, checking it was still slumped by the shed, just picking out his sprawled feet. Fear galloped into my stomach, and I pushed myself to go quicker before it bolted and took me with it. I lunged into the dark shed—somehow even darker than the dark outside, ever increasing depths of darkness—and clawed at the radio receiver. The wires tangled round the bed posts, and I whimpered as I tried to pull them free; the sprinting panic wanted me to rip them out, but I fought to keep thinking: *I mustn't break them or leave vital parts behind.* I slid the machine into the bag, folding the wires and cables on top. I felt all around the bottom bunk; nothing left. I had it. When I picked up the plastic bag by the handles, one snapped and the set clattered to the floor with a crash that made me yelp like the fox in the field. I gathered it all up, pushing wires back inside, and cradled it in my arms. Back out of the shed and down the steps in one leap, but the Maglite flew from my hand and landed ahead of me in the grass, pointing straight at Horatio, lighting him up. His eyes still open, his teeth showing, his stomach eviscerated to the white ribs. I grabbed the torch and ran past him to the car, throwing the radio set into the passenger seat, hauling the wheel round to get away. I screamed down the track to the camp, back into the acrid fox musk. *Stinking animals. Fucking scavengers.* Pounded through the trees to the grave. But Woody wasn't there.

Back by the car, his bike was already gone. I set off toward the mine. *Reckless little*—I squeezed my eyes closed for a second. *What did I expect? Teenagers think they're invincible.* I raced along the road with my lights dimmed, more from an instinctive urge to hide than a belief that it would let me go undetected by the helicopter. I only realized I had missed the turn to the railway when the dark bulk of the Bury Ditches rose up ahead of me. My wing mirror clipped the gatepost as I skidded into the car park, grinding to a halt on the scree. I dropped my forehead onto my fists that gripped the wheel. I could still smell Horatio's blood on my shoes. Peter was inside that tree, totally exposed. What did it matter, I tried to console myself, there were bodies everywhere. In the road, in cars, in homes. Nature would take its course. What difference did it make if nature took its course with one more boy?

The difference, I thought as I got out of the car and lifted the boot, *is that I promised his mother I'd look after him.* I gathered all the bags of charcoal and a half-full petrol can. After seeing what became of Horatio—no, I had to do it properly. This was how we did things. With dignity.

Chapter Nineteen

Back at the mine, the truffling noises of sleeping children echoed down the tunnel from the main chamber. I stayed close to the entrance to unpack the shortwave radio. Willing it to work, to find a signal, scrabbling around to turn down the volume when it crackled into life, then feeding the antenna out through the bars of the locked portcullis gate.

My hand fluttered around the tuner like it was the knob of a closed door, and I wasn't sure what was on the other side. I closed my eyes and tried to remember the most populated frequencies, though it had been years since I'd tuned in regularly. I started somewhere in the middle. Static. Whistling. Wailing. I had to be patient. I let the sounds squall around me as I started a fingertip search, seeking contact in empty space. *Maybe William Moton had been lying—or delusional—maybe there was no one out there after all?* I shrugged the negative voice off my shoulder. Fingers back on the dial. A sudden loud click, and a woman's voice said, "BBC." It sent a shock through me. I homed in on the signal until the interference receded and her voice came through:

"Emergency broadcast. We will shortly cross live to BBC Broadcasting House"—whiplash of the heart—"for an important announcement. Please stand by." I stood by, dry-mouthed with hope. My hands hovered over the radio set like a medium conjuring shadows in a crystal ball.

"This is a BBC emergency broadcast. We will shortly cross live to BBC Broadcasting House for an important announcement. Please stand by." Long empty pause. I descended into the light, a bright filament that zipped across the ether and dropped me, blinking, into a dusky studio, bunker lighting, competent Aunties bustling past in secretary skirts. "This is a BBC emergency broadcast. We will shortly cross live to BBC Broadcasting House for an important—" With a long sigh, I was dragged from this comforting place of stoic women, the dank walls of the mine came back into focus, and I realized the sound was my own breath releasing. My hands stilled as the adrenaline drained; my heart returned to downbeat. After a few seconds the message repeated. I checked my watch: just gone midnight. I listened to her voice every thirty seconds for fifteen minutes: thirty times, the same; thirty times, I stood by. Just as she asked. Of course, we never crossed to BBC Broadcasting House. But the balm of her voice, warm as mother's milk, was intoxicating. After thirty messages I found the willpower to let her go, and she walked away like my own mother, never looking back.

Farther up the dial, voices looming in the dark. Sounds like dripping water, as though I'd been plunged into the drains. The monotonous rhythm of a foreign language. Then a nasty buzz cleared to a strong signal and a man's voice: "Good morning." I sat up straighter, as though he could see me. But then—strange words with the odd English phrase: "stumbling block," "prime minister," "half past nine." Some kind of Pidgin English. I jabbed the dial, punching in frequencies, skipping bands. Sloppy now. I crashed around in the ether until I detected a wavering signal, just clear enough to hear that Radio Revival Sweden was "keeping shortwave alive." An English-accented newsreader:

"Broadcasting on the half hour, this is *The Newsroom*. The headlines this morning: The International Rescue Committee has expressed concerns about Portugal's decision to force a ship carrying asylum seekers back into international waters during a severe storm. All contact with the boat and its estimated five hundred passengers has been lost. The ship was approaching the Azores when it was intercepted and turned away by Portuguese naval patrols. In a statement, the Portuguese government reiterated its sovereign right to close its borders in response to the English Plague. The crew reportedly denied that the boat had sailed from the United Kingdom, claiming instead to be owned by people traffickers before—" A violent wail swept the voice away. I searched above and below the frequency, hands shaking again with the effort of maintaining a false calm—inside my head I picked up the radio set and dashed it on the stones, crushed it with my boots, lifted the iron gate, and smashed the black box to pieces—but I couldn't find Radio Revival Sweden again.

I spent a long time pacing the frequencies, each click one more step into the wilderness, the blurring static rushing around me like a snowstorm—disorienting—and I started to wonder if the voices I had heard were real at all, or if they were recordings stuck on a loop like the BBC emergency broadcast. Echoes, the light from dead stars. It would help to hear a date or anything that told me it was live, real, coming from the flesh and blood mouths of actual living beings. I tried to visualize lips moving close to a microphone, feel the intimacy of breath on my ear. But all I could feel were the dark mineral walls of the tunnel pressing around me. And anyway, I'd forgotten what the date was, so even if they said it, it could be today or yesterday. The day before. If they were alive then, they could be dead by now.

I pressed on through the storm, until: "Zero, zero, four, zero." For a beat I thought I'd lost it, but then the recorded voice picked up. "Aviation weather update: Amsterdam, report missing; Dublin, report missing; Shannon, report missing; Prestwick, report missing; London, report missing; Paris, report missing. Atlantic Flight Information Service: report missing. Time, zero, zero—" The signal bled into some kind of old-time jazz. I fine-tuned until I heard the recording again, but it was back to "Prestwick, report missing; London, report missing—"

I turned down the volume and sat with my hand over my mouth. The smell of petrol made me heady.

"What was that?" Joni stood behind me in the tunnel.

"Didn't mean to wake you," I said.

"Was it flight information?"

"Just a list of airports. Weather updates. I don't know what it means."

"It means someone is still checking the weather and broadcasting the reports." She waved a hand at the volume dial. I edged it up. Static again.

"Maybe they're trying to resume flights?" She sounded upbeat.

"Well, they can't if all the information is missing."

"But they're trying, right? Keep going, see if we can find the signal again."

I did as she asked—it was hard to resist her newfound zeal—but I suspected that she just felt buoyed by the American accent, letting it take her home. I didn't want to hear a long list of "missing" places, a reminder of the state of my country, my people. I let the radio scroll. I couldn't remember what I did want to hear. It was like walking into a room and forgetting what you came for. With my hands over the radio set again, I had that same sense of it being a crystal ball, but instead of conjuring the outside world in its mists, we were the ones trapped inside, screaming, unheard behind the glass. It was pointless. *If they can't hear us, if they think we're all dead already, then we might as well be ghosts.*

"It's late, Joni. Let's get some sleep—"

"Shh!"

A sudden break in the static, like a patch of blue in a cloudy sky, and a male voice, hard American drawl: "I could care less about politics.

217

I don't know if we should go save these people. But I do know this—I am frightened for their souls."

Joni huffed in response. "Move on."

"We brung it on ourselves," I said, imitating the accent.

"Don't take the piss. Just move on."

But I didn't. I let the fundamentalist rant. It was fine; his fire and brimstone warmed the cockles of my heart.

"And for two generations now," the voice went on, "these people, these dark-sided people, have never gone to church. I hope you can understand this. God gave them free will. God gave his son so they could live in purity and righteousness—and they turned their back on him. A poll, a recent poll, found that ninety percent of people in the Great British Isles do not go to church. Ninety percent! This is what happens when we turn from the house of God and—what? Worship a boy warlock?" Whoops, screams. "More people read a book about a wizard than they do the book of God. Please—"

"Why are you listening to this horseshit?" said Joni.

I shrugged. "At least they know we're here." I clicked the dial and let it scroll. "Maybe you can go home, Joni. If we get ourselves off this godforsaken island."

I was fast running out of frequency. Bubbling water noises told me we were in the vicinity of scrambled military channels. I turned down the volume as we passed through patches of piercing tone. Then a waft of jazz, like the one we'd heard before, faint and ethereal, as though it were coming not through space but through time, a scratchy gramophone, a man's thin voice trembling over a piano, "The moment I left, you came home to me." Grinding interference and another accented voice:

"—systematic abuses of the most basic human rights. Of course we need movement restrictions to ensure public health, but these must be proportional. Mass quarantines must have a legitimate objective and be based on scientific evidence—"

"But Ambassador Nygaard"—another male voice in the deep, soothing tones of a news anchor—"surely the legitimate aim of these measures is to prevent the English Plague from becoming a global pandemic?"

"Naturally, this is desirable—"

"Desirable? Surely vital?"

"Yes, vital, but my point is that the responses of the past week have lacked coordination—and frankly, we still don't know what kind of atrocities have been sanctioned—"

"Atrocities, Dr. Nygaard, you are using that word?"

"What else shall we call it? The aircraft leaving the UK that were quarantined on the first day, the passengers left to die on the runway or shot dead when they tried to disembark. The other planes that were refused permission to land and turned back—lost—we don't even know how many."

I heard Joni shift at the mention of planes, her feet scattering stones. My hand found her arm and squeezed.

"Now, we hear about this ship sunk off the Azores. And the isolation camps—"

"Well, there are many conflicting reports about the existence of these camps—"

"They exist. We are hearing about thousands of survivors, no food or water or medical assistance, children separated from parents, healthy people locked in with the sick—"

"Well, we must leave it there, Dr. Nygaard. The Norwegian ambassador to the United Nations. We can cross live now to our correspondent in New York, Charles Carter, who is at the UN. Charles, is there much sympathy for the Norwegian stance?"

"Well, the secretary-general today praised international efforts to stamp out the virus"—a strain of music stole over the reporter's excited words—"the unprecedented scale of the"—a languid trumpet shushing him—"new legislative powers"—until the drowsy mood washed his voice into oblivion, as though he, too, had succumbed. I let the music play. In the darkness, a woman's voice all around, clear and pure and hard as my rocky pillow when I lay back against the wall of the tunnel. Joni joined in when the woman sang "Stormy Weather." How she and her man weren't together, while outside the mine, it was raining all the time. The pitter-patter came down like the scutter of lazy drums and, as though hypnotized, I knew the words. In the dark I closed my eyes and sang along.

Chapter Twenty

"Giant jungle nymph," said Charlie.

"We'll squeeze into two cars," I said, scraping the bottom of the jam jar.

"Hercules beetle," said George the First.

"I had driving lessons," said Jack. "Well, one. I could drive your old car, and then we'd have three?"

"Assassin bug," said Charlie.

"Could you boys play Bug Bingo somewhere else?" I said. "We're trying to talk." Jack kept pressing the button on the car fob, the LED reddening his face as the dingy morning light seeped into the cavern. I took it off him, before the battery was also a thing of the past. "We don't have enough petrol for three cars. And anyway, it's a moot point until we find Woody. What do you think, Joni?"

She was kneeling over a gas stove that wouldn't light. "It's too risky to go outside." She looked at Lola, checking that she was listening. "So he's going to have to find his own way back. We have one more day, tops, before we need supplies. Then we need to move on. And Harry's burnt fingers look infected too, no fever yet, but—"

"So we need to get something for him," I said. "Maybe we could get to a shopping center. Hide inside—"

"Listen to this, Mum," said Charlie. "The assassin bug wears a coat of ant corpses! Perfect disguise—its only natural predator thinks it's a giant ant."

"Seriously, boys, sit over there and play your game."

"It's educational," Charlie said.

"Good. Educate yourselves over there."

They shuffled across the cavern, past the younger kids building rock towers, taking the crackers and jam with them.

"All right," said Jack, "I'll check the map for one of those out-of-town shopping centers."

"But what if the Cleaners are watching them?" said Lola. "Seems kind of obvious."

"If we're out of food, we don't have a lot of choice," I said. "We have to move."

"Sacred scarab," bellowed Charlie.

I slapped myself with both palms on the forehead.

"Are you okay, Mrs. Greene?"

"We can hide in plain sight"—I pointed at the roof of the cavern to indicate the sky—"so the Cleaners think we're giant ants."

I was about to explain the full genius of my plan when a shrill whistle from outside got Woody's gang running toward the clearing. We trailed after them down the tunnel, into the thin daylight.

Woody stood at the center of his minions' orbit, his arms limp while they exalted in his glory. He was covered in mud, apart from his face; maybe he'd splashed it with water in the river, or he'd pushed the tears away with the backs of his hands until they formed two curtains of grime, pulled aside to reveal his anguish. His friends didn't acknowledge his distress—or didn't know what to do with it—and instead harried him for details of what he'd done on his adventure.

He scythed them down with a dismissive "Stuff."

"I'm glad you came back," I told him, after his friends gravitated away.

He looked off down the ghost railway and made one of his soft pops. "We don't need you to look after us."

"Apart from all the food—and the car," I said. He stepped around me toward the mine. Like my kids, he didn't realize that I needed them.

The sound of scuffling feet brought my attention back to the clearing, where a line of boys was breaking into a run, scuttling toward the portcullis gate. Instinctively, I turned to check on the whereabouts of my kids. Then Jack appeared from the trees on the other side, pulling up his trousers and hollering. I scooped Billy up in my arms and caught Maggie's hand as I started to run toward the tunnel, away from the spanking sound of a helicopter.

———

"You led them right to us, *Woody*!"

I could hear him protesting as the last kid scurried in through the gate, which Lola struggled to lock with a padlock. I glanced around the yard outside, but there were no obvious signs of habitation. Car hidden. No rubbish. Jack had us well drilled. But the sound of the helicopter expanded to a rapid heartbeat. I could imagine trees cowering in the downdraft.

"Hurry, Lola," I said, just as the lock ground home, and she raced into the darkness ahead of me. I staggered behind her, Billy bumping against my thighs in the crouching run. We reached the cavern, which was full of noise and orange light.

"Stupid little pecker!" one of Woody's own minions yelled.

"It's not Woody's fault," I said, "and we don't have time for squabbling."

Joni moved round the cavern, extinguishing lamps as she went.

"Where does that tunnel go?" I asked Jack, pointing to the passage on the far side from the entrance. "We should get deeper into the mine."

"There are tons of them. We haven't explored them all, but if we stay left, we'll come to an old water shaft that leads to the surface in case we need an escape route. Comes out by a big farm, like a dairy. There're other ways out, but they're flooded—"

"No, the dairy is perfect," I said. "Let's hope the cows are still alive. If we get in the shed, the helicopter won't tell the difference between our heat and theirs."

"Assassin bug," said Jack.

"Exactly."

Angry shouts of "little pecker" bounced off the hard stones of the tunnel. Scuffles broke out in the darkness. Woody moved toward the tunnel that led back to the bolted portcullis. I blocked his way.

"Where you off to?"

"I must've led them here," he said, staring down the tunnel, the sound of the helicopter rising over the hubbub.

"And you're thinking you could lead them away again?"

"Why not?"

"Because I'm not going to let you, Woody. Look, I can never make it up to you, what happened to Lennon, but I can at least do what's best for you now. And you know, if there's one single thing I've learnt from my half-arsed attempts to be a mother, it's that you don't give kids what they want; you give them what they need. Even if they hate you for it. So going out there, getting yourself shot, that's not what you need. It won't bring your brother back. But these kids, they follow you. You can help them."

His hand went to his mouth, knuckle between his teeth. I took hold of his wrist and drew it down. From beyond the iron gate, the spanking of the helicopter was unmistakable. It had found us.

"Please?" I said to Woody.

He snorted, but turned into the cavern, back to his boys. When I stepped into the fray, Charlie and Billy gripped my legs. The cavern was teeming with shrill voices and the clattering of rocks underfoot. Chaos.

Joni emerged out of the dark next to me. Maggie was standing with the Lost Boy, holding hands, talking close into his ear. In fact, I realized, she was singing to him. I nudged Joni and pointed two fingers at my lips. She gave one of her long piercing whistles. Silence, but for one of the Harrys, who stumbled and got shushed.

"We're leaving right now. Quickly and quietly. Jack will lead the way. We go crocodile-style, do you remember that from little school? So get into twos, like this." I pushed Maggie and the Lost Boy into the center of the circle to show how. Pulling other pairs of boys into line, clamping their hands together. Most of them groaned. "You will hold hands," I said, "because we need to help each other. The path is rocky, uneven, and if one of you stumbles, the other will hold him up. But if one of us goes down, the rest will fall over him. And we don't have time. Understand? So hold hands. And we're going to sing—quietly, mind—a marching song. To keep in time, and so we don't get split up, right?" I moved along the line, spacing the pairs out. Joni came along the other side, telling them to leave their stuff, it wasn't important. "Who knows a song?" I asked.

"Dumb Ways to Die," came a wobbly voice from the front, feet stamping a rhythm on the spot. The others picked it up.

"Not that one," I snapped. "What about this—'I don't know but I been told.'"

"I don't know but I been told," Jack echoed as he set off down the tunnel.

"St. Govan boys are made of gold," I said, pushing the first pair after him.

"St. Govan boys are made of gold." The next two strode away in time.

"I don't know but I believe," I sang, gesturing at Lola to go halfway down the line.

"I don't know but I believe." The whine of the helicopter engine threatened to drown me out, and I had to shout over it.

"Chopper's coming, it's time to leave." I hefted Billy into my arms.

"Chopper's coming, it's time to leave."

The light faded as the lamps swung down the passage. Joni ducked in a few pairs behind Lola. I counted them all out; seventeen people, with my party and the St. Govan boys. When all the kids had gone, I pushed Maggie and the Lost Boy ahead of me. The cavern dropped into darkness with the leaving of their lamp. Outside, the trees thrashed beneath rotor blades, obliterating the echoes of footsteps in the tunnel, the small voices still chanting. I pushed my Maglite into Charlie's hands. "Stay close," I said and gave him a little shove into action.

"I got one," he said, matching his stride to mine, pointing the torchlight so that we both hurried to catch up with it. "I don't know but it's been said."

His voice whispered round the tunnel: "I don't know but it's been said."

"Let's get gone before we're dead."

———

Down the mine proper, the air was swollen with noise and effort. There was the odd cry as someone stumbled and twisted an ankle, scraped a knee—but tears were for later; we all sensed that. The boys were quicker than me, and I lost sight of them when the tunnel bent farther into the hillside. I lumbered on. My arms were so numb that Billy's body fused into my own. His skull beat a steady rhythm against my collarbone. The darkness loomed behind me, so that its heat bore down on my neck like an outstretched hand. *The Cleaners must move faster than us, even in those biohazard suits. And I won't even hear their footsteps over all this racket.* I could sense fingertips on my collar. Once, I glanced over my shoulder, but the movement spun me off course into a jagged wall. There was no one there. Just darkness. I staggered past the occasional dark mouth that led to one side tunnel or another, but I pushed ahead, not wandering from the path: kept my head down, kept my boots straight, kept expecting a shot through the back of the head.

"Billy," I whispered to him, "if Mummy falls down, you start running, okay? Okay?"

But his head just nodded against my shoulder as it had all the way down the tunnel.

The passageway slowly cleared of rocks and leaves until it was smooth and flat. We might have walked for hours or just minutes; I was quarry now, intent only on eluding that outstretched hand. We descended again onto bigger stones, a rockfall perhaps, and a few puddles had formed along the path. Billy drew his legs up from the splashes. Then the tunnel narrowed again, and I had to bend at the shoulders to fit under a corrugated iron tube that fed us into a small, wet cave with a jagged, flinty ceiling and further corrugated iron tubes shooting off into the rock. Lola was there, and Charlie and Maggie clung onto her, but I urged them on, my voice brusque. Now we were climbing. An orange glow ahead caused my breath to stall in my throat—*we're back at the cavern!*—but then the light glowed brighter and whiter, and I saw it wasn't oil lamps but real sunlight. The ground was again littered with rocks and leaves, and the scrabbling of feet over stones was joined by a hiss of wind in the trees. Stick-figure silhouettes stepped into the sunshine ahead of me, and I followed, until we all emerged into painful brightness.

I dropped Billy onto cushiony grass at my feet and rubbed my fists into my eyes like a blubbing baby. As my blindness cleared, I could literally not believe my eyes. We stood outside a stone hut, which looked more like a privy than a mine shaft, on the edge of a manicured garden. The shag-pile lawn was fraying at the edges, but the topiary hedges retained their shape—nothing fancy: pyramids, balls—and the flower borders were thriving with late-summer blooms. A long row of purple agapanthus heads stood bolt upright on long stalks, caught in the act of sunning themselves.

I got my breath back along with my focus. This didn't seem like a farm. We must have come out at the wrong place. It was impossible to see outside the tiny walled garden—we could be right near the mine for all we knew. But then the boys started filing away around the side of a greenhouse, following Jack's voice, and I hauled Billy back up off the grass before I could lie down in it and just capitulate.

———

It *was* a farm. We stepped out of the secret garden and dashed across to the dairy. Gangrene clogged the air. The kids recoiled, but we pushed them inside and slumped down in groups next to the high metal gates, where the surviving cows kept themselves away from the dead ones. One heifer came and leaned over us, breathing a hot reminder down my neck, making me shudder back up to my feet. Their water trough was trickling and fresh, so I got Charlie and Maggie to drink and scooped up some handfuls for Billy. The cow just stared at me with her big eyes. I told her I'd open the gates before we left.

We sat down on the concrete. I rubbed the back of my neck, trying to scratch out the feeling of being prey. The helicopter had been coming in to land as we left the cavern. Surely the Cleaners realized right away that we were inside the mine. We must have left footprints. By rights, I should have felt that shot, that hand in the dark.

I twisted to speak to Lola, just as Jack bent to the ground and pressed his face into his hands. He gave a short bark of anguish. Lola spun toward me, one hand spread in a starburst of shock over her mouth.

"Do the roll call again," she said, pulling at the neck of Jack's shirt. "I'll do it myself." And she ticked her long finger at each of the boys. "There's sixteen of us here. Is that right?"

Eeny, meeny, miny, moe, I heard in my head, *who got left back down the hole?*

"We were seventeen, including myself," I said. "I counted as we went out."

"Harry from 5b," said Jack, muffled by his hands. "Harry Whatsisface."

"Berman," someone said.

"Harry Berman," Jack confirmed.

There was a long silence. Two of the cows pushed at each other and seemed to stir up the air, so the gangrene reek caught in my throat, and my mouth filled with saliva. I swallowed it down.

"Do you think they got him?" Lola whispered. The question mingled with the rotten air.

I nodded. "I think maybe he distracted them from us."

Jack stood up. "I'll go back for him."

"I'll go. I led the Cleaners to us." Woody.

I squeezed my nose between my fingers until flesh-colored stars appeared. I had taken a short philosophy course at university once, half a module when I was trying to round out all that maths and economics, and I remembered a problem the ethics tutor set: *There's a group of you, hiding from a murderer in an old house, and you have a baby that won't stop crying. If the murderer finds you, he will kill you all. Do you suffocate the noisy baby for the sake of the group?* There was another example: something to do with being trapped in a cave and a fat person gets stuck in a hole that's the only way out. "The morally good action benefits the greatest number of people," we parroted. We were eighteen, narcissistic; we killed the baby, we hacked the fat kid with our crampons. We held aloft our hefty moral code and brought it down repeatedly on the heads of anyone who threatened our principles. I looked over at Charlie and Maggie sitting on the dungy ground, Billy sucking his thumb. Nowadays, my principles were about as firm as my pelvic floor. And yet the outcome was the same: neither maternal instinct nor higher intellect has time for heroism.

We had to leave Harry Berman. It was the right thing to do, a no-brainer: sixteen lives versus one. Morally good odds. And yet—and yet

I couldn't formulate the words. Woody and Jack were still bickering over who most deserved to go back and get themselves killed, when Lola jumped up and raced outside. Coming round the corner from the walled garden was a sopping wet Harry Berman, who ran into Lola's arms and let her drag him inside the cowshed.

"What happened, you numpty?" said George the First, who had been crying for his classmate only moments before.

"Lost a shoe and stopped to put it on. I shouted but no one else stopped, and I didn't have a torch. Took the wrong tunnel into a flooded bit." He squirmed under all the eyes turned on him. "I wasn't in a pair, was I?"

They all slapped him on the shoulder and congratulated him on finding his way out in the dark. I stood back and watched my hands shaking with relief.

"Thing is, Mrs. Greene," he said. "The Cleaners are down the mine. I could hear them in the tunnels." We had to go. Hiding among the cows would shield us from heat cameras overhead, but not the Cleaners on foot. We had to run again. Outside the dairy, on the far side of the yard beside the farmhouse, stood a huge double cab pickup truck. It wouldn't be comfortable for the kids under the tarpaulin in the back, but we didn't have a lot of choice.

"Right." I pointed at Jack and Woody. "If one of you still wants to be heroic, you can get into the house and find the keys to that truck."

Woody felt most inclined to redeem himself, and while he braved the buzz to get the keys, I marched through the stackyard, into a shed, where I found a selection of lawn mowers and a stash of fuel. I slid a can behind each seat of the truck. Then we loaded the schoolboys into the bed of the pickup, lying top to tail like sardines, and secured the tarpaulin so we wouldn't lose any more on the way.

———

The cab stank of petrol and stale smoke and unwashed bodies, and even opening all the windows did little to improve the air quality. The truck clawed at the gravel as we spun across the yard and out through the gate. We followed the narrowest roads, heading as directly east as we could manage, putting distance between us and the mine. The long chassis pitched and rolled like a boat, and I nearly lost it on a tight corner, swearing as I slowed down, before my speed crept up again, one fear taking precedence over another. We shot across a junction, not bothering to stop and look, and the miles clocked up. Our knuckles returned to flesh color. Eventually, we started speaking again.

"What am I looking for?" Lola fished in the glove compartment, pushing aside CDs and empty cigarette packets to produce a lurid map of tourist attractions: England was covered with enormous standing stones, roller coasters, and llamas. She spread it out across her and Jack's laps, both crammed into the front seat next to me.

"I bet there are Cleaners everywhere by now," he said. "Especially in high-density areas." His fingers slid over the gray blob ahead of us.

"Let's stay on the back roads and out of the towns," I said. "Take us somewhere remote. What about all this national park?" I waved my hand over the green areas that flanked us. *Cannock Chase. Hop up into the Peak District. On into the Moors. But then what?* Jack was right: we were probably moving from one search area into another.

"I'm hungry," said Billy, but without much urgency. I twitched the rearview mirror down to see him in the back seat.

Joni sat by the far window. My three and the Lost Boy were crammed in the remaining space. Two schoolboys who couldn't squeeze in the back were scrunched into the footwells.

"Have you got your belts on?"

Charlie helped the younger ones cross the strap over their laps and click it home. I smiled at him via the mirror, but he just stared back. The rolling of the vehicle swayed his chin from side to side in a repetitive motion that made me think of disturbed animals in a zoo.

They were all doing it. I tilted the mirror up so I could watch the sky behind us.

"We'll get something to eat soon, kids," I said.

"There are mints down here." Jack started rummaging in the center console, stretching out his long legs to make room to open the flap and get at the sweets. His knee banged into the radio and the car filled with loud static. I jabbed at the illuminated buttons, but only set the thing searching through stations with the same high-pitched wail and rhythmic tone that had provided the weird soundtrack to my night-time search for Billy. It was only then I remembered that I'd left the shortwave radio behind in the cavern. I looked away and caught sight of myself, silent screaming in the wing mirror: gargoyle face, all teeth.

"What about this?" Lola yelled over the noise and held up a section of map. "There's a wildlife park. About"—she measured the distance in thumb-sized increments—"eighty to one hundred miles away?"

"Good, but no motorways," I yelled back. "Turn that bloody noise off."

Jack was prodding at the radio. I found the right switch on the steering wheel, and with a final beep it cut out.

"No!" he said. "Turn it back on, Mrs. Greene. Listen."

I pressed the switch and he swore under his breath, until the dial came round to a high frequency, where it locked on to a signal.

"There," said Jack. "Listen."

A rush of static and then a montage of repetitive pips and birrs. It meant nothing to me, but still I knew it was a lifeline. Morse code.

Chapter Twenty-One

A couple of miles along the narrow forest road that led to the nature reserve, I stopped and got out to inspect the roadkill. It was the third lump of flayed mess we'd seen since we'd followed the brown tourist sign off the main road. It was fresh. A deer. Whatever hit it must have dragged it along the road because half of it was missing. I got back into the cab and moved on.

"What do we do if we meet another vehicle?" Lola asked.

I shook my head. It made sense that there would be other people like us, but I didn't know the social conventions on how to engage in these circumstances.

"Friend or foe," said Jack under his breath.

I drove on. We crept under old oaks and then out into barren drifts of gorse. The road was held aloft by a landscape that had never let it bed in. Every lump of roadkill made my knuckles whiter, as though the carcasses were jinxes that would make unknown vehicles come racing round the next corner. I found I was hunched over the wheel, head between my shoulders, in that dumb, instinctive way that people have when they drive under a low bridge.

I steered us as far as the next brown sign and turned into a narrow lane that was blessed with a little tree cover. After a short way, it widened into a small car park beside a high metal fence. There was no visitor center, no buildings of any kind, just a stony track—a walking path as wide as a road—leading past the fence, down a steep slope into the valley. I idled at the top of the hill.

"Is this it?" I asked Lola.

"I guess. But I thought it would be—more than this."

If we couldn't find a hideout here, we'd be forced to camp in the forest again. Or worse, on the open moorland.

The pickup crunched onto the path, and we rolled down the slope in first gear. Behind the fence, red deer grazed, their heads bobbing up as we passed. In the next pen were curly-horned sheep.

"Look, Mum-may," said Billy, "sheeps."

"Mouflon," said Charlie.

How long since we've eaten meat? I didn't think I could slaughter a sheep. Joni probably could, if we could get her back into hippie-homesteader mode. The road hugged the flank of the hill and lowered us gently down. Another large pen spanned the valley floor, its steep sides thick with trees. We passed the information board, and I saw that it contained lynx. Charlie pressed against the window, but couldn't spot one. We skirted the lynx enclosure and reached the end of the path in front of a log cabin–style shelter. Under the overhang were some information boards and a few screwed-down tables and chairs. A shuttered window suggested there might even be a small snack kiosk.

"Bingo," said Jack.

Lola looked at me for confirmation that she'd done well, and when she saw my face, allowed herself a small smile.

"If we can just hide the car, this is perfect," I said. "Good job, Lola."

We all got down from the cab, and I pulled off the tarp to let the kids out of the back. They took in the new place with a lot of blinking. One of them ventured behind the building and gave a shout of joy: there was an adventure playground with zip wire! They all raced off.

"Hey, hey!" Jack called after them. "We need to get under cover."

"Give them five minutes to stretch their legs," I said. "Just while we get sorted. We're going to be out in the open anyway."

"All right. What shall we do with the car?"

Behind a set of gates at the far end of the building stood a couple of four-wheeled bikes and just enough space, if we shifted some stuff about, for the pickup. Even if the shelter was open on one side, we figured it was better to get the car under cover. We parked it and hefted a couple of bales of hay onto the bonnet for good measure, to disguise the heat or infrared or whatever the helicopters might be able to detect.

"If there's some food here, we've really hit pay dirt," Jack said.

"Ta-da," said Joni. She had taken the crowbar to the door of the kiosk and waved her hand at a basic kitchen.

"Mummy?" Charlie appeared from the opposite direction.

"Come on, love, we need to get inside."

"I think you should see this." He took my hand and led us back past the building, following the line of the lynx enclosure. He trailed his other hand along the chain-link fence, coming to a halt with his fingers looped through the diamonds.

"There," he said.

Just beyond where he stopped, the wire gate of the lynx enclosure was propped open with a brick.

"There's more," he said.

"What?"

"You won't like it." He walked down a short path that led to another high enclosure that stretched out of sight ahead of us. Charlie stopped short of a small log cabin.

"Hide," said Charlie.

"What?"

"It's a hide. Where you view the animals."

He led me forward a few paces, and then pulled my arm to make me stop.

Beyond the hide, alongside the high wire fence, a corpse lay spread-eagled in the dirt. My body sucked in air with a small gasp.

"That's not the bad thing," Charlie said.

I followed his pointed finger to an information board detailing the behavior and habitat of the Eurasian wolf, and beyond that to the wide-open gates of the wolves' enclosure.

———

"What about us?" I threw a small rock at the body, disturbing a few languid flies. "Haven't we got enough to contend with, without wolves and wild cats roaming the forest?" I launched a handful of gravel at the keeper, and it spattered down onto the desiccated skin of her wax jacket.

"That's not very nice, Mummy." Charlie pulled at my arm. "The wolves would have died in there. Like the cows—you let them out."

"Cows are not going to attack us in the night, Charlie! Have some sense."

"Wolves aren't actually nocturnal; they could attack us during the day, too." He stopped when I thrust my hands into my hair. "Anyway, she just gave them a chance to survive."

"What about giving us a chance?" I sounded like a petulant toddler.

Charlie walked over to read the information board. I joined him, looking over my shoulder into the surrounding stand of trees. They could be anywhere. Watching us. Some of the half-eaten carcasses we'd seen on the road—which I'd assumed were roadkill—were large animals, easily as big as a small child. As big as Billy. *Billy! What if he wandered away from the zip wire into the trees?*

"Come on, Charlie, we need to get back."

"Just look at this, though." Charlie was pointing at the board, where there was a map of the wolf enclosure. "There's another building over here. It says 'Research Station.'"

"I don't think we'll be doing much research. Let's get back to the others before the wolves do."

Charlie sprang into action and raced ahead of me up the path. I took the opportunity to throw another rock—hard—at the body of the treacherous keeper, but I missed, and it rattled the wire fence. Such a high fence: must be ten feet and topped with razor wire. Designed to keep wolves in and idiots out. And that gave me a new idea.

———

"Tell me again. Why are we planning to lock ourselves into the wolf enclosure?" Woody was not convinced.

"Because this shelter is completely open, so the wolves or lynx could get to us. But we'll be safe from the animals inside the wire fence. And if the helicopters pass overhead, they'll think our heat imprint is just the wolves."

"There are nearly twenty of us. That's a lot of wolves." Woody held his ground.

"If we break into that building on the far side of the enclosure, then they can't detect us at all," Lola said. "If we have to sleep outside, the Cleaners think we're wolves, and if we get inside, then the heat cameras can't see us: full stop. Win-win."

"We could also let a couple of the deer and sheep out of their enclosures." This was Jack. "The wolves would surely take them before attacking us?"

"Good idea," I said. "Do that, too."

Jack strode off, full of purpose.

"And what if the Cleaners do spot us, and we're stuck inside a wire enclosure? How would we get away?" Woody's cronies were lingering within earshot. He had reinstated himself as their leader, and challenging me seemed to be his favored method of regaining lost status. He swaggered about, hiding his anxious restlessness with exaggerated movements.

"If we're hidden, the Cleaners won't find us, will they?" said someone from our side of the divide. "Unless you run off and bring them back again, Little Pecker."

Woody's gang stood behind him, but didn't leap to his defense. Hedging their bets.

"The wolves could still be in there for all you know." Woody was shouting now, losing it. "Then you'll be shut inside with them. And you'll be eaten like the meatheads you are."

The meeting degenerated into yelling. Charlie held tight to my hand, rattled by the aggression. I squeezed his hand three times, our code. He squeezed back: *I love you, too.*

Woody was railing now. Jack was back in the fray. Lola held her head in her hands. The last thing we needed was for the group to splinter and break apart. What we needed was cohesion. Or failing that, compliance.

"Boys!" I shouted. They couldn't even hear me. "Hey, boys!" Nothing.

A loud clanging broke through the hubbub. Everyone spun round. Joni had a massive saucepan in one hand and a wooden spoon in the other. She clanged again.

"Enough," she said. Her thick hair had matted into a magnificent, frizzy aura that glowed like Aslan's mane in the late sun. "There's food here for one decent meal. It'll be served in the building inside the enclosure." She stomped inside the kitchen and slammed the door. The moment hung around us. I stepped into it.

"Right, let's get ready for a slap-up dinner. Jack, can you let out some of the sheep like you said? Woody, could you and your boys raid the vending machines for drinks and snacks? Lola, take three boys and load as many hay bales into the back of the pickup as you can. You two"—I pointed at a couple of the younger boys—"go and ask if you can help Joni."

They hesitated. For once, I realized with a degree of relish, I was not the scary one.

"She won't bite you. Go on." They moved toward the kitchen.

As I hoisted Billy onto my shoulders and got Charlie to put on his backpack and help Maggie with hers, there was a loud crash of glass and a whoop. Woody's boys had smashed their way into the vending machine. The noise of industrious vandalism followed me down the path toward the high wire fence.

As we rounded the corner, there came a swinish cry behind us. The Lost Boy ran from the shelter, dashing a few steps in the wrong direction before Maggie called out, *"Boy!"* and he spotted us. His skinny legs blurred in his frantic rush to catch up, and he slammed right into me, his face buried in my hip. His body was too stiff even to shiver. Maggie took his arm and placed it round my waist, and he let it rest there. Charlie's and Maggie's wide eyes moved between the boy and my face.

"What happened?" said Charlie.

The Lost Boy, of course, said nothing.

"He thought he'd been left behind. Maybe he got left behind once before." I waited in case there was a nod, but he was still rigid. "We promise we won't leave anybody behind, especially this boy." I gave his shoulder a jiggle. "Okay?" The slightest pressure against my hip could have been acknowledgment. "Now, let's go and get settled down in the wolf enclosure for the night."

———

The research station was an underground bunker. It was clear that the wolves spent their time on top of and around it—the area was littered with bones, lumps of fur, and trodden-down patches of grass. But it was deserted now. The land sloped down to the entrance of the bunker, and I lifted away a wooden slat that secured a big set of double doors. There was no lock. We stepped into a short tunnel, wide but barely higher than my head, that led into a cave-like room. Two horizontal windows at head height gave a wolf-level view of the surroundings. There was nothing in the room beyond the dirt floor, just a couple of benches that the kids could stand on to peer out. A single door opened to the outside of the enclosure: that would placate Woody. Even though I'd given him the plum job of vandalizing the drinks machine in the hope of getting him on my side, he still behaved like a mistreated dog in a shelter; he tolerated me giving him food, but snapped if I got too close.

Jack arrived with a few more boys. After all the activity, they sat down on a bench, rendered awkwardly idle. Jack bustled about with our few belongings, but soon ran out of things to do and stood with his hands on his hips. His hair just brushed the roof.

"This is ideal, really." He sounded disappointed.

"It's underground, but dry. Even better than a cave," I said.

"Hmm."

"What do you want, Center Parcs?"

He still looked glum.

"Too posh for Center Parcs, okay. Club Med?"

He almost smiled.

"I can't stretch to the Four Seasons, I'm afraid. Not for all seventeen of us."

He finally laughed, but still shook his head. "When it said 'Research Station,' I thought there might be equipment here. You know, like a radio."

"Ah, but we do have a radio." I held out the car keys. "Do you want to fetch the truck?"

He grabbed the keys with a muted "yes!" and jogged along the tunnel into the light.

"Did you learn how to reverse in your one lesson?" I yelled after him, but he just waved the keys in the air and kept going. *He won't crash it,* I told myself. *It's not very far, he can't possibly crash it.* I turned to my kids. Charlie sat on a bench, unpacking the contents of his backpack in a neat line. Maggie was struggling to lift Billy up so he could see out the window. He pressed his face against the glass.

"Oooh," he said, in wonder at the outside world where he'd been only moments ago.

"I don't know why you're saying that because there's nothing even there," Maggie said, dropping him unceremoniously back down.

They were all being so perfectly themselves that it made me smile.

"Sit with me," I said, and pushed my bum between them onto the bench. Billy planted himself on my lap; Maggie and Charlie snuggled up on either side. The Lost Boy squeezed next to Maggie. "I feel like I haven't spoken to you in days."

"You run in and you're there," said Billy, "and then you run out and you're not there."

"I'm sorry," I said. "You must be frightened. I should be with you more."

"It's okay, Mummy," said Charlie. "We know you're trying your hardest."

I closed my eyes. A lump of emotion appeared in my throat, and I fought to keep it down. Life seemed so complicated and, of course, it took a kid to see how simple it really was. A bubble full of pitiful gratitude burst inside me. No one else ever noticed that I was *just trying my hardest*. Not Julian, of course, who had seemed to think I was driven to work hard just to annoy him; and not the school or the other mums or the *Daily Mail*, who implied that being the breadwinner was somehow selfish; and not even me, my own hardest mommy-shaming critic, whose long finger of guilt damned me if I did and damned me if I didn't. Charlie squeezed my hand three times, and my eyes fizzled as tears fought their way out. I cried for Marlene Greene, who never managed to have it all despite trying her hardest. I cried for Charlie and Maggie and Billy, whose mother was adding to their fear by crying in front of them. I cried for Peter and Lennon, who had the great fortune to survive the virus only to end up saddled with me. I cried for Horatio, who came back for me. And I cried for Joni, who loved so hard but still lost. I cried, and my kids wrapped themselves around me like vines until I was squeezed dry.

Maggie stood up on the bench. She took my face in both her hands and turned it up to her own. She smiled and clumsily wiped my cheeks with her hands.

"Don't worry, Mummy," she said. "You can go back to work soon. For a rest."

I laughed out loud at my own snide joke echoing through my daughter. I gathered all the children into a hug that contained too many knees and elbows to be comfortable, and only let them go when we saw the pickup truck arrive outside with music blaring and kids hanging off the back like the world's least threatening gang of child soldiers.

———

I took the wheel and reversed the truck into the tunnel of the research station, folding in the wing mirrors because it was a "honeymoon fit," as my father would have said. As dusk slid down the hills into the valley, the rest of the kids came home to roost. I'd brought the hay bales with the intention of parking the pickup outside and covering it over, but once we saw that the conspicuous vehicle would fit inside, we burst the hay open and made a soft bed on one side of the room. Joni and her helpers brought the food down in a wheelbarrow, and there was plenty. Woody's gang doled out cans and crisps. After a head count to make sure everyone was inside, I stood for a moment in the entrance and listened to the night. Like a traveler in a foreign land, I had grown accustomed to the strange soundtrack without ever needing to understand it. I was just reassured by its constancy. Not a part of it, but not threatened, either. And there were no howling wolves. I slid the wooden plank into place to seal the doors and closed our hideout into near darkness.

Inside, I accepted a plate of beans and mini sausages with a can of Tizer. I sat down in a circle with our kids and Jack. Joni sat close to us, but up on a bench. She had gone quiet again after her burst of activity. I let her be.

"But it's not much use having the car radio if we can't understand the Morse code," said Lola.

"What is Morse code?" asked Charlie.

"It's a way of sending messages without speaking. You use dots and dashes instead of letters."

"Why don't you just speak?"

"Maybe you can't speak. Or you're trying to be secret. Like when we squeeze hands." I grabbed his wrist and did *I love you*: three squeezes. "Or I could signal by flashing a torch—dot, dot, dash, dash, dash—like that. It's very useful."

"But I don't understand what the dots and dashes are," he said.

"Well—" I struggled to find a better way to explain.

"I only know SOS," Jack cut in. He wrote the letters in the dirt with his finger and made three dots next to the first *S*, three short-line dashes next to the *O*, and another three dots next to the last *S*. "I saw that in a film."

Charlie got up to peer at the writing. "Oh, is *that* what that is?" He reached over to rummage in his backpack. He pulled out the *Survival Skills* book and flipped to the inside back page. He turned it so it was the right way for me to see and handed it over.

"Is that Morse code, Mummy?"

It was.

Jack was up and heading toward the car with most of the others following him. I sat in the dirt with Charlie for a few seconds longer.

"Well done, Charlie." He flushed all pink around the ears. The fact was, we'd had everything we needed right from the beginning, but I had been running around too quickly to realize it.

———

We easily picked out the phrase "SOS," and the book listed an individual code that meant "start." We listened again and again and got the start and the SOS, but beyond that it was too fast to make out the letters.

"This is rubbish," said Charlie. "You could get a computer to do this."

"Unfortunately, we no longer have an app for that. Or, indeed, anything else," I said. "Let's just take it one letter at a time. There's a tiny gap after the letter, like in SOS it goes, 'dot dot dot, gap, dash dash dash, gap, dot dot dot,' right?" They agreed. "Okay, then let's concentrate on the first one after the gap after SOS. See if we can get it."

We let the rhythm of the Morse code wash over us. Eventually, there was a pause, followed by the code for "start."

"This is it," said Lola.

"Shh."

"Dot dot dot." *S*.

"Dash dash dash." *O*.

"Dot dot dot." *S*.

"SOS," said Charlie.

"Shh!"

"Dash, dot, dash, dash, dot, dot." The signal ran on, and I turned down the volume.

"It's too hard," said Charlie.

"It's so quick," said Jack. "I got dash, dot—then what?"

Lola sang the rhythm out. "Bah, bup, bah, bah, bup, bup."

We all agreed. Bah, bup, bah, bah, bup, bup: dash, dot, dash, dash, dot, dot.

"That doesn't make sense." Jack scanned the book. "There are no letters that long."

We sat through the message again. Picked out the pause, the "start," and the SOS. Then: bah, bup, bah, bah, bup, bup.

"That's definitely right," I said.

244

"Okay, well, 'bah, bup' or 'dash, dot' is the letter N. So that would make 'bah, bah, bup, bup' the letter Z."

I wrote "NZ" onto the windscreen with a stub of crayon. We all looked at it. The Morse code melody niggled away in the background.

"What does it mean?" Charlie asked. "New Zealand? Capital is Wellington."

"It can't be right." Jack turned the pages of the survival book, as though there might be an explanation readily available.

"Let's just carry on with the next letters and see what we have," I said.

There was groaning. "It's too hard." "We don't know what it means." "What's the point?"

"Just keep your eye on the ball, kids."

"What?"

"Look." I spun in my seat to face them all. "What is our long-term goal?"

"Find somewhere safe."

"Right. And how do we do that?"

"Work out this message."

"And how do we do that?"

"Listen to it over and over until we get it."

"So shall we get on with it? Or would you prefer to sit here whining about how difficult it is until the Cleaners find us?"

"Get on with it."

"Right." I turned the volume back up, but the dots and dashes washed over us. There was more groaning.

"Stop thinking about how hard it is," I said. "You're wasting your brain power on thinking."

Jack sat back in his seat and closed his eyes.

The electronic rhythm surrounded us. Lola was right about the bahs and the bups: it was easier to hear it as music than try to translate it to dots and dashes. We reached the long gap at the end of the trans-mission and then the start signal and the SOS.

"Ready," said Jack.

"Shh."

The code for NZ rushed by and then: "bah, bah, bah, bup, bup." Lola sang it and we all joined in.

"Bah bah bah bup bup!" Jack ran his fingers down the page.

"A number eight."

I wrote "8" on the glass.

Then we got "6," followed by "0," "4," "1." Painfully slowly, having to listen through the whole message again and again, we picked out a sequence of ten numbers.

NZ8604112884

"But what does that mean?" asked Lola.

"Coordinates," said Jack. "We did coordinates on the orienteer-ing course. It should be written like this." He grabbed the crayon and wrote it again. "'NZ' indicates a square on a map, and then the first five numbers give a westerly point, and the second five give the northerly point. It's quite a specific location."

We carried on listening to the message until we had deciphered the second part, which returned to letters again.

My writing spread across the windscreen: NZ/86041/12884/ DONT/GO/SOUTH.

Chapter Twenty-Two

Woody and his little gang, which had dwindled to three of the younger boys, occupied the space in front of the single door to the outside, hunched beneath an invisible dome of bitterness. Every now and then, the whole group turned, a many-headed beast, and glanced our way before ducking back down to whisper their grievances. Only the fool-hardy would dare to approach this little stronghold. The exclusion took me back to my own school days. At least now, though, I had a pretty good idea of why I found myself on the outside.

I watched them without looking their way, while the conversation swaggered around my own group. Hyped-up on the unexpected success of deciphering the Morse code, my kids were already celebrating, their noise engulfing the room. Of course, we had no idea where NZ 86041 12884 actually *was* in layman's terms. And we didn't know what we would find there. But we boasted confident speculations about getting a map and being out of danger by this time tomorrow.

"See ya, wouldn't wanna be ya," said Charlie.

Out of the corner of my eye, I saw Woody's finger slip inside his mouth, and, though I couldn't hear it over our delirium, I knew he gave a soft pop while he took it all in.

"Shh." I laid a hand on each of my kids' shoulders to calm them down. "Others are trying to sleep." What I was trying to convey to their immature consciences was: some of the others might not feel like celebrating quite so soon, leaving behind loved ones without knowing if they're dead or alive. Or leaving them in a shallow grave in the middle of a field. We might be battling away, but we had long since lost the war.

"Let's lie down to sleep now."

There was a lot of grumbling about the scratchiness of hay, but they eventually settled. Joni stayed on the bench, munching through a bag of trail mix. Lola and Jack propped themselves against the wall and whispered behind the barrier of their knees. I lay back in the hay between my boys and watched a cool sliver of blue-black sky framed in the long window.

A change in air pressure disturbed me. Or maybe even woke me. The light was different—it was so black, I couldn't tell the windows from the walls. It must have clouded over. It must be much later. A soft click told me the outside door had been open and was now closed. I tried to reach silently for Charlie's backpack, where I knew there was a torch, but the hay rustled beneath me, setting off ripples of sound as my noise prompted other bodies to rearrange themselves in their sleep. With stealth no longer an option, I rummaged in the bag and clicked on the Maglite, flickering the beam first over my own brood, who were all there, and then straight to Woody's corner. He was gone. I checked behind the pickup, where we'd left a slop bucket for overnight emergencies, but there was no sign of him. I swore behind my teeth and stepped over sleeping bodies to the door.

Outside, the torch was pathetically inadequate against the bulk of the darkness. The door clicked behind me, and I heard a crunch of gravel to one side. The light barely made it the few feet between me and Woody, who was fastening his trousers. I dropped the beam so that it pooled between us, and we both stood in the dark outside the circle of light.

"What are you doing out here, Woody?"

"What do you think?"

"We brought a bucket inside for that."

"Go back in then, if you're scared." The hard edge of his voice bounced my concern away.

"We shouldn't be taking risks now, not when we're so close to getting there."

"Getting where?" His question faded into the dark.

"I don't know until we find a map. But I feel sure we have to check it out."

"As sure as you were when you thought my brother was involved in some plot to kidnap your son?"

The wind drew a long breath through the trees.

"That's what I thought." He walked toward the door, and my torchlight trailed after him. "You're just winging it. For all you know, the Cleaners could be sending that Morse code so we go straight to them. Save them the bother of finding us."

"That could well be the case, so we'll have to be careful. But what else are we going to do? Do you really think if we hide, they'll just leave us alone? If they find us, they will kill us."

Woody's feet turned back into the light, the white rubber caps of his trainers glaring.

"How many people have the Cleaners killed?" His voice was quiet.

"I saw them shoot the hermit, and they killed our dog. But who knows how many others—"

"And how many people have you killed, Mrs. Greene?"

I licked my thumb and used it to rub away the hard little scab behind my ear, then tasted the tingle of blood.

"I have killed one person. By accident. It was an appalling mistake, but—"

"And what about the other kid? Peter. Was he an accident?"

"Yes! He got burnt, he couldn't survive those injuries, it was a mercy killing. And that wasn't even me." My whiny voice hung in the air like the steam rising off Woody's piss. I sounded like Maggie: *It wasn't me, Mummy; it's not fair, Mummy.*

"And you wanted to leave Harry Berman behind at the mine."

"Nobody wanted to leave him behind."

"Well, I make it one for the Cleaners and two for you." Woody stepped forward so that his eyes flared for a second and were doused by shadows. "So tell me, Mrs. Greene. Who should I be running away from?"

———

Back in the hay, I rolled over in my sleep and gasped aloud as something sharp pricked my cheekbone. I sat up, and found it had drawn blood. I sifted through the green strands of grass down to the hard-packed earth below. There I found a white tooth. I lifted my hand to my mouth, and when it came away, a second incisor came with it in a puddle of bloody drool. My tongue slid into the gaping hole left behind, and I whimpered as the pressure popped out my canine, which arced in a languid rotation down onto the soft hay, where it bounced once and slipped between the strands. I pulled my lips over my teeth, as though that would keep them in, but my mouth filled with blood, and I had to swallow it. I lay back down in the hay to tongue my wounds. But the movement set off a bloom of warmth beneath my legs, and I bolted up again to see blood dilating out from between my thighs, and I screamed exactly the way I had once when I was pregnant with Billy and thought I was losing the baby—which only the day before I had considered aborting because Julian didn't want to know about another child, and I didn't see how I could manage a third as well as the business, and it took a bloodletting, a moment of horror, for me to realize that I could never let that baby go. I pressed my thighs and my mouth together to keep my blood inside.

I sat up in the hay. My heart kicked me in the ribs just like Billy had later in the pregnancy. He was there, sleeping beside me. My teeth were there, safely in my mouth. The dawn was there. I got up and downed the dregs of the can of Tizer to wash away the taste of blood that came from picking at the scab behind my ear. It was bigger than ever with strands of hair dried into it like a fetid little nest. I needed scratch mitts, like a baby. I headed for the door, expecting to navigate past several boys. But the space was clear. Woody and his gang were gone.

Outside, as I followed the path toward the main shelter, Charlie's warning about the wolves hunting at first light ran round my head like an earworm. When I glanced over my shoulder, the high fence of the wolf enclosure was already out of sight, shrouded in a mist that would make perfect cover for predators. Stones clattered to my right. I faced the misty wall again, expecting to see one of the boys. Instead, there was a clang of metal. The noise was smothered by the fog. Silence.

"Woody?"

Scuffling over hay bales. I was near the main shelter.

"Woody, are you there?"

My feet turned themselves back toward the wolf enclosure. But the gate to the lynx pen was closer—I should run there instead, get inside. Another metal clang from the shelter, and the mist ahead of me started to swirl. I backed away from whatever was stirring it up, and my heel caught on the lip of the grass verge so that I rattled back against the fence. I groped along in the direction of the propped-open gate. The footsteps crossing the gravel were light, stealthy. I found the gate and stumbled to get inside, grappling it shut.

"Mrs. Greene?"

A boy emerged from the mist. I was standing with my arms rigid to keep the gate closed. We stared at each other through the metal diamonds.

"Were you scared?" He made this sound like it defied the laws of physics.

I unfurled my fingers from the gate and came out from inside my pen.

"Unlike Red Riding Hood, I can comprehend the possibility of being gobbled up by a wolf. So, yes, I was scared."

"Sorry."

"Not your fault. What's your name, anyway? Where're the others?"

"Kofi. And they've gone."

I pushed my hands into my hair and tipped my head to the sky. *Make it stop.*

"What do you mean 'they've gone'?"

"They took one of the ATVs from the shelter."

"I don't even know what an 'ATV' is."

"All-terrain vehicle. Four-wheeled bike."

"For God's sake."

"They're going back to school."

"I don't believe this."

Kofi waited with a patient face, as though I simply needed time to believe this.

"Why?" I asked.

He hesitated: a good kid, torn between a rude truth or a downright lie.

"Don't worry, Kofi. I know Woody hates me and doesn't trust me for toffee, which is quite understandable in the circumstances. What I mean is, what does he hope to achieve by going back to the school? Why is he going *there*?"

Kofi shrugged. "I suppose—it's home?"

First Joni, now Woody. Why this fixation with home? Making homes was my living. Or, at the very least, playing house. But now the concept had as much relevance to my life as some arcane point of algebra.

"Fine. We'll go after them. How many went?"

"Woody and Joss Hartnell and Mo Hassan."

I set off back toward the research station. "So how come you didn't go, too?"

"There wasn't room."

I glanced down at him. He was one of the smaller ones in Woody's gang, a late bloomer. He stared straight ahead, as though he weren't used to anyone looking at him. The mist was retreating from the morning sun into the cool edges of the valley. Heavy dew revealed a skein of ossified spiders' webs on the metal fence of the wolf enclosure, their intricate bone-work ragged beyond repair. As we walked past, I slammed my hand against the chain link, and it thrashed, showering us with chilly droplets as the sound roared through the valley. Children's voices answered, carrying across the flatland from the den. They were up and about. I hurried on, but Kofi was digging deep in his pocket for something.

"It's not true, what I said before," he announced to his hip. He pulled out a huge and filthy handkerchief to dry his dewy face. "I couldn't decide whether to go with Woody or not. I cried."

"You cried! Did the heavens open and a divine voice call you a sissy?"

"No. But Woody said I'd have to make up my mind or they'd go, and then I went and sat in the shelter and they left."

"It sounds like you *did* make a decision."

"I was too scared to go."

"Or maybe you were brave enough to make up your own mind." I put my hand on his shoulder, which he shrugged off straight away, but carried on walking beside me back to the den.

———

Breakfast was meager. A catering-size tin of cheese crackers without the thrill of cheese. The meal from the previous night had stretched our bellies again, reminding us how it felt to be full. Now we echoed with hunger, and it was all too much for Billy, who screamed for food until he was puce, and then collapsed into a snotty heap. While I calmed him down, Maggie raided another boy's rations and stuffed his crackers down her maw before he could stop her. The den felt very small all of a sudden.

We should have been packing up and moving on, but once again we were stuck, debating which way to turn. By Kofi's estimation, the boys had left over two hours ago. We could backtrack and try to catch them, but we didn't know which route they had taken. If they even had a map. Or petrol. Or a clue. We could let them go, hoping they would reach the safety of the school and stay there, so we could send help once we found it. Or we could split up: Jack wanted to head to the school on the other four-wheeled bike, while the rest of us found a map and worked out the location of the coordinates. Then we could rendezvous at an agreed point later that night.

"I'll go with Jack," said Lola.

"No."

"I can help persuade the boys to come back."

"Two words, Lola: *your mother*. It would finish her off. Besides, I need help herding these cats." I waved my arm around to take in my three, the Lost Boy, and the rest of St. Govan's.

"I really don't think Jack should go alone—" Lola started protesting.

Joni emerged from beneath the tarpaulin on the bed of the pickup and let a heavy canvas rucksack drop onto the dirt floor.

"No." Her voice landed with the same dull thud. "Not happening."

"But if you think it's too dangerous for me, then why are you okay with Jack going? Is he expendable?"

"He's not my child," Joni said. She hauled the bag to the bench and started unpacking, her side of the conversation closed.

"I'll go with him." Kofi stepped forward. "I was thinking perhaps we should find a map and work out the coordinates first? Then we can tell Woody where we're headed, convince him it's safe, and it won't seem so bad."

While this was a good suggestion, Kofi was ignored. Behind him Joni had reached the bottom of the canvas bag and, with no fanfare, produced a map and a compass, the ones she had been carrying since we came to the woods. The compass she laid behind her on the bench. One by one, everyone followed my stare and turned to watch her. She lifted the cardboard cover of the Ordnance Survey map and unfolded each side until it was held wide in her arms, settling herself into a more comfortable position on the floor before inspecting it. She seemed oblivious to our rapt attention. After a few seconds, she folded the map up, ensuring the creases bent in the right direction.

"Joni?"

"Wrong map."

Jack held out his hand. "Could I see it please, Mrs. Luff?"

"It's the wrong map."

"I'd just like to—"

"Check if you want to." The map ruffled through the air toward Jack like a hen in flight. "But I'm telling you it's the wrong fricking map. It's grid square SO, not NZ. This map is for South Shropshire. NZ is somewhere else. Up north."

I flapped my hand at Jack to prevent him from further startling the horses.

"At least we know now that OS maps show the right grid references," I said. "Where can we find more hiking maps?"

"The library." "Motorway service station." "Camping shop." The kids were full of good ideas.

Lola went to the pickup and came back with the tourist map she'd used to get us here. She folded out our section and tapped it with a fingernail. "What about an airfield? They'd have detailed maps, right?"

Charlie was at my side in a moment with one finger in the air.

"No," I said to him.

He let the finger slump to his side.

"No light aircraft," I said to him. "No hang gliders. Definitely no hot air balloons."

"Paramotor?"

"I don't even know what that is."

"It's like a backpack with a giant fan attached—"

"No, Charlie. We will not be escaping by air. We're not thrill-seeking. Quite the opposite, we will be thrill-avoiding."

Now that we had jettisoned so much stuff, we were on the move in minutes. We jolted across the wolf enclosure, pausing only to contemplate a pile of sheep's wool near the gate, which no one could recall being there before. I glanced into the dark spaces of the tree line as we drove past and was glad to power up the hill to the open moorland above. Jack appeared in my rearview mirror on the bike, and we followed the rolling road toward the town, in the direction of the airfield.

The grid reference was still daubed on the windscreen, and I found myself racing toward it. A donkey chasing a carrot. *Could Woody be right?* I thought. *The Cleaners came after us with the stick, and now this is the carrot?* I forced myself to slow down so that Jack could keep up.

The road turned quickly into a single-lane commuter route, and we rushed past nondescript houses, business units, and then farms. Although still semirural, this was the most populated area we had encountered for days. There were frequent crashed cars, mostly military, and the occasional corpse by the roadside. The bodies were slightly inflated, as though they had died while wearing a fat suit. No one inside the car said a thing. I flicked on the radio, and we listened to the bahs and bups of the radio signal, rolling through the Morse code message. Prompted by Lola, I turned off onto a smaller lane.

After we passed a massive garden center, the road bent round under some trees, and I slammed on the brakes. Cars, all facing away from us, blocked both sides of the road. Jack came to a jerky halt next to my window. I wrenched the pickup into reverse and backed down the lane.

Jack spun the bike round and stopped beside me again. He gestured at me to roll down the window.

"There are people in the cars," he said.

"Bodies," I corrected him.

"The airfield is just at the end of this lane." Lola tapped the map.

"Charlie's not the only one who thought of flying away from trouble," I said.

Jack switched off the bike and wandered into the car park of the garden center. Lola opened the door to go after him.

"Don't—" I started.

"I won't go near any bodies. I'll just see if there's another way to the airfield."

I scrunched round in my seat to face Joni and the kids in the back.

"Pee pee?" said Billy.

"I want to go to a café," said Maggie.

"Plane," said Charlie, pointing to the other side of the road.

I scrunched round the other way and saw the tip of a white wing sticking up behind the hedgerow.

"Joni, can you keep the kids in the car? We shouldn't be out here. Too much buzz."

"I got it." Joni opened her door and went to shout something under the tarpaulin.

"Mummy—" started Billy.

"Always comes back. Just stay in the car."

I trotted across the lane and through the surreal line of palm trees that welcomed me to the garden center. There was a special offer on spring bulbs and pond netting. I turned from the buildings into the car park. Jack and Lola were clambering over a wooden fence on the far side. I yelled at them to come back, and they stopped to consider whether or not to ignore me.

A few cars looked abandoned, presumably by people who had decided to walk to the airfield. I cupped my hands round my eyes and peered inside the first one. There were no maps in the seat backs and no GPS. The second was the same, though there was a big cooler on the seat. I tried the door and it opened, but the stench told me that whatever was inside the box was beyond edible. Jack and Lola returned, and I told them to check the other cars. I tried another one, but the only map was a large-scale atlas of France and the Low Countries. Behind me, glass smashed. Lola punched the jagged edges away with the end of a brick and reached through to pop the door open. From inside the glove compartment, she produced a hidden satnav device.

"How did you know that was there?" Jack asked her.

"Circle on the windscreen," she said, "left by the holder."

While Jack was congratulating her on being "totes *city*," I ran over and plugged the GPS into the cigarette lighter of the pickup. It burst into life with a beat of drums. I hit the button for home, just to test if it still worked. The screen went gray, and it started calculating a route.

"Hello, satellites," I said to the sky. "Don't be alarmed, but we're still alive down here."

Chapter Twenty-Three

I walked between the jammed cars, averting my eyes from the faces behind windows. It was unnatural. As though I were the dead one and they were all alive, stunned by seeing a ghost. Only my sense of smell suggested I was still living.

"Are you sure about this?" Lola said, with the brick still in her hand.

"The hermit was inside the kitchen alongside a body for long enough to bake bread, so he said, and he didn't catch it."

"But you'll be really close to them. You might have to touch them."

I peeped into a hatchback with two bubblegum-pink suitcases pressed against the glass. I couldn't do that one. Lola bent down to the window from the other side and gave a little sigh before also moving on. Most of the vehicles had satnavs, but we weren't wasting our time on those anymore: they didn't work with grid references. Jack gave a shout from the grass verge next to a battered Land Rover. He had his hands on the roof and was staring in through the driver's window. Inside was a man and a mound of yellow dog, both well concealed by a blanket of black that flickered occasionally like the flank of a horse. There was also a spiral-bound road atlas on the dashboard. I stopped on the passenger side and ran my fingers over the glass, which was etched from the inside with claw marks.

"Why am I more upset about the dog than all the people?" asked Lola, scrubbing at her eyes.

"Because it's a manageable amount of grief," I said. "It's like releasing a bit of water from the dam so the whole thing doesn't burst. It's a survival instinct."

"Is that why you're not upset about Uncle Julian?" she asked.

"Julian? I am upset about Julian. And Peter. Lennon." I rubbed a fist on the glass, as though I could scour out the claw marks. "Don't forget about Horatio. William Moton. All these poor buggers in their cars. Do you want me to go on?"

Lola shrugged to show that she didn't.

The atlas was tucked down close to the windscreen. I would have to climb inside the car to get it.

"Right, then, you two. Sod off and leave me to it."

"But—"

"There's going to be flies and all manner of smells, some of which will be me vomiting, so please just do it."

They retreated down the row. I pulled out a scarf from my back pocket and wrapped it twice around my face. It reeked of petrol fumes that made my head woozy. I'd also commandeered a pair of thick gloves with a built-in ice scraper. I pulled these on and checked that the others had gone far enough away. Then I took a deep breath and wrenched open the passenger door, hitting the ground as the swarm of flies pelted over my head. I scrambled up and grabbed the door handle to haul myself inside the vehicle. The stench absorbed me like a sponge, and I found myself trying to palm it away with one hand while I reached for the atlas with the other. The map splatted down into the footwell, and I fell back onto the road, pulling the scarf down just in time to heave onto the back wheel.

"Told you," I said to Lola and Jack, who were watching me from three car-lengths away. When my stomach settled, I crept low along the road and slid my hand inside to grab the atlas, slamming the door shut as soon as I had it and scurrying away in a crouch like a rat with a morsel. I threw the map at Lola, who caught it in gloved hands, and ripped my scarf off. Jack handed me a packet of wet wipes, and I disinfected my face and hands while he did the same to the cover of the map.

"Tell me it has grid references," I said, through a mouthful of lemon-scented tissue.

Lola flipped through the pages.

"It has grid references," she said, after settling on a page and folding the book open to inspect it. "Could it be the Yorkshire Moors?"

"Let me see," Jack and I said, at the same time.

"No, somewhere over here." Lola made a circle with her fingernail. "On the coast. They're taking us to a harbor."

———

"I never realized the Yorkshire Dales was different to the Yorkshire Moors," I said. We had broken into the garden center café, and the kids were spread out between the tables, munching organic apples and knobbly carrots from the farmers' market stalls and tasteless fair-trade chocolate from the display by the checkout. The air was humid with the pall of rotting salad leaves.

"What goes on in all these places?" Lola asked, tracing over the map all the neatly labeled villages and towns that lay between us and the coast.

"I know more about the Serengeti than Yorkshire."

"That's not surprising; you grew up there." Lola glanced to where Joni was hunched over a barbecue tray out on the patio, toasting sweet-corn cobs to eat on the long drive. "Mom still thinks home is Pennsylvania. I know it's my roots and all that. Don't tell her I said so, but the place doesn't mean anything to me."

"People are jigsaws, I think, made up of all their experiences. Home may be one big piece or lots of little pieces, but it's only one part of the picture." I whisked creamer into my tea, trying to break up the archipelago of powder lumps on the surface. "When I was a kid my mother went through a phase of saying 'there's no place like home' in this ominous voice that she had when she'd been drinking. I guess I hadn't seen *The Wizard of Oz*, because I thought she meant there was *no such thing as home*. I thought it was a bit brutal, even as a six-year-old." I laughed a bit to show Lola that no harm was done. She just gnawed her lip in response. "In retrospect, I think she was very unhappy. But, of course, you never consider that your parents might be happy or unhappy or anything in between. But anyway. Jack's an expat kid, too, right?"

"His parents moved to Hong Kong after his father left the army."

"Right." I sipped the tea and shoved the plastic drink away.

She poured some Snapple into a teacup and savored it while she studied the map. Jack and Kofi had gone back for Woody. We would go ahead to check out these coordinates from a vantage point on a cliff top. The map showed a lookout symbol, and I thought I knew the place: Whitby Abbey. I'd never been there, but it was a famous tourist attraction, the site of picturesque ruins. It would be sign-posted and easy for Jack to find. We planned to rendezvous there later. But Lola was still with Jack in spirit if not in body, her finger tracing his route to the school. It wasn't far, but our world had shrunk, and its dangers, concentrated. My scale had shifted so that I could no longer see the big picture, only the next mile and the one after that, as though I were driving at night with my headlights on. We traveled a land of little terrors, a place where one misstep might kill: one gulp of tainted air, one wound we couldn't treat, one single bullet. Death would be small. Tiny. It would snatch us in the space between one breath and the next.

"Where is Jack now, do you think?" Lola snapped me out of it.

"He'll be fine." *Because what could go wrong for an untrained teenage driver who has "borrowed" a brand-new Audi for a race across the countryside to find three lost children?* "We'll see them tonight at the coast."

Lola scraped her chair back from the table with a grating protest and gathered up the map. "I can't believe I'm going to say this, but I'm excited about the prospect of sitting on a real toilet."

I watched her high-step across the shop and into the ladies, and I closed my eyes and said a quick prayer for Jack. *Come back safely, Jack,* I whispered inside my head. *Don't make Lola hate me forever, you cocky little bastard.*

The peaceful interlude created by the snack break degenerated into bickering between the boys. I sent them off to the loo in batches, while the others went scavenging for more drinks and rations. Billy scooted onto my lap, and I wiped his mucky face with a napkin dipped in Snapple. I don't know why I bothered: his clothes were stiff with filth. The genteel setting of the garden center café threw our dishevelment into the spotlight. Quite frankly, we were a shambles.

Joni came in looking for carrier bags for the food. She sniffed the air in the café. "We stink." She walked over and hammered on the door of the boys' toilet, yelling at them to get washed.

"Let's pick out some clean clothes." I pulled my kids over to the gift shop.

"Isn't that stealing?" Charlie asked, his eyes fixed on a cabinet of Swiss Army knives.

"In the circumstances, I think it's known as looting."

His eyeballs swiveled back to mine. "Isn't looting naughty?"

"Are you my conscience now? Anyway, we've already cleaned out a supermarket. I don't see why keeping clean is worse than keeping fed. Just grab some clean socks. Get those funky ones with sharks: we might be going on a boat later."

Billy was already looting with some enthusiasm. He plumped down on his bum to pull on a pair of women's spotty wellington boots that came up to his hips. Charlie finished twisting his trouser legs into hard balls of guilt and succumbed to temptation, jimmying open the knife cabinet with a stick. Even the Lost Boy sat next to me clutching a new pair of deck shoes. He pulled them on, biting his lip while tying the laces. Maggie appeared holding a dress decorated with prancing ponies, but stopped to watch the Lost Boy. I smiled at her open admiration of his skills. Shoe laces remained Maggie's nemesis; any attempt to show her how to tie them ended in a tantrum—on both our parts. I had long since realized that teaching Maggie basic life skills would have to be done surreptitiously to avoid wounding her hypersensitive pride. Rather like slipping extra money into a poor relative's wallet, we could never acknowledge my helping hand.

The Lost Boy got the laces into two loops, but when he pulled them tight, the knot tumbled apart. "Almost." I crouched down next to him. "Can I show you a trick? I'll have to touch your hands, though." He moved his arms a little to allow me access. I guided his fingers to make bunny ears and perform the tricky switcheroo. When I took my hands away, he pulled the laces tight the first time. "Nicely done," I said. A ripple of satisfaction passed his lips as he tied the other shoe. From the shelf behind me, I picked up a bar of artisanal soap and some bamboo-cloth towels. "Come on, all of you. Bring your new clothes in here."

Inside the disabled washroom, I filled the sink with water and lathered up a cloth. I stripped Billy bare and laid him across my legs. While I wiped him down from head to feet, the others undressed and stood in line. I rinsed gray water out of the flannel, and Billy shivered in his wet skin, so I wrapped him inside a big towel and eased the water from his eyes with my thumbs.

"Better?"

"Make me a sausage, Mummy."

I swaddled him tight inside the towel, so that his arms and legs were trapped by his sides, and picked him up like a baby, rocking him dry and warm. Then I dressed him in his bright new clothes and correctly sized spotty wellies, of which he was mighty proud. He toddled out to show the others his new going-on-a-boat shoes.

Charlie had already started washing himself, too self-conscious to stand naked for long. The Lost Boy joined in with his back turned to me, wiping his thin limbs with studious care. I held another flannel out to Maggie, assuming she, too, would want to do it herself.

"Mummy wash me."

"Okay."

I laid my daughter across my legs and wiped the soapy cloth over her face and neck. She stretched her head back to offer me her throat. Charlie slopped his cloth into the full sink behind me, so that watery bubbles tickled onto my scalp. I bathed Maggie's soft torso and the creamy skin of her arms. All the way down to her mucky feet, where I slid the cloth between each toe and rolled it into a ball to scrub the blackened soles.

The smoke from Joni's barbecue curled in through the window. It took me back to another echoing white-tiled bathroom in Africa: my mother smoking a cardamom cigarette while I huddled under tepid bathwater. I had her attention at last, but could only bob under the water with my eyes protruding like a frog, my throat bulging with all the things I wanted to say. When she decided I had stewed for long enough, she threw a scratchy sun-dried towel round my shoulders, rubbing my hair so hard my eyes watered.

"This towel is very soft, isn't it?" I said to Maggie.

She agreed that it was.

"It's made of bamboo."

"Like pandas!"

"Pandas aren't made of bamboo, silly!"

Maggie giggled. I finished drying her hair and pulled the new tennis dress down over her shoulders.

"Are you all right, sweetheart?"

"I miss you." Her eyes winced, as though it caused her a little pain to admit it.

"But I'm right here."

"Sometimes I miss you when you're right here." The wince spread until her whole face was bunched up with the effort of finding words. I cupped her jaw in my palms and ran my thumbs over her eyebrows to smooth the furrows away.

"I miss you, too, Maggie, all the time." She folded into me for a cuddle, and I felt her heart beating against my belly. I pulled her in tighter, so she could hear my heart in reply. Her eyes closed and her shoulders dropped, so that I held her full weight in my arms for a few moments.

"Daddy does this when you go away."

"What?"

"Holds me tight so I can pretend to hear your heart beat like when I was a baby."

"He did that?"

"Daddy said I mustn't be scared that your plane would crash, because we loved you so much it would keep flying. And you loved us so much, you would keep it flying, too."

Daddy. Julian. One person or two? This didn't sound like Julian. But maybe Daddy was different. How was I to know, I hardly ever met the guy. But I think I would have liked this Daddy. I would have been able to grieve for him.

"Daddy was right," I said, as Maggie pressed her face into my stomach. "I always came back, didn't I?"

When Maggie stood again, she drew a little brown comb out of her pocket and plucked the teeth with a fingernail.

"Do you want me to do your hair?" I asked.

She shook her head once, and her mouth made a strangely adult movement of magnanimity.

"Can I do yours, Mummy?" She rasped the comb again.

"You can. And Maggie?"

"Yes, Mummy?"

"I'll never leave you again."

I sat down on the white tiles to watch the sweet-corn smoke drift past the window while my daughter held my head back in her pudgy hands and wrenched the knots from my hair.

———

"What's that?" asked Charlie.

"What?"

"That."

"What are you talking about?"

"That thing."

"I'm driving, so use your words, Charlie."

"There's a thing. Up in the sky."

That got my attention. I pulled to a stop by the side of the road and wound down my window. Wind bustled past me into the car. A group of white wind turbines stood on the neighboring field, their long ballerina legs stretching through their rounds. I got out of the pickup and accepted a pair of binoculars that Charlie held through the window. The sky flowed overhead, and I followed the gray torrent of cloud to a point beyond the turbines, where a single dark shape hung in the sky. The wind was loud, so I couldn't hear much, but I focused the binoculars as best I could and concluded that it wasn't a helicopter: no noise and too small. I got in the truck and passed the binoculars to Charlie, who resumed his watch.

"Just a bird riding the thermals. Good spotting, though."

As planned, we had started the drive to the coast. Jack would meet us after dark at Whitby Abbey, from where we should be able to observe the harbor. If it seemed safe—based on what criteria, I wasn't sure, but gut instinct and the absence of gunshots would be key—we would wait for Jack and the other boys before approaching.

"What if it is a trap?" Lola asked.

"Then I'll kick and punch them in the willy," threatened Billy, demonstrating his moves on his sister, who took him out with a single ninja elbow to the eye. His plan was as good as anything I could offer. Being realistic, if this wasn't a rescue mission by friendly forces, then we had very little chance "going forward."

"We'll go hide in a cave," said Joni.

"What will we eat?" asked Billy.

"Baked beans."

"I hate baked beans!" Maggie reacted as though baked beans were a fate worse than death.

We sped across land that featured nothing higher than a telegraph pole. The route wound through nondescript villages whose whitewashed houses and garden walls flanked the road, leaving no room, even for a pavement. We raced from the corral of each settlement to the exposed flatlands beyond. There was nowhere to hide here, so we ran. I muttered apologies to the kids bouncing around under the tarpaulin in the back.

Lola reached over a hand and tapped my wrist on the steering wheel.

"You're doing it again," she said.

I gripped the wheel to prevent myself from drumming my thumbs to the rhythm of the tires. Instead, I counted the letters of the place names we passed to see which ones were prime numbers. Took a while to get a nineteen. Whitby was a perfect number.

"What's that?" asked Charlie.

"What?"

"That."

"Words, Charlie."

"In the sky again. It's bigger this time."

I stopped outside a boarded-up pub and reached my hand back for the binoculars.

"There," said Lola, pointing past my nose out the window.

I didn't need the binoculars. Something small and black was hovering over the massive steeple of the village church.

"It's a ginormous spider," said Charlie.

"It does look like a spider," Lola whispered. "Or a fly."

I pushed the truck into gear and bumped down the curb into the street. A muted scream told me the boys in the bed had really felt that one. I accelerated away, watching the church spire and its strange hovering angel recede in my wing mirror.

"It's a drone," I said. "And so was the one before."

The pickup pitched through the village, round some traffic cones, before a sharp bend outside the local school. We picked up speed again as the road swept past a long row of stone cottages.

"What's a drone?"

"Can it see us?"

"Where is it now?"

I ignored them and drove. Joni scooted round on her seat to face backward on her knees. She took the binoculars and crouched to peer out of the rear window.

"Anything?"

"Nope."

"Hold on." A hump in the road. Her head hit the ceiling, but she righted herself and lifted the binoculars back to her face.

"I can't see it anymore."

The road bent round another sharp bend. A long wall ran alongside us as the street narrowed for several hundred yards to a single lane. The sign told me to give way to oncoming traffic. Instead, I drove straight ahead, right up to the rear bumper of a crashed car that forced me to stop just before the narrow section widened again.

"Fucking stupid place to crash your car," I said.

I wound down the window and scanned the sky, but I could see nothing, not even the tip of the steeple that must be a mile or so behind us already. We were stuck between the houses to the left, the crashed hatchback in front, and the drystone wall to the right. The land beyond the wall was higher than the road, so that the stones strained to hold back the weight of an overgrown graveyard. Brittle crests of dried grass flooded over the wall in waves.

"I think I see it," said Lola.

"Where?" Joni squinted into the binoculars.

"I'm not sure."

"Can you see it or not?" I asked her.

"I'm not sure!"

"All right," I said. "Let's work on the assumption that you can."

I let off the hand brake, and the pickup made contact with the back of the hatchback. It resisted for a second until I gave the engine more power, and then the car's nose pulled away from the house with a teeth-grinding scrape and rolled toward the end of the narrowed section. It picked up speed and trotted obediently along. The kids gave a little cheer. But then its tires turned out into the road and it veered to the opposite side, and not even all my swearing could prevent it from embedding itself in the very end of the stone wall, just a few feet shy of a gateway that led into the graveyard. I rolled up behind the hatchback and gave it a shunt that budged it another foot out of the road. But a second bump creaked a metallic warning through my bonnet. I reversed a little to straighten up and then squeezed between the back end of the stricken car and the brickwork of the houses. Lola wound down her window to pull in the side mirror. The cab pulled clear of the car, and Charlie started celebrating again. But then we jerked to a halt as our wider back end wedged. I forced the pedal down and the pickup writhed like a fish, catapulting past the crashed car with a screaming wrench. As we drove away, the red brick wall of the house collapsed into the road behind us, blocking the narrow lane once and for all.

Chapter Twenty-Four

We crossed the river to reach the cliff top, driving into a purple sunset, the same bruised color as the clouds of heather drifting over the moorland that had brought us here. It seemed that the land ran seamlessly into sky. After our long days of confinement—forest, mine, wolf enclosure—I felt like I had stepped onto a parapet, an impression that was heightened by the buffeting wind on the exposed road. The wide view offered a vertiginous freedom, as though we could drive straight over the edge and just keep going.

As we approached the Gothic face of Whitby Abbey, the sun dropped behind one ruined window socket and split into an orange frangipani flower. The glow streamed across the surrounding pastureland so that the dry grass lit up, its windblown movement swilling like the yellow hair of a drowned girl. It shifted direction to beckon us toward the cliff tops. We rolled along in silence, tires rumbling like distant thunder.

"Is this real?" asked Maggie. I assured her it was. We rumbled on until I stopped the pickup beside a tall stone cross, so weathered its ornamental top was worn down to a nub.

"I see the sea, and the sea sees me," said Charlie. As though in response, a wave drummed on the rocks below.

I got out and walked to the stone cross, up the little steps to its base to gain extra elevation and look out over the coastline. Mercury water pooled in the sheltered river inlet down in the town. But the wide swathe of beach running up to a distant headland was batted by shallow waves, slow blinking eyelids. Lola climbed up beside me, fighting to open the map in the wind.

"There's nothing down there," she complained.

There was, though. Through the binoculars, I scanned past the darkening town and along the coastal path to the north, where the cliffs of a headland began and a road slid down a sharp slope into the water. It wasn't the harbor we were expecting, but it was access to the sea, and it was certainly low profile. I pulled the binoculars away and squeezed my eyes to focus better. Looking again, I made sure of what I thought I could see: the glinting signal of the sun's last rays on the white coat of a person walking up the slipway.

The last time I had seen a white outfit, it was marching away as Horatio buckled onto the forest floor. I squinted through the binoculars again. This was different. His movements were swift, unrestricted: no biohazard suit. Then there was a second figure, going down toward the beach and disappearing from view behind an old wooden pier. *Into a boat that was moored out of sight, maybe?* I scanned back up the slipway to a white tent, like a small marquee, set up on the road. There was a flag, which I couldn't make out. Red and white. *Red Cross?* No, the red was in the background. I called Charlie over, passed him the binoculars.

"Your eyes are better than mine. What's that flag?" I said. "It's not the George Cross—"

Charlie peered down. "Norway."

"Are you sure?"

He held the binoculars out to me. "Blue-and-white cross on red. Easy. Norway. Capital: Oslo."

I looked again, and then I could make out the blue. Joni scrunched over the gravel to join us and took the binoculars while we studied the map.

"Looks like the place," said Lola. "Right coordinates."

Way below us, the sea slapped the land.

"They're too far away," I said at last. "I need to get closer to see if it's safe."

"Let's just go," said Joni.

"But we don't know who they are," I said.

She made an impatient sound and stared out over the water. I faced the other way, to check the kids in the pickup. Billy pointed two fingers to his eyes and turned them to point at me. *I'm watching you.* I copied the motion in response.

"What choice do we have?" Joni asked.

"I'm just saying we should check it out first," I said. "You can stay here, under cover." I pointed to the abbey, where a deep stone archway led to a visitor center. "I'll run along the coastal path until I reach a vantage point." I measured the distance on the map with my thumb. "It's about five miles there and back; I'll be gone less than an hour."

"And what happens if you don't come back?" said Lola.

"Then you revert to Plan A: hide in a cave."

"And leave you?"

"Yes, Lola—if I get killed, you and Joni must leave me and get the children to safety."

Lola chewed her lip. "I guess an hour might be enough time for Jack to catch up."

"If it's safe down there"—I nodded in the direction of the white tent—"we can keep watch until he turns up."

"Okay."

Joni turned to face me, her eyes slipping over my shoulder into the distance. I followed her gaze. Way beyond the yellowed grass, a flock of birds rose up as silhouetted darts against the sky, too distant to hear their cries, but their disarray clear. Something had disturbed them from their roost.

"Let's go now," Joni said again.

Charlie pointed a finger. "Drones."

Two black dots, small as gnats, growing in size as they headed toward us. An unnaturally coordinated movement amid the floundering birds.

"Back in the truck," I shouted at two boys who'd slipped out from under the tarpaulin. "Get in!" They scrambled up as though scalded by the ground. I started the engine and spun the wheels over the gravel.

"Which way?" I said to Lola.

"There's only one road. Back the way we came."

If we followed that road, it would take us in a wide loop to the south before we reached the route that led north toward the headland. We would have to pass right beneath the drones, which were approaching now in a kind of pincer movement.

"What about this path down toward the town?" I pointed to a wide avenue of stone steps ahead of us.

"It goes straight down the cliff."

"They're coming, Mummy," hissed Charlie. Maggie broke out into a high-pitched keening.

I edged the pickup forward to the top of the steps, which curved round the escarpment between black iron railings. Once committed, there would be no stopping.

"What do you think?"

"It's too steep," said Lola.

"How far does it go?"

"There's one hundred and ninety-nine steps. It says on the map. We can't even see right to the bottom."

"Mummy, they're coming!" Charlie said. Maggie gave a loud yelp and clamped her hands over her ears, the keening louder.

I teetered on the top. These were not the undulating hills of Shropshire. If I rolled it down this cliff, it would leave us with more than a busted headlight and a few dents. If I lost control on the steps, it would kill the boys in the back. Little buggers wouldn't stand a chance.

Maggie was thrashing her legs now, lashing out a hailstorm that pelted everyone around her.

"Quiet, Maggie!"

"It's too steep." Lola.

"Let's just go." Joni.

Billy sobbing.

Maggie keening.

The boys in the back under the tarpaulin, waiting.

In the rearview mirror, one black fly came into view. Still too distant to hear, I nevertheless felt its buzz. All the voices receded, and I was left with a weightlessness, like I'd had for one calm second when I'd rolled the Beast, as land turned into sky. A moment when the worst had already happened, so there was nothing left to worry about. I wanted to stop forever in that pause between cause and effect. A place where I didn't have to be responsible for everybody all of the time. I blinked and the drone was still coming at me, bigger, faster. I hauled the pickup into reverse, and we shot back from the precipice, over the gravel, and straight under the cover of the stone cloister.

"Get out," I said. "Joni, take all the kids and get out."

"Mummy!" Three voices in unison from the back.

"You have to hide." I turned to face Joni and Lola, appealing to them. "Take the kids under cover and when it's clear, start down the steps. I don't have time to explain. Just do it." Nothing moved except the wind through the dry grass and the drones in the sky. "Ah, Jesus!" I flung open my door and jumped out to wrench off the tarpaulin. While the boys clambered out like clockwork robots, the others emerged from the cab, and Joni rounded them up into a darkened corner.

"Where are you going, Mummy?" Charlie clutched at my hands while I struggled to clear everything from the cab, making me drop the petrol canisters, which I scrambled up off the floor and dropped into the open back of the pickup.

"It's okay. Just go with Joni and Lola, right? Down the steps. I'm right behind you." I squeezed Maggie's chin as I passed her. She held hands with Billy and the Lost Boy. "Look after them."

"Yes, Mummy."

I turned the wheel and sped away, just as the two drones skimmed over the blank face of the abbey.

The pickup flew through the long grass with a sound like the wind in my hair. Faster. The speed gauge went into the red. I steered straight toward the cliff edge, all the while checking the sky behind me. It was hard to judge the distance of the drones. They seemed to move closer together and apart again. With a small gasp, I realized they had turned and were following me.

I let them grow larger in the rearview mirror, and when I was sure they were flanking me, I braked hard, the truck stopping abruptly in the dry grass. Out of the cab and into the bed, I unscrewed the tops of the petrol canisters and laid them down. Fuel sopped round my feet. I vaulted over the side, back behind the wheel, jerking away across the field again, veering in a wide arc toward the cliff. In the wing mirror: two drones, up high, eyes in the sky. The petrol sprayed up in a wake behind me. I held the wheel steady with my knees and started scrabbling in the center console. The driver was a smoker, that much was obvious from the smell. There must be a lighter, matches. I scooped the detritus onto the seat. Nothing. "Fuck's sake!" The truck swerved as I leaned to reach the glove compartment. I pulled the satnav cable out of the socket and fumbled the cigarette lighter into place instead. Ahead, the cliff edge approaching. Behind, the drones approaching. My thumb found the small knob and pressed it down. *Come on, come on.* I opened my door wide, the hinges screaming, the truck filling with the roar of wind buffeting, grass thrashing. *Come on.* The cliff was just yards away now, my body's cells straining to keep me away from the edge. Click. I pulled the red-hot lighter from the socket and gripped it tight in my fist as I rolled out the open door, through the soft cushion of long grass, and onto the ice-hard ground that lay beneath.

———

I didn't see the pickup go over the edge. I may have heard an explosion, but my head was ringing from the fall. I pulled my limbs back into their rightful places and got up. There would be pain later. But the smell of petrol was all around me, scattered wide from the back of the vehicle. I ran a little way along the path that the car had scythed through the grass, and held the lighter to a clump of sodden stalks. A flame caught right away, and I started to run, fast. A loud slap—like someone shaking out a bedsheet—and I knew the wind had taken control of the fire. It skirted away from me, racing with ruthless energy along the line of fuel toward the abbey. I ran counterclockwise to the galloping flame, praying that the kids had already started down the steps. I risked a look back at the drones, couldn't see anything beyond the reams of smoke, my hot shield. I ran on, hiding in plain sight, until I reached the stone steps.

A dozen small figures straggled down the hill ahead of me. Joni brought up the rear, slowed down by Billy in her arms. *Thank you, thank you.* I took the steps two at a time, a shooting pain through my right shoulder telling me it had taken the brunt of the landing.

"Mum-may!" Billy called out as I caught up on the steep incline. Joni stopped and turned to grin at me. But I shooed her on; the whole hillside was covered with dry grass, the landscape volatile. Already, smoke poured over the cliff edge, the abbey face lost to us.

"We have to get across the river," I told her.

"Carry me, Mum-may," cried Billy.

With the elbow of my right arm swaddled in my left hand, the pain was bearable.

"I'm sorry, Billy, I can't. Joni's got you."

She caught my eye and nodded once, noting my discomfort. "I got you, Billy. Let's get out of here."

We reached the final curve, stepping onto cobblestones just as a roar of flame came tearing down the hillside. The narrow streets quickly clogged with smoke, blowing all ways in the wind, and as the waiting children started scrubbing at their stinging eyes, I urged them down a side street that seemed to descend toward the sea. A spike of panic at a dead end. My shouts lost amid coughing as the smoke came after us like a monster I'd created. But then: "This way," shouted Lola, and we plunged into an alley that brought us onto a larger road beside the river inlet. Outside the labyrinth of cobbled streets, the smoke cleared, and we stopped running, caught our breath. A quick head count, and we were all there. I gathered Billy into an awkward, one-armed squeeze. Over the ragged rooftops, smoke blossomed. The fire must have been huge, but it wouldn't conceal us forever. I turned back to the coastline. The headland was a dark shape beyond the town, which was itself beyond the river.

"Why's there no fricking bridge?" said Joni. The wide river inlet was flanked by storm barriers—a concrete cervix—that protected the harbor. But we couldn't cross it. A stone wharf that jutted out into the water led only to an ornamental anchor.

"It's further up." I herded the kids onto the reeking mudflat left behind by the receding tide, and we staggered upriver to the same bridge we'd crossed not half an hour before. A tattered line of Union Jack bunting struggled against the wind. The children pattered across the span of the bridge, silent and watchful. A flag rope dinged against its pole. Boats nodded in the water. Charlie tugged at my arm.

"Couldn't we—?"

"I don't know how to sail a boat, Charlie."

Gray swells of the river beneath our feet. The sound of water smacking every surface: keel, pillar, rock. Maybe on a calm day, it might have seemed possible. Maybe if I had the time to work out how to start a boat, the sea would be the most direct route to the white tent with the red flag, which was still probably three miles up the coast. But without that option we had to keep moving north as best we could.

I directed the kids along the coast road that bent around steep curves until we mounted the cliff top opposite the abbey. I scanned the sky for drones, but it was marbled with smoke, fire raging across the grassland and also, it seemed, through several buildings on the edge of the town. The heat must surely be a distraction—cover—but the smoke meant we wouldn't see approaching drones until they were on top of us. In the other direction, looking north, the headland beneath which the Norwegian tent was hunkered was still in the distance. We had to move faster. Going straight along the beach would take too long, and that option would leave us totally exposed with nowhere to hide if the drones came. We stayed on the cliff top, the grand Victorian hotels as blank-eyed as the long-ruined abbey. We kept moving along the promenade, past endless memorial benches, all facing out to sea, as though that were the rightful place for grief. Billy whined, and I scooped him up with my left arm, wincing at the pain. A shout on the wind; ahead of us, Lola was pointing over the grass to a weatherboard shed, which advertised rental bikes. "Pier-to-Pier Cycling." By the time I reached her, she had smashed the lock off with a rock and was hauling open the doors. We wheeled out the bikes—one boy asking, robotically, for a helmet—and straggled onto the coastal path, dipping below the promenade, which meant we wouldn't be seen from the land.

"We can do this!" I shouted to Joni, who weaved unsteadily in front of me. Ahead of her, the younger kids hunkered over their handlebars, stabilizers taking the brunt of their lurches. Maggie and the Lost Boy wobbled away. Billy was perched on my crossbar, his shaggy hair blown back from his face. Despite the pain throbbing through my shoulder—it was my collarbone, I could feel it—I arched forward and kissed him on his soft spot.

The hard-earth path swooped downhill toward the headland. I could make out the dark shape of the slipway and the incongruous white gleam of the tent, though it was still too far off to see any detail. Billy shouted "whee" as we started to freewheel. My chest jumped with giddy relief, and I could have thrown my head back and laughed, larking along in the salt spray like it was a bank holiday. But then the bikes that had been streaming ahead of me clogged into a messy jam, and the expectant faces turned to me again. As I approached, I saw that the coastal path turned away from our destination. I swore into my teeth. A development of holiday cottages interrupted the path and forced it inland. The headland retreated behind the houses. I braked hard and had to grab Billy round the middle with my sore arm. My head swam with pain.

It was too steep to go down to the beach. And in any case, we couldn't cycle on the sand. Better to move quickly on the road. I glanced back. The pall of smoke had consolidated into a column over the town. Charlie backed up until he was next to me.

"Looks like a volcano," he said.

"Can you manage to cycle a bit further?" I asked him.

He nodded, still looking back: "You burnt down the town, Mummy."

"Not all of it, love. Come on." I cycled past the waiting children and round the dogleg that took us inland, thighs burning up the long slope, until it came out onto a road beside a windswept golf course. Once again, I could see the headland, which pointed out to sea like a long black finger. It was hard to tell in the darkening light, but it seemed far away again. Like a dream, where it slid off every time I got close.

The drones could be on us in minutes, and what would we do—a dozen kids on bicycles? Inside me, contractions of panic multiplied in my gut.

Huge white shapes in the field opposite reflected the last of the daylight. I squinted down the road and read "Edge of the World Caravan Park." I lifted Billy over to Joni and let my bike fall onto the grass verge.

"Wait here," I said. "Whistle if you spot drones."

I ran across the road and straddled the rickety wire fence. The dry grass was thigh-length, but I waded through it, past the static caravans to a row of motor homes that were lined up beside electrical boxes. *Needs must.* I hesitated by the driver's door. I put a foot on the step and held the handle, then swung myself up to look inside. Four bodies, thick with flies. I jumped back. Too much buzz. I pressed my lips together to keep the nausea inside. The next motor home: a face slumped against the front window. I walked right past it to the third, put my foot on the step to look in, but when I heard Joni's whistle I swung myself up onto the bonnet to see back to the road.

"Drones?" I shouted.

Charlie stood on the road, holding binoculars to his eyes. He lowered them as the other boys started running their bikes down the road, hopping on after a few steps and streaming away.

"Is it drones, Charlie?" I shouted again.

He lowered the binoculars and shook his head. "Helicopter," he shouted. "There's a helicopter coming."

Of course there was. The drones were only trackers. The helicopter would have to make the kill.

I jumped down from the bonnet and hauled open the driver's door. A body tumbled past me in an explosion of flies—the smell slamming me in the face—to land in a heap between me and the cab. I darted to the side door. Inside, another body. *Needs must. You must.* I pulled my sleeves over my hands, gulped down a breath, and went in, flailing my arms at the flies, grabbing the two feet, and using all my strength to pull the body out through the door. I fell backward down the steps, leaving the body slumped in the doorway. I went back, grabbed the back of the old woman's jeans, and dragged her clear. In the door, through the hatch, into the cab. Retching from the smell. The engine shuddered to life. I pushed the gear stick into drive and the vehicle shot forward, ripping the campervan's cables from the power supply and crunching over the grass, picking up speed as I approached the fence, opening the windows to let the sterile salt air blow through.

The motor home burst through the wire and bounced onto the road. I braked and jumped out. Joni was already running down the road, carrying Billy. Lola followed, herding Maggie and the Lost Boy ahead of her. I screamed at Charlie who was still staring through the binoculars. He scampered over.

"How far away is the helicopter?" I asked him, as he went in through the side door.

"Them," he said. "There's two of them."

I left the door pinned open, ran back to the cab, and the campervan sprang forward. We raced alongside a high grassy bank, hemmed into a rat run between moorland and sea. The other kids were ahead of me, spread out all over the road. I leaned on the horn as I approached the first group, and they automatically veered to the sides. I slowed down, still rolling, while Lola hung out of the side door, shouting at the boys to dump the bikes and get in, Joni hauling them inside. The first one vomited immediately onto the carpet. As I accelerated, I checked the wing mirror, but couldn't see anything.

"How far away were the helicopters, Charlie?"

"Over the town."

"Coming this way?"

"Yep." He got up and staggered through the swaying cabin to look out the back window.

I braked for the next group of boys, who'd seen what was happening and stopped, leaving their bikes on the verge. Lola and Joni manhandled them on board. The motor home picked up speed again, lumbering along. The land dropped away and was replaced by a line of Victorian seaside villas as we raced into the next town. The final group of boys was ahead, still peddling. I sounded the horn, and they turned, swerving across my pathway. My mind flashed back to another set of bikes, a boy's legs pumping, Woody's brother. Lennon. But I shook it away. *He is gone. We are still here. Focus.* The boys ditched their bikes and were inside.

"That's it!" yelled Joni.

There was a muted cheer. I pushed my foot down to the floor, as though I could force the motor home to go faster by sheer willpower. I swore at it, and the thing seemed to respond, building up momentum on the downward slope. Finally, the headland took on definition. It was maybe half a mile north.

"Charlie?" I shouted to him, but at that moment his face appeared next to mine.

"They're here," he said.

I resisted the urge to slow down as the road bent out of sight ahead of me, both arms held straight against the steering wheel as we pounded past parked cars. The road dodged over a bridge, and I was forced to brake heavily to make the turn, Charlie tumbling into the footwell, the cries from the back making me wince. The motor home was too huge, its front scraping against the stones as we ploughed across the bridge and barreled away. Charlie hauled himself into the passenger seat. As the road curved, it allowed a brief glimpse back down the coast road—the way we'd come—and we saw the intent shapes of two helicopters bearing down on us. But as the road twisted us to the north again, Charlie gave a shout, and his hand hit the dashboard. I squealed to a stop in front of a roadblock.

Solid red and white barriers prevented us from reaching the slipway. We sat in silence as the buffeting slaps of the helicopters caught up.

"Mummy!"

I switched off the engine. Rested my heavy arms against the steering wheel. Ahead, the white marquee on the road. People moving inside. Tables of equipment, food, medicine. A flag flying, a red, white, and blue standard snapping to attention in the wind. Now, a man in a white coat and hat running toward us, shouting words I couldn't hear over the thumping of blades. His hat blew off and rolled twice before settling the right way up on the pavement. He hung over the barrier, waving his arms. His eyes bulged. I opened my mouth to reply, but my lips seemed to stick together.

"Mummy!"

The furious wind got louder, and my hair streamed in front of my eyes. I lifted an arm to hold it back. Joni and Lola had opened the side door and were on the road outside, Lola's mouth moving as she shouted at me through the window, the sound of feet scuffling as Joni launched children toward the barrier, which the man shoved aside with his bulk to let them through. Greeting each boy with a huge hand on the shoulder, pulling them behind him, paternal.

"Mummy?"

In the rearview mirror, three sets of eyes fixed on mine. Then Charlie broke away to look out his passenger-side window and started to yell. The dark shadow of a helicopter slid down his face. A panicky whine of engines as it came in to land on the beach below.

"Mummy. Move. You have to move, Mummy." His eyes flickered back to mine, and then he was tearing at his seat belt.

Move, I told myself. *Get your children and move. Make this stop.*

I scrambled my knees onto the seat and leapt into the back. I carried Billy in one hand and reached back with the other to pull Maggie through the door. Charlie hurtled straight into the arms of the man, who gathered him and the Lost Boy up and ran behind the roadblock. I covered the same few yards in what seemed like a single bound, and we hit the ground behind the barrier, where the man in the white coat had already stopped and placed Charlie onto his feet, holding his hips for a few seconds to make sure his legs were steady. The other boys tottered about, bewildered, like exhausted marathon finishers. Joni and Lola pressed against the iron railing, watching the helicopters like they were animals in a zoo.

"You're safe now," the man said in a heavy Scandinavian accent.

"Here? We're safe here?" I was panting like I'd run a mile when I'd only taken a few steps.

"Behind the road break, yes."

"Here is safe, there is not safe?" I indicated both sides of the barrier. "That's it?"

He gave a tight smile. "That's politics."

Chapter Twenty-Five

Inside another tent. This one was white and tasted of salt. I couldn't be sure if that was from the sea air or the rehydration fluids. The man, Dr. Larsen, looked up from his clipboard to monitor the Cleaners, who leaned on the barrier, masks lifted to smoke. One by one, they dropped their fag ends on the road and returned to the helicopters down on the beach. When the doctor turned back to me, he still had one white eyebrow raised.

"Who are they?" I asked.

"They do not exist." After a couple of seconds, he smiled, as though that were the only option left. His latex-covered thumb raised my hair to stroke what remained of the laceration from the car crash. He had already strapped up my arm, but it wasn't broken. Now, he selected a pencil from his front pocket and puzzled over the clipboard for the correct place to write.

"The helicopters look real enough to me," I said.

He lifted a pair of round steel glasses from his button nose, which was too small for his hearty baker's face. His eye contact was like a pat on the shoulder. My body gasped in a sudden breath, and I used it to push down the tears that threatened to surge up and out. Dr. Larsen slid a drink across the table and busied himself with paperwork while I gulped at it. He checked the time on his watch and wrote down the exact hours and minutes.

"They're covert," he said, after I pushed the plastic cup away. "Black ops. While the UN is holding another meeting and agreeing on the exact words for a statement, someone—we don't know who, we have ideas, but we can't prove it—someone is paying these guys to eliminate the virus. Kill the host, kill the virus."

"But if we had the virus, we'd be dead already."

"It is possible for people to carry a virus without getting sick. Maybe that is also the case with the English Plague, but we don't know for sure. It is like nothing we've seen before."

"But you're not wearing protection?"

"Earlier in the week, I did. But no one is coming in sick anymore. We think the virus is dead or dying, but it's too soon to be certain. There is a theory that it was accelerated by carbon monoxide—no people, no cars, less carbon monoxide, so it died, see?—but everyone"—he waved his arms about to indicate that everyone was *crazy*—"very scared."

"And the UN? NATO? Why aren't there peacekeeping forces?"

"The world does not want your epidemic. That is the only matter on which they all agree. And NATO—the terrorists were homegrown, an attack by British nationals on British soil. So people are saying it is not NATO's problem. NATO should use their resources to stop it spreading, so yes, they are patrolling borders, securing ports, this kind of thing, but—" He shrugged.

Inside my head, a flickering spool of images from the past ten days. *Frightened eyes. Flames. Remote stars. Billy lying in my arms like a baby.* A swell of anger murmured deep down. *No one came to help! What had we done to deserve that?* And then I looked at Dr. Larsen's hands, a scar across one knuckle from some other disaster—one I had probably read about in the newspaper and immediately forgotten—and I wondered how many times he'd sat in a tent while a woman composed herself. Maybe a woman who'd lost more than I had—lost her children—and waited for the outside world to care. Maybe these women were there now, in Nepal or Syria or Somalia, listening to the coverage of the

English Plague on the radio and thinking, "Now you know how it feels, now you know." Maybe the African version of Marlene Greene was holding a charity auction, just as I had once. *(Was it for Darfur? Or Haiti? Or maybe Aceh?)* Maybe the Indian Marlene Greene was clearing unfashionable clothes from her wardrobe into black bin liners that she would deposit outside a secondhand shop in the rain. Maybe it would make them feel better, pretending they were doing something, just as it had done for me. Dr. Larsen wiped a cold swab across my arm and followed it with a needle.

"Tetanus," he said.

"So why aren't the mercenaries attacking us?"

He picked up his iPhone and showed me my face on the screen. "Say 'cheese'—I'm recording. Live streaming, actually. If they come, we would have the evidence to expose them. And there would be questions about whoever is paying. In the meantime, we send eyewitness accounts to the UN. And they put them in a bottom drawer."

"Surely it's a crime against humanity?"

"Oh, there will be an inquiry. In about ten years. A tribunal."

"What about the other survivors?"

"There are no survivors. Not officially."

I waggled my fingers in the air and gave a sarcastic little "hello."

He shrugged. "If the people in the camps around Folkestone and Calais continue to kill each other, it will be true soon enough."

Don't go south.

He turned my hand palm up, squeezed the end of one finger, and jabbed it with a needle. We both watched a pearl of blood surface.

"So who are you?" I said. "Red Cross? UN Refugee Agency?"

Dr. Larsen drew the blood into a tiny tube and stood it in a tray behind him.

"A blood test. If there's nothing unusual, you can board the hospital ship. You'll be the last. We're full."

"Médecins Sans Frontières?" I said.

"Just a concerned neighbor. I came out of retirement. It's okay, I was bored." He asked if my arm was hurting, did I want painkillers? I looked at my kids, ripping open packet after packet of medical supplies until fat white cotton wool balls plumped the floor around their feet. They were safe, so nothing hurt anymore.

"What happens to us now?" I said.

"We take you to Norway, and then the world is your oyster. Or Norway is your oyster."

"So I'm a refugee?"

"Asylum seeker, actually. Until your application for refugee status is processed. But most countries in Europe are refusing applications, and France has the camps, so—"

"Fuckers."

"Fear brings out the worst in people, especially groups of people. Anyway, you'll be quite comfortable in Oslo." He said it "Ahzz-lo." *Will I ever feel comfortable saying* Ahzz-lo? I thought. *Will the children?* "Apart from the military police and the heat scanners and the curfew and the rumors. The hysteria. But it's better in Norway than most of Europe. You might want to seek asylum further afield. Australia has agreed to take British refugees, but it is difficult to go because Singapore and Dubai have closed their borders. The U.S. and Canada are taking refugees also."

"The U.S. is okay? We have family there. Her husband and mother." I nodded my chin toward Joni, who was talking intently to another doctor, perhaps having the same conversation.

"It's okay. The virus hit so fast here that the U.S. had time to quarantine aircraft from your airports. Some were turned back, some rerouted to remote isolation zones. There are rumors that one plane was shot down when the pilot tried to land because he was short of fuel, but who knows if that's true. Human rights groups are complaining, but no one cares because the measures worked; they contained the virus.

There've been some protests and unrest in a few cities, but nothing out of control. Her husband is likely fine."

The children came over, followed by the young doctor who'd been talking to Joni. The doctor was improbably pretty and clean, an angel to supervise this sterile place. Her white teeth matched the tent, which felt like a decompression chamber outside heaven's gate. She gave Dr. Larsen an update on the kids' condition. All good, blood count normal, minor injuries—ready to board. She waved Joni into a chair and started her tests.

Dr. Larsen called the children over. "So who do we have here?" He turned to a fresh sheet on the clipboard and wrote the names of my children. Charles Luff-Greene. Margaret Luff-Greene. William Luff-Greene. Dr. Larsen reached the Lost Boy, who returned his gaze through huge, dark pupils. "And what is your name?" When the boy said nothing, Dr. Larsen turned to me.

"What will happen to all the other children?" I pointed to the Wild Things who were sitting in little clumps on the slipway.

"It is a matter for the authorities. Your children stay with you, of course, but these boys will go to care families. What do you call this?"

"Foster homes."

"Yes."

The Lost Boy stood next to Maggie, their contrasting fingers entwined.

"His name is Peter Luff-Greene," I said.

"He is your child?" Dr. Larsen's eyes flicked up to mine from the clipboard. "You are saying this boy is also your son?"

"Absolutely, his name is Peter Luff-Greene." I put my hand on the back of the Lost Boy's head. "Isn't that right?"

He looked up at me and opened his mouth.

"Yes," he said.

The doctor held my eye for a moment and then gave a single nod and wrote down the details.

"Good. Then the Greene family can please make your way to the boats. We sail in half an hour." He checked his digital watch. "Oh. Ten minutes. Because of the tide."

We walked out of the tent onto the concrete slip. A rubber dinghy with a solid-wooden floor was moored in just a few feet of water, its massive outboard motor raised to avoid the rocks. An identical orange boat came scudding over the sea toward us, and I realized that the dinghy would ferry us to a much bigger ship that was moored offshore. Despite Larsen's reassurances, I glanced along the beach at the helicopters, but they were hidden behind the stanchions of a dilapidated wooden jetty. The concrete slipway nestled in its lee.

"We need two boats as you are so many." Dr. Larsen surveyed all the boys. "Where did you get all these children?"

In an instant, the dreamy state induced by the white tent and its serene inhabitants lifted, and a familiar tension returned. We were still waiting for Jack and Kofi, and hopefully Woody and the other two boys. They could be at the abbey, waiting for us. Or on their way.

"There are more boys," I told him. "We have to wait—"

"Larsen?" It was the angel, calling from the tent. She said something to him in Norwegian, her head tilted toward Joni.

"It's your friend, one moment." He carried his bulk nimbly up the slipway.

"Sister-in-law," I said, pointlessly.

The dinghy pulled up to the slipway. The driver, who was probably a decade younger than I, had ragged stubble that deepened the creases of a face that had seen it all before. He came onto the concrete and hunkered down next to the first group of schoolboys, speaking quietly until they rose to their feet and followed him into the boat. He threw life jackets onto their laps; "It will get choppy," he said. He turned and called me to get in.

"I have to wait to speak to Larsen," I said. I put my good arm around my children. They weren't going anywhere without me.

"We don't have long," he told me, but went over to the next group of boys and led them into the dinghy.

I counted the boys in the boat. The Wild Things were all there. And I had my four kids. Joni was in deep conversation with Dr. Larsen and the female doctor in the tent. *So where is Lola?* I looked up the slipway to the tent and beyond. Along the coastline, a smoking hillside marked our rendezvous point with Jack. *Where the fuck is Lola?*

I herded the children back up the slipway. Behind me, the sputter of an outboard engine as the dinghy full of schoolboys pushed off.

"Joni?" I called to her.

She turned, and her face was brimming with tears.

"What happened? Where's Lola?" I grabbed Joni's arm, but she was intent on the young doctor, thanking her over and over until the woman moved away, busying herself with packing up supplies.

"She goes first." Dr. Larsen waved Joni ahead. And to his colleague, "Radio the ship. Clear a berth."

"What's going on?" I asked.

Joni glided past: a sleepwalker. Her body moved away from me, but her eyes locked on to mine, her head rotating weirdly, like a ventriloquist's dummy.

Her mouth opened and she said, "I'm pregnant, Marlene. I'm pregnant."

"That's—" I said. "Congratulations."

And she floated down the slipway toward the dinghy.

"And she could lose it if she doesn't get treatment." Dr. Larsen was throwing boxes of gear onto a trolley. "So we go now."

"But what about Lola? And the other boys?" I followed Larsen, catching one of the boxes as it slipped. My kids bobbed along in my wake.

"The tide is going out." He stopped and looked me in the eye. "We have only five minutes. You got yourself lucky we are still here."

"We can't go without Lola."

Dr. Larsen released his breath in a quick sigh that seemed too delicate for a man of his scale. "Is she here?"

I scanned the empty tent, the desolate street beyond. Obviously, she wasn't, but I jerked my head about, as though she might appear from nowhere. I asked Charlie. Maggie? They hadn't seen her, either.

"I'm sorry, then we leave now." Dr. Larsen called a command, a brusque seal bark, to the driver of the second dinghy, who pulled the ropes tighter to hold the rocking boat steady against the slipway. "The hospital ship is full. And the tide—"

"But there are more refugees. We have to go and find Lola and the boys."

"My other patients need urgent attention—your sister-in-law included. The ship must leave now for Oslo. This is the last transfer." With that, he pushed the trolley to the edge, and the driver hauled the plastic boxes on board, stacking them under the wooden seat where Joni sat, huddled inside her life jacket. Larsen stepped in next and turned to offer a hand to us. Maggie jumped on and scooted next to Joni. Then the boys. Larsen nodded at me and pulled life jackets out of a locker. I stepped onto the heaving boat.

Joni smiled and looked along the seat next to her—taking in the four young ones. She glanced behind her into the prow of the boat: empty. She turned and looked out to sea, toward the hospital ship, as though she might see Lola there. She turned back to me.

"Marlene? Did—"

"Lola's not here, Joni. We don't know where she is."

Water slapped against the rubber hull.

Joni stood just as a wave rolled the boat. She staggered to keep her balance, ending up with her knees bent, one hand on the seat behind her and the other on her stomach. I had a sudden vision of her heavily pregnant. Dr. Larsen stepped in to take her by the elbow and make her sit.

"I have to find her." Joni's voice was shrill.

"Severe anemia can lead to premature birth or even miscarriage. Your baby is at risk—" Larsen tried, but Joni grabbed him by both arms and hauled him down toward her face. Pencils fell from his jacket pocket and tumbled across the floor.

"My daughter is at risk!" She shook him once by the arms, and then turned her face into his chest and started to cry.

A slow chill crept up my veins, blown in on the salt air, drenching me in cold sweat. I looked at my own children, safe and warm in blankets. At Joni carrying her unborn child, who should surely be given a chance. Somewhere else, somewhere cold and dangerous, were Lola, my niece; Jack and Kofi, good boys who'd helped us; and Woody, whom I had promised to protect. Two others, whose names would be forgotten.

Around us, the sea had grown dark, layers upon layers of gray dragged this way and that. Joni's screams drifted away, like a gull's cries. *Lola. I won't leave her. I'll go after her.* My mouth filled with a marine tang that was pure and lonely.

"No, Joni," I said. I couldn't bring myself to look at my children as I stepped off the boat. "I'll go after her."

Chapter Twenty-Six

Billy's fingers dragged hairs from the back of my neck as they were wrenched away. His broken fingernails scratched stinging claw marks along the length of my chin. Sea salt blew into the wounds. Joni tried to wrestle him into a hug, but he wriggled away. He leapt into my arms again, a soft body that fit mine like a jigsaw puzzle. My missing piece. I put my hand to the back of his head and slid my thumb to the place behind his ear. He gripped me even tighter and shuddered.

"When are you coming back, Mummy?" Charlie asked, twisting his trousers into knots. "How many sleeps?"

"Quite a few sleeps, Charlie," I told him. "Can you look after the others for me? Stay together. Joni will be with you. You're safe now, okay? That's better, isn't it, now that you're safe? That's better." I stopped and took a calming breath. Charlie clung to my hip, wide-eyed.

"We will keep them safe," said Dr. Larsen.

"Until I get back."

Not a single muscle shifted on the man's face. "Of course."

Maggie sat on the bench seat, arms wrapped around herself like a straitjacket.

"Maggie?"

She ignored me, staring hard at the rocks that were emerging from the water and growing up around the boat.

"Maggie, I have to go now." I tried to move Billy so I could hug her, but he clamped on. I shifted him onto one leg to crouch down. "Maggie?"

"Why are you going?"

"To bring Lola home. She's all alone. And it's dangerous."

"But you promised."

I had. I had promised never to leave her again. My mother's voice in my head: *Never make promises you can't keep.* It reminded me of something. I worked my fingers into my jeans pocket and drew out a velvet pouch.

"I want you to take this, Maggie. Look after it for me." I opened the string and drew out my mother's huge brooch.

"It's beautiful," she said, turning the jade in her hands. She struggled with the pin, and I helped her fix it in place, holding the blanket closed across her chest. She looked like a tiny Celt, a warrior child raised under Boudicca.

"Mummy?" she said. "What if you die?"

Billy's arms tightened around my throat.

"Then one day, Maggie, you will give that brooch to your own daughter. Even though you love it, and it's hard to let it go, you will give it to her. And you will understand—because you will be a mummy by then—you will understand that what you want doesn't matter. You don't even have a choice. You will tell her that someone gave you a precious thing, but with it came the responsibility to protect it—"

"You're trying to say that Lola is the precious thing, aren't you? And the other children."

"Yes, Maggie. That's right."

"But they're not your children. We're your children."

"I know, I know. It's hard to explain, but—" The jumble that I was trying to define coiled up inside me. I tugged at a few frayed edges in my mind—*I can't let them die: couldn't live with myself; after all that Joni has done for me; I owe Woody; I'd never leave you if I thought you were in danger; you're safe but they're not*—only the knot just got tighter. "Maggie, I'm—I'm just trying to do my best."

Once again, I saw myself reflected in her eyes: her train jumping the tracks, a pause while she gathered herself up and carried on.

"We'll be stuck on these rocks if you don't go soon," she said.

I kissed her scraggly hair. "I love you, Maggie."

Now Charlie. I turned to him. "Do you understand? I don't want to leave you. I love you. But—"

"I get it."

"Really?"

"It's like Peter when he slept by the gate that time. He said he wasn't scared, but"—he raised his arms and let them fall against his sides—"he *was* scared."

"But he did it anyway."

"Can I come with you?" he asked.

"No."

"I could help—"

"You'd be brilliant, but no. The only way I can go back in there, Charlie, is knowing that you are safe. Do you see?"

"Yes."

I hugged him for a long time, until Larsen put his huge hand on my shoulder and drew Charlie over to a seat.

Like all toddlers, Billy sensed my need to leave and gripped me tighter than ever. The boat rocked as he flailed in my arms.

"Billy," I said. At least I didn't need words for him. I crushed him to me, as though I could press his soft body into my own, as though our separation weren't yet complete, and we could go back to one flesh.

His forehead pressed hot against mine, and I thought fervently about how much I loved him, hoping that the strength of feeling would burn through our skin and deep into his mind, leaving him branded with it. *Whatever happens, you will remember this,* I told him silently, *you will remember that there was this much love.* His tears were hot salt on my raw skin. His kissy lips one more time. Then Larsen pulled him away. I slid over the side of the boat into ankle-deep water.

"It is time to go," he said. He called out to the driver, and the engine raged.

I took a step away.

"Don't let them see you," he said.

The slipway hid me from the helicopters, but I crouched down anyway, one hand against its slimed wall.

"When will you be back?" I pushed my tears away into the sea.

"It is not my remit to come back."

"You like having a remit, do you? Lots of lovely paperwork?"

The doctor smiled into Billy's golden hair.

"If you get bored again," I said, "feel free to come and rescue me."

The driver pushed off. The dinghy rotated slowly, so that Joni drifted past me. She reached out and made sounds of gratitude and promise, but her words were lost in the roar of the engine. The boat edged into deeper water, and then the outboard motor dropped, and it surged forward. Larsen gathered Billy into a bear hug, and the motor roared again, the dinghy rearing up into the waves.

I watched them and they watched me; I would never turn away; I would always look back. By the time the small figures of my children were out of sight, my feet stood on sand, the tide cutting me off, stranded and alone.

———

The sea breeze carried the voices of the Cleaners from the beach. They sounded closer than they were, but I kept myself low as I scrambled over a rocky breakwater to reach the cover of the houses that faced the sea. I clambered into a back garden, looking for somewhere to hide in case the helicopter took off again.

The engines started and built up to the familiar spanking din, whining into action as I pulled the handle of a shed that refused to budge. No other cover. For a desperate second I eyed a rabbit hutch, before simply pushing the back door, which swung open. I stepped into a huge living space that ended with a vast picture of sea and sky framed in the bay window. Way out, amid the deep grays, a small light wavered in the darkness. They must have reached the ship by now.

With a blast of light, a shape rose into view, and the room was plunged into brightness. I hit the floor. The helicopters turned, and lights spiraled across the walls and away. I raised my head and watched them slide out of the frame, though their heartbeat thudded for a long time in the quiet night, heading inland. I stayed facedown on the living room rug. The dark rushed back in. My children were safe. What more could a mother hope for?

By the time I pulled myself back up off the floor, the moon had risen, shining a long path across the water, as though taunting me. It had forced the tide to turn, and now it dared me to follow. Instead, I went back to the kitchen and started packing up food from the cupboards. For the first time since I'd entered the house, I noticed a buzz in the hallway, so I slipped out the back door and down the side alleyway onto the coast road. Staying close to the cover of houses, I broke into a jog and, as I got into my stride, a run. When the road bent away inland, I dropped down onto the beach and the hard, wet sand slapped under my boots. My lungs felt huge, swollen from salt air and crying. But I felt I could run forever. I raced toward the blackened cliff that I would have to climb to reach the abbey. The rhythm of my boots on the sand like a drum. But then there was something else, another rhythm, clashing with mine. Instinctively, I clicked off my torch and threw myself down, crabbing over to hide behind the ribbed remains of a breaker. But no light in the sky. No beat of helicopter blades. The sound—slowing, arrhythmic now—came from the sea. I squinted into the dark. A tiny light bounced across the waves. Then a voice calling my name as a bulky figure jumped from a dinghy onto the beach.

"You're supposed to be looking after my son," I said.

"I am. A boy needs his mother."

For a moment, I thought Larsen was going to grab me, force me on board. I wouldn't have had the will to resist. But instead he said, "Take this," and pushed a canvas bag into my hands. I fumbled open the buckle, and he shone his torch inside: medication, a transistor radio, and, wrapped inside another canvas bag, a gun with ammunition.

He nodded once and turned back to the dinghy. "The boat has sailed, we need to catch up."

"Thank you," I said.

He reached the dinghy in a few strides, pushing it away from the sand as he rolled inside.

"I'll see you then," he called out. "Same time, same place?"

"It's a date."

The engine roared, and his small light bounced away into the gray.

———

Later, I reached the bridge over the river and looked for the light out at sea. It was gone. The ship must have sailed. This was a good thing. When I had been pregnant with Billy, after the bleeding made me think

I'd lost him, I used to close my eyes and convince myself that the white sunspot I could see was the light of my baby. I closed my eyes now and saw the sunspot. But when I opened my eyes, the light out to sea was still gone. *Gone to safety,* I told myself. *Gone to safety.*

It was easy to follow the uphill curve of the cobbled streets through the old town to the base of the hill. The abbey peered down again, the smoke, cleared. The hillside reeked, and the stone steps were black with charred debris. Along the top of the cliff, buildings smoldered, but the grass fire seemed to have burnt itself out. I paced myself and reached the top of the steps with burning thighs but enough energy to run, if needed. The moonlight played with the night's proportions, so I felt I could reach out and touch the top of the ruined facade. Push it down like a cardboard cutout. But the sea breeze howled through the empty window sockets, reminding me that it was real.

I climbed back up to the base of the stone cross. It was still warm from the day. I pressed my scratched face against it and closed my eyes. I smiled at the white sunspot. But then a scraping footstep from the other side of the cross filled my body with an electric surge of adrenaline. A thin figure scuttled across the gravel toward the hillside, a cloak streaming out behind. I slipped down the steps and landed heavily on my backside on the grass with a huff.

The figure reached the top of the steps and turned toward me into the moonlight. Lola's narrow face shone white beneath what I now saw was not a cloak but a raincoat.

"It's me," I called out.

"Aunt Marlene?"

"The same." I got up and pressed my hand into the hip that always seemed to take the brunt of every mishap. The fall, the run, the withdrawal of adrenaline—now my right arm and shoulder throbbed back into action, too.

"What are you doing here?" Lola asked. "I watched you all leave."

She stayed at a distance, behind the iron railings of the steps. It was just as well. Anger pooled in my hands, which twitched with an urge to wring the truth into her: *You made me leave my children; I could die without seeing them again.*

Lola gave a hiccup and started to cry. "I thought you were the Cleaners. I thought I was going to die." She sat on the top of the 199 steps and wept into her hands.

I walked over and hugged her from behind, my arms around her delicate neck.

"What about Mom?" she asked, barely audible.

"Well, put it this way. If we see her again, she'll be too happy to hold a grudge, and if we don't, then it's not really your problem, is it?"

"Is that supposed to make me feel better?"

"Quite the opposite, actually. But it is better than throttling you, which is the other option."

Lola detached herself from my embrace.

"I didn't think they would just sail away and leave us," she said.

"The tide went out. And there are other survivors on the ship who need treatment. And your mother—"

"Are they coming back for us?"

"Maybe." I let the bit about Joni go. We could deal with that later. "So what's your brilliant plan, Lady Lola? What happens now?"

"Rescue Jack."

"That's it?"

Apparently, it was.

It was cold at the top of the 199 steps. The wind picked up. Wisps of cloud scuttled across the moon, sending huge shadows over the waves like dark glimpses of sea monsters. Lola shivered and zipped up her coat. We needed shelter for the night. Tomorrow, a vehicle. And supplies. A new plan.

I hauled Lola up by the elbow, and we started down the lonely steps to the town, accompanied by the hiss of waves dragging stones across the sand, making wishes as they went.

"Do you think we'll get back, Aunt Marlene? Will we make it?"

"Oh, yes, Lola," I said, through a mouthful of salty air. "We'll make it back. Mummy always comes back."

ACKNOWLEDGMENTS

Thank heavens for a serendipitous #mswl tweet that led me to Danielle Egan-Miller at Browne & Miller Literary Associates in Chicago. It's humbling that Danielle chose to invest her experience, enthusiasm, and editorial nous in me. I'm grateful also to agents Joanna MacKenzie and Abby Saul, who continued reading about a nasty virus even while poorly.

Massive thanks to Jodi Warshaw at Lake Union Publishing for her leap of faith and for seeing into the heart of a prickly mama bear. Her thoughtful development of the manuscript brought me to Caitlin Alexander, whose craft and eagle eyes prompted me to clarify ideas, characters, and language. Ginger Everhart and Karen Parkin also worked their magic on the text. I'm grateful for the skill and dedication of all my new Amazon Publishing colleagues.

I've been blessed with many nurturing readers during the gestation of *All the Little Children*. I began the novel for an MA in Professional Writing at Falmouth University (UK), where my tutor Emily Barr was encouraging and exacting in just the right measure. The support of Helen Shipman and Susannah Marriott also gave me confidence when it was needed, while the critical insights of fellow student Neill Bell-Shaw proved invaluable.

Members of The Singapore Writers' Group endured numerous drafts, with only minimal sighing when presented with yet another opening chapter. Alice Clark-Platts asked questions that provoked vital answers and assured me that "it's ready." Sometimes a small comment made a big impact, so sorry to anyone I've missed and thanks to: Sarah Carlson, Shankah Chandrashekar Iyer, Vanessa Deza Hangad, Matt Schnetter, Marion Kleinschmidt, Shola Olowu Asante, Magali Finet, Marc Heal, Helena Ryan, Sarah Salmon, and, of course, Lucia Orellana for resisting the urge to punch Marlene (or me) in the face.

Catherine Carvell is sorely missed from our Brownies circle. Damyanti Biswas and Clarissa Goenawan are fellow survivors on the road to publication. As is Melissa Nesbitt, who spotted that fortuitous #mswl tweet and sent many a "don't give up"–type message at weak moments. Thanks also to Anna Davis from Curtis Brown Creative, who generously offered guidance long after the workshop in Singapore, where we Brownies first met.

I'm grateful to my friend Dr. Elizabeth Biggs for giving medical tips and teatime Tiger Beer, while engineer and power-outage expert Crispin Holliday helped me blow up a paint factory. The farming Furnisses of Shropshire offered inspiring walks and countryside lore. And the force of nature that is Carlotta Indermaur gave Joni her Pennsylvania patter.

To residents of the "blue remembered hills" of Shropshire or the Yorkshire coast: I'm sorry for moments when I've rearranged the geography of your beloved landscape.

Finally, I'm thankful that my children, Lydia and Frank, are so patient with their mummy. They may not have the right sport kit in the right bag on the right day, but I'm always, always thinking of them. Carol and Ray Foster fed me a childhood diet of Ladybird Books; thanks for starting me off as I was meant to go on.

The last word, as is so often the case, goes to my husband, who is my greatest supporter and best friend. Mark once said I was his "wild card." He should know that he's the ace in my pack. Thanks, Ace.

ABOUT THE AUTHOR

Photo © 2016 Emily Newell, Littleones Photography

After spending a decade as a broadcast journalist for the BBC, Jo Furniss gave up the glamour of night shifts to become a freelance writer and serial expatriate. Originally from the United Kingdom, she has lived in Switzerland and Cameroon and currently resides with her family in Singapore.

As a journalist, Jo has worked for numerous online outlets and magazines, including *Monocle*, the *Economist*, *Business Traveller*, *Expat Living (Singapore)*, and *Swiss News*. Jo has also edited books for a Nobel Laureate and the Palace of the Sultan of Brunei. In 2015, she founded *SWAG*—an online literary magazine for writers in Singapore.

All the Little Children is Jo's debut novel; she is at work on a second domestic thriller to be released in 2018. To learn more about the author and her work, you can connect with her on Facebook (JoFurnissAuthor) and Twitter (@Jo_Furniss) and through her website, www.jofurniss.com.